SNEAKING OUT

DUNEMERE
Books

NEW YORK
SAN FRANCISCO

BOOK
1

SNEAKING OUT

BY
CHUCK VANCE

PUBLISHED BY DUNEMERE BOOKS

DUNEMERE
Books

Copyright © 2018 by Chuck Vance
www.dunemerebooks.com
chuckvanceauthor.com
Cover illustration © 2018 by Jill De Haan
www.jilldehaan.com
Book and cover design by Jenny Kelly
ISBN: 978-0-9984997-7-2

SNEAKING OUT

"It's time," said Oscar, flinging off his comforter. Despite the fact that he was in bed, he was fully dressed. All he had to do was put on his shoes and fleece jacket. That, and open the window and jump out.

Luke felt the blood rushing to his head. Was it really time? He glanced at his phone to be sure: almost two in the morning. Unlike Oscar, he'd been too nervous to sleep. Instead, he had done his history homework and studied for next week's Spanish quiz. Then he'd watched a bunch of *College Humor* videos before collapsing in his faded armchair with a copy of *Field and Stream* magazine.

A brisk October breeze dragged scratchy tree branches across their window. The moon was full and bright, but at this hour it was pretty much a given that everyone on campus was sound asleep—everyone except the two girls who were preparing to meet them outside. All Luke and Oscar had to do was sneak out of their dorm and make it to the woods without detection.

Easier said than done.

St. Benedict's—their boarding school, nestled in the heart of Connecticut—treated sneaking out of the dorm after hours as a serious infraction of the honor code, so if they got caught, they'd be up for a Disciplinary Committee hearing. If they were lucky, the D.C. would be in a good mood and simply put them on probation, but if the members were feeling cranky they could just as easily rule it a strike. One strike equaled suspension; two was expulsion. Oscar already had one strike—due to his habit of skipping classes and illegally signing out—and even if Luke got off with probation, it would be a big problem. Colleges, not to mention parents, cared a lot about that stuff.

Of course, Oscar would take it in stride. Hell, he'd probably go down in a blaze of glory. He'd brush his dark hair out of his eyes, smile lazily at the members of the D.C. and move on, as if getting kicked out was all just part of some grand plan. Luke was the opposite; if he got expelled he might as well go straight to the tattoo place in town and ink the word "failure" across his forehead, because that's what he'd feel like.

"Dude, come on, let's bolt," Oscar said.

To outsiders, they were an unlikely pair. Oscar was ornery and aloof and had the reputation of being a rebel. He excelled at sports but was not necessarily a team player; he participated in no extracurriculars other than what was required, and had no problem challenging authority. That attitude, coupled with the self-confident swagger of someone who knows he is good-looking, made him the kind of guy who would give any parents pause when he showed up to take their daughter out on the town. Not that Oscar would even bother getting out of his car to knock on the door; girls went to him, not the other way around. Luke, on the other hand, was the all-around good guy: clean-cut, a great student and athlete, a Student Rep, a dorm prefect, president of the Outdoors Club, and a member of STEAM—St. Benedict's Environmental Action Movement. Luke knew some people viewed him as some sort of perfectly packaged college-app striver, and it bothered him, but what could he do? He liked doing those things and he wasn't about to change just to avoid conforming to other people's perceptions.

Luke was certain he and Oscar would probably have steered clear of each other had they not been placed together as roommates freshman year. But they both fell out of their public roles when they were in the quiet of their own room, and they'd become best friends.

"Come on, Chase. Hurry up."

"Okay, okay. I just need to stuff my bed." Luke moved his pillows under the covers so that it looked as if he were still in it, sleeping.

Tonight, Oscar had arranged to meet Kelsey, a preppy blue-eyed blond who giggled a little too much for Luke's taste. Luke, in turn, had invited Pippa, a recent transfer from England.

"If I were you, I'm not sure I'd risk keeping Pippa waiting. But sure, by all means go ahead and arrange your bed perfectly."

Luke made one last adjustment to the comforter. "You don't like her, do you?"

"What's to like? She's totally stuck-up and she's not even that hot."

"I think she's hot," Luke countered. He pictured Pippa in his mind: she was tall, with very blond hair and nearly translucent skin. There was something almost otherworldly about her. She had really smart things to say in American Lit—ideas that were distinct from those of all the other kids in the class. She made him think. Plus, it was unusual for St. Benedict's to accept any new students junior year, so that gave her an extra layer of allure.

"I guess I shouldn't be surprised. You have a thing for 'different' girls," Oscar said, using air quotes the way he always did when this subject came up.

"Come on," protested Luke, even though he had to admit that it was partly true. All his friends expected him to only like girls who resembled him, as if couples should pair off like a set of matching salt-and-pepper shakers. Just because he had a preppy, all-American sporty vibe didn't mean that's what he looked for in a girl. In fact, he was attracted to girls who were a little unexpected.

"Sure you do. Different girls are totally your thing, man. This girl's got a posh accent and no one really knows anything about her. She's a mystery, and you love that stuff."

Oscar snapped his fingers. "Hey, you know what? I think it's because if you took off her omnipresent beret she looks like Daenerys from *Game of Thrones*. You've got that whole fantasy world fetish going on, right?"

"Fantasy world? Me?" Luke rolled his eyes.

"You know, Mother of Dragons, and all that?" Oscar thrust out his chest and clasped his hands in front of himself like a princess.

Luke pulled his pillow out from underneath the comforter and tossed it at Oscar's head.

"Yeah? Well, I'd rather go out with a badass dragon girl than silly little Kelsey."

"Now it's official," Oscar said, catching the pillow and spinning it in the air. "You are actually *trying* to make us late, aren't you?"

Luke held out his hand for the pillow and Oscar threw it back.

Luke finished with the bed and stepped back to look at it critically. In the dark and without a close look, it might look like a person was actually in there. Right now, not so much. But it would have to do.

Time to go. Luke opened the window and reached for the thickest tree branch. It shook a bit, weakened by his weight, but it was secure. Luke had spent most of his summers climbing trees at his grandparents' farm in Virginia, and nowadays he spent a few Sundays every month camping and climbing in the nearby Berkshire Mountains with his club. Always pushing himself, he had taken a month-long outdoors course at the Appalachian State Park last summer to pick up new skills.

He didn't have a choice; he *had* to push himself. Those skills were way more than just a hobby: they'd actually saved his life three years ago.

He laughed to himself. It was sort of funny to think of where he was now, using some of those lifesaving skills to sneak out to meet a girl. Mac, his group leader from the Appalachians, would actually be proud. He was always urging Luke to go further, push himself harder, in every way. Luke was doing that tonight, all right. Pushing his rule-abiding self right over a disciplinary line he had never crossed before.

Luke reached down and dove for a lower and thicker branch, working his way down the tree easily and landing smoothly on the ground. Oscar followed less gracefully, hitting the ground first and then falling backward with a thud. His backpack—holding the orange juice they'd snuck out of the dining hall at breakfast and a water bottle half-filled with vodka—landed a few feet away.

"Careful with the goods!" Luke warned.

"The way back, we're going through the basement," whispered Oscar, standing up and wiping dirt off his jeans before picking up his backpack.

"Wimp."

The central campus of St. Benedict's was scattered with brick buildings and the occasional white clapboard or modern structure, all clustered around a man-made pond with a small fountain in the center. Just beyond the pond was the chapel, its enormous lit steeple piercing the sky. The entire campus was big: four hundred and sixty acres. To the north, through the playing fields, was Everett, the gigantic athletic center where all the indoor sports took place. On the front side of campus was Route 443, which cut through the town of Southborough—a blink-and-you'll-miss-it village. On the opposite side, to the west, where Oscar and Luke were now headed, the extended terrain was hilly, heavily forested and crisscrossed by narrow river valleys, stretching all the way to the Berkshire Mountains.

Their dorm, Wilcox, was the closest one to the woods. That meant they could go out the back and hide in the shadows and survey the scene until they found a safe time to rush across a clearing of about a hundred yards up a hill into the woods. The girls' journey was a little trickier because their dorm, Hadden, was farther away.

Luke scanned the scene, and gave the all-clear signal. "Go!"

Once they had run through the clearing and made it to the tip of the woods, Luke felt a rush of accomplishment. Sneaking out of the dorm in the middle of the night was basically a rite of passage at boarding school.

"Yes! Chase, you finally did it!" Oscar tackled him, wrapping his arm around Luke's neck in an affectionate chokehold. "You're not an after-hours virgin anymore. I'm so proud."

Luke ducked out easily. He didn't really want Pippa to see them messing around.

"Now, where *are* those girls?" murmured Oscar, straightening up to scan the darkness. Their designated meeting place, on a hill right at the edge of the woods, afforded a good view of the campus below, but there was no sign of any movement other than waving tree branches. It was windier than Luke had expected. He was glad his hair was cut short; Oscar kept having to shake his out of his eyes.

"Maybe they bailed," Luke said.

"Well, Pippa may not be coming but Kelsey definitely is."

"How can you be so sure?"

"She texted me before we left the room."

Luke regretted not checking his phone one last time before leaving the dorm; there wouldn't be any signal here. Would Pippa bail? He had asked her to join him impulsively the night before. They were talking after study hall, both waiting on line at the vending machines, and she was complaining about how prudish the school was compared to her old school in England. So almost on a dare, he had asked her to meet him at the Dip, knowing that Oscar was planning to hang with Kelsey. He didn't think she would say yes, but she'd eyed him coolly and grabbed her bag of potato chips from the vending machine with a casual *I suppose so* that had made Luke's stomach flip.

"Hey, look," Luke said. Below them two figures were running across the clearing, brightly illuminated by the moonlight. Pippa wasn't wearing her beret, which Luke was grateful for after Oscar's earlier comment, but if any girls should have worn hats or hoods it was those two: the moonlight practically reflected off their fair hair. Not exactly the best camouflage.

Two minutes later, the girls arrived at the meeting spot, breathless.

"You made it," Oscar said, pleased.

"Of course we did," said Kelsey with mock offense, adjusting her ponytail. "I told you I was coming."

Oscar leaned over and kissed Kelsey, taking her by surprise. Luke looked away in embarrassment and his eyes met Pippa's. She gave him a look of disapproval as if to say, *Don't even try that on me.* Or maybe she was merely grossed out by PDA.

"Glad you came," said Luke, moving to Pippa's side.

She shrugged. "No worries."

Luke smiled. Oscar had been right: that accent did him in every time. "Did you have any problems sneaking out?"

Pippa motioned toward Kelsey. "Other than waiting for *her* for twenty minutes? No."

"I told you, I had to wait until Mrs. Chester went to sleep. She's an insomniac and her apartment is right next to my room."

"It just seemed like an overly long time, that's all."

"Well, I'm sorry," said Kelsey in anything but a remorseful tone. "But I really don't want to get busted for this. Coach Rosenberg just gave us a huge lecture last practice about risking our recruitment. She hasn't done any of my college intros yet and I don't want to give her a reason not to put in a good word for me with the field hockey coach at UVA."

9

Pippa looked irritated. "We all have something to lose, don't we?"

Luke had never seen Kelsey shrink from anyone—she was usually at the center of any group—but she held back from making a comment and edged toward Oscar.

Pippa turned back to Luke. "It's quite odd. Once you get out of the dorm, it's amazingly simple to sneak out. My school in Devon had alarms on the doors, but there's no security here whatsoever."

"Which is insane, considering the crime history in this area," Luke joked, trying to lighten the tone.

"Yeah, we'd better watch out for the Southborough Strangler," Oscar added. "They never caught him."

"Don't freak me out," Kelsey begged, holding tighter to Oscar's arm.

Luke saw Pippa roll her eyes. It was clear that Pippa and Kelsey were not the best of friends. Actually, now that Luke thought about it, despite having been at school for almost two months it didn't seem like Pippa really had any friends. That didn't really deter him; he liked to make up his own mind about people. Still, it was interesting to note.

"Come on, let's get going," Oscar said. "We're too exposed here."

Luke watched as Oscar effortlessly, almost carelessly, took Kelsey's hand and started walking deeper into the woods. He wanted to take Pippa's, but she had folded her arms firmly across her chest.

They fell in line as a pair behind Oscar and Kelsey.

"So what will we do when we get to this mythic spot in the woods?" asked Pippa.

Luke pointed toward Oscar's backpack, slung casually over one shoulder. "We may have brought some refreshments."

Pippa smiled, and Luke gave a silent prayer of thanks that Oscar and Kira Matthews had only had a few shots from their stash last weekend after the dance, leaving enough to bring tonight.

"Luke Chase, Mr. Rule Follower, living on the edge tonight," Pippa said, teasingly.

"Uh oh. I see my reputation has preceded me."

"It has indeed," Pippa said. "In more ways than one."

Oscar turned around. "Hey, hey. No talking about reputations. Mine'll be next and I don't want Kelsey here to get second thoughts."

Kelsey swatted him playfully, and even Pippa smiled. The girls thought the banter was just a joke, but Luke and Oscar exchanged a glance. Oscar was a good wingman, always able to block people from digging into Luke's past, and he was pretty sure that was where the reputation talk was headed.

They continued deeper into the woods, carefully maneuvering over errant twigs and rocks as they headed into the autumn darkness. In the moonlight, branches and trees took on more sinister aspects. Random wildlife noises made them all look over their shoulders more than once. They were jumpy, but in a fun kind of way. Luke understood why so many students took the risk to sneak out. He was feeling the same run of emotions that made horror movies worthwhile: fear and dread, mixed with anticipation and relief.

Their place of debauchery had already been selected for them, because students of St. Benedict's had stolen away for years to the very spot where they were headed. "The Dip," as some unknown alum had christened it, was at the base of the remains of a hand-laid rock wall of mysterious origin. Rumors about the wall abounded: witches were burned there in the old days; it was part of the Underground Railroad; it was a farmhouse that had burned and the whole family had perished, and so on. The forgotten partition jutted out of the gravelly earth in the middle of nowhere, and ended just as abruptly ten yards later. It would look innocuous to most, except that on one side there was a deep drop-off mostly shielded by saplings and birch trees. Shadowy figures could hide in plain sight (and leave their vodka bottles and cigarette butts behind). Luke had passed by often enough during his daily runs but had never been there at night.

Suddenly a rush of memories from three years ago flashed in Luke's mind like a series of snapshots. He shivered involuntarily, and shook his head as if to clear his mind. That was weird. He'd spent tons of time outdoors in the three years since *that* episode, never once thinking about it. Why tonight? Maybe there was something about the danger of sneaking out that echoed his ordeal three years ago, bringing it all back to the surface.

Not now, he told himself. *Don't think about that now.*

"You okay?" asked Pippa, with real concern.

"Yeah, I'm fine."

Pippa scrutinized him carefully, but before she could say anything, Oscar spoke.

"Okay, we're here." Oscar hopped down into the hole and turned around to lend Kelsey a hand.

"Ready?" Luke asked Pippa.

"Quite." She dropped down into the Dip without waiting for assistance.

Luke looked down, hesitating for a second. What was wrong with him tonight? This was fun. They were having a good time.

Everything will be fine, he told himself. *Nothing bad is going to happen.*

He followed Pippa, descending into near darkness.

2

Everything was going well so far. They'd been in the woods almost an hour, and they'd nearly finished the vodka. Luke was having a good time. He and Pippa had the same Spanish teacher, although different periods. While Oscar and Kelsey made out, he and Pippa slowly moved closer and closer to each other on the log, laughing over the telenovelas Señor Diaz liked to assign for homework.

"The new one, about the huge family in the tiny apartment, is on Netflix now. We should watch it together during study hall next week," Pippa suggested.

"Shh!" whispered Kelsey hoarsely. "What was that?"

It was the third time she had thought she heard something. They all froze and waited in silence. If there's one thing Luke had learned about sneaking out, it made you really paranoid. It also gave him an excuse to pull Pippa closer. He felt a rush when she leaned up next to him.

"Kels, it's nothing," Oscar said impatiently.

"One might think you were looking for a reason to go home," Pippa told her.

Kelsey frowned. "Why would I do that? God. Excuse me for wanting to save all of our asses."

"I think we can look after ourselves," Pippa said. "And don't forget, we have the Kidnapped Kid here."

Luke winced. It had been a long time since someone called him that, at least to his face. Usually he went weeks, or even months, without ever thinking of what had happened to him three years ago, but now this was the second time tonight he'd been pulled back to that dark time. It made him uneasy. And worse: now he knew for sure that Pippa knew all about it, too.

"Hey, that's not cool, Pippa," Oscar told her. "That subject is off limits."

"It's okay," Luke said.

"No, it isn't," Oscar insisted.

"I'm just saying out loud what everyone says behind your back. I wasn't even on campus a single day before people told me about your history, Luke. How you were kidnapped and had to escape by—"

"Okay, moving on," Oscar said. "He doesn't—"

Oscar abruptly stopped. This time there was definitely a noise. At first no one said anything, hoping it was another mistake. But then the sounds came again, unmistakably the soft sweep of footsteps crackling through the fallen autumn leaves. The velvety darkness was broken by splashes of moonlight, but the small glimmers were enough to illuminate the girls' horrified faces. Pippa's sharp features were a stark patchwork of dark and light.

"What was that?" she whispered.

Luke felt his body go cold. Were they about to get caught?

"I heard it, too," said Kelsey, her voice wavering with fear. She twisted her ponytail nervously and sunk deeper into her dark blue Patagonia fleece jacket. "Oh my God, if I get busted my dad will kill me."

"It's probably just some animal." Oscar wrapped his arm around her. "No one knows we're here, don't worry."

The footsteps snapped again through the crisp air. They all froze; the only sign of movement was their eyeballs flitting from left to right, trying to locate the source of the noise through the cracks of light. Was it a teacher searching for them? They had felt so safe curled in the darkness, but now it was proving a liability. They could hardly make anything out. Luke's heart was thudding in his chest and he began to perspire under his flannel shirt.

"I'll go check it out," said Oscar, rising.

Kelsey tugged at his jeans, attempting to pull him down. "I don't think that's a good idea. What if they see you?"

Oscar tipped his head and gave her a sideways smile, the one Luke had seen a million times. The smile that said *No worries, everything will be fine.*

"Better they see me than you, okay?" he told Kelsey.

Kelsey, unsurprisingly, was not immune to his charm. "Okay," she whispered, dropping her hand.

"Dude, I'm not sure you should do this," said Luke. The

last thing he wanted was for Oscar to be the sacrificial lamb. Oscar had the most to lose out of all of them—it would be his last strike.

"Don't worry about it. I've been here a million times before. I know my way around."

Oscar brushed some bushes away and quickly disappeared into the night.

"What if Mrs. Chester did a bed check, realized we were gone, and came out to search for us?" Kelsey said. "Or what if someone saw us running across campus? We are so dead."

"Guys, it'll be okay," said Luke without conviction. "It's probably nothing."

He felt along the cold, damp ground until he found the log to sit on again. His legs felt heavy, and he was increasingly uncomfortable in the small cave. The confinement was really starting to bother him. He rubbed the thin, two-inch scar that ran along his right jawline, a remnant of that first night three years ago. Rubbing it was a habit he'd developed during times of stress. Over time it had flattened out and now he could barely even feel the ridge. He could feel Pippa staring at him.

"Wait, what's that barking?" asked Kelsey. Luke tensed up, not sure if he was reacting to the barking or to the fear in her voice. Where was Oscar?

"A dog, perhaps?" Pippa not-so-helpfully pointed out.

The dog's agitated wail sounded closer and closer. No one spoke while the dog continued barking. Luke cocked his head to the side and listened. His whole body filled

17

with dread. A dog. That made a third thing tonight that echoed his past. What was going on? He had to stay calm; make his senses focus on other things. He could hear Pippa's labored breathing, smell the slight scent of her rose perfume.

The dog abruptly ran off. A minute passed in silence. Then two. The tension in the veiled darkness was oppressive.

"I'm cold," whispered Kelsey.

Luke took his phone out to text Oscar. No signal.

"I think I'll go check on him," said Luke, but it was more than that. His heart was racing. Hearing the dog had made it impossible to push all the memories of that night—of his kidnapping—aside. He couldn't sit still.

"Wait," Pippa said. "Don't go."

"I don't want to leave Oscar out there." He started to pull himself up, but suddenly they heard voices.

"What did you want?" a woman asked.

Luke stopped dead in his tracks. He could hear Kelsey suck in her breath behind him. As carefully as possible, he turned and slunk down, feeling his way backward. Whoever was talking was right above them, but had no idea they were there. Luke put out his hand and gently pushed Kelsey and Pippa back, away from the edge of the Dip and further into the pit underneath the wall. They slunk down until their backs were snug against the mossy stones. All they could see above were trees and shadows. And darkness.

"Just want to talk, that's all."

Luke couldn't tell if it was a man or woman speaking. It sounded like a man, but if it was, he was speaking in a weird falsetto.

"Why are you talking like that?" asked the woman.

The wind started up again, sending leaves rustling along the ground and making the conversation indecipherable.

Luke and the girls waited, all three breathing hard, trying not to make a sound. Kelsey had grabbed his wrist tightly and was furiously digging her nails into him. Luke prayed Oscar wouldn't stumble back and interrupt whoever was up there. He wondered if he should reach for Pippa's hand, but she had wrapped her arms tightly around her chest and tucked her hands under her armpits.

"You're crazy," they heard the woman say when the wind momentarily died down.

The man's response was muffled.

"We're done," she said. "How many times do I need to tell you?"

"But he's wrong for you," whined the man. Again, his voice sounded girlish and unnatural.

"Just leave me alone," the woman said. "Please. That's all I want."

They heard footsteps through the leaves. Okay, good. Someone had walked away. Kelsey started to move forward as if to make a break for it, but Luke pulled her back and put his fingers up to his lips to shush her. He motioned upwards with his shoulders, indicating that he thought the other person was still up there. They waited for what seemed like an eternity. Then suddenly they heard movement, footsteps, and it was clear the second person had left.

Luke counted his heartbeats, waiting to see how long before they could talk and then the three of them exhaled, slumped to the ground, and collapsed into silent, heaving laughter.

"Well, whoever that was, they weren't looking for us," Luke finally said. "We're safe."

Relief washed over him.

"Who do you think it was?" breathed Pippa.

"I couldn't tell," Luke replied. "I was just glad they weren't calling our names and saying things like *suspended* or *expelled*." Or worse, he wanted to add, but didn't.

"At first I thought it was two women, but now I think one of them was a guy," whispered Kelsey.

"I know. What was up with that?" Luke said. "He was talking like a freak."

Suddenly there was another noise, sharp this time. "What was that?" asked Kelsey furtively.

Luke cocked his head, listening carefully. "It sounded, I don't know, like a yelp." It had come and gone abruptly, almost as if it didn't happen.

"I didn't hear anything," said Pippa.

"You didn't?" asked Kelsey. "I don't know, it didn't sound human. Maybe it was the dog."

"I heard there are coyotes in these woods," said Pippa.

"Coyotes?" Kelsey inched closer to Luke.

Suddenly, out of nowhere, Oscar jumped down into the

Dip. Pippa and Kelsey shot back, startled, then the nervous laughter started again.

"Miss me?" asked Oscar, as casually as if they were all hanging out in Main Hall instead of the woods in the dead of night.

"What the hell, dude? Trying to freak us out?" asked Luke.

"Sorry. I've just been out there on my ass, waiting for Heckler's wife to scram so I could climb back in here."

"That's who that was? Dean Heckler's wife? The first wife or the second?" asked Luke. Dean Heckler was one of two deans at the school. There was Mr. Palmer, who was the dean of students, (always referred to as "Mr. P.") and Mr. Heckler, the dean of faculty.

"Wait, both his ex-wife and current wife live here?" asked Pippa. "On campus?"

"Well, they both work here. I think the first Mrs. Heckler moved off-campus after everything. That's the messed up thing about boarding school faculty. They become entrenched. They don't leave even after getting ditched for a newer and better-looking version," explained Luke.

"With certain, shall we say . . . more impressive assets," added Oscar, rounding his hands out in front of his chest. Kelsey yelped in mock irritation and swatted his arm.

"So which wife was it?" Luke asked again.

"Well, old Mrs. Heckler was up there with her dog—"

"His first wife?" asked Luke. "Weird. Who was she with?"

"I just told you. Her dog."

"No, we thought we heard a guy, too," Kelsey said.

"Yes, there was definitely a bloke there," insisted Pippa.

"Nothing gets by you guys, does it?" Oscar said. "Okay, this is where it got bizarre: *both* Mrs. Hecklers are in the woods tonight. The first one was here first. Wait, that sounded funny; I mean, that's who we initially heard. She was walking her dog. Nearly gave me a freaking heart attack. The dog was totally onto the fact that I was hiding in the bushes, that's why he was barking like crazy. Luckily she thought he was flipping out over a squirrel and didn't take the time to investigate. Otherwise, I would've been toast. But just as I was about to come back, Heckler's second wife showed up with a dude. They stopped right next to you."

"We thought they'd find us for sure," said Kelsey.

"So she was with Dean Heckler?" asked Luke. If the dean was out patrolling the woods, that was a big problem. If Luke had to choose a faculty member to find them, Dean Heckler would literally be last on the list. He was hardcore. It had never been confirmed, but there were rumors that he'd been in the military at some point, maybe even the CIA.

"No. In fact, one of the few things I heard the guy say was that her husband was a 'pretentious windbag.' Honestly, I can't argue with that. Seems like a pretty accurate description of Heckler to me."

"If it wasn't Heckler, then who *was* the guy?" asked Luke.

"I don't know, couldn't see him. She was facing me, he

was blocked by a tree, and then he took off without her."

"Couldn't you tell by his voice?" asked Pippa.

"Nah, it sounded weird. Like he was pretending to be someone else."

"You're right," agreed Luke. "We heard him, sort of. It was like he was talking in a fake voice."

"Do you think we can go now? I really need to use the bathroom," said Kelsey.

"Me as well," said Pippa.

Luke looked at Oscar.

"I don't think we should risk leaving yet. Let's give all those Heckler wives a minute to get back to campus. What if they run into each other and stop to have a catfight or something?" said Oscar. "How about you two go find a nice tree up there where you can do your business?"

"Fine," said Kelsey. "I can't wait anymore. I'm about to pee in my pants."

She took a step forward and tripped, falling into Luke with a loud cry of alarm.

"Shh . . ." Everyone else hissed in unison.

"Sorry!"

Oscar bent down and felt around on the ground.

"Just a bottle," he said, rolling it into the back corner where it clinked against a rock. "You okay?"

Kelsey nodded.

"Good. Just be quiet out there, okay? We've made it this far. Let's not get busted now."

The girls scrambled out of the Dip.

"Dude, I was *freaking out*. I thought you'd gotten busted," admitted Luke as soon as the girls left.

"The dog scared the crap out of me for sure, but luckily old Mrs. Heckler had no idea I was there. She seemed kind of scared, like the dog was trying to take off into the woods, and she was begging it to go back. I even heard her dragging it away."

"Well, what about Heckler's new wife? Do you think she saw you?"

For a few seconds, a strange look of derision twisted Oscar's chiseled features. "No way. Joanna Heckler was pretty heated about something. Really pissed, talking harshly to the guy she was with. There's no way she was paying attention to anything else."

"Yeah, well, one word to her husband and we're history."

"Even if she saw me, she wouldn't rat me out," said Oscar confidently.

"You never know," said Luke, suddenly exhausted. "Geez, I'm done for tonight."

The last of his adrenaline drained away and all he wanted was to be under his duvet in bed. He had a long day tomorrow; classes, followed by soccer practice. A big game was coming up on Saturday. But things with Pippa seemed kind of cool; he felt a little glimmer of hope as he thought about hanging with her tomorrow after study hall.

"Hey. Do you still not like her?" Luke asked, breaking the silence.

"Who, Pippa? Yeah, that's still a no. Did you hear her try to shut me down when I told her to stop talking about stuff that was none of her business? Just shows she thinks she's better than everyone," said Oscar.

"Well, I'm not sure she thinks she's better than *everyone*," said Luke. "Maybe just you?"

"Fair point." Oscar smiled and took out his phone to check the time. "Man, it's getting late."

"I know. I'm beat."

"Girls take forever going to the bathroom."

"No kidding." With three older sisters, Luke was no stranger to waiting for girls in bathrooms.

Oscar leaned back against the muddy wall and closed his eyes. Luke was tempted to do the same when he heard a rustling noise. This time it sounded closer than before.

Luke waited, hoping it was the girls so they could get out of there.

"What's that? The girls?" hissed Luke.

"No. Sounds like . . . I don't know, something sliding."

It did sound like that. Almost like something was being pulled through along the leaves.

"Should we go check it out?" asked Luke.

"Nah, the girls will think we're spying on them."

Luke listened again, but this time he heard nothing. Maybe one of the girls had been scraping the leaves to cover where they went to the bathroom? He didn't know. It felt like minutes before Pippa slid back down to the Dip.

"Ready to leave?" asked Pippa. Her voice was back to be-

25

ing cold and sharp, having lost any of the friendliness Luke had thought he'd heard before. Great.

"Where's Kelsey?" asked Oscar.

Pippa didn't answer.

"You didn't leave her out there, did you?" asked Luke, concerned.

"What, was I supposed to hold her hand while we peed?"

Neither boy wanted to address that.

"Did you sort of, I don't know, kick the leaves around when you were out there?" asked Luke, finally.

"No, why?" asked Pippa.

"It sounded like someone was sweeping or dragging something; definitely heard a weird noise. It sounded man-made. Girl-made."

"Well, I didn't hear anything," said Pippa.

"You didn't hear *anything*? Do you have really bad hearing?" asked Oscar.

"No! What the hell? I went as far away as possible to pee so you guys wouldn't have to enjoy the sound effects. And you're the one who's hearing all this stuff. It's probably your imagination."

Suddenly the branches were brushed aside and Kelsey practically fell down into the hole, shaking and out of breath. Her hair was tousled, and she had leaves all over her fleece.

"Shh!" she said, fairly aggressively. "Someone's out there!"

"One of the Mrs. Hecklers?" Luke whispered.

Kelsey shook her head. "No! Someone else."

"Kels, don't worry. We're fine. No one's going to bust us,"

said Oscar in his most assured voice. "It's probably the guy Mrs. Heckler was with, and it seems like he's got other things to worry about."

"Oh yeah? Well, why would he be in the opposite direction? Behind the Dip?"

A chill went down Luke's spine. Why would that guy have come back around? Had he seen them after all? But if he had seen them, why would he just be waiting and watching? Things were starting to get very weird. Luke didn't like it. All his earlier nervous energy came roaring back.

"What do you mean?" asked Oscar.

"There's someone else out there," Kelsey hissed. "Someone just standing there, hiding behind a tree. He's out there, *watching* us."

3

No one moved for what seemed like an eternity. They didn't know what to do. Was someone really out there? And if so, was it someone from the school waiting to bust them? Or worse? Luke was really feeling déjà vu now.

They waited, frozen in fear, their ears straining to hear any sound. But it was completely quiet.

"Kelsey, are you sure you saw someone?" Oscar asked quietly.

"Yes!" Kelsey was practically crying now.

The near misses weren't funny anymore. Even Pippa had dropped her reserve and looked scared. Things had gone beyond a fear of getting in trouble; now their safety might be in jeopardy.

Luke's senses were on high alert. He pulled up his sleeve. His running watch said ten past three.

He looked at Oscar and tipped his head back toward campus. Oscar nodded, understanding. They needed to leave.

"Okay, guys," Luke said, keeping his tone light. "I don't know who is out there, if anyone, but it's time to call it a night, am I right?"

The girls nodded in unison, finally agreeing on something.

"Oscar's going to go up first, then Kelsey, then Pippa, and I'm going to follow. We're going to hold onto each other and move through the woods as fast as possible, together. Okay? Once we're ready, we're going to run and we're not going to stop until we get to the meeting spot. Don't worry about being quiet. Let's just move, as fast as we can. Got it?"

Luke's heart was racing, but he was glad to be planning and moving. Action always made him feel better.

"I'm scared," whispered Kelsey as Oscar helped her up the Dip.

"Just hang on to me," he said, taking her hand.

Luke hopped up last, looking around quickly to take everything in.

The other three kept their eyes on him until he gave the signal.

"Go," he said, motioning toward campus before grabbing onto Pippa's hand. The two of them took the lead.

They ran, all of them, as fast as they could, jumping over logs and flinging branches aside. If anyone was out there looking for them, they had definitely made themselves a target, but it was better than staying back in the Dip where they'd be sitting ducks for whoever was out there.

Luke shot backward glances as they ran.

Was that a person or a branch? A stalker or a squirrel?

"Nearly there," Oscar said.

"Yay," Kelsey replied weakly.

Finally, the chapel's steeple appeared in the sky like a beacon. They had made it back to the meeting spot. Not quite home, but close enough where it felt safe.

Everyone was breathing hard.

"I must say, I have no love for this school, but right now I'm quite glad to see it," said Pippa.

"Yeah, home sweet home," said Luke. He really meant it. This night had been unexpectedly grueling.

"Are you okay now, Kels?" Oscar whispered in his most concerned voice, pulling Kelsey into a hug.

Luke turned to Pippa. He realized they were holding hands again, after dropping them during their sprint through the woods. He reached for her other hand and pulled her closer.

"Well, that was certainly an adventure," she said, smiling at him.

"It was," Luke agreed. "And not at all what I expected."

"Nothing wrong with unpredictability, is there?"

"Not at all," Luke said. He would have preferred to get to this point earlier in the night, back in the privacy of the woods, but he knew he should kiss Pippa now or he'd regret missing his chance.

Oscar cleared his throat.

"I hate to break this up," Oscar said. "I really do. But hello, we may have just escaped the Southborough Strangler in the woods and I'd kind of like to call it a night, if you don't mind."

Luke reluctantly broke away from Pippa.

"Tomorrow," he said to Pippa. "After classes end. You, me, and that telenovela."

"As you Americans say, 'sounds like a plan,'" Pippa replied.

They were about to make a break for it and run through the clearing when they saw a figure walking with a flashlight down by the dorms.

"Stop," whispered Luke, putting his arm out.

"Nooooo," whined Kelsey. "Oh my God, I just want to get back to my room."

Whoever it was disappeared around the corner.

"I couldn't see who it was," said Pippa, looking at Luke. "Security?"

"Security leaves at midnight," Oscar said.

"Then who?" asked Kelsey.

"It couldn't be who Kelsey saw in the woods, could it?" Oscar asked. "How could he have beat us back?"

"There's no way," Luke said.

"But why would someone be walking around so late at night?" asked Pippa.

"Dorm duty?" offered Oscar.

"This late?" Luke knew what they were all thinking: a teacher was out looking for them. Funny, all that fear in the woods had made getting busted seem like a lesser problem, at least for a little while.

They waited, but the person with the flashlight didn't reappear.

"Okay, listen," Oscar said. "Let's just go. If we're busted, we're busted. But I think it's clear, and you know what, I can't take it anymore."

"Agreed," said Luke, the girls joining in.

All four ran down to the edge of Wilcox, whispering quick goodbyes before Kelsey and Pippa split off and ran down the path toward Hadden. By unspoken agreement, Luke and Oscar waited to go inside.

"I know you're into her, but I just want to go on record as saying that girl is trouble," Oscar murmured.

Luke knew he meant Pippa. "Why do you say that?"

"For one thing, where'd she go? Why did she ditch Kelsey like that? I bet she wanted to freak her out, and she was willing to jeopardize us just to mess with her."

"What? No way." Luke frowned. The thought hadn't occurred to him.

"Yes, way," Oscar said. "Mark my words."

When the girls disappeared at the end of the path, Oscar slid open the basement window in the laundry room of their dorm and wiggled his way inside. Luke followed.

"Why didn't we sneak out this way? It's much easier," whispered Luke.

"Mr. Crawford lives right above here. You know how he stays up super late, watching movies. We couldn't risk it."

Every dorm had at least one faculty member living in an apartment per floor, depending on the size of the dorm. Mr. Crawford was chill, and they hung out a lot in his apartment eating pizza or watching TV, but no matter how relaxed he was, he would have no choice but to turn them in if he caught them sneaking out.

Luke turned to shut the window and glanced out at the clearing toward the woods. Something caught his eye. He could swear he saw a man standing there against the backdrop of the forest. Watching him. He pressed his forehead against the glass and this time he was certain.

The warm, fuzzy feeling he'd had from thinking about Pippa disappeared, and Luke felt a familiar rush of terror wash over him.

A man. In the woods. Watching him.

No, not this. Not again.

Luke shut the window harder than he meant to, his stomach churning. He'd felt so safe for so long. Had it just been an illusion?

4

Luke heard about the murder during Spanish class.

All morning he had been feeling as if something bad had yet to happen, but he didn't expect anything like this. Señora Gonzales rapped on the door of their classroom and when Señor Diaz huddled with her in the corner, he returned pale and ashen, even under his dark beard. Before he spoke, the chapel bells sounded and the class knew then that something was amiss.

"Students, I have an announcement," said Señor Diaz in English, another sign something was wrong. It was supposed to be all Spanish, all the time. He clutched at the air behind him until he found his desk, then he lowered himself awkwardly onto it. "Dean Heckler's wife, Joanna, was found dead this morning. On campus."

There was a surge of chatter in the classroom.

"Damn," Andy Slater said to Luke. "That's some morning announcement."

"Dead? What do you mean, 'found dead.' Did she have a heart attack or something?" asked a girl in the front row.

Señor Diaz's eyes flickered across the room nervously. "Um, unfortunately, no. It appears to be . . . *unnatural* causes. She was found in the woods . . ."

The blood drained from Luke's face when he made the connection. *She was there! And now she's . . . dead! That means Oscar was one of the last people to see her alive!* His head started spinning. This couldn't be happening.

"Before I say more, Headmaster Thompson has asked that everyone go to the Chapel. So, class dismissed."

It took about twenty seconds for the class to react; there was a beat of quiet, followed by the rush that came with the discovery of being in the middle of a unique event, spectacular and salacious, albeit gruesome and tragic. Something had finally happened, here, in the middle of nowhere, at their tiny little school that had been founded by an undistinguished American president's brother. And not only that: they got to miss class for it!

The hallways grew louder as students poured out of classrooms and made their way to the chapel. In 1890, it had actually housed the original St. Benedict's School, and classes were held there until the turn of the century when the rest of the school was built. On the steps by the doorway stood a bronze statue of Randolph Troffet, the first chaplain of the school. It had been a gift of the class of 1932, and ever since then it had become a custom of every student who passed by to rub his nose for good luck. The entire statue was dull and oxidized except for the nose, which was bright and shiny.

"Mrs. Heckler was a damn fine-looking woman. What a friggin' waste," exclaimed Gupta, one of Luke's lacrosse teammates as they walked across the path toward the chapel.

"But think about it. Being married to Dean Heckler was also a waste," said Andy Slater. "Why would a hot chick marry an old, uptight dean of faculty at a boring boarding school in central Connecticut? That will still go down as one of life's great mysteries. Who shot JFK, do aliens exist, are spaceships responsible for crop circles, why did Joanna marry Dean Heckler . . . ?"

"Another mystery is why there didn't seem to be any drama," said Luke. "One minute he's with his first wife, Mary, the librarian, then summer break two years ago, he comes back with a new wife. And there's like no public fighting or screaming and crying."

"Yeah, that was bizarre," Andy said. "Your husband leaves you and then marries someone else and you have to see your replacement everyday 'cause she works in the alumni office. Who could deal with that?"

"Maybe the first wife left *him*," said Gupta.

"Yeah, she could have turned into a lesbian," said Andy.

"She wouldn't need to be a lesbian to get turned off by Dean Heckler," Luke said. "Plus, you never know what goes on. It's not like they had kids. People seem to stay together for the kids. Take them out of the equation . . ."

"Do you think when they found her in the woods she was naked?" asked Gupta. "Because if I had to find a dead body, a naked one wouldn't be that bad. Especially a looker like Mrs. Heckler."

"Naked?" Luke asked. "Gupta, what the hell? She's *dead*."

Gupta shrugged. "The Southborough Strangler's victim was found naked, right? So maybe Mrs. Heckler was, too. You never know. Wonder who found her? I'd like to ask him . . ."

Luke was disgusted by how gleeful his friends seemed. He walked ahead on the path, collecting his thoughts. Did it happen while they were there? Was there anything he could have done to save her? Maybe not. Maybe she was found far away from the Dip. The woods were big, after all.

"This is so major. Who do you think did it?" asked Andy, jogging along beside Luke to keep up with his pace.

"Don't know," said Luke, clenching the straps of his backpack.

"Obviously you don't know, but who do you think? Heckler, right? Isn't it always the husband? Or maybe it was someone who broke into the house after she was asleep and took her into the woods."

"Dunno."

Suddenly Andy's eyebrows shot up. "Ooohh, I get it. Sorry, man. Too close to home, right? Okay, fine. I'll leave you in peace."

Andy fell back to talk to another group of students who were more than eager to discuss the cause of death. Luke heard "strikes a nerve" and "Kidnapped Kid."

The truth was, Andy was right. It did strike a bit of a nerve, and Luke wished it didn't. For three years, he had avoided talking about his kidnapping, or abduction, or whatever people wanted to call it, and now suddenly it was the topic of conversation for the second time in not even twenty-four hours. Even worse, he could barely admit to himself that he felt a ping of relief. He wasn't connected at all to Mrs. Heckler. He barely knew her, which meant the watcher in the woods hadn't been there for him. Of course, that made him feel guilty. Someone had just died, and he was relieved?

Just stop thinking about it, he told himself.

Instead, Luke focused on Joanna Heckler. Talk swirled all around him: "decapitated" and "strangled" and "naked." He racked his brain to see if he could remember anything important that Mrs. Heckler had said when she was standing above them. But it was impossible; the wind had been too strong. Wait! *He's wrong for you.* That's what the guy had said. *He's wrong for you.* Was that some sort of clue? It just seemed insane, crazy, that of all nights they decide to sneak out, they heard Mrs. Heckler and now . . . Luke shuddered.

Throngs of students squeezed through the double doors, rubbing Troffet's nose on the way, and Luke took his seat in the fifth row. Seats were assigned both by grade and alphabetically by the first letter of the student's last name. They had "chapel" for thirty minutes every Monday, Tuesday, and Thursday before sit-down dinner. Wednesday and Saturday were athletic game days and Friday was, well, Friday. At every chapel they would say the Lord's Prayer, then there would be a few announcements followed by either a teacher giving a speech about a topic or a guest speaker. Luke's friends back home thought it was strange that his school required so much time in a church, but it was actually a nice break in the day.

But today, not so much. Luke glanced around at his classmates' animated banter and wished he were able to feel that detached. He was overcome by a sinking feeling. He would have to come forward and admit that he was out there last night. It would destroy everything. Forget getting a strike—he would probably get kicked out. But what else could he do? The thought sickened him. His parents would be so disappointed, although they'd probably be even madder that he'd jeopardized his own safety.

He glanced around and spotted Pippa a few rows down to his left. She held her head up haughtily, as if unfazed. Or maybe she always just tried to appear that way. Why had she been so unfriendly to Kelsey? Could she really have left her out there on purpose?

Pippa must have felt him staring at her because she turned, and when their eyes met she lost her icy demeanor. She was sitting too far away to have a conversation, mouthing the words *oh my God* instead, looking at him with the same mix of fear and incredulity that Luke was feeling. They signaled back and forth a few times. Well, at least something good was coming out of this.

"This is so scary, don't you think?" asked Liz Collins as she slid into the seat next to him. Liz was a good friend of Luke's. Initially it had been the alphabet that drove them together through all the assigned seating, but it hadn't taken long before the friendship became genuine. Oscar had always told Luke to go for her, and even though she was definitely pretty—she looked just like a younger Halle Berry—Luke liked having Liz as a friend and he didn't want to risk ruining it.

"Unbelievable," Luke said.

"They better have a very good reason why they are not evacuating campus right now. It has to be that they know who killed her."

"That or they don't want their endowment to go down."

"True. It's always about the almighty dollar," said Liz with a laugh. "Oh, here they come."

Anthony Thompson, the headmaster, and Robert Palmer, the dean of students, walked up onto the stage, accompanied by two men wearing blue police windbreakers. They leaned in and whispered to each other before Mr. Thompson went up to the podium and cleared his voice. He was a large, bald, African-American man who was normally very smiley, but today he looked drawn and serious, and under the fluorescent lights the gleam of sweat on his pate was visible. It usually took a while for the school to quiet down, but not in this case. The noise level dropped immediately, and a hush fell across the room.

"Good morning, students. I am sure by now all of you have heard the tragic news about Joanna Heckler's death. First of all, on behalf of the entire St. Benedict's community, I want to extend our deepest sympathy to Dean Heckler and the rest of Mrs. Heckler's family. I hope each and every one of you will keep them in your prayers. Although Mrs. Heckler had only been with us a short time, we will remember her vibrant personality and her winning smile. Her work in the alumni office was a great help to the school, and I know we will all miss her.

"Of course, the circumstances surrounding Mrs. Heckler's death are horrific, and quite unprecedented for our school. As you may know by now, we believe that Mrs. Heckler's death was not accidental. We will be working very closely with the Southborough County Police Department to find a quick resolution to this matter. Some of you may be questioned by the police in order to assist them toward a speedy conclusion, but we want to make it clear that no students fall under the umbrella of suspicion and a faculty member will be with you at all times. A lawyer will also be available to you. In addition, we will be contacting your parents to let them know, and we will be offering a leave of absence to any student who wishes to take it. But please note we have also hired Amon Security Systems who will be providing us with dozens of security guards as well as creating other security measures to ensure your safety. As of now, classes are cancelled for the rest of the day; please use this as a time of reflection. Counselors will be visiting each dormitory to meet with students as a group and they are also available for individual sessions. Dorm heads will communicate timing with you all. In addition, all off-campus volunteering activities are suspended, and going to town will require a sign-out at all times, even during permitted hours before five o'clock. The safety of our students is the most important . . ."

As the headmaster droned on and on, Luke surveyed the room. Pretty much all of the faculty were present—well, except for Dean Heckler. Luke's eyes slid from one faculty member to the other. Someone in this very room might be a murderer. If only he had heard who was talking to Mrs. Heckler. Or maybe it wasn't the funny-voiced guy who had done it. The original Mrs. Heckler had been out there in the woods walking her dog. What if *she* had done it? Maybe she was pissed about being dumped for a younger, prettier wife. Could it have been revenge? Maybe all that fake amicable stuff was a lie and she was laying in wait for the right moment to strike her rival. Some people wait years plotting and planning how to kill someone. It wouldn't be the most unusual thing.

"Until further notice, we do not want to make any assumptions that this crime can be linked to previous crimes in our area. I realize many of you will jump to this conclusion, but I am asking you to withhold your suppositions. The police department has assured me that they have no reason to believe that Mrs. Heckler was the victim of the Southborough Strangler."

The Southborough Strangler! As soon as those words were uttered, the chapel erupted in frantic whispering until several teachers rose from their seats and roamed the aisles quieting students down. The Southborough Strangler was the subject of urban legend among the St. Benedict students, but Luke had never heard an adult reference the story before.

What Luke knew was this: About a decade ago, a woman was found dead in her apartment near the Mobil station on Route 443, strangled with her own bra. Police initially thought it was a crime of passion. Her ex-boyfriend was a suspect, but because of a lack of evidence he was never charged. A few months later, two towns over, another woman was strangled. Police eventually arrested the second woman's husband, who insisted he was innocent and it was the work of "the Southborough Strangler," but the jury sent him to prison. There was still a small group of his supporters who believed that there was still a Strangler at large, and they had perpetuated that legend over the past ten years. But no one really knew if he (or she?) actually existed.

"All right, settle down," said the headmaster. "Chief Corcoran and Officer Bluth will speak now about our additional safety measures."

An hour later, as the students were pouring out of the chapel, Luke tried to catch up with Pippa but instead found himself falling into line with Mrs. Palmer, Mr. P.'s wife, who had been the faculty parent in Nichols, his freshman dorm. She had always been polite with the boys, although not too involved with them because she had been so busy with her twin preschool-aged sons. Like most faculty spouses, she worked on campus, and she was editor of the St. Benedict's Alumni Bulletin. Luke recalled she was also a deacon at the local Presbyterian church.

They greeted each other, Mrs. P. murmuring about how terrible the situation was. Luke nodded along, not really wanting to get into it with a member of the faculty, but not wanting to be rude, either.

"Were you, um, friends with her?" he asked.

A quick look of horror flitted across her face. "No," she said sharply, with a vehement headshake for emphasis. But then she seemed to reconsider and hastily amended her sharp tone. "But not for any particular reason . . . I . . . uh . . . Our paths didn't really cross."

That was odd. Why would she have minded Luke knowing the two women weren't friends?

She started talking again, seemingly eager to change the subject.

"I got great feedback from your article on the Appalachian Park program in the recent bulletin," she said. "Thanks again for taking the time to share your experience with us. You have quite a skill for storytelling. You should definitely do Mr. P.'s nonfiction senior seminar next year."

Luke had forgotten how she always referred to her husband as "Mr. P." and never by his first name or as Mr. *Palmer*. She always said it in some sort of reverential tone, as if Mr. P. was some sort of god. He was technically good-looking, although a bit nerdy, but then so was she, thought Luke as he studied her. She had clear skin and pretty green eyes but her hair was sort of a nondescript brown worn pulled back in a ponytail, a casual look that didn't exactly go with the suits she always wore.

"Yes, good idea," said Luke, although he had no intention of doing so. He had heard Mr. P. was a harsh grader and he intended to steer clear.

Pippa was far ahead of the crowd exiting the chapel. Why hadn't she waited for him? Luke said good-bye to Mrs. P. and veered away from Pippa's direction, confused and a little hurt. This girl was all about mixed signals. He decided he'd better find Oscar, anyway.

The art classes, music rooms, and Black Box Theater, as well as all of the administrative offices, were housed in an enormous castle-like brick building called Archer. Looming three stories tall, Archer covered the equivalent of an entire city block. When Luke entered through the side door he saw Oscar standing by the stained-glass windows in the alcove of the official school entrance, Main Hall, checking his phone.

"We've got to talk," Luke said tapping Oscar on the shoulder.

Oscar looked up and squinted at him. "Pretty major."

"I know," said Luke. "We need to figure out what our plan is."

"What do you mean, 'what our plan is'?"

Students flooded through the doors. Main Hall was the nerve center of the school's social gatherings, offering the opposite of privacy. Luke pulled Oscar down the marble-floored gallery toward the admissions offices. They slipped into an alcove and sat down in the plush red velvet window seat. One of the best aspects of the building was the shaded alcoves, small octagonal meeting rooms, obstructed balconies and window ledges that made for discreet meetings.

"We're not doing *anything*."

"But we've got to do *something*," insisted Luke. "We were the last people to see her alive."

"We don't know that," said Oscar, leaning back on the window seat, arms out with his left ankle resting on his right knee. Oscar always had a way of sitting so that he took up the most amount of space possible. "Besides, we have no information. I'm sure the police already have this case all wrapped up. They obviously know who did it, otherwise they would have shut down the school and sent us home. They're not going to keep us here with a killer on the loose."

It was just what Liz had said, and it did make sense. They would never keep the students at the school if there were any chance a maniac was running around. There would be too many lawsuits, for one thing.

"But don't you think they may need our testimony or something?" asked Luke.

"What for? We're useless. Trust me, *we have to remain silent.* No one will gain anything if we tell them we were out there."

Luke nodded. "Okay. Okay. You're right. I know." He let out a huge sigh of air he hadn't realized he'd been holding since Señor Diaz's class ended. He was glad Oscar was talking him down. Luke's thinking was definitely clouded by his own experience. "So what should we do?"

"Well, first off, we need to talk to the girls and tell them to keep their mouths shut," said Oscar, a little harshly. "Pippa seems like she'd have no problem ignoring this whole thing. Kelsey, on the other hand . . ."

"Yeah," agreed Luke. Kelsey seemed to be the kind of person who liked to fan the drama flames. "Okay, let's talk to them."

"There's one more thing, but I don't want you to panic."

Luke felt his chest tighten. "What is it?"

Oscar reached out and patted his shoulder. "Don't stress, it's probably not a big deal, but I can't find my ID card."

"What do you mean?"

"Look, it's probably in the room somewhere. I'm hoping, but I'm just worried it fell out of my backpack last night."

"You're kidding, right?"

Oscar shook his head without any sign of his usual careless smile. "I wish. Look, worst-case scenario, I dropped it in the clearing when we were running back to our dorm. I can always say I was on a morning walk if someone finds it."

"*That's* not the worst-case scenario," Luke protested. "Worst-case scenario is they find it in the woods, or the Dip. Jeez, Oscar. How could you be so careless? You're going to get us busted!"

Oscar nodded. "Dude, chill. Let's just hope it doesn't happen. Maybe I can go look for it out there during my next free period."

But Luke wouldn't be placated. "There are cops everywhere! There's no way you can go look for it. You just better pray it's buried under some pile of leaves and no one will ever find it."

"I was never a religious guy," Oscar tried to joke. "But maybe it's time for some prayers. Have you seen Mrs. P. around? I'm sure she can give me some Bible passages to study."

"Dude, it's not funny," said Luke, angrily. His cheeks were flushed, his head was spinning, and everything felt out of control. "We have to try and find that card. And in the meantime, we have to make sure the girls are on the same page. Let's text them to meet us at Main Hall tonight."

5

Kelsey's eyes were red from tears. She was gripping a big ball of Kleenex tightly in her fist. Luke and Oscar were attempting to calm her down, but it was difficult with Pippa continuously expressing her irritation.

The day had been a flurry of phone calls between stressed-out parents and nervous students. Besides sports and classes being cancelled, much of the campus was off-limits during the day. Even the Jigger Shop, aka "the Jig," where they could buy snack food like bagels and fries, was closed. So was the school store. Instead of the requisite chapel session before sit-down dinner, students had met in their dorm common rooms with the counselors and dorm heads. They were supposed to listen to a lecture on safety, then discuss "how they felt about things." Fortunately, Mr. Crawford hadn't forced the boys in Wilcox to discuss their emotions or how they were doing. They had met briefly and awkwardly as a group with a counselor and then watched a few episodes of *Blue Mountain State* to kill time before dinner.

Some parents had arrived and yanked their children out of school, but the administration had gone into overdrive to prevent that from happening by promising amped-up security. Luke had been able to calm his parents down on the phone. Surprisingly, it hadn't taken much. After his past incident his parents had made him go to a psychologist for a year, and Dr. Carey's biggest advice for his whole family was that they had to move on and not live in crippling fear. Luke just had to invoke Dr. Carey's name and his parents backed off.

Besides, Luke had never seen so many policemen and security guards in one place. The school was teeming with them. And everyone on campus was looking over their shoulders, watching their backs, checking each other out. *If I were the killer, I'd be pretty nervous right now*, thought Luke.

Both Oscar and Luke turned their room upside down to search for Oscar's ID card that day, but they couldn't find it. They retraced their steps from the tree they climbed down to the basement where they reentered. Unfortunately, their search stopped abruptly at the edge of the woods. The cops wouldn't even let them get within ten yards, so Oscar was forced to retrieve a new ID card at the dean of students' office. Fortunately, Mr. P. was tied up with all of the murder mess, so Oscar only had to deal with his assistant. He told her that the card had fallen out of his cell phone case that morning.

At night, after study hall, the students were let out of their rooms for thirty minutes for what was affectionately known as Animal Hour, which was when everyone met up to look for their crush or get snack food, not necessarily in that order. Tonight they weren't allowed to be outdoors because of the murder, but that was fine because everyone usually ended up inside Main Hall anyway. Despite the fact that the fluorescent lighting was garish, the headmaster's office was centrally located right on it, and there was absolutely no privacy, this is where the students mostly hung out. If a boy talked to a girl in Main Hall after dinner, by study hall every single student knew about it. Same for any Animal Hour meet-ups.

There were usually only one or two teachers at most lingering around Main Hall, but that night there were several watching everyone nervously. Fortunately, they were mostly preoccupied with whispering their theories to one another, so Luke, Oscar, Kelsey and Pippa were able to surreptitiously slip away one by one and regroup in one of the soundproof music rooms in the basement. It had been their first opportunity all day to meet. Luke was glad for the excuse to see Pippa, even if she had blown him off after chapel earlier.

"Look, calm down, Kelsey. You have nothing to be upset about," said Oscar.

Luke was sitting in one of the small chairs leaning forward so his hands were resting on the music stand. Kelsey was on top of the piano, while Oscar sat at the piano bench and every now and then played some of the keys in what was a misremembered version of "Yankee Doodle," much to the others' irritation.

"I just feel like we need to come clean, like, go to the headmaster and tell him that we were out there and just, like, pray he doesn't do anything," she said, sniffling.

"Yeah, right, Kelsey. What he's going to do is expel us. Or at least me. I'm on thin ice here. Thanks to Dean Heckler, one more infraction and I'm out," said Oscar. He banged on the piano and then stopped and shook his head. "Gee, Dean, karma's a bitch."

"But maybe they'll forgive us because of the circumstances . . ." sighed Kelsey, hopeful.

"We'll just become suspects," said Pippa tartly. She was standing in the back of the room leaning against the poster of Beethoven. "It's never a good idea to go to the police, ever. They turn everything on you. Trust me, I know. My mother is a barrister—a lawyer, as you Americans call it. The second we admit anything, they'll have us all go against each other and next thing you know one of us is on the line for this murder."

"Whoa. I don't know about that," Luke said.

"One of *us*? No way! We can all vouch for each other!" Kelsey exclaimed.

"Actually, we can't," said Oscar. "You went out to the bathroom and separated from Pippa."

"I didn't *separate* from her, she ditched me!" Kelsey said, dissolving into tears. "Why would you say it like that? You think *I* could have done it?"

"None of us thinks you did it, Kelsey," said Luke, exasperated. He knew Oscar well enough to see that his roommate was probably losing interest in Kelsey already, which could be disastrous. A scorned woman is an outspoken woman, and Luke had seen it happen before with other girls Oscar had tired of and heartlessly discarded. "We just need to stick together right now because we don't know what other people might think. There's no need to go to the headmaster because right now, we don't really have any information to offer them. We know she was out there, but so do the police, obviously. What else can we add?"

"Well, we know that she was talking to some bloke who was really mad at her, and we know the first Mrs. Heckler was out there with her dog. I'm sure they'd love to know that," said Pippa, before adding, "But hell if I'm going to tell them anything."

Luke was surprised, but gratified, that Pippa was so intent on not saying anything. He wondered why she was so determined not to go to the police, but at the same time, he didn't want to press it.

"What about the creepy-voice guy?" whispered Kelsey, almost to herself. "That was so weird and scary."

They were all silent for a minute, then Oscar slapped his hands down hard on the piano, making a jarring discordant clang and causing them all to jump. "We don't know anything about that, so as of now, our lips are sealed. Just carry on like nothing happened. Don't act suspicious. Play it cool," advised Oscar.

"Fine by me," Pippa said.

Kelsey didn't say anything. She was probably waiting for Oscar to reassure her. Luke glared at his roommate and tipped his head toward Kelsey, signaling him that now was not the time to withhold attention.

"Deal, Kels?" asked Oscar, getting the message. He stood up from the piano bench and gently tucked a strand of Kelsey's long hair behind her ear. She visibly relaxed. Ordinarily Luke would be rolling his eyes at this classic and cliché Oscar move, but tonight he was just glad Oscar had both the ability to calm Kelsey down and the willingness to do it.

"All right, that's settled, can I go now?" said Pippa, moving off the wall toward the door.

"Sure," Luke said, but he was confused. They had talked about hanging out tonight, hadn't they? Telenovelas and all that? Murder was a real romance-killer.

Pippa bolted out the door without waiting for anyone else.

"Bye, nice hanging out with you, let's do it again soon," Kelsey said sarcastically to the closed door.

Luke couldn't help it; he laughed. Kelsey smiled, appreciating the break in tension.

"Okay, I'm going to go up now," Kelsey said. "Wait a few minutes before you leave so people don't see us coming up the stairs together."

"Sure."

Oscar began playing "Heart and Soul" on the piano and Luke fiddled with the music stand. After a few minutes they stood and began walking up the stairs.

Outside, the air had cooled considerably since the morning, and cold hovered over the campus. Luke felt a shift in the campus mood since last night. There was a creepy stillness; it was definitely the scene of a crime.

"Why do you think Pippa's going along with us?" asked Luke as he zipped up his Barbour jacket. That was actually secondary to what he was really wondering, which was whether she liked him at all. If he had to admit, he wanted Oscar to say she was going along with it because she liked Luke. But Oscar didn't take the bait.

"Protecting her ass, probably," said Oscar. "Oh, excuse me: her *arse*."

Luke ignored the dig. "But she hates it here. I doubt she cares about getting busted."

"I think she just plays it that way. Wants to be a tough guy. I think she's all facade."

"There is something a little . . . unsettling . . . about her," admitted Luke.

"No doubt about it. Glad you're finally seeing the light," said Oscar, as they turned the corner down the path that looped around the pond. Other groups of students were on their way back to their dorms too, with several security guards and teachers moving them along.

"Do you remember anything else that guy said to Mrs. Heckler?" asked Luke suddenly.

Oscar looked up at the sky. "He said something like, 'You'll regret this.'"

"Like a threat?" asked Luke.

"Kind of. She definitely seemed sketched out by the guy. Like she couldn't wait to get away. Plus that creepy voice . . ."

Luke stopped. He had a sickening thought. "Hey, remember that sound I heard? That yelp?"

"No," Oscar shook his head. "I wasn't there for that."

"Oh, right. Well, there was this weird little yelping noise. Like the sound my dog makes when someone steps on her foot by accident."

Oscar waved to a girl he'd hooked up with two weeks earlier. "Maybe it was the first Mrs. Heckler's dog," he suggested, distractedly. "Hey, honey!" he called to a freshman he was scoping. She blushed and turned back to her friends, giggling.

"I was thinking maybe it was when she was being killed," said Luke quietly.

Oscar snapped back to attention, He stopped and contemplated that idea. "Whoa. That's nasty."

"Yeah."

"And that sound you and I heard afterward was the killer dragging her body," said Oscar.

Luke shook his head. "Ugh. I don't want to think about that."

"I know; it's insane."

They were almost to the dorm.

"Do you think it could have been the Southborough Strangler?" asked Luke.

Oscar used his new ID card to unlock the door. "No. I don't think there's a Southborough Strangler. I think the

56

killer is here, on this very campus, walking among us."

Luke's tensed as they entered Wilcox, looking over his shoulder before the door slammed shut. Again, he had the unshakable feeling that someone was watching him.

6

The media had caught on to the murder and their vans and satellite trucks were camped outside the school hoping to nab some hapless student for an interview. As a result, the administration had put major restrictions on social media and Wi-Fi access and had the security company monitoring everything.

Students always had to use their ID cards to get into their dorms, but generally the school had been pretty relaxed about locking up the academic and sports buildings. Now every building was locked all the time, requiring an ID card for entry, and there were additional security checkpoints in the main buildings. Mostly this was inconvenient, because when the weather got cold students liked to cut through the buildings instead of following the paths.

There was a claustrophobic atmosphere on campus. Everyone felt it. Security guards seemed to be around every corner. Teachers were omnipresent. Lights out was actually being enforced. Police fanned through the woods, bringing sniffing German shepherds with them. All the kids were talking about the surreal "Big Brother is watching" vibe and how it was like living at home with your parents.

Luke and Oscar had both tried to continue their normal routine while pretending they hadn't seen or heard anything in the woods that night. Oscar was having an easier time doing that than Luke, which made sense. The scariest situation Oscar had ever been in was over last year's Christmas break in New York City, when a devout taxi driver had objected to him making out with Caroline Rossi in the backseat, started waving a knife, and kicked them both out thirty blocks from Caroline's apartment. But for Luke, this whole murder thing was a lot more personal. It was a connection to his past, as much as he wished that wasn't true. He'd been able to save himself before, and he'd escaped death this time as well, but someone had still died. It weighed on him.

"Hi, Luke."

Luke was on line at the school store when Pippa breezed past him on her way out. He had been talking to Liz, who was in front of him, and he hadn't even noticed Pippa paying at the register.

"Oh, hi, Pippa," said Liz.

"Hey," Luke said, hopefully.

But Pippa barely looked at him before exiting. He felt his

face flush from an irrational wave of anger at Mrs. Heckler for ruining his chances with Pippa.

Luke was holding a giant bag of potato chips, replacement batteries for his graphing calculator, and deodorant—just some of the miscellany that he was always rushing to the school store to buy. Liz's basket was full of packs of Post-its, printer paper and a bag of Bic erasable pens. The school store, which was located on the ground floor of Talbot, a white clapboard building with black shutters that housed all of the language classrooms upstairs, was always buzzing with students buying all of the random supplies needed for life at boarding school. It was stuff they really couldn't find in the small town of Southborough and since the nearest mall was about thirty minutes away, St. Benedict's provided students with the opportunity to buy what they needed on campus. In essence, the school was this little self-contained entity, a microcosm that existed in its own little world, supplemented by a daily avalanche of Amazon packages.

"Are you guys friends?" Luke asked Liz when Pippa was fully out of earshot.

"Friend-*ly*," said Liz. "I don't really know her, but she seems cool."

"You're the first person I've heard say that."

Liz shrugged. "A lot of the girls get threatened when a new girl comes, especially if she's pretty. And look, Pippa isn't exactly the warmest person I ever met, but I think it's kind of intimidating to be the only new girl in your grade."

Luke nodded, and Liz laughed.

"Yeah, you're nodding your head like you know what I'm talking about, but you have no idea. Girls can be brutal. Cliquey, and they totally close ranks. A few weeks ago I walked past Pippa's dorm room and popped my head in and I could tell she was upset. She told me how tough it was. She's a little different, not your typical American boarding school girl, but she wants to be liked just as much as the rest of us."

"Good point," Luke mused.

The line was moving slowly, with kids stocking up on several baskets worth of supplies, as if preparing for a hurricane. Luke shifted his bag of chips into his other hand.

"It's so weird here right now, don't you think?" asked Liz.

"Yeah. Police state."

"Apparently the police are leaving soon. There have been a lot of complaints from parents that they were freaking the kids out with their giant 'Crime Scene' windbreakers and dogs. Two more girls from my dorm left this morning."

"Really?"

"Uh huh," she nodded. "It'll just be the security guards after the cops leave."

"But don't the police have to solve the crime?"

"I guess, but maybe they have a suspect."

"I haven't heard anything, have you?" asked Luke.

"No, but . . . I'm getting the impression it was kind of a 'take a number' thing. A lot of people hated Mrs. Heckler."

"Really?" asked Luke intrigued. "Like who?"

Liz leaned in closer. "Well, Mrs. Palmer is my adviser so I

61

had to meet with her this morning, and when I got there she was talking to Ms. Chang—the new English teacher, who's actually my dorm head."

"Yeah, I know who she is," said Luke. So did every other male on campus. Attractive teachers were definitely noteworthy.

"Well," Liz lowered her tone and glanced around. "When I got there I was waiting for them to finish their conversation and I was kind of outside the office but they were talking, and you know how Mrs. Palmer is kind of conservative? Well, she was saying something about 'if you behave a certain way and go after other people's husbands, it's not going to end well.'"

"Really?"

"Yeah, and then Ms. Chang started to whisper that she heard something about Joanna being a man-magnet, but she didn't know the details and frankly she didn't really see the attraction because Joanna was so obvious, and Mrs. Palmer said she would fill her in later but it would take a long time to tell her the backstory, but something about 'reaping what you sow' and 'playing with fire and getting burned.' "

"She loves her Bible quotes, doesn't she?"

"Yeah, but I'm not into slut-shaming. Not that women should go for married men, but it takes two to tango, you know?"

"Next!" the cashier called. Liz plunked her stuff on the counter and Luke noticed she was buying shin guards.

"You play field hockey, don't you? Kelsey's on your team, right?"

62

"Yeah, she's our star offensive player."

"I heard she's good. Hard to imagine. She seems a little . . . fluffy."

Liz shook her head. "That girl is a shark out there. I won't say vicious, but she's sent some of the other teams home battered and bruised. No question she'll go to a D-1 school."

"Wow. Interesting."

Maybe Kelsey wasn't so weak and helpless after all, thought Luke. *Why did she pretend she was whenever she got around Oscar?*

"Come quick! You gotta see this!"

Luke was just exiting Talbot and walking toward the quad behind the library when Andy Slater called out to him. He stopped and waited for Luke as several students ran past, taking the path toward the pond.

"What is it?"

"Just come! They think they found something."

By the time Luke and Slater made it to the pond there was a large group of kids clustered in the northwest corner pointing at something. Luke could see two security guards in front of the pack, furiously talking on their walkie-talkies, and one on his knees by the pond.

"What is it?" Luke asked.

Andy elbowed through the crowd, with Luke following. There was frenzied excitement in the air, and everyone was pointing and talking nervously.

"It's a bra!" said Andy, who had a better view from his vantage point.

The news rippled through the crowd, setting off a cacophony of comments and outbursts.

"Is it Mrs. Heckler's?" some student called out.

"The Southborough Strangler was here!" shrieked a girl's voice.

"Was someone else murdered?" another girl called out.

"Okay, everyone, move aside." Mr. Hamaguchi, a science teacher, pushed his way through the crowd. "Step back right now or you will be receiving demerits."

The students dispersed enough to make a path for Mr. Hamaguchi and the additional security guards. Mr. Hamaguchi bent down next to the security guard, who was using a stick to pull the bra toward him. Luke heard footsteps slapping the pavement and glanced to his side to see Mr. P. running from the direction of Archer. His tie was askew and his hair windblown.

"What is it?" asked the dean, moving toward Mr. Hamaguchi.

The guard pulled up the bra in time for everyone to see that it was a lacy and red. He immediately bagged it in a Ziploc and sealed it closed.

Mr. Hamaguchi and the dean conferred in hushed tones, and everyone stood still, craning to hear what they were saying.

"Is it Mrs. Heckler's?" Andy called out.

Mr. P. put his hands up. "Everyone back to class."

"Should we be worried?" a girl's plaintive voice called out.

"No. This was obviously a prank, and not at all funny," warned Mr. P. "We will be looking into this."

"How do you know it's a joke?"

"Yeah, maybe someone else was strangled and dumped in the pond."

That set off a new wave of frenzied discussions.

The teachers ignored them and began walking through the crowd back to the main building with the security guards following.

"Come on, tell us!"

Suddenly, Mr. Hamaguchi whipped around. He was a thickset man with a full head of coarse dark hair, an imposing figure when he squared his shoulders. He stared at the crowd with watery dark eyes. "You know, this voyeurism into a horrible tragedy is disgusting. You should all be ashamed of yourselves. Students of St. Benedict's should know better. How dare you speculate this way? A woman has lost her life."

Mr. Hamaguchi abruptly turned and walked away. Mr. P. followed.

"Whoa," Luke said. "Why was he so mad? And what if that was evidence? Shouldn't they have called the police to come get it themselves? It might not have been a prank."

"Yeah, it was. I caught a glimpse," Andy said. "'Juicy Joanna' was written in Sharpie."

Everyone groaned.

"Are you serious?" Luke hadn't noticed Liz join the group, but there she was, looking outraged. "That's not a prank, that's the sign of a seriously deranged individual. Who would do that? You, Andy?"

"No!" Andy said. "God. Definitely not me. It was probably just a senior prank."

It was a rite of passage at St. Benedict's for the seniors to play a series of pranks during their last year, culminating with an enormous prank in May. Last year's class had somehow driven the football coach's car into the center of the pond in the middle of the night—that didn't go over very well. But it wasn't as bad as the year the class of 2010 had stolen the delivery of fetal pigs that the science department was going to use for dissection and threw them from the balcony of the chapel onto the laps and heads of all the students, who were wearing their Sunday best. Some of the seniors actually got expelled for that one, but year after year the pranks kept coming.

"Don't say *senior prank* like it makes everything okay," Liz said. "Senior pranks should be funny. This wasn't funny. It's misogyny, plain and simple, and I'm so tired of this school giving students a pass when they do dumb or disgusting things and claim it's tradition."

Liz was furious, and rightly so.

Andy had his hands up. "Hey! I didn't do it, I swear."

"But you thought it was funny. Oh, haha, 'Juicy Joanna.' What about you, Luke? You think that's funny, too?"

"No! Not at all."

The crowd was gathered around, listening, some of the girls nodding. "You go, Liz! Tell them."

66

Luke grabbed Andy's arm. "I think we should go."

The boys retreated, murmuring apologies. *Wow*, Luke thought. The murder was definitely stirring things up on campus. First Mr. Hamaguchi, now Liz. Everyone was on edge.

The worst part? If people he considered friends could turn on him so quickly for something he didn't even do, what would happen if they knew he'd actually been there when Mrs. Heckler was killed? Luke hoped he never had to find out.

7

The following day Luke and Oscar were on their way to the chapel for the memorial service for Mrs. Heckler. Dress code was enforced. Coat and tie for the boys, dresses for the girls—clothes usually reserved for chapel talks and sit-down dinners.

"Hey, Luke, do you have a second?"

Luke felt his heart go a little faster. It was Pippa. Her cheeks looked pinker than usual, maybe from the wind, and it made her look softer, not as fragile. He'd avoided her at Animal Hour the night before; he'd decided to wean himself off his interest in her. But now here she was again, and looking good, too.

Luke glanced at Oscar who rolled his eyes and kept walking. "Try not to be late," he called over his shoulder.

"Aren't you heading to the service?" Luke asked Pippa.

"This will only take a minute."

They veered off the path to go under the sycamore tree.

There was a bench there, donated in honor of a member of the class of 1998 who had died in a car accident, but neither of them sat down. It was an unwritten rule that only seniors were allowed to sit on the bench, and you could get hazed if anyone caught you there. Luke had never attempted to see what would happen if he tried, and he wasn't about to start now. Still, it would have been nice to have a seat. It was sort of awkward standing there.

Pippa took off her striped scarf and rewrapped it around her throat. Luke plunged his hands into his pockets and was trying to think of something to say when she finally spoke.

"Listen, I'm sorry if I've been a little brusque lately."

"Oh. It's okay."

"No, it's not. I've been quite rude, really. I don't mean to, it's just . . . well, I've been burned a bit of late, and I have a hard time trusting people."

"I can relate," confessed Luke. He thought about all of the new "best" friends he acquired after his abduction. There are so many people who just like to coast on other people's fame or notoriety. When he had first arrived on campus his classmates wanted to make him into some sort of celebrity because of what happened to him, and his story was told over and over with great embellishment. But Luke wanted no part of playing the victim, or the hero, for that matter. So he had learned early that the best way to deflect unwanted interest was to keep his cards close to his chest, and to confide in a select few.

"I know you can relate, and that's why I quite like you,

Luke," Pippa said. She looked him squarely in the eye. "You're what my friend Tamara would have called a brilliant egg."

"A what? I've never heard that one before," Luke said, embarrassed but also kind of psyched.

"It suits you."

"Um . . . thanks? I think."

"Don't worry, it's a compliment. I wish you could have met Tamara . . . Look, I know I'm a bit cagey, but I do have good reason . . . "

She tapered off. Luke could see in her face that she was conflicted.

"Is there something you want to talk about? I mean, I want to say you can trust me, but that sounds like something strangers say to each other on one of those online dating sites."

Pippa smiled. "It does, really. But I do think you're genuine. I can't talk about it now. It's not you, it's me, as the saying goes. But I just want to let you know that . . . I don't know . . . just bear with me, if you will. I need to get some things sorted. And I emphatically don't want anything to do with this whole Mrs. Heckler murder. The last thing I need is more police in my life."

"More police?"

"Police. Police in general," she added quickly. "You remember, I told you my mother was a barrister."

"Oh. Right."

"Luke! I've been looking for you."

Luke was startled. He turned around to find Mr. P. approaching. He glanced back at Pippa, who was pulling at the ends of her scarf nervously.

"Hi, Mr. P.," Pippa said. "Text me," she whispered before slipping away.

The dean waved at her but was all business.

"Luke, could you please follow me? We'd like a word," said Mr. P.

Luke nodded. "Sure." *Who's "we"?* He wanted to ask, but he didn't dare.

They walked together toward Archer, making small talk along the way. Just as they were about to enter the building, Luke saw Kelsey, who took in the situation and flashed an even more panicked expression than he'd just seen on Pippa. Luke gave her a quick nod as if to assure her that everything was cool, but he felt a pit forming in his stomach. What if they knew something? But then why single *him* out? Maybe because they thought they could break him. He decided to be strong. He'd stick to the plan. He only hoped the girls would, too. But judging from Kelsey's reaction, it didn't look good.

Instead of turning left into Mr. P.'s office, the dean made a right turn into Headmaster Thompson's office. Luke surveyed the room nervously. He had only been in the wood-paneled office a handful of times before, and every time the atmosphere had been light, with so many other people crammed inside the rectangular room that it had felt festive. There was a decidedly different feeling today, one of tension and gloom. Even the subjects of the framed oil paintings on the wall seemed to stare down at him with suspicion. Although a fire crackled softly in the fireplace, the room felt cold and unwelcoming. Besides the headmaster, one of the policemen from the assembly was seated in the leather armchair, reviewing a manila file. He looked up and studied Luke carefully.

"Come on in, Luke," said the headmaster. "Have a seat."

Luke prayed the beads of sweat forming on his forehead were invisible. His tie felt tight around his neck. He quietly took a seat and felt three sets of eyes boring into him. The headmaster remained behind his desk, and Mr. P. sat on the radiator next to the window, folding his arms and staring at Luke.

"Luke, this is Chief Corcoran. I think you'll remember he spoke at the assembly." The headmaster motioned to the policeman.

"Yes, hello," Luke said.

The chief didn't say anything. Luke shifted uncomfortably in his seat.

"Luke, you're a leader here at school. I was telling Chief Corcoran that you have been on the student government since you were a freshman, and it's most likely that you'll be elected student body president next year. You're a varsity soccer and lacrosse player, and a dorm prefect. A solid B+ student," said the headmaster, smiling.

Luke nodded, stifling an irrational urge to laugh at the headmaster lauding his average grades.

"I thought we'd bring you in, talk to you a little bit about what the situation is here. Maybe hear what you have to say," said the headmaster.

"I'm not sure how I can help," Luke said. "I barely knew Mrs. Heckler."

The chief cleared his throat. "We're more interested in collecting perspectives from around campus the night of the murder. Did you notice anything unusual?"

"No, sir." Luke's voice didn't betray any of the panic he was feeling inside. Anything unusual? Holy crap. They obviously knew he'd been out of the dorm.

"Nothing at all? Nothing out of the ordinary that night? Everyone where they were supposed to be?"

Luke kept his gaze steady. "Yes, from what I recall."

Inside, his stomach was roiling. He didn't know what to do. If he admitted he'd been in the woods, there was no going back, and the consequences would be huge and irreversible. On the other hand, if he didn't say something now, it could be worse for him if it ever did come out—he was breaking the school's honor code by lying, and that was grounds for immediate expulsion. Not to mention, he didn't like the idea of withholding any information that might help find the killer.

The chief continued staring at him, waiting for Luke to blink. Luke met his gaze, refusing to back down, feeling as if his life depended on it. Or at least, his life here at St. Benedict's.

"Is there something specific you're wondering about?"

Luke asked. "Things have been pretty crazy, so my memory isn't the best right now, but I want to help. Maybe if I knew exactly what time or place you're wondering about, I can think harder about it."

"Let's talk about your roommate," the chief said. "Oscar Weymouth. We found his student ID card in a very unusual place last night."

Luke gulped, surprised by both the directness of the revelation and the fact that the ID was turning out to be the exact worst-case scenario he'd feared.

"Oh?" he asked, cursing himself that his voice came out all high pitched and nervous. "Where?"

The chief didn't answer. "Did Oscar leave your room at all the night Joanna Heckler was murdered?"

"No."

"No? Are you certain?"

Luke was definitely at a crossroads. It was now time to make a choice, one that he could not go back on, but he wasn't going to turn on Oscar, not now, not without a chance to talk to him first about a plan.

"I'm certain I didn't see him leave."

Technically, that was true. Luke hadn't "seen him leave." He had "left with him." He hoped they didn't call him out on the semantics.

"Luke, I've heard a lot about you from Headmaster Thompson. And glancing through your folder, I'd say you pretty much toe the line," said the chief.

Luke flinched. The chief was looking at his file? Was that

legal? Suddenly Luke wished he could have a lawyer present. He shifted in his leather armchair.

"Luke has always been a fine member of the community," added Mr. P.

Luke felt awash with relief that Mr. P. was coming to his defense. Mr. P.'s words carried weight. He had actually gone to St. Benedict's, and Luke was certain he had *never* ended up in the headmaster's office for any sort of infraction. Even though he was still in his early thirties it was hard for students to ever imagine him as a teenager. He was always so serious.

"There is one thing that I don't quite understand, though," said the chief, again staring at Luke intently. "Your friendship with Oscar. I've been learning quite a bit about him today, and it doesn't seem as if the two of you are the most compatible."

Luke tried to remain cool.

"Well, Oscar's been my roommate since freshman year. We were placed together, and well, we've roomed together ever since."

Luke thought of the first day of freshman year. At the time, Luke was a shy and slightly nervous fourteen-year-old who was escorted to campus by both of his overprotective parents as well as his oldest sister, Katie. He was from Georgetown and possessed some of the savvy that comes from growing up in a city, but the kidnapping the year before had turned him into an international celebrity. He was feeling pretty vulnerable starting at St. Benedict's, knowing that everyone on campus knew everything about him. He didn't want people to treat him differently or befriend him for the wrong reasons, like some of his groupies had at home. But that didn't happen with Oscar. By the time Luke and his family found his room on the second floor of Nichols, Oscar had dismissed his own parents and coated the wall with posters of old rebel bands like The Clash, Pink Floyd, and The Sex Pistols.

"Don't expect any royal treatment," Oscar had warned. "I'm not going to think you're cool just because you've been on YouTube."

Oscar had been the only one who was straight with Luke in those days and it was totally refreshing. It was exactly what Luke had needed and they had been best friends ever since.

"Yes, but why?" asked the chief. "Surely you can switch roommates, can't you, Mr. Thompson?" He turned to face the headmaster.

"Of course," nodded the headmaster, now looking more serious than before.

"So why stick with Oscar?" asked the chief again.

"We're friends," said Luke.

"But you don't seem to have much in common," said the chief.

"That's not true," protested Luke. "We're both on the lax team, we both like obscure British sitcoms, and newspapers like *The Onion* . . ." Luke's voice faded. It all sounded so trite when you had to outline the reasons you liked someone.

The chief looked at him carefully. "It seems like Oscar is on his last legs here."

Last legs? Why was he saying that now?

"Well, I know he likes to challenge authority but—"

"Challenge authority?" interrupted the chief. "How so?"

Did he say the wrong thing? It wasn't anything new; for sure the chief had Oscar's file there. "I don't know, I mean, yes, he's been busted before for certain things . . ."

"Then I'm sure you also know who suspended him last year for going into New Haven for the day without signing out."

Luke's mind raced. "Um . . ."

"Dean Heckler," said the chief. "He's the one who put Oscar one step away from expulsion. Came down hard on him, as I understand. I'm sure Oscar is not too fond of Dean Heckler."

Luke didn't know what to say. It was true, Oscar was no fan of Dean Heckler, but he really didn't like any member of the faculty. He didn't even really trust the cool teachers like Mr. Crawford—who Oscar insisted had arrested development and still wished he were a student at St. B's rather than a teacher. But if they were trying to imply that it was reason enough for Oscar to retaliate against Heckler's wife, well, that was ridiculous.

"Oscar talks a big game," said Luke. "But underneath, he's a good guy."

The chief gave Luke a look of disbelief that made it clear he was skeptical. *He's the type of guy that could extract con-*

fessions from innocent people, thought Luke. He wondered if the chief had ever met Dean Heckler before the murder. They were a lot alike.

"Look, sir, I understand how he might come off, but your perception of Oscar is all wrong. I feel like . . ." Luke hesitated. It was hard to describe how he felt about Oscar without sounding overly sentimental. "I'm definitely a better person because of Oscar. He's sort of, you know, always looked out for me."

"Did he?" asked the headmaster.

Luke turned to him and nodded. "I'm not sure I would have survived here without him. This place can be really intense."

"But you've survived intense situations before, Luke," the chief pointed out. "On your own."

Luke nodded, knowing what the chief was alluding to but hoping they weren't going to go there.

"I read all about you this morning, Luke. And I remember seeing you interviewed on, what was it? *Good Morning America?*" asked the chief.

Luke shrugged. "Could have been." The fact was, Luke had been interviewed on most of the national morning shows. He'd gotten all sorts of attention after his abduction.

"You don't like to talk about that, Luke?" asked the chief.

"It's ancient history," said Luke, pulling at his jacket cuff. The room was getting even hotter.

"You were pretty brave," said the chief.

"Luke showed tremendous courage," interjected the

headmaster. "To remain calm and show the strength and determination to escape, even in his weakened condition was an impressive feat very few could have achieved."

Luke squirmed. He hated this conversation. He felt the chief studying him carefully.

"May I show you something?"

"Sure," said Luke, with the hope that this would change the subject from sneaking out.

The chief glanced at the headmaster who nodded, before taking a large manila envelope off the desk and sliding out some large photographs.

"What you are about to see is privileged. We don't want you discussing this with any of your classmates, you understand?"

"Yes," said Luke.

"These are crime scene photographs. Are you choosing to see them?" asked the chief.

"Uh huh," said Luke.

"What's that?" snapped the chief.

"Yes, sir," said Luke. He stomach was twisting into a knot.

"We can have your parents present for this, son," said the headmaster, reaching his hand over the table.

"No, it's okay," said Luke.

The chief handed him the stack of photographs. Luke looked at the first one. It was of a body—Mrs. Heckler no doubt—face down in a pile of leaves. Her dirty blond hair was splayed around her head and her arms were opened wide by her sides, as if she had been reaching out. She was wearing jeans and a dark green coat, with a maroon scarf around her neck. He felt sad. She probably had no idea that when she chose this outfit that it would be her last, and then some kid would be in the headmaster's office staring at pictures of her dead body. He wondered if her parents were alive. His parents would be devastated if anything happened to him or his sisters. His kidnapping had almost killed them.

Luke looked at the next photograph. It was a close-up of Mrs. Heckler's head. There was no blood or anything. All he could really see was her hair and the scarf. He could tell it was a St. Benedict's scarf, the one most students and teachers bought from the school store.

He wasn't sure how long he was supposed to take looking at each picture, and he could tell that everyone in the room was watching his reaction carefully. The thing was, at this angle, the pictures could be of anyone. Of course he knew that it was Mrs. Heckler, but he couldn't see her face or anything. And besides, he'd seen so many episodes of *Law and Order* and *Criminal Minds* that pictures of dead bodies didn't seem that outrageous. Sure, the ones on TV were fake, but they didn't look any different from these pictures.

"What do you think, Luke?" asked the chief.

"I think, it's . . . um . . . sad."

"It is sad," said the chief, reclaiming the photographs and sticking them back in their envelope. "Any idea from those pictures how she was killed?"

"Strangled, maybe? By the Southborough Strangler?"

"And did you notice what was around her neck?" asked the chief.

"It looked like a St. Benedict's scarf," admitted Luke. He didn't know what they were after. Why did they show him the photos?

"Good deduction," said the chief. "It was in fact a St. Benedict's scarf. And do you know whose it was?"

"No, I have no idea."

"It was Oscar's scarf. His name was sewn right there into the tag."

Luke flushed. He hadn't been prepared for that. Oscar's scarf was the murder weapon? Luke felt suddenly dizzy. But no, this was *Oscar* they were talking about! His roommate of the last three years! There had to be an explanation. There was no way that Oscar had killed Mrs. Heckler. Right?

"Someone could have stolen his scarf."

"Do you think so? Did he mention anything like that?" asked the chief.

"No," Luke admitted.

"No," the chief repeated smugly, leaning back in his armchair. "Which makes sense, because as it turns out, there were yearbook pictures taken two days ago, the day of Mrs. Heckler's murder."

The chief pulled out another photograph from his folder and slapped it on Luke's lap. Sure enough, there was Oscar in the back row, wearing his St. Benedict's scarf.

Luke felt a rush into his head and for the first time realized that he was in over his head. Way over.

"So now we have Oscar's ID at the scene of the crime, and his scarf used as the murder weapon . . ."

"Well, the ID is not really . . ." Luke was about to blurt out the fact that they were all there but immediately stopped himself.

"The ID is not really what?" asked the chief.

Luke shook his head. "Nothing. I was just going to say that people lose those all the time. And scarves."

"Luke, now is the time to tell us anything you can think of about Oscar's relationship with Mrs. Heckler," said the headmaster.

"Relationship? I don't think he really knew her."

The headmaster and the chief exchanged knowing looks. Relationship? Luke wondered. Was he missing something?

Luke took a deep breath. "I promise you, I can't think of anything."

"Well then, we'll have to start at the beginning and you'll have to tell me everything you know about Oscar from the first day you met him," said the chief.

Great, thought Luke. That would take forever.

"I'll leave you to it," said the headmaster rising. "Dean Palmer will stay with you. I have to make a speech at the memorial service, but I will be back in twenty minutes. Make sure you're forthcoming, Luke."

"Of course."

What about all that talk at the assembly on how kids were not under suspicion, Luke wanted to ask. Was that all a crock?

8

By the time Luke left the headmaster's office the memorial service was over and it was time for soccer practice. He had spent the past forty-five minutes listening to the police tell him that Oscar was a troublemaker while pushing him to agree. At the end nothing was accomplished. Luke rushed up to his room to change, and was thankful that Oscar wasn't there. The room was still a mess from the ID search. He had neglected to send out his laundry, so he had to fish his old practice uniform out of his dirty hamper. Gross.

He was about to leave his room when he paused at the threshold. He glanced over at Oscar's side of the room. Making sure the door was firmly closed, he walked over to Oscar's desk. It was the usual mess: stacks of notebooks with papers spilling out of them, a St. Benedict's pencil holder overflowing with pens, Oscar's laptop, a small case of paperclips and a stapler. The usual stuff people would have on a desk.

Luke slid open the top drawer. There were photographs of Oscar and his friends from summer loosely strewn about. Girls and guys that Luke had heard about, some that he had met, looking like every teenager on Nantucket. Girls in bikinis and brightly colored dresses and guys in khaki shorts and Sperry's. Luke picked up one of the photos: Oscar, shirtless, wearing aviators and swinging off the mast of a sailboat. It was impossible for that guy to take a bad picture. Luke shook his head, and put it back on the pile. Next to the pictures were glue sticks and a small pack of monogrammed stationery with Oscar's initials. That was about it. Luke shut the dresser. Why was he snooping around Oscar's drawers? Oscar didn't have a "relationship" with Mrs. Heckler. Was he really actually taking the chief's words seriously? And what was he hoping to find?

He started to leave when something caught his eye. On the bottom of Oscar's small trash bin, underneath some Xeroxed papers announcing the Autumn Harvest Fair was a cherry red Post-it note. The adhesive had stuck to the white plastic garbage bag. Luke bent down and pulled it out.

On the top of the Post-it note was the St. Benedict's logo, followed by *JOANNA HECKLER, OFFICE OF ALUMNI AFFAIRS*, stamped underneath. Then in bubble handwriting, presumably Mrs. Heckler's, it said *The Pink Taco*. With a smiley face underneath. What did this mean? Why did Oscar have this? And more importantly, why had he thrown it away? Luke folded it up neatly and rummaged through his closet for a place to hide it. He retrieved of one his LL Bean boots and stuck it in the toe until he decided what to do with it. It was too weird. Was Oscar lying to him? Did he know Joanna Heckler a lot better than he had led on? And what did "The Pink Taco" mean?

Luke took a deep breath. He wanted to give Oscar the benefit of the doubt. For the past few days all of the students had gone crazy trying to dig up any info on Mrs. Heckler. Maybe someone got a hold of her pad and was writing weird stuff and spreading it around. It had to be some gag. That's why Oscar threw it away.

Luke calmed himself down enough to make it to practice on time.

"**D**ude, what did you think of that service?" asked Gupta as they put on their cleats in the locker room.

"I didn't go," said Luke.

"Dude, you bagged? That is *badass.*"

Luke didn't bother correcting him. "What did I miss?"

"Usual boring speeches. Nothing interesting. Although get this: Mr. Hamaguchi was bawling like a baby."

"Mr. Hamaguchi?" asked Luke, with surprise.

"Yeah, it was bizarre. Big, blubbery tears."

Luke remembered Mr. Hamaguchi's reaction at the pond. "Sounds like he's taking it hard."

"I'll say."

Luke had Mr. Hamaguchi for science, and he was the faculty adviser to STEAM, which basically met every few weeks and tried to keep St. B's on its toes about finding ways to be greener. Mr. Hamaguchi's role was limited; he showed up at meetings when they needed him to intervene with the faculty, but that was pretty rare. He never seemed very emotional and was actually kind of a stiff, so it was surprising to hear he was getting so upset over Joanna Heckler's death.

"Maybe they had something going on?" added Gupta.

"Come on, no way."

"Why not? You never know."

Luke was about to protest but then he stopped. *It's true, you never know.*

Luke reached the field with no time to spare. Coach Saunders told them they would do fifteen minutes of laps, and rather than groaning, Luke was actually grateful to have the time to run and clear his head. Nothing like the crisp October air to take his mind off everything.

The fields were a luscious green, glistening in the buttery afternoon sunshine. Pretty soon buckets of snow would cover them but for now, it was the kind of bright New England day that made it into the St. Benedict's brochure. The field hockey players were in their red kilts scrambling after the ball, the Big Red football team was doing drills—everyone looked alive and hearty. Luke started out running with the pack, but when everyone started talking about the murder, even slowing down to banter about it, Luke accelerated so that he could run alone and avoid any conversation. He was all talked out.

The chief had been relentless, pounding Luke and trying to convince him to turn on Oscar. He wanted Luke to disclose everything Oscar had ever said about Dean Heckler, any mention of his wife he may have made, and any streak of violence Oscar had exhibited. They continued to ask Luke if Oscar had left the room that night, or had ever snuck out, weaving it back in as if to trick him. Luke had been tempted to come clean, to tell them that yes, they had all snuck out that night; but it went against the plan and he worried that would only implicate Oscar further. Plus there *had* been those missing minutes, when Oscar was outside the Dip, presumably waiting for Mrs. Heckler and her friend to take off so he could return. Of course, Luke could try and cover for him, but what if they questioned Kelsey and Pippa? Would someone say something and it would all unravel? Would Luke be revealed as a liar and if so, what would happen to *him*? And most of all, what did Luke really think about Oscar now?

Luke wanted to believe that there was no way that Oscar could have done anything. Sure, Oscar had gotten into fistfights before. There was one bad one when they were at a party in New York City one weekend, but that was because some jerk had accused Oscar of hitting on his girlfriend and spit on him. Oscar was only defending himself. After that one incident, there had been no other violence. He hadn't even tried to fight that taxi driver who'd pulled the knife on him. And as for Mrs. Heckler, Luke had never heard Oscar say anything in particular about her. In fact, her name had never even come up.

But now there was a warning signal buzzing in Luke's mind that was forcing him to question Oscar. The missing minutes. The scarf. The weird yelping noise when Oscar was gone from the Dip. The fact that it was Oscar's idea not to come forward—and how he had insisted on it, even pressuring Kelsey. The recently discovered red Post-it, and the fact the police seemed to suspect him of something. The tension was gnawing at Luke, and a debate raged inside his head. On one side was the belief that his best friend would never do anything like this, but on the other, all those unanswered questions.

The headmaster had told him in no uncertain terms that he was not to confide in Oscar about the pictures or the suspicions they had against him, but Luke didn't think he could keep silent. Did they really expect him to act natural, like nothing happened, when he had to sleep three feet from the guy every night? It was absurd. Maybe they wanted him to crack and grill Oscar? Their room could be bugged.

Fifteen minutes was almost up but Luke didn't want to stop running. It felt so good to be outside in the open air, trying to forget about everything.

"Do you think I could do one loop in the woods?" Luke called out when he approached the coach's bench. "I really could use the exercise. Want to get out of my head."

The coach hesitated. "I don't know if that's a good idea."

"But there's a security guard right there," said Luke, motioning to a guard walking along the stone wall that ran the entire edge of campus. Coach Saunders eyed the guard, before nodding.

"Okay, you're off drills today so you can work on endurance. But tomorrow back to the schedule."

"Thanks, Coach," said Luke. He made his way up the hill to the Loop, the path that ran around the campus. He'd have to go through the woods, even near the part where Mrs. Heckler had died, but he wasn't scared. Actually, he *wanted* to be close to it, as if it would bring him some answers.

Inside the woods everything darkened immediately. The tall pine trees obscured the waning sunlight, and shadows flickered off surrounding rocks. All Luke could hear were his own footsteps, pounding along, smashing the crackling leaves below. His breathing sounded loud and panicky in the quiet. Luke twisted his head from one side to the other, studying the clusters of century-old trees. Soon they would be completely stripped of their shaggy leaves and turn into tangled knots of twisted branches. Everything was dying now.

Luke was starting to feel winded; he hadn't run this much in a long time. Maybe he'd been overly ambitious and should have stopped before with the others. He felt a slight cramp in his stomach, so he slowed his pace. There wasn't much further to go before getting back into the open, thank God, because Luke was starting to register that weird feeling again, like someone was pursuing him.

A strong sense of déjà vu descended on him and he was

instantly crushed by the vivid memory of the mad dash he'd made through the Virginia woods three years prior. His pulse quickened as thoughts of those harrowing days drifted back into his mind.

All of his senses were on fire, exploding with overstimulation. The warblers' songs echoed off the large oak and weathered hickory trees that engulfed him. Their cooing calls to one another seemed more ominous than joyful. The woods were steaming from a recent rainfall and Luke inhaled the strong odor with every heaving breath. His feet pounded over the muddy forest floor, splashed through puddles and over rust and copper-colored leaves, searching for an exit. Out of the corner of his eye, in the dark underbrush, he saw glimpses of woodchucks and groundhogs darting furtively out of his way, as scared of him as he was of his pursuers. The dazzling beauty of nature that his grandfather had introduced him to was now lost on him, and relegated to a dizzying and haunted backdrop for his worst nightmare.

By the grace of God, he had fled the cabin in the woods that his kidnappers had locked him in for two days. He'd taken off in the early hours of the morning when the moon was filmy and the sun just a promise. But not before he snuck into the cabin, holding his breath, praying his abductors wouldn't wake up, to grab some necessities for his escape into the dark woods. He had been well trained by his grandfather and knew what he needed to survive. He had stolen the thick wool sweater that he found dangling on a hook by the entrance and the large black-handled knife he had discovered in the top kitchen drawer. Luke had sifted through the cabinets, desperate to find any other portable provisions. A coil of rope, and a plastic bag into which he poured some household cleaning powder that he located under the sink. Ammonia. He had read about it in one of his grandfather's military books. Ammonia can hide human scent.

And so like Hansel and Gretel, Luke left his own version of a bread trail as he moved through the woods. He would run for approximately half an hour before slowing for ten minutes and sprinkling ammonia to conceal his scent. The slobbering, sharp-toothed attack dog that his captors kept tied to the front door would have a harder time finding him now. He preferred his running escape to slowing down. It was when he was still enough to hear his heart beat that he felt the pounding sense of fear commingled with claustrophobia. He was angry. Why had he been torn away from his family? Was it all for money? But what made him the angriest was that they had made him view the woods, so poetic and magical for his entire life until that point, as something sinister and fearful.

He only realized he was hungry when he stumbled upon a patch of teaberries. He knew they were edible, and so he would plop down amidst the spicebushes and other shrubs and eat the sticky berries until they stained his fingers a light pink. He'd take a second to watch the salamanders slither under the rocks, and remain motionless enough to hear the rustle of skunks and other wildlife make their way through the thick brush. Fortunately, there were natural springs in the woods, and when he would come across one, he'd slurp as much water *out of the palm of his hand, water that he'd scoop up fervently and drink until he couldn't. Then he would continue on. There was never a second where he wasn't aware that he was being hunted.*

Suddenly, Luke snapped back to the present, back to the St. Benedict's woods and stopped dead in his tracks.

Someone was there.

"Come out," Luke demanded in an even voice. He waited a beat before adding, "I know you're there."

Out of nowhere, a figure jumped down from a high tree branch, not three feet in front of him. Luke instinctively raised his fists, but dropped them at once.

"Mr. Tadeckis?"

"Very well done, Luke. Kudos," said Mr. Tadeckis, dusting himself off. "You always were an excellent tracker."

Mr. Tadeckis ran the Outdoor Survival Program. He was an awkwardly large man with creepy Napoleon Dynamite glasses and an unusual haircut—shaven on the sides with a large flop of dull brown hair on top. Everything about him was strange, from his camouflage outfits to the bulky knapsack that he always carried with him. He also had the annoying propensity to turn every question into a challenge.

"What are you doing out here, sir, if I may ask?" inquired Luke, still winded from his run.

"The better question is, what are *you* doing here?"

"I'm doing laps for soccer," Luke said.

Mr. Tadeckis looked in the distance. "Fair enough. I'm out here working on survival exercises. My unit is going up north in a few weeks and we're expecting some harsh conditions. You should join us, Luke. Why do you confine your survival courses to summer programs? Is my class not good enough for you?"

"I belong to the Outdoor Club," Luke said defensively. "We go camping and hiking twice a month, at least."

Mr. Tadeckis snorted. "Please. That club is for babies and you know it. My classes teach you actual skills. Or do you think you've already learned everything you need to know?"

"It's not just that," said Luke quickly. "I have soccer and basketball and lacrosse. I don't have a lot of time."

Mr. Tadeckis frowned. "Those sports will come and go. I'd be surprised if you even pursue them in college. Survival skills are useful for life. But then, you know that."

Mr. Tadeckis had been trying to get Luke to join his outdoor class since freshman orientation week, when Luke had been the only one of his classmates to make it through the obstacle course. He'd had to climb rocks, take a zip wire over the river, and hike through uncharted paths. Apparently, no freshman had ever succeeded at it before. Luke had considered taking Mr. Tadeckis's class, but was promptly informed by the older students on his soccer team that Mr. Tadeckis and his "pupils" were regarded as an odd band of misfits and outcasts. "Dorks" was how the soccer captain referred to them. Luke ultimately declined Mr. Tadeckis's invitation and had avoided him ever since.

But in retrospect, it *did* seem like a stupid reason not to take the class.

"I'll think about it," Luke said honestly.

"Think hard," urged Mr. Tadeckis.

"I'm sure it's been busy in the woods these days. Cops and security all over the place," Luke said, somewhat lamely attempting to change the subject. The guy freaked him out; he didn't know what to say to him.

"Just between us, Luke, the cops are morons and the security guys are a joke. I've had about twenty of them walk underneath my perch today and not one noticed I was there. Hell, *I* could be the Southborough Strangler for all they know."

Luke took a deep breath. He was starting to question the wisdom of continuing this conversation. "Well, I just hope they find the killer."

"Oh, they won't," said Mr. Tadeckis, leaning down to examine something on the ground. Luke watched him pick up an orange leaf dappled with large black veins and scrutinize it.

"They're on the wrong track."

"The wrong track?" Luke asked weakly.

He twirled the leaf between his fingers. "Come on, Luke, don't play dumb with me. You were there. You know it's not the Southborough Strangler."

Luke felt like someone had punched him in the stomach. Adrenaline pumped through his body.

It took everything he had to keep himself in check. "I don't know what you're talking about," he said slowly.

Mr. Tadeckis laughed. Then he threw his leaf back onto

the ground. "You kids are so naïve. But okay, Luke, play it that way."

Luke was dumbstruck. If Mr. Tadeckis knew they were there, then . . . "Okay, hypothetically, let's say there were kids out there that night. Not me, but other kids . . ."

"I'll play along," said Mr. Tadeckis abruptly.

"Well, why wouldn't you tell on them?" asked Luke.

"What would be my incentive?"

"Well, you're part of the faculty."

"No, I'm not," said Mr. Tadeckis briskly. "The administration makes that very clear. I am not part of the faculty because I teach no academic courses. Or at least, I don't teach what they consider to be academic courses. Unfortunately, my work is relegated to a different arena. Therefore, I am not given the title of "faculty member." I am a "staff member." I do not get to participate in assemblies and I do not get to assign grades. They do stick me with dorm responsibilities, however, just to make me pay for my accommodation."

Luke could tell that this was a sore subject for Mr. Tadeckis. He wanted to steer him off the topic before he got all riled up. "Okay, but still, why wouldn't you tell on them?"

Mr. Tadeckis put his chin down.

"One: I don't care if kids sneak out at night. In fact, I consider it a worthy initiative, as it exhibits both boldness and cunning. Both are useful survival skills. Two: I have little desire to reveal my coordinates at night. I enjoy moving freely in the dark, and quite frankly, you would be surprised at how many of my colleagues, as well as your fellow students, feel the same way. I catalog what comings and goings I witness for possible further usage. And three: I have very few personal vendettas. The ones I do have, I address in quite a different manner. Reporting intel to the headmaster would not be my preferred modus operandi."

"So if you did see who was out there, does that mean you know who killed Mrs. Heckler?" asked Luke.

Mr. Tadeckis stared at Luke, before a sly smile crept across his face. "We'll get to that later."

Luke felt chilled. His body temperature had dropped since he stopped running, and now the cold sweat was clinging to his body. "Don't you think you should tell the police if you know?"

"Don't you think you should tell the police what *you* know?" countered Mr. Tadeckis.

Luke didn't know what to say. "But I don't know anything."

"That's probably true, Luke," laughed Mr. Tadeckis. "There is a lot you don't know. Take Pippa Eaton, for example. What do you *really* know about her? Yes, she's a cute Brit and you would probably like to engage in coitus with her, but do you know why she's here? Did you ask her why she left England? Why she was *run out* of England?"

"Run out? What are you implying?" asked Luke, voice wavering. *Pippa?*

"Nobody but a hacker can find anything on her, because she's not who she says she is. Look at the student handbook. She's a blank. What is she hiding?"

"There were other people out there," Luke blurted. "What

about the first Mrs. Heckler? Her husband ran off on her. Maybe she was blind with rage and wanted nothing more than to kill off her successor."

"I'd consider her a worthy suspect," concurred Mr. Tadeckis.

"And you," said Luke, feigning laughter to lighten the statement. "You were out there, too."

"Yes, I was," said Mr. Tadeckis. He dropped his knapsack on the ground, and slowly walked closer to Luke, so close that Luke could feel his breath on him. There was something menacing about the way he approached him. Mr. Tadeckis fumbled in his pocket, retrieving something. Luke was tall—a good five foot eleven, but Mr. Tadeckis had about four inches on him. Should he run? Where were the police? Didn't the headmaster say they would be everywhere?

"I have something just for you," said Mr. Tadeckis.

Then Luke saw it. His blood curdled. The metal caught the sun's reflection and flashed Luke in the eyes. It was a knife. Luke raised his fists, and took a few steps backward to get his bearing, all the while with Mr. Tadeckis coming at him forcefully. Luke felt his back press against a tree. There was nowhere else for him to go. He'd have to fight for his life. Mr. Tadeckis slowly opened the knife, lifted up his arm, and . . . *bam*! Stabbed the knife into the tree behind him.

Luke exhaled.

"Relax, Luke. I'm giving it to you for your own protection."

"You couldn't have just handed it to me?"

"I could have, but it wouldn't have been as much fun."

"You have a strange idea of what's fun," said Luke.

"Danger tends to follow people, Luke," said Mr. Tadeckis in an abrupt tone. "Just because you had a dose of it before, doesn't mean you're vaccinated. I'll bet, with your history and your character, you'll find yourself in lots of challenging situations before your life is through."

"Therefore, I should arm myself?"

"Preparation is key," said Mr. Tadeckis.

Luke turned and pulled the knife out of the tree. "You want me to stuff this in my shorts and bring it back to soccer practice with me?"

Mr. Tadeckis grabbed the knife from him and put it back in his pocket. "You'll find it in your desk drawer when you get back to your room."

"What if I don't want it?" asked Luke.

Mr. Tadeckis scooped up his knapsack and started to walk away.

"Oh, you'll want it, Luke," he said over his shoulder.

9

The rest of the day crept by. The school had determined that the best course of action was to make it business as usual on campus. Formal sit-down dinner had returned, which meant all the boys were back in coat and tie, and the girls in skirts or dresses.

After dinner Luke entered his room and was relieved that Oscar hadn't returned yet. He had successfully avoided him all day—it was fortunate that they were assigned to different dinner tables this semester—but he braced himself for the two hours of study hall behind closed doors where they had only one another to stare at. Now the room would be full of secrets. Luke wasn't sure how long he could keep up the facade.

He slid into his desk chair and opened his Spanish book. Maybe he could pretend to be really stressed about school to avoid talking to Oscar. That would be the best solution for now, until he figured things out.

Suddenly remembering Mr. Tadeckis, he pulled open his desk drawer. There in the back, next to some loose paper clips and thumbtacks, was the knife. Creepy.

"That dinner sucked," said Oscar, banging the door closed behind him. Luke was so startled, he practically jumped out of his chair. Recovering, he immediately slammed his desk drawer.

"Yeah, so what else is new?" Luke asked, feigning casualness.

"All they ever talk about is how organic and local everything is, but how about making it actually taste good? For once, why can't they serve pasta that's not a pile of gluten-free, dairy-free, taste-free mush? Bolognese sauce instead of vegetarian. I am so sick of broccoli in everything."

Oscar threw himself on his bed and stared up at the ceiling.

"Remember when we used to get garlic bread on pasta nights?" Luke said.

"With cheese, dripping with butter," Oscar added mournfully.

Oscar was silent for a minute. "Hey, you want to play Scrabble?" he asked, sitting up and pulling the game out from under his bed. "I can't play Words With Friends anymore now that the Wi-Fi sucks."

"Um, no thanks. I really have to study."

"Come on . . ."

"No!" snapped Luke.

Oscar stared at him with surprise.

"Sorry, I just . . . I'm stressed about this Spanish home-work. I just don't get it at all."

"Need help?"

"No, no, I just need to practice," said Luke.

Oscar gave him a strange look. "Are you still stressed about us getting caught? Don't be. I think we're totally in the clear."

Luke gritted his teeth. He couldn't look Oscar in the eye. "Maybe I'm just being paranoid."

"I'm not worried anymore. No one suspects a thing."

Luke pretended to stare at his book, while he watched Oscar retrieve his ratty copy of *War and Peace* and turn to his marked page. Luke sighed with frustration. He focused on the trash bin by Oscar's desk. Had Oscar noticed the Post-it was missing? Of course not. Luke felt stupid for be-ing so nervous. What he should do was just ask Oscar what the meaning of The Pink Taco was. Maybe Oscar and Mrs. Heckler were playing word associations or making up book titles or something. But that again would mean that Oscar had more interaction with Mrs. Heckler than he led on.

If only he could ask him. But the chief and the headmas-ter had been absolutely adamant: do not talk to Oscar about the murder; do not let him know you have any suspicions about him. At first he thought that would be easy because he didn't have any suspicions, but now he did. Damn.

If it was one of his other friends it might be easier. His friendship with them was less complicated. For example, Andy Slater. He was definitely one of Luke's best friends, if you had to assign that honor. They had sports and student council in common, and they spent a lot of time together, but they had never had really intense conversations so Luke wouldn't feel awkward keeping something from Andy. But Oscar and Luke's friendship was different. Probably because Oscar was smart as hell. In fact, he was reading *War and Peace* for pleasure; it wasn't even for a class. It was so like him to always do the opposite of what was required just to thwart authority. St. Benedict's was no place for Oscar. His father and grandfather were alums, and probably even a string of other Weymouth men before them, but Oscar would have been much better off at a more progressive school.

He couldn't be a murderer. Could he?

After staring at his Spanish textbook for an hour, and then writing a quick study guide for his English reading, Luke used his phone to go online and open up the St. Benedict's website. Cell service was usually spotty but Luke bet the press had brought some kind of booster to their encampment outside the school gates; he had three bars where he'd normally have barely one.

The student handbook was on the portal, and this was where they listed students' photos, names, their parents' names, and what school the student had attended prior to St. B's. Everyone's cell phone numbers and home addresses were there, too, and you could even click on a link that sent you to the Google Maps view of their house.

When Luke found Pippa's picture, he discovered Mr. Tadeckis was right. Under *Pippa Eaton* there was only a post office box in London, England listed. No cell phone number. How could she not have a cell phone? There was no mention of her previous school, her home address or even her parents' names. Zilch. It was strange that he hadn't noticed that before, but then he wasn't really the type to pore over the handbook like some of his friends.

He went to Facebook and typed in Pippa Eaton, but there was no one with that name. There was a Catherine Pippa Eaton, but it wasn't the Pippa he knew. That was strange. Why wasn't she on Facebook? Almost everyone at school was on it, even if it was just for fantasy football or to form groups for class project discussions. Maybe Pippa didn't want to receive any messages? Maybe there was a reason she was so aloof?

When he Googled her name, a zillion pictures of Pippa Middleton—the sister of that princess or duchess or whatever—appeared. There were however two Pippa Eatons on the Linked-In site, but when Luke clicked on that he learned that one was a vet and the other a marketing manager. No pictures were available, but he didn't need to see them to know neither of them was his Pippa. Luke was now totally intrigued. Where was her cyber footprint? Everyone had one; it was unavoidable. He located a few more Pippa Eatons, but the age didn't fit. Luke was about to do a search for arrest records for her but suddenly stopped. What if someone could trace it? Or a school administrator wanted to see his phone? Even if he cleared his browser, they could probably resurrect his history if they really wanted to. Right now, no one knew that he had any connection to Pippa. Mr. P. had been the only one to see them together, but he had barely noticed her. No one would ever guess they had been in the woods the night of the murder. He was probably being paranoid, but still, it was pretty clear the administration was watching them. For once, Luke was glad his cautious tendencies came in handy. He glanced back at his phone. Nine fifty-five. Five minutes until Animal Hour.

"Study hall's just about over," said Luke. "I need to check something out at the library. You want to go out?"

Oscar, engrossed in his book, just shrugged. "It's cold. I think I'll just stay here."

"Okay," Luke said, relieved.

He put his jacket on but paused right before leaving, his hand on the doorknob.

"Do you think I need a scarf?"

If there were anything Oscar wanted to tell him, this would be the time.

"How the hell would I know?" asked Oscar. Typical. Luke smiled.

Luke bypassed the gaggle of students heading to Main Hall. It was funny to see how some of the girls had reapplied their makeup and obviously brushed their hair. It was an effort wasted on him. He was definitely not attracted to high-maintenance girls.

A lone security guard checked his ID at the library door. He only saw a few other students there—day students who were probably using the reserved textbooks before returning home. Mr. Hamaguchi was hovering over some papers with a freshman. Probably a tutoring session.

Luke walked to the computers in the back and sat down in a carrel. Everywhere you turned in the library there were giant glass walls inter-spliced with jagged gunmetal-gray rods and concrete beams. The design didn't exactly fit with the rest of the traditional architecture at St. Benedict's, but it had been designed as a gift from a famous architect whose son went there in the 1970s. There was really no way the administration could say no when he offered it. At night it could be pretty creepy because you knew that everyone outside could see in through the glass, but you couldn't see out. Luke took off his jacket and quickly got online.

There was no point doing a generic search again, given what he'd seen on his own phone. He had to think. What did he know about Pippa? She was from London, yes, but so was that damn royal sister, so that complicated any search. And apparently it was a very common first name there. He needed to think. What had she told him about herself? Very little. He really knew nothing. Was that possible?

Luke leaned back in his chair and rubbed his temples. She must have said something personal, no matter how guarded she was. He closed his eyes. Ever since he had been in captivity he had learned to play a game where he tried to pick up on clues from the small things people said about themselves. Sort of like honing his powers of inference, Sherlock Holmes style. He had started it because he never wanted to be surprised by people he thought he knew again.

His mind returned to all of his encounters with Pippa. Slowly, bits of conversation began floating back to him.

"My school in Devon . . ."

"Trust me, I know. My mother is a barrister—lawyer, as you Americans call it . . ."

"You're what my friend Tamara would have called a brilliant egg."

"I wish you could have met her . . ."

"The last thing I need is more police in my life."

Luke sat up abruptly. It wasn't much, but it was a start. He typed in Pippa; barrister; Devon; England; police; and Tamara.

Within seconds 48,230 entries popped up.

"Wow," Luke said under his breath. He glanced around, leaning into the screen when he was certain no one else was around.

At first, Luke wasn't sure if he was on the right track. The entries were about someone named Pippa Binns. But as he continued to click on the links, he found a picture of his Pippa—Pippa Eaton, only the photo had been captioned *Pippa Binns*. And to his horror, she was being led by two police officers into a courthouse. Luke felt a growing sense of dread as he read the accompanying articles. Pippa Binns, or Eaton—whatever she wanted to call herself—had been linked to a notorious crime in England. There were pages and pages of news items. Some of the headlines were salacious, screaming out, "Body of Teenager left to rot!" and "Did Pippa leave her to die?" After trying to piece it together, Luke finally found an article in the *Daily Mirror* that laid everything out:

28 February 2017

HOMICIDAL FRIENDS

It's a scandal that is rocking one of Britain's poshest boarding schools. Who killed Tamara Alderton? Was it her best friend?

Kentshire police confirmed today that Pippa Binns remains "a person of interest" in the murder of fellow classmate Tamara Alderton. Mr. Gordon Asher, of Kent, discovered the 14-year-old schoolgirl's body at seven-thirty p.m. on February 2nd. Miss Alderton was found lying in a brook, her face smashed and a victim of blunt force trauma to the head. After several days in coma, she succumbed to her injuries on February 6th.

Miss Binns and Miss Alderton were classmates and unlikely best friends at the exclusive Castogan School. Pippa Binns, 14, is a child of privilege, hailing from Devon, the only daughter of a prosperous anesthesiologist father and barrister mother. Less fortunate was Tamara Alderton, hailing from council housing in Essex, and the fourth child of a pub keeper father and realtor mother. Neighbors remark that they did not witness conflicts at the Alderton home, but do mention that the parents are rarely about and the children were left on their own quite often. Family finances are "often tight," confessed a neighbor, so the family was thrilled when "Tamara's remarkable grades awarded her a free spot at that posh school."

By all accounts neither Binns nor Alderton was popular. Miss Binns was tall and gawky and towered over the other children her age. She was thought of as 'cold' and 'snobbish' and made little attempt to befriend her peers. Miss Alderton was nervous and immature, the subject of some ridicule amongst peers. But both girls had each other. For the first two years the girls were inseparable. Miss Alderton became a frequent guest at Binns' house and a 'second daughter' to Miss Binns' mother, a witness attests. But then something turned horribly wrong.

Eyewitness accounts confirm that Miss Alderton was last seen alive in the company of Miss Binns. Several members of the Essex track and field team spotted them walking by the brook at four o'clock. One student (name withheld because of age) says that at approximately five-twenty p.m. he saw the girls quarreling as he rounded the corner on his way to football. He swears under oath that 'the tall girl' appeared menacing. However, a groundskeeper claims that at approximately six p.m. he saw the girls embracing, holding hands and laughing.

Miss Binns through her cousin and family spokesman Samuel Eaton has made one public statement: "Tamara was my best friend. I would never harm her. We had a brief disagreement at the brook, but quickly made up. When I left her, she was alive." Miss Binns has now engaged the services of barrister Mary Tremble, and through her attorney refuses additional comment.

"No one would leave anyone alone out there at that hour," says Constable Martin of the Essex police. "It was cold and it was dark. The story is unlikely."

Classmates agree. The few that knew Miss Alderton well say that she was a fearful girl, clingy, and disliked being alone. "Rubbish," one classmate said when asked if they believe Tamara remained at the brook alone. "It's a weird lesbian fight. Pippa killed her."

No more statements were made by police as the investigation is still pending. The Alderton family has released a statement, saying: "We will miss our pride and joy, our darling Tammy."

Luke's jaw dropped in disbelief. Had Pippa really killed her best friend? He scanned through various other links, but they just rehashed the story. The more he thought about Pippa the more it dawned on him that it was possible she could be the type of person to harm someone else. There was something detached and heartless about her. His instincts had been so wrong; she was not his type at all. Luke liked independent girls, and he had liked the way she appeared so unfazed when he asked her out. That she had said yes wasn't surprising. Girls gravitated toward Luke; not the same as with Oscar, but they felt comfortable with him. He knew part of it was the whole hero-fame thing, and he also knew he was considered attractive, but he thought it was probably mostly due to the fact that he wasn't immature like his other friends. His older sisters had trained him well since day one, teaching him to respect girls, and advising him on what and what not to do with women. They had been determined to make a gentleman of him, and he had to say, they were right on a lot of stuff. He thought he had a pretty good read on people, but now with Pippa, he realized he wasn't so sure.

And yet she had seemed so vulnerable when she told him to "bear with her." She couldn't have killed her friend. Or was she playing him? Luke was confused. Did this mean Pippa could have killed Mrs. Heckler after all? That night at the Dip, Kelsey was so upset that Pippa had left her, making it very clear that Pippa had *left her.* Maybe Pippa took the scarf without anyone seeing and ran out and strangled Mrs. Heckler? Had there been enough time? Luke had to think. Possibly. But how would Pippa have known that Mrs. Heckler would be in the woods? It was too random. Not to mention, what was the motive?

Luke absentmindedly drummed his fingers on the keyboard. He wished he had more experience in the art of deduction. Maybe he should take some Agatha Christie books out of the library. He arched back in his chair and glanced around. It was pretty empty now. The day students and Mr. Hamaguchi had gone. It was just Luke and the librarians now. *The librarians!* Suddenly Luke remembered that the first Mrs. Heckler, the dog walker, was a librarian. Mr. Tadeckis has said something about her . . . what was it? Oh right: he had called her "a worthy suspect."

Luke clicked off the Pippa story, cleared the browsing history, and set the computer back on the St. Benedict's home page. He rose from his chair and walked over to the front desk where Mrs. Pemberly, the ancient white-haired librarian, was sorting through a card catalog.

"May I help you, dear?" she asked sweetly.

"Um, I was wondering if Mrs. Heckler is here," Luke said nervously.

"No, I'm afraid not. Can I help you with anything?"

"No, she, um, she was helping me pull some primary source materials for a history paper . . ." He was not good at lying. Mrs. Heckler *had* helped him, but that had been last year. And besides, what was he going to say if she *was* here? *I heard you in the woods that night? Did you kill your husband's new wife?* No, he'd make up some lie. Like he found some old dog toy and thought it might belong to her dog. But if she wanted to see it, he'd be screwed. He should have planned this out. He was very lucky Mrs. Heckler wasn't there.

"I'm so sorry, dear, but Mrs. Heckler's taking the next few days off. If you want, I'm sure I can help you. Is this for Ms. DeStefano's American Voices class?"

"No," Luke said quickly. "That's okay. The paper isn't due until next week. I'll look for her when she comes back."

"I just turned off the lights upstairs and down the back, Evelyn," said a voice behind him. Luke turned to find Mrs. Nelson, the other librarian, approaching the front desk from the stairs.

"Wonderful, let's get everything all locked up. It's closing time," said Mrs. Pemberly as much to Mrs. Nelson as to Luke.

"Okay, I'll just snag my jacket," said Luke. The back of the library was now dark, the only light coming from the glow of Luke's computer screen in the distance. He continued past rows of bookshelves, plotting his next move. His feet were noiseless on the soft carpet and it was so quiet he could hear himself breathing.

Suddenly Luke saw something out of the corner of his eye. It was just a flash, for a quick second. He quickly looked to the side, but there was no one.

"Hello?" asked Luke weakly.

Silence.

"Anybody there?" Luke mustered.

Again, nothing.

I'm becoming a lunatic, Luke told himself. Was he being extra skittish because of his past? But no, he didn't think so. He continued on and went and grabbed his jacket off his chair. He was about to take off when he paused and pressed the mouse key on the computer. The story from the *Daily Mail* was up on the screen. Luke stared at it. Hadn't he cleared the history already? That was weird. He went through the steps again. *Yes, I'm sure, yes, reset top sites.* He shut down the computer and started to make his way back to the front door. It was like walking out of a tunnel now, trying to follow the light. His paces got quicker and quicker. Suddenly, he heard the front door slam. He squinted, but couldn't see who had just left.

"Goodnight, honey," said Mrs. Pemberly when he passed the librarian's desk.

"Goodnight," said Luke.

"Goodnight," echoed Mrs. Nelson as she exited the office.

But wait a minute, he thought. *If both librarians were still here, who just left?* Luke spun around.

"Did you see who just left?" asked Luke.

Both of the librarians looked confused.

"No," said Mrs. Pemberly. "I heard the door shut, but I was getting my bag." She said, motioning to the bottom of the stairs where her handbag was plopped.

"Did you?" he asked Mrs. Nelson with perhaps too much interest.

"No, I was in the office."

"I think we're all a little on edge these days," said Mrs. Pemberly nicely. "Don't worry dear, the security guard has been standing at the entrance all night. We're safe in here."

"Right, thanks. Have a good night."

So there was someone there. Someone who wanted to see what I was looking at. The police? Mr. Tadeckis? The killer?

Luke turned and walked to the exit. The security guard was still there, busy talking football with a fellow guard. Luke paused, internally debating. Should he ask them who just left the library? Or would that just bring suspicion on himself? Maybe it was better to lay low. Besides, the guards didn't really seem to know anyone personally, and whoever had been in here was obviously normal enough that the guards had assumed he or she had a reason to be there.

Luke walked hurriedly past the guards down the path. The wind whipped his face as he exited, and he buttoned up his coat to his neck. Winter was definitely coming. He saw a figure ahead of him: a woman wrapped in a dark coat. He was trying to make out who it was when suddenly he heard a thud.

"*BOO!*"

Luke jumped and turned around, fists up.

"Got ya!" shouted Andy, laughing. He had popped out from behind the bush.

"You scared the hell out of me!" Luke said. "You fricking idiot!"

"Dude, did you think I was the Strangler?" asked Andy, waving his fingers in the air before wrapping them around his own neck and feigning choking.

"Shut up," said Luke. He thrust his hands in his pockets and started walking toward Wilcox. Andy followed. He was wiry and bouncy, one of the fastest runners on the lacrosse team. He really should have done track instead, but he didn't click with the guys on that team so he had always stayed with lax.

"Where the hell have you been lately? Shacking up with some mid-chick?" asked Andy, using his nickname for the sophomore—middle grade—girls.

"Hardly. Just kind of laying low in light of the murder and everything."

"Yeah, it's pretty nuts." Andy blew some of his shaggy hair off his forehead. "The sweet part is the freshmen girls are all too afraid to go anywhere alone. I had Dana Waitt hanging all over me this morning, and Kira Matthews couldn't keep her hands off me after dinner. I swear dude, this murder was the greatest thing to happen to my social life."

"Don't let Liz hear you say any of that," Luke warned. Usually he found Andy funny, but now after Liz had called Andy out, Luke couldn't help picturing her and his sisters looking on with disapproval, which meant hearing all of Andy's smack talk with a different ear. "Besides, you already hook up plenty."

"Yeah, but now I don't have to pretend I like them."

"Jesus, do you have any idea how horrible you sound?" Luke asked.

"I'm not horrible. Whoever killed Mrs. Heckler is horrible." Then Andy leaned in closer to Luke. "Did you hear she was like, banging half the faculty? I even heard she was getting it on with a student."

"How'd you hear that?" asked Luke with interest.

"I dunno, maybe Brooks or Gupta. They said they went into Mr. Crawford's office and heard him on the phone with someone and he said something about Mrs. Heckler and some kid who worked with her in the alumni office. Doesn't really make sense, 'cause only losers do that volunteer stuff, and Mrs. Heckler was pretty hot if you ask me."

As Andy continued to talk, Luke's mind raced. A student? What student had Mrs. Heckler been with? Could it have been Oscar? Luke tried to remember. Oscar *did* have to work in the offices a lot when he got demerits. Could he have met her then? Maybe that's why the school was convinced Oscar was guilty? Maybe that explained the Post-it? Luke shivered. How could he be so naïve about his friends?

He shivered again. It was entirely possible that the two people he was closest to at St. B's were killers.

10

Luke had a restless night. He had already been pretty wound up after his talk with Andy and then his parents called and wanted him to give them a blow-by-blow update on what was going on. Normally, you weren't supposed to talk on the phone after lights out but the school was letting everyone speak to their families "to work their way through the murder." He understood now why it was a good idea not to talk to your parents before bed; they just got him all hyped up about everything and made it hard to sleep. He understood their concern, what with everything that happened before, but he didn't need to talk them down. It was a long time before he fell into an anxious sleep.

He woke with the sun as it first bled through the trees. This morning (had it been two days? Three? He didn't know) he found himself high up on a tree branch. His ears were alert and he listened carefully. In the distance, he heard a dog. THE dog, his enemy. He had been rationing his ammonia and per-

116

haps had not used enough to fully hide his scent. Hoisting himself down and sick with the growing dread that his time may be up, Luke feverishly snapped a sharp branch off the maple tree. He peeled apart the bark and hacked at it with the knife so that the end of the stick was as pointed as possible. It was dirty and crude, but it was sharp. He drove the stick furiously into the mushy ground by the base of the tree then he covered it with the pile of fallen leaves from the ground. As quickly as possible, he scrambled back up the tree, and concealed himself in its limbs. The seconds felt like hours. Drops of sweat poured out of Luke's forehead and dripped down his face. The dog came closer.

Luke squinted to see as far as he could. Finally, the dog strolled right under his tree and stopped. Luke deliberately snapped a branch. The dog, startled, looked up and barked. Then he leapt up toward the trunk of the tree and landed with a whimper on the hidden spike in the pile of leaves. The dog moaned in agony, his chest cut wide enough for Luke to see the red gash from his perch in the tree. Even though he was an animal lover, Luke watched without pity as the dog writhed on the ground. The dog had spent a week strutting around Luke's cage, snapping his nasty mouth at Luke, desperate to tear him to shreds. His wild eyes and angry jaw had tormented Luke in his dreams, and now he was no longer a threat.

"Kato!"

Luke held his breath from his perch. He finally had a view of one of the men behind the masks. He was big, with wild curly black hair and large hands. Luke watched him bend over the *dog to check on him and knew it was his only chance. Clutching the knife that he had taken from the cabin, he dropped down onto his abductor's back.*

The man collapsed with a grunt. Luke closed his eyes and plunged the knife down with all his strength. He slashed him as much as he could. His captor was so surprised that he was only able to let out small gasps. Luke thrust the knife into his flesh and twisted. The man fell gasping against the tree and onto his deadly, now dead, dog. Luke took off in a frenzy without looking back. It took him another two days to make his way out of the woods, to a small dirt road that led him to a county road and a camping site. By the time he approached the front desk there, weakened and almost dehydrated, his face was on every newspaper and he was already being called a hero.

Luke woke up sweating. He was relieved to look around him and see his dorm room; not those horrible Virginia woods, or the Georgetown hospital, or the D.C. police station with the swarms of media outside. He remembered that he was at St. Benedict's, and it was Saturday.

Saturday meant they only had classes until noon, and then a soccer game in the afternoon. Luckily it was a home game, so he'd be done by about four o'clock. He had a plan. Today he was going to walk over to the first Mrs. Heckler's house and find out what the deal was there. He just wanted to know if she might be a suspect before he pinned everything on someone else. Like, why was she walking her dog in the St. Benedict woods at three in the morning, especially if she lived off campus? He also wanted to try and figure out who that creepy-voiced guy was that was talking to the other Mrs. Heckler the night of her death. Mr. Tadeckis knew for sure, but Luke didn't know if it was even worth pumping him for the information. Mr. Tadeckis was so damn freakish. In fact, there were a lot of people on campus that Luke now considered creepy. It was weird; two weeks ago he would have said this was the most normal, banal place in the world. It had been a real safe haven for him. *Murder warps everything*, he thought.

"Wanna go to breakfast?" asked Oscar, pulling a worn green cashmere sweater over his head.

"You can go ahead," said Luke as he buttoned up his shirt. "It's going to take me awhile."

Oscar stopped and looked at him. "Dude, are you avoiding me?"

"What are you talking about?"

"Since the murder you've been so out of it."

Luke still couldn't look Oscar in the eye so he turned to the mirror. His hair was so short that it didn't need brushing, but he had a cowlick by his left temple that he liked to try to smooth to the side.

"You don't call, you don't write. No bedtime chats. I don't know, it's kind of weird . . ." continued Oscar.

Luke noticed his eyes were bloodshot from lack of sleep. Great. That would help with the soccer game today. He leaned into the mirror. His eyes were normally a very pale blue. His best feature, he'd been told, but not today. The combination of red bloodshot vessels and the piercing blue made him look like some kind of wacked-out zombie fresh off a film set.

Oscar was still talking. Why was he still talking? Couldn't he just leave it alone?

"Do you somehow blame me for sneaking out?" asked Oscar.

Luke whipped around. "Shut up!"

Oscar gave him a quizzical look. "Relax! What's *wrong* with you?"

Luke ran over to Oscar and put his hands over his mouth. Oscar tried to whip his hands off but Luke shook his head. He leaned into Oscar's ears and whispered, "They're listening."

Oscar tried to say something, which sounded a lot like "You're crazy" but Luke's hands muffled his voice.

"Come on, let's go to breakfast," said Luke, and he practically dragged Oscar with him out of their room, down the stairs, and out the front door.

When he finally released him Oscar shook away. "What the hell?"

Luke led him over to some trees just off the path by their dorm.

"Look, I haven't wanted to tell you but . . ." he paused.

"But what?" demanded Oscar.

"The headmaster and the chief of police think you might have done it," said Luke. There. He said it. Now there was nothing he could do.

"You're crazy," said Oscar for the second time. "You're making this up."

"I'm not lying. They hauled me in there the other day and grilled me for over an hour about you."

"Why would they think I did it?" asked Oscar, visibly shocked.

"She was strangled with *your* scarf," said Luke. "But dude, you can't tell anyone."

"Holy crap! Holy crap!" said Oscar, putting his hands to his forehead and turning around in circles. "Did they find my ID?"

"Yes."

"Damn."

Out of the corner of his eye, Luke noticed Mr. Crawford and Ms. Chang walking on the path. They waved at Luke and Oscar, who returned their wave. Luke pulled Oscar off the path toward him to avoid a conversation with them.

"Be cool. Seriously, people will notice if you freak out," said Luke.

"How can you tell me not to freak out? This is bad, really bad. I have to call my dad," said Oscar. It was the first time Luke had ever seen him lose his cool.

"No! You can't tell your dad. Then they'll know I told you," said Luke.

"This is my life! We're talking about *murder*!"

"Okay, just listen. Talk to me first. Tell me about your scarf."

"I don't even know! I couldn't find it a few days ago; I

don't know where I left it. Obviously, the murderer took it."

"But you were wearing it in the yearbook picture."

Oscar gave Luke a look of astonishment. "Oh God . . ." he said.

Luke felt his stomach drop. "What?"

"They showed you the picture? They must really think it's me."

"But what about the scarf?" Luke asked urgently. "How did you wear it in the picture?"

"Dude, that's *your* scarf."

Luke felt a sudden sense of elation. He and Oscar didn't often share clothes because he was a little bulkier than Oscar, but things like scarves and belts were definitely passed between them. Asking wasn't required, but usually one of them would give a heads up, but Luke was so grateful Oscar had borrowed his scarf without asking that it was as if he had just received the best Christmas present of his life. He started laughing, he was so happy. How in the world could he have ever thought it was Oscar? There was no way.

"Why are you laughing?" asked Oscar suddenly.

Luke couldn't stop.

"My life is over. Stop laughing like a goddamn maniac!"

"Sorry, I'm just so stoked that it was my scarf," said Luke.

"Did you actually *believe* them?" asked Oscar in horror.

Luke's mind flitted to the Post-it. Better to not say anything. If Oscar knew he'd been snooping around his desk, he'd be both hurt and pissed.

"No!"

"Oh my God, you said they hauled you in the *other day*. How long ago? You didn't tell me right away? You believed them, didn't you? How could you?"

"No! It wasn't that I believed them. I just didn't know what to do. They were messing with my mind."

"I can't believe it! I thought you trusted me!"

"I do, I swear, but they were like grilling me, asking me all sorts of stuff. And then I remembered that you were out there for awhile without us, and then Andy told me that Mr. Crawford said there was some student that Mrs. Heckler was having an affair with who worked in the office with her, so—"

"Oh my God! What the hell?" asked Oscar, now furious.

"I was scared!"

"After all these years living together? Okay, first off, I was out there but it wasn't like, oh, I'll scam on Kelsey then run out and kill Joanna. I'd have to be literally insane because I have no motive. Secondly, yeah, I did do a demerit thing in her office but it was me filing while she gabbed on the phone with Dean Heckler the whole time, saying all this whispered lovey-dovey stuff like, 'Oh, that weekend in Vegas was so fun,' blah, blah. Come on! Why would I be messing around with her when I could be with someone like Kelsey? Do I look like a cougar lover to you?"

Oscar looked the most serious Luke had ever seen him. Luke suddenly felt horribly guilty. How could he have even entertained the thought that it might have been Oscar? He knew him inside and out. It was a total betrayal.

"You're right, you're right," said Luke. "I'm sorry."

Oscar glared at him before stopping. "If you of all people think I could have done it, then . . ."

"I was wrong. I don't know what I was thinking. They were so convincing and I was scared."

"Have I ever lied to you?" asked Oscar.

Luke shook his head. "No," he admitted.

"God, I thought you were like the one person I could count on."

"You can count on me."

Oscar got quiet.

"But what's the Pink Taco?" Luke blurted out.

"What?" asked Oscar with confusion.

"I saw the Post-it from Joanna Heckler in your trash," said Luke.

"Jesus!" exclaimed Oscar with frustration. "So you *do* suspect me!"

"No, but I thought it was weird that you had something from Mrs. Heckler."

"She recommended a restaurant in L.A.," said Oscar. "I told her I was going spring break for my cousin's wedding and she said I should check this place out."

"Oh," said Luke feeling guilty.

"Oh my God. I really can't believe this."

"Well, sorry, it was in your garbage, you didn't say anything . . ."

"I forgot! Until she was knocked off and then I found it and thought I should trash it. Now do you believe me?"

"I believe you," repeated Luke. And he really wanted to.

"Right," said Oscar with a shrug.

"I swear. I do."

"Anything else you want to ask me about? Speak now. I can't sit in our room thinking you're hoarding all these unasked questions."

"Well, there is one thing," Luke said.

He saw Oscar tense up.

"Cougar lover?" Luke said, spreading his arms out, palms up. "What the heck? Where did that come from?"

Oscar loosened up and ducked his head. "Yeah, okay, that was a little cheesy, I admit it. But you know what I meant. Desperate times call for desperate words, or so the saying goes."

They stood in silence for a minute.

"What the hell am I going to do?" asked Oscar, stuffing his hands in his pockets and chewing on his lip.

"It's not what *you're* going to do, it's what *we're* going to do."

"We? You sure about that? Because it doesn't really seem like you're on my side."

"I am on your side, cougar lover. One hundred percent."

"Jeez, I said I *wasn't* a cougar lover. Something wrong with your ears?"

"Nope, I hear you brother. So let's go. We've got stuff to do. *We* need to find Mrs. Heckler's killer before it's too late."

11

Luke and Oscar came up with a plan on their way to the dining hall. Now that they knew that Mrs. Heckler was killed with a St. Benedict's scarf—*Oscar's* St. Benedict's scarf—they knew that the killer was someone in the St. Benedict's community and not the Southborough Strangler. This meant in all likelihood they knew the killer. Therefore, they decided to make a list of suspects and go through each one until they got the killer to confess. With the police focusing on Oscar, they wouldn't be looking elsewhere. It was up to them to do it. So they would.

At breakfast they huddled at a corner table in the enormous dark-wood paneled dining hall, replete with vaulted cathedral ceilings and stained-glass windows. Over puffy Connecticut bagels and wet scrambled eggs, they took out a spiral notebook to jot down their list of suspects.

Old Mrs. Heckler (librarian): *she was ditched by her husband for a sexier version. Must be bitter. Most likely jealous. Was in the woods with big dog. Possible that Oscar left his scarf in library and she nabbed it.*

Dean Heckler: *Why not? His wife was probably cheating on him, and she was in the woods with another guy; maybe he got fed up, esp. because he's a tough guy. Possibly CIA. Also, husband usually prime suspect.*

Mr. Tadeckis: *weird. Hangs in woods all the time. Is creepy and could be one of those psycho guys who keeps women in caves and cuts them up after feeding them dog food for weeks.*

Mystery Dude: *the guy that was arguing with Mrs. Heckler in the woods. Was clearly pissed that he was blown off. Who was he? The last person to be seen with her, and they were fighting. Weird voice thing.*

Pippa: *offed her best friend. Had those missing minutes in the woods.*

People to think about: **Mr. Hamaguchi:** *a formerly emotion-free robot, why is he so upset over Mrs. Heckler's death?*

Also, female teachers were not fans of Joanna Heckler. Something to consider.

That was it. Luke had told Oscar everything that he knew, including his interaction with Mr. Tadeckis and all of the stuff he had learned about Pippa. Oscar gave Luke a know-it-all look and reminded him that he knew that girl was a "shifty limey" from the start. They broke up the list and decided they would have to go through each of their suspects and find the killer. It had to be someone on the list.

"Who do you think it really is?" asked Luke.

Oscar examined the list. "I don't think Pippa is our killer. Maybe she's killed in the past, but realistically . . . with us up there, it was too risky. And how would she even know Joanna Heckler would be in the woods that night? Not to mention, I can't see a motive."

"Shall we cross her off?"

"Leave her on for now. Why not? If anything, it helps us to be more cautious."

"Yeah, and in any event, it's always better to eliminate suspects than add them," said Luke.

"Exactly. You never know."

Luke glanced again at the list. "I think the mystery dude is key. He was pretty heated that night."

"Yeah."

"And Dean Heckler clearly had motive."

They both stared at the piece of paper, deep in thought.

"I still feel like we're under surveillance," Luke said.

"Obviously. I'm sure we are."

"In fact, last night when I was in the library, I could swear someone went over to my computer and checked out what I was looking at."

"We should burn this list," said Oscar.

"Totally."

"Hey, guys."

They both looked up. It was Kelsey. She was holding her breakfast tray, although it didn't look like anything was on it other than a ceramic coffee mug.

"Hey, Kelsey," said Luke. He discreetly shut his notebook so she wouldn't see the list. He could tell by the awkward way she was standing there that things between her and Oscar probably weren't going so well.

"What's up, Kels?" asked Oscar, barely feigning concern.

"Are you holding up okay?" Luke asked, a little too enthusiastically, as if to cover Oscar's lack of it.

"Mind if I sit here a sec?" Kelsey asked nervously. It was rare to see Kelsey by herself. Usually she was surrounded by several friends.

"Of course," said Oscar, sliding down and giving Kelsey his seat across from Luke.

Kelsey looked around anxiously then sat down. She flipped her long hair over one shoulder and took a deep breath. "Listen, I'm really freaked out . . ."

"Don't worry, Kelsey," said Luke. "No one knows we were out there in the woods. You don't have anything to be worried about."

"It's just . . ." she began, but then trailed off.

"What is it?" asked Oscar.

"I don't know . . . I mean, if anyone found out, they would have the wrong idea," said Kelsey.

"Is this about Matt?" Luke asked. Kelsey's boyfriend, Matt, had graduated last year. Luke had heard they were still sort of together, although Kelsey hadn't been acting like it lately. "Look, no one wants anyone to find out about you and Oscar. We all know you have a boyfriend," said Luke, shooting Oscar a look. Oscar just shrugged.

"I know, and he would absolutely freak if he had any idea about . . . that . . . but that's not what I meant."

Kelsey was nervous, and it seemed to be more than just concern that Matt would hear about her hookup with Oscar. "I mean that everyone knows how much I hated Mrs. Heckler, and if they knew I was out there in the woods when she died, and going to the bathroom alone and all, they'd get the wrong idea . . ."

Luke was floored. "Wait, what?"

"You hated Mrs. Heckler?" asked Oscar, confused.

"Didn't you know that?" asked Kelsey, her brow furrowed. "*Everyone* knows that."

"I didn't know that," said Luke and Oscar in unison.

Kelsey stared at them blankly. "Because of last year . . . my father . . ."

Both Luke and Oscar shook their heads no.

"I thought you knew. I thought everyone knew," Kelsey said in disbelief. When Oscar and Luke just kept shaking their heads, she continued. "Okay, last year during parents weekend my dad came. My parents are separated, so he came without my mom, which sucks, but anyway, he went to school here so he stopped in the alumni office to get some sort of form or something. It had to do with his reunion and Mrs. Heckler was there and she was *all over him*. I am not kidding. She was touching him, and laughing with him, and telling him that she's down in Maryland a lot for recruiting and could she hook up with him there. And she was like, doing a double entendre on the words 'hook up' because she wanted me to think she meant meet up, but then she'd lean in and say *hook up*, wink wink. And when I got back to the dorm I screamed to everyone how much I hated her. But I didn't want to kill her, I swear."

Luke's head was swimming by the time Kelsey finished her diatribe. They hadn't even considered Kelsey a real suspect, but here she was, supplying a motive. But Kelsey? There was just no way.

"Look, no one, *no one,* would ever think you did it, Kelsey," Luke said.

"You'd be the last person anyone would suspect," agreed Oscar.

"Really?" asked Kelsey, visibly relieved.

"Really," said Luke and Oscar in unison. Oscar was a much better suspect, not that Luke was going to admit that to her.

"Okay, that makes me feel so much better. I was just worried after we talked in the music room, when you guys pointed out I'd been out there alone . . ."

"Don't worry," Luke said, although he noticed it wasn't until Oscar nodded that Kelsey perked up.

"Great," she said. "And about that other thing . . . Matt's been texting me like crazy, and I would feel so bad if he heard anything about us, so . . ."

"Don't worry," Oscar said. "We're cool."

We're cool? What was that? Jesus. Luke hoped Kelsey was serious about working things out with Matt, because if this was just a play to make Oscar jealous, things might get rough when she realized Oscar probably wasn't interested in her at all anymore.

Suddenly, the noise in the dining room died down, and heads started turning toward the back of the grand room. Headmaster Thompson was walking past the enormous marble fireplace that flanked the west wall. He was followed by the chief of police and none other than Dean Heckler. No one had seen the dean since his wife was killed, so there was a palpable excitement in the air. *What were they doing here,* Luke wondered. The room was basically silent as the odd triumvirate took their seats and began to eat their breakfast.

"Do you think he was craving the dining hall food so bad that he broke mourning and returned?" whispered Oscar.

Luke looked carefully at Dean Heckler's face. He was serious and grim as he leaned in to say something to the chief. But then again, that was nothing new; he was always serious and grim.

"That dude is no barrel of laughs. I wonder what Mrs. Heckler saw in him?" asked Luke.

"She was clearly disappointed, judging by the way she was all over my dad," said Kelsey, folding her arms indignantly.

"Do you think they're interviewing him?" asked Luke.

"I think this is our cue to head out," said Oscar, who was in no rush to put himself in front of the police.

As they were depositing their trays and throwing out their trash, Mr. Crawford approached to do the same.

"How's it going, guys?" he asked.

"What's the deal down there, Mr. Crawford?" asked Oscar, motioning toward the back of the room.

Mr. Crawford glanced back at the headmaster and his breakfast guests. "I don't know. I'm pretty much the last to know anything around here. Some days I think they still think of me as a student."

Probably because you look and act like one, Luke thought. Instead he said, "I would think Dean Heckler would take some time off. Are they making him come to work already?"

"I doubt that. But you never know how people process death."

"Dean Heckler's heartless. I can't imagine he's too broken up over it," said Oscar.

"Now, now," chided Mr. Crawford. "That's not nice. The dean's a good guy." But he said it in that chastising tone of voice adults use on kids when they privately agree but can't say so out loud.

"So, Mr. C.," said Kelsey, leaning in flirtatiously. All the girls were in love with Mr. Crawford. He had boyish good looks despite being in his early thirties, and he dressed like a student, in Patagonia clothing and baseball hats. He was of average height, slight with blue eyes and dark hair, and had the chiseled features of a male model. Still, Luke wondered whether this was just another show put on by Kelsey for Oscar, to incite some kind of jealousy.

"Who do you think did it?" Kelsey smiled flirtatiously.

Mr. Crawford gave Kelsey a smile, as if enjoying the attention. "I'm flattered you think I know everything, Kelsey, but in this case I have no idea."

"Hmmm. But do you think it was a crime of passion?" asked Kelsey, tipping her head to the side.

"Could be, but whenever I strangle my girlfriends, I try not to kill them," said Mr. Crawford.

They laughed.

Suddenly Mr. Crawford's demeanor got serious. "But seriously, I'm sorry, I shouldn't be joking about this. Who do I think did it? I have no idea."

"Come on, you must have some theory," prompted Kelsey.

Mr. Crawford sighed, clearly torn between whether he should be candid or assume his teacher role. The latter won. "Okay, only a theory. The Hecklers' house is on the edge of campus by Route 443, so maybe someone came to her house first and then took her into the woods under duress? Why else would she be in the woods?"

Kelsey, Luke, and Oscar remained silent. *They* knew that Mrs. Heckler had not been taken into the woods under duress, but of course they couldn't say anything.

"But do you think she had a boyfriend?" asked Luke.

Mr. Crawford frowned. "No. I didn't hear anything like that."

"Someone told me you said a student who worked in her office was under suspicion?" asked Oscar brazenly.

Luke shot him a warning look, which Oscar ignored.

"I said that?" asked Mr. Crawford, incredulous. "I don't

think I would ever conjecture out loud about another teacher with a student. Not that I even think that."

"Well, someone thought they heard you on the phone," Luke said hastily.

"Am I being spied on?"

"No, no, I guess it was just a rumor," said Luke. "There are so many of those going around."

"Well, I don't know any privileged information. I barely knew Mrs. Heckler. I might have said one word to her the whole time she's been here. She wouldn't even know who I was," Mr. Crawford laughed. "I do feel a bit guilty though."

"Why?" asked Luke and Oscar in unison.

"I was on dorm duty that night. And, look, I don't want to scare you kids, but I heard something around two in the morning. So I went outside to check. Then I went back again at three. Something didn't seem right."

Luke and Oscar exchanged glances. Had Mr. Crawford heard them sneaking out?

"You shouldn't feel bad, Mr. C.," said Kelsey. "You had no idea. There's nothing you could have done."

Mr. Hamaguchi approached with his tray in hand. Whereas Mr. Crawford was considered fun and outgoing, Mr. Hamaguchi was very reserved and quiet. That's why his tears at Joanna Heckler's memorial service were totally out of character.

They had been standing and holding their trays, but Mr. Hamaguchi's arrival prompted everyone to start moving down the line to dump their food and napkins in the compost bins.

"Kelsey, ready for frog dissection today?" Mr. Crawford asked.

"No! Mr. C., it's so gross, I really don't think I can do it."

"It's not gross, it's fascinating," protested Mr. Crawford. He tossed his silverware in one bin and his plastic plate in another. "Dissection is one of the highlights of my class."

"Don't you think it's mean?" asked Kelsey, getting rid of her plate and utensils. "These frogs are born and raised in captivity and then killed just so we can cut them open."

"It is kind of cruel," said Luke.

"Not at all," said Mr. Crawford. "It's the cycle of life."

"I'm sure you'll find it captivating," interjected Mr. Hamaguchi. "Each of the frogs has been injected with dye so that you can see the different systems. There's really nothing like the first slice."

"I doubt it," Kelsey said, making a sour face.

"I agree," said Luke, stacking his tray on top of the pile at the end of the line. "Kelsey, time to visit the infirmary to convince the doctor to let us take a sick day."

Luke, Kelsey, and Oscar said good-bye to the teachers and continued on toward Main Hall. The image of the frog, spending its entire life in a cage and awaiting its death, troubled Luke. He knew what it was like to be kept in a cage, not knowing your fate. He had dreamed of being liberated but was also terrified of what would happen if he were. His hours were spent with a killer dog salivating for the opportunity to sink its teeth into him. Sure, science teachers think that the cycle of life is captivating, but try being on the other side of it.

12

They slaughtered them. It was embarrassing. St. Benedict's scored five goals, and Rutherford Academy didn't even get one. Luke was elated; it was a nice end to a very stressful week, and it was a good omen for the big game coming up with their main rival, Brewster Hall. After showering, Luke left the locker room and set off toward the first Mrs. Heckler's house. Oscar had wanted to go with him, but they agreed that with Oscar under the "cloud of suspicion" it was better for him to lay low. Especially since they couldn't be sure, but they had both sensed that Oscar was being watched by the hired security guards. The last thing they wanted was a tail. So while Luke went, Oscar was going to snoop around and try to get some intel on the other suspects on their list.

Luke had tried to get Mrs. Heckler's address from the campus directory, but her name didn't show up anywhere. When Luke Googled her, he found out she lived off campus, on one of the small cul-de-sacs off Banks Road. Once again, it confounded him as to why she would be walking her dog on campus at three in the morning if she didn't even live there? Something was not right about that.

As he set out, he realized he should have taken his bike. He thought he would be less conspicuous if he walked, but it was a lot farther than he had thought, and the sun was dropping, leaving only about an hour of twilight before dusk. On weeknights, students had to be on campus by six but on weekends they were given a bit more leeway in case they wanted to go to the movies. Other schools had stricter sign-outs, but the town was so small, St. B's probably felt there was no need to bother. This week, though, Luke was supposed to get permission to leave campus due to the murder, but he hadn't been able to find Mr. Crawford after the game. He had slipped him a note under his door and hoped he would be back before it was dark. It wasn't so much the darkness that worried him but more the "townie" factor.

Unfortunately, Southborough was not a prosperous town, and St. Benedict's was a prosperous school, so that led to tension between the kids at St. Benedict's and the kids who attended the public high school in town (aka the "townies."). Sometimes the students from St. Benedict's would be walking to Pizza Hut or one of the only two other restaurants that Southborough boasted—Pizza Hut and a local Italian called Antonucci's—and some kids would drive by and throw stuff at them. In return, the St. Benedict's kids would yell back all sorts of snotty stuff about SAT scores and future welfare recipients, and the fights would escalate. Luke hoped he wouldn't have to deal with that tonight.

Suburban and country living was a lot different from growing up in Georgetown. Every time Luke returned to St. Benedict's, it took awhile to readjust to the quiet rural setting. He was glad that he had the opportunity to experience this type of school, which was full of pep rallies and football games, but there were times he preferred the anonymity of city living. His parents had decided to send him to St. Benedict's abruptly right after the incident. They had thought he would be safer tucked away in a quiet boarding school in a sleepy town. That was laughable now. And it was frustrating to Luke, because what had happened to him before was circumstantial. It wouldn't have mattered where he was living; it had to do with his family, not him. He felt better prepared these days. The trick was to learn how to sense danger. In a city, danger followed patterns: you learned to avoid certain kinds of people, certain kinds of areas. But in the country, danger was more random, which made it feel far more sinister. Desolate houses along poorly lit streets had all the makings of a horror movie.

When he finally turned down Mrs. Heckler's street, he had three split-level houses to choose from. He wanted to see if he could guess which was hers without looking at her address in his pocket. The first one had a ton of kids' toys in front, and since he knew she didn't have kids, he looked at the second, which had two Harley Davidsons in the front. A biker librarian? No way. So Luke turned his attention to the third. It was pretty nondescript, dark brown with green trim. Neat. A Prius in the driveway. Bingo. That's the type of car a librarian would drive. With utter certainty, he waltzed up to the door and rang the bell. Minutes later, a big man with a mustache came to the door.

"Can I help you?" he asked.

"Um . . . is Mrs. Heckler here?" Luke asked nervously. He hadn't expected a man to be there. He'd thought she would still be single.

"I think you want that house over there," he said, pointing to the house with all the toys in front.

"I don't think so. She doesn't have kids."

"The woman who works at the prep school? With the dog?"

"Yes."

"That's her house," he said sternly.

"Oh, okay," said Luke. "Sorry to bother you."

Luke stepped off the man's front porch and pulled the crumpled-up paper out of his pocket. Sure enough, the address of the toy house was the one he had written down. Damn. He really needed to improve his sleuthing skills.

He walked over to her house, examining the abandoned tricycles and soccer balls, as well as a tiny pink plastic stroller. Definitely not dog toys. It was so odd. No one had ever said she and Heckler had kids.

Luke rang the doorbell; certain there was some mistake. As soon as he did, he heard barking.

"Hush, Blackie! Hush!" someone said from inside.

The door opened, and there was Mrs. Heckler with a black Lab.

"Luke," she said. "What a surprise."

She was surprised? Not as surprised as Luke. He never thought she would know who he was.

140

"How did you know—" he started to say, but then stopped when he realized she obviously must know him from the Kidnapped Kid story. He would never get used to that.

"Oh, I know all the students," Mrs. Heckler said. "I remember referring you to some books for your history paper last year? On child labor in the Colorado mines?"

Luke nodded. He didn't trust himself to say anything. This wasn't exactly turning out the way he thought. She had a good memory, recalling not only that she'd helped him, but the topic, too.

"What brings you out here? Another paper?"

Luke blinked. "Oh, no, nothing like that. Um, is this yours? Well, not yours, I mean. Blackie's?" Luke held up a small-checkered sweater that was clearly fashioned for a dog. Oscar had "borrowed" it from his adviser's daughter (unbeknownst to her) and would return it when Luke brought it home. It would only be missing a few hours. It was the only ruse they could think of to get to Mrs. Heckler.

"No, it's not his," said Mrs. Heckler. "But that was very thoughtful of you to come all this way to return it."

Luke looked at Mrs. Heckler. She wore big glasses that took up most of her face, but if he squinted, he could imagine that she was probably pretty when she was younger and not as exhausted as she looked right now.

"Well, sorry to bother you," said Luke.

"Hey, Mama M., when's dinner?" asked a small girl who wrapped her arms around Mrs. Heckler.

"In ten minutes, sweetie," said Mrs. Heckler. "Go tell your brother to wash his hands."

141

Mrs. Heckler had kids? Things were getting more and more confusing.

"Sorry about that, it's dinnertime," said Mrs. Heckler.

"Oh, I won't keep you," said Luke, taking a step back. "It's just that I saw you in the woods the other day and when I found the sweater I thought it might be Blackie's."

"You saw me in the woods?" Mrs. Heckler's eyebrows rose.

"Well, not in the woods. Going into the woods. I live in Wilcox and I saw you out the window of my room late one night."

"You kids stay up way too late studying. I worry about all the pressure you're under. It's too much. I've been working with the administration to come up with some homework guidelines because they don't see what you kids go through the way I do."

Luke shifted uncomfortably. It was difficult to picture her as a cold-blooded killer when she was doing things like remembering his history topic from over a year ago and talking about how worried she was about her students.

"Mary, who's there?" said a male voice from behind the door.

"It's *Luke Chase*," she said.

And then out of nowhere, Dean Heckler was suddenly standing in the doorway.

"Luke Chase? What are you doing here?"

Luke wanted to ask him the same question. What are *you* doing here? Isn't she your *ex*-wife? And whose kids are these? But he knew he couldn't. Before he could answer, Mrs. Heckler jumped in.

"He's very sweet. He brought this dog sweater over because he thought it was Blackie's."

"Huh," was all Dean Heckler said. He stared at Luke, looking him up and down. Dean Heckler had that look of someone in the military. Close-cropped silver hair, a strong chin, and he always stood totally erect, as if he was prepared at any time to salute a commanding officer. Anyone who dealt with him knew he was as harsh as a military officer. And there were those CIA rumors, too.

"Well, I'll be going now," said Luke. "Sorry to have bothered you."

"You going back to campus, son?"

"Yes, sir."

"I'll drive you then," he said before turning to Mrs. Heckler. "Thanks, Mary."

"You take care, Carl," she said, squeezing his arm.

Luke was embarrassed to witness this moment between them. What was the deal here? They were divorced, so shouldn't they hate each other? Why were they hanging out? Luke silently followed the dean down the path to the bottom of the driveway where the dean's Toyota Camry was parked. He got in the passenger seat and as soon as the dean put the key in the ignition the seatbelts swung forward and strapped both Luke and the dean tightly into their seats. It was a bit disconcerting.

"That was awful nice of you taking time out of your Saturday evening to come and return a dog sweater," said the dean.

"Oh, well, the weekends are really the only time I can get off campus, so . . ."

The dean continued driving in silence. Luke became nervous. Then he realized that he hadn't said anything in the form of a condolence to the dean. He felt weird. What should he say? What if the dean started crying? No, he wouldn't. But the silence was too strange.

"Sir, I just want to say I'm sorry about your wife. I've never been through anything like that, obviously . . . um, but I know it must be painful."

"Thanks, son," Dean Heckler said. "It's the worst thing that ever happened to me."

Luke was surprised to see an expression of emotion transform his face. Especially since he had just been at his ex-wife's house.

The dean cocked his head to the side, as if he were debating something, and then abruptly spoke.

"A lot of people are interested in this. A lot of reporters have been poking around. And I know the students think this is the most exciting thing to ever happen. But to me it's a tragedy, and I hope people will respect my privacy."

Luke nodded. But then it dawned on him that maybe the dean was accusing *him* of poking around. Which he actually was doing, but still.

"Sir, I hope you don't think I am interested in the . . . salacious elements of this situation," Luke said. "I just found the dog sweater, and as a dog owner myself I would hate to lose something like that, so I thought I'd track down your wife, um, your ex-wife."

Dean Heckler nodded. Luke glanced outside the window

at the trees that were now enveloped in shadows. This time of year, night just seemed to seep into daylight earlier and earlier. He was actually glad, as awkward as it was, that he got a ride home. It would have been a bummer to walk back.

When they reached a stoplight, the dean turned and looked at Luke. "I can tell you're wondering what I was doing at Mary's tonight. And though it's not your business, and I have no reason to tell you, I will, simply to stop any potential rumors from starting. Mary and I are still close friends. Sometimes people grow apart, as we did, and we decided to do the mature thing and end it amicably. Mary lives with her sister, Tilly, and she's now a foster mother and is very happy in her life, and I was happy, too, until this week. I just don't want anyone to think Mary could have done something like this . . . I see you shaking your head but there has been talk, and I can tell you now, Mary wouldn't hurt a fly. She is a good woman."

"She's very nice," Luke said when the dean paused. He added lamely, "She helped me a lot last year with some history research."

The light changed and they continued on; Luke could tell the dean was pensive. He was definitely shaken up, that was for sure. Luke had never heard him talk so much in his life.

"You know, people want different things in life," said the dean, almost to himself as much as to Luke. "Mary loves small children, and well, I'm a teacher, so of course I love kids," he said, without much enthusiasm, "but I don't need my own. She did. And then Mary's a homebody, and I got the itch to travel, see some more of the world."

"Right," Luke said. "Like Las Vegas."

"Vegas?" asked the dean, with a little laugh. "Is that where you'd go first when you decide to see the world? Never been, myself. But Joanna and I went to Paris and New Orleans. We were planning a Christmas trip to Vancouver, and then maybe back to Europe. Italy next time."

"Sounds nice."

"Would have been. Would have been."

Luke could make out the jagged castle-like edges of St. Benedict's against the inky sky and knew they were fast approaching school.

"Wilcox?" The dean asked, and when Luke nodded, he rounded the loop and stopped in front of the dorm.

"Well, thanks for the ride," said Luke.

"No problem," said the dean, as Luke exited the car and shut the door. The dean rolled down the window. "Oh, and Luke?"

"Yes, sir?" asked Luke, leaning into the window.

"I know you bringing that sweater over to my ex-wife's house was a pile of horse crap. I've got my eye on you now, boy. You watch out."

The dean pulled out of the driveway leaving Luke in the dust.

13

"That was not cool," Luke reported to Oscar when he got back to his room. Then, as a safety precaution, he went over to his desk, put his iPhone in its speaker dock, and turned the volume to the maximum. Seconds later, Vampire Weekend came blasting out of the speakers. Luke went and sat on the edge of Oscar's bed where he was spread out, lounging.

"Dean Heckler was there, and now he is totally onto us, or me, really. Just what I need."

"What happened?"

Luke told Oscar everything that had transpired at Mrs. Heckler's house, as well as the car ride home. Oscar listened with rapt attention, and interjected the appropriate profanities when Luke paused for effect.

"And check this, I asked him about their trip to Las Vegas, and it turns out he's never been."

Oscar perked up. "She was definitely talking to someone about her weekend in Vegas. I heard her!"

"I know. I believe you. But she didn't go to Vegas with him. Probably with the boyfriend."

"Do you think the dean knows?" asked Oscar.

"I'm sure. If *we* know then she probably wasn't very discreet."

Oscar stood up and began pacing. Then he turned to Luke.

"Why do you think he's still hanging with his ex?" asked Oscar.

"That's what I want to know," said Luke. "They were so friendly that it practically seemed like they were still a couple, so I was thinking, what if they did it together? You know, like, co-conspirators. He divorces one wife as part of a plan, then marries the new one, maybe takes out some insurance money on her, offs her, then gets back with the old wife."

"That's interesting, because based on what I discovered, that could make a lot of sense," said Oscar, pulling out some printed pages from under his pillow. "Take a look."

Luke scanned the Google searches that Oscar had printed out. There were tons of articles on Mrs. Heckler's death, and plenty more about her life.

"Joanna was loaded! Or at least her father was."

Luke nodded. "That theory would fit, then."

"Totally. He wouldn't even need insurance. Now Dean Heckler probably stands to inherit a buttload. No wonder he married her."

"The better question is, why did *she* marry *him*?"

Oscar pulled the papers out of Luke's hand. "Look at

this, it's textbook. Her dad has been married like three or four times. She was married before to another much older guy—who she snatched from his wife, no less. It's the classic daughter of divorce, 'love me, Daddy' routine. Joanna wanted her dad's attention, so she kept marrying dad-types, acting like a flirty little girl, you know."

"You think?"

"Yeah. It makes perfect sense. She'd make you feel like, so special, that you were the best, the only one she wanted, and then she'd use you and abuse you."

Luke examined Oscar's face carefully. He was talking about Mrs. Heckler as if, well, as if he knew her.

"You got all this from that one time you worked in her office?" Luke casually asked.

"I told you, I know her type," said Oscar. Then he turned back quickly and looked at one of the articles again.

"God, your rep really takes a beating when you die a gruesome death."

"All those local reporters are freaking stoked! Finally, something to write about."

"Okay then, so we have to work overtime. We have to come at this from a different angle. We're the students. We have the advantage of having been there in the woods that night. We know she was having an affair, we know her husband's ex-wife was there and we know Pippa was there along with Mr. Tadeckis. And that Kelsey hated her. That's all stuff the police probably don't know," said Luke.

"I'm sure they know about the affair," said Oscar. "I mean,

one look at her picture and then her husband's and it's pretty obvious."

"Okay, but still. We have to use the resources we have that they don't have. They're focusing on you as a suspect."

"Don't remind me," implored Oscar.

"But we have to prove them wrong. The best way is eliminating the suspects. We have to talk to Pippa—"

"That crazy psycho," interrupted Oscar.

"—and we have to find out who Mrs. Heckler was having an affair with. I think that's the key."

"My bet is that the dean is the killer," said Oscar. "Husband spurned? Case closed. And all that CIA stuff. Where was he the night of the murder?"

"Yes, I know you want it to be him, but we need to wait to check him out because he's already suspicious of me. Let's try and find the boyfriend next," said Luke.

"But I thought we agreed he took off that night? Left her alone?"

"But maybe he came back. Maybe that's who Kelsey saw."

"Don't you think we would have heard her say something like, 'I told you to get lost or something'?"

Luke paused. It was true. She had sounded angry, so no doubt she would have made a fuss if the guy came back to try to talk to her again. She definitely seemed like the type who wouldn't like a guy who was all over her. Luke saw her with a more standoffish type. The dean was actually kind of like that. Reserved, the type who would withhold compliments and be really critical. Someone with low self-esteem might be into that. Thank God Luke had been paying attention to everything during his sisters' "insights into women" tutoring sessions.

"I think if we find the boyfriend, we might learn more about how or why she died. He's the key."

"How can we find him?" asked Oscar.

They both sat quietly for a minute, listening to the music and trying to figure out their next move. Finally, Luke smiled.

"Okay, I have it. Mrs. Heckler and her man knew about the Dip. I mean, they didn't go underneath it, but they knew enough about it to meet at the wall. The Dip is *the* place for booty calls. What is the second place where people meet to hook up?" Luke asked, raising an eyebrow to prompt Oscar.

Oscar sat up and snapped his fingers. "The audiovisual equipment room."

"Bingo!" said Luke.

"Let's go," said Oscar.

Luke stood up. "Okay, but on our way, let's try and track down Pippa before she heads off campus or something. I heard a lot of the girls are going downtown to hit the movies, and I think we need to ask her a few things in case she takes off."

"Man, these girls are a lot of work."

"That reminds me," Luke said. "Can you please not blow off Kelsey? At least not so obviously. If she cracks, we're in trouble."

"She's so needy," Oscar said. "I don't know how Matt can

deal. It was fun at first, making her feel better all the time, but it's old now."

"Yeah? Maybe you should go watch one of her field hockey games. Liz says she's an animal out there, so maybe the whole 'rescue me' thing is an act."

They walked toward Hadden in silence. Luke couldn't help thinking how so many people, and things, were turning out to be different than they seemed.

Pippa smiled when she entered Hadden's common room and saw Luke waiting.

"Hey!" she said brightly.

"Hi!" said Luke.

"Hello, Pippa," said Oscar, leaning his head out from the armchair he was sitting in. The armchair faced the fireplace so he hadn't been initially visible to her. It was obvious at once by her deflated look that she was less than thrilled to see him.

"Oh. Hi," she said warily.

"Now, now, if I didn't know you loved and adored me, I would have thought you were unhappy to see me," taunted Oscar.

Luke shot Oscar a look. He didn't want him to be his obnoxious self, which would really rile Pippa. In fact, he had debated not bringing Oscar along at all, but then he thought he might need him. Pippa would be hard to intimidate, and they had to find out what the hell happened in England,

and then basically accuse her of doing the same here. Oscar would be way better at that than Luke.

"Ignore him," Luke said. "He's being an ass. And he's going to stop right now."

"I should hope so," said Pippa.

"Listen, can we talk to you a sec? It's important. Outside?"

Pippa shrugged. "I have to get my coat."

"We'll wait," said Luke.

She went back upstairs and disappeared for what seemed like hours. Luke was irritated, and sat in his chair fuming. Why did Oscar always have to put Pippa on the defensive? Come to think of it, Oscar had a way of always alienating the girls Luke was dating. Was it jealousy? If yes, why? Oscar could get any girl he wanted. In fact, right now he was thoroughly enjoying flirting with every girl that came through the door. They all adored him; the bad boy myth was alive and well, no matter how intelligent or educated girls were. So why did he have to give the girls Luke liked such a hard time?

"Why are the common rooms in the girls' dorms so much nicer than in the boys dorms?" mused Oscar, swiveling around in the armchair. "I mean seriously, they have a Nespresso machine. We don't have a Nespresso machine."

"We don't drink Nespresso."

"And look, no stains on the carpet."

"Ready," snapped Pippa as she came flying down the stairs. She didn't wait for Luke or Oscar, so they both rushed to follow her out. Oscar still took one last second to say something to a pretty sophomore before exiting.

The threesome walked in silence over to a bench in a clearing under some trees. It was completely dark now, and most people were getting ready for Saturday-night activities. There were shuttles, accompanied by security guards, going off campus for the students who wanted to go to the movies or to restaurants, and the Jig was loaded with people who skipped dinner and just went to eat French fries and hang out. There was usually a dance on Saturday nights, a pathetic event with a local DJ and punch that was pretty much frequented exclusively by freshmen and sophomores, but it had been canceled out of deference to the deceased.

Pippa sat down on the bench and folded her arms defiantly. Oscar put one leg up on the bench, while Luke stood in front of her. They waited for a security guard to pass. Luke wondered if the security guards even knew what they were supposed to be on the alert for. Or was this guard here because he'd been told Oscar was a suspect and should pay particular attention to him? If that were the case, they'd have to make sure they kept their voices down so as not to be overheard.

"What's up?" asked Pippa briskly.

"We just wanted to talk to you again," Luke said. How would he bring up the fact that he knew she was accused of murder back home? This was more awkward than he thought. "But I think we should keep our voices down," he added, motioning to the guard, who now seemed to be hovering by the garbage can about twenty yards away. Definitely loitering.

"What do you want to talk about?"

"Well, it's about the murder," said Luke.

"I'm listening," said Pippa.

Oscar was getting impatient with Luke's stalling. "We want to eliminate you as a suspect," he said.

"Me?" she asked with astonishment. "Why would I kill her?"

"We don't think you killed her," said Luke hastily.

"Well, Luke doesn't think so, but I'm not quite—"

"Have you gone mad?" Pippa said to Oscar. "You're really a wanker."

"Did you call Tamara a wanker?" asked Oscar with a wicked smile.

Luke watched the blood drain from Pippa's face. She opened her mouth to say something, then snapped it shut.

"Look," said Luke in his nicest voice. "We don't want to be jerks here. But we found out about your past, about your friend who . . . who was killed."

He stopped in hopes that Pippa would interject, but she remained quiet. He watched her eyes carefully, to see if she had tears in them, but she didn't. Her mouth was curled into a frown, her face white, but she displayed no other emotion.

"You have a homicidal past, from what we understand, so we want to know, when you ditched Kelsey, did you take a second to kill Mrs. Heckler?" asked Oscar.

Pippa glanced at him and then at Luke, as if debating what to say. Finally, she spoke. "That situation that you are referring to was a truly tragic and horrific part of my past.

I had hoped to never discuss it again. I can assure you that things in the paper are not always true, and I could sit here and defend myself but I won't. If you think I murdered Tamara, fine, I murdered her. If you think I murdered Mrs. Heckler, fine, I murdered her. You can think what you want and do what you want. I don't care."

She paused and turned to Luke. "I'm sorry I ever trusted you. I thought you were a different person, but clearly you're not."

And with that, she stood up and walked quickly back to the dorm. Luke and Oscar just looked at each other.

"Why do you always go for these insane girls?" asked Oscar finally.

Luke felt awash with guilt, although he wasn't sure why. He had been right to question her, hadn't he? But if so, then why did he feel as if he'd just betrayed her? He probably should have done it without Oscar being there, but then he and Oscar both knew he would have chickened out.

"Let's go check out the audiovisual room," Luke said finally.

14

The Audiovisual Equipment Room was hook-up central primarily because of its location off a desolate hallway behind the Black Box Theater. The only other rooms nearby were used for storage of theatrical sets, and were accessed only once a season when students were setting up for a performance. Therefore, the foot traffic on this particular spot of campus was limited to those teachers in need of a DVD player, television or projection screen, and with technological advancement in phones and computers there was less and less demand for this stuff. There was a sign-up sheet outside the classroom where faculty and students (who were supposed to get teachers' permission but often didn't) were required to note the time and date they checked out equipment. As soon as Luke and Oscar rounded the corner, they made a beeline for the sheet.

"I'll take it," said Oscar, swiping the clipboard before

Luke could reach it. "Hmm . . . very interesting," said Oscar, flipping through the pages.

"Are you going to show me or what?"

"Patience, my friend. Patience."

"Come on."

"Here," said Oscar, turning the clipboard around so Luke could finally see it. "Bingo."

Luke leaned in. On October 6—the Friday six days before Mrs. Heckler's murder—she had signed out the DVD player. Luke felt a flash of sadness when he read her careful bubble print. That handwriting was now extinct. One day, she's signing out equipment, the next day . . . gone.

"So, what do you think?" asked Oscar.

"I don't know."

"Why does someone in the alumni office need the DVD player?" asked Oscar.

"You're right. But maybe she had a presentation or something?"

"Seems fishy. I worked in the alumni office. Seemed like all she did was mailings. Pretty boring. That's why she wanted to talk all the time."

"Maybe we need to ask someone who's working there now?" asked Luke. "I can check with Zaid. He does the student work schedule. I think he even runs the student-alumni committee, which would put him into direct access with Mrs. Heckler."

"That kiss-ass is all about padding his college applications," sneered Oscar.

"Dude, if you don't want to go to University of Nowhere, you should think about doing that crap too."

"No thanks."

"Whatever. Okay, so are we thinking that Mrs. Heckler was here hooking up with the mystery guy?"

"Totally. Checking out the DVD player was a cover. We both know this room has seen a ton of action. She had to be discreet, obviously, but she wanted a quickie."

"It seems kind of risky."

"That's why people cheat," said Oscar, as if he were an expert on the topic.

"How do you know why people cheat?" asked Luke. "Who are you, Dr. Phil?"

"No, I just know; it's more about the thrill. Not so much to do with the person."

Luke turned and gave Oscar a quizzical look. "You seem to have a lot of knowledge on this topic."

"Hello? Kelsey? She has a boyfriend. And she's into him. She clearly wanted some sort of high from me."

"You sure its not the other way around? Because it kinda seems like she keeps bringing him up to make you jealous," Luke said, his eyes still locked on Oscar. "And anyway, Kelsey isn't married. Have you ever been with a married woman?"

"No," said Oscar, quickly averting his gaze and glancing back down at the clipboard. He started flipping through the pages.

Luke was about to press him when he noticed something on the list.

"Hey, look who checked out the DVD player the next day."

Oscar leaned in to where Luke's finger was pointing. *CARL HECKLER* was written in block letters, followed by *OCTOBER 7.*

"Coincidence?" asked Oscar.

"Come on, the dean definitely had no reason to check anything out. He's a *dean*. All he has to do is administrative stuff."

"And bust people for minor infractions," reminded Oscar.

"Right," said Luke. "And maybe he was busting his wife."

"You think he was onto her?"

Luke raised his eyebrows. "I think he followed her here."

"And came back the next day to see if he could find any evidence."

Luke nodded. He scanned the rest of the list. There were several teachers and a few students who had signed out stuff. He turned the pages back and searched for names of people who signed out the equipment just prior to her death. On October 3rd there was another name.

"Mr. Tadeckis was here too," said Luke.

"Geez, two of our suspects. Wonderful."

Luke flipped the pages over again, comparing all of the different names and dates and handwriting. Something was bothering him. He looked again at Mrs. Heckler's name and then scanned down to her husband's. After that was Mr. Hamaguchi on October 6, then Mrs. McNamara, a math teacher, followed by Mr. P.

"Wait a second," said Luke. His finger pointed at the date Dean Heckler had written.

"October 7, the day after Mrs. Heckler was here. So what?" asked Oscar.

"Right. He wrote October 7. But then right below him, Mr. Hamaguchi signed out equipment and wrote October 6."

"So it goes October 6, October 7, October 6," said Oscar. "Someone messed up."

"I don't think so," said Luke. "I think Dean Heckler was here right after his wife. I think he wrote the wrong date so it wouldn't seem suspicious. He had no idea Mr. Hamaguchi would come by later and write the correct date."

"Nice catch," Oscar said.

"Yeah. Dean Heckler was definitely covering his tracks. The question is, what else does he have to hide?"

"Let's go inside and see if we can find anything," Oscar said.

Luke opened the door and they entered the darkened room. It was filled with all sorts of audiovisual equipment, and most of it had not seen any use in years because it was becoming rapidly outdated. There was a stack of VCRs on the window shelf, but now that cassettes were practically extinct, they were rendered useless. There were also carts to wheel televisions and radios around to various classrooms, and old computers from the 1990s.

The black shades in the room were drawn and Oscar flipped on the garish overhead light. One lightbulb promptly flashed and then died, and the one remaining bulb had little success in illuminating the room.

"So, where do you do it when you come here?" asked Luke.

"A gentleman never kisses and tells," said Oscar.

"Come on."

"Over here," said Oscar. In the center of the room there was a giant bookcase filled with reels of film and miscellaneous instruction manuals. It was as if whomever had brought it in there had gotten tired and rather than placing it next to the wall, just abandoned it. The benefit was that it created a nice little nook behind it, where illicit trysts could take place and go unnoticed even if anyone walked in the door. Someone had even been brazen enough to drag a giant beanbag chair behind the bookshelf, and there was an old wool St. Benedict's blanket that could probably have used several rounds in a washing machine. Luke followed Oscar to the beanbag and they both crouched down.

"This is kind of nasty. Do you really think a teacher would come here to get some?" asked Luke.

"I saw Mr. Larkin and Ms. Wakefield coming out of here last year, looking all disheveled."

"Gross."

"Yeah, but now they're engaged."

Luke looked back at the beanbag. He tried and failed to imagine Mrs. Heckler and some guy getting all hot and bothered here. He thought she'd go for a classier tryst, maybe at the Hyatt in Waterbury or something. She always did dress young and kind of jazzy for a boarding school, wearing flirty-type clothes that were stylish and showed a lot of skin. He got the impression she identified more with the students than with her husband. Maybe she was trying to relive her youth? Maybe her boyfriend was? That could be one of the kicks for them.

"People are so careless, I don't know why it's such a problem closing this door," said a man's voice.

"Maybe it blew open?" asked a woman.

"The windows are shut, I doubt that."

Luke and Oscar stared at each other. Yikes. They were not alone anymore. What should they do? How to explain that they were just lurking around the audiovisual room? Oscar turned to Luke and mouthed 'What now?' Luke shook his head.

"See, the windows are sealed," said the man, who had obviously gone over to check them.

I know that voice, I know that voice, thought Luke.

"So what do you need the DVD player for?" asked the woman.

"I'm showing my freshman class *The Fantastic Voyage.*"

Oscar and Luke both looked at each other at the same time. *Mr. Crawford!* They mouthed in unison. That was best-case scenario. He would be cool. What should they do? Reveal themselves?

"Oh, I love that movie," said the woman.

Luke felt like he was holding his breath. Both he and Oscar remained motionless, but it was getting uncomfortable down in their crouched positions. Should they expose themselves?

Oscar tapped Luke on the hand. *Ms. Chang* he mouthed.

Luke nodded in recognition. She was the smoking hot new English teacher who looked like a badass James Bond heroine. There had been rumors about her and Mr. Crawford. What if they were going to hook up here?

"You think they'll like the movie?" asked Mr. Crawford. "If I'm trying to teach them human anatomy, maybe I should show them a different kind of film. Have you seen any dirty movies that you can recommend?"

"Ha, ha, very funny," said Ms. Chang. Although to Luke it sounded like she didn't think the joke was very funny at all.

"Come on, you seem like that type," said Mr. Crawford.

"Okay, I'm over this conversation," said Ms. Chang with irritation.

"Let's go," said Mr. Crawford. "Wait a second, what's that?"

Luke panicked, thinking Mr. Crawford was referring to him, so he abruptly stood up.

"Hey, Mr. Crawford."

Mr. Crawford's face dropped in astonishment. Luke's heart skipped a beat when he realized that Mr. Crawford had been leaning down to pick up a DVD and not headed toward the hook-up place where Luke and Oscar were hiding. They could have easily evaded detection if Luke hadn't panicked.

"What are you doing in here?" asked Mr. Crawford, his brows furrowed.

Ms. Chang, who had been a few steps ahead of him out the door, came back into the room and gave him a puzzled look.

"I . . ." Luke was at a loss for words.

"We were just talking," said Oscar, popping up.

Mr. Crawford and Ms. Chang appeared even more confused.

"In here? You guys are roommates. Don't you get enough of each other in your room?" asked Mr. Crawford.

"I don't think students are supposed to hang out in here," added Ms. Chang.

The teacher they had previously described as a "hottie" went down three points in Luke's book.

"We were walking around the hall, trying to track down, well, let's just say a certain girl, and we wandered over here and I swear I thought I saw some animal in here, like a rat or a dog or something, it was big, so we came in here to check it out," said Oscar.

Mr. Crawford appeared skeptical.

"Animal? Wasn't the door closed?"

"No, someone had left it open," said Oscar, fumbling.

"Yeah, it's true," added Luke. His face was reddening. He was definitely not a good liar. "So we poked around. But no animal."

Mr. Crawford and Ms. Chang looked at each other, then back at the boys. Finally, Mr. Crawford spoke.

"Okay, well, I think you guys better hit the road now."

"Yeah."

Mr. Crawford smiled. "I know this place is where kids come to you know, get together. Is there something I should know about you two?" he added, teasingly.

Luke and Oscar were relieved. "Don't ask, don't tell," said Oscar with a wink.

15

Sundays were all about sleeping as late as humanly possible. Although Luke and Oscar had agreed that they had to go find the first wife of Joanna Heckler's first husband, they still refused to let anything come between them and their slumber. It was literally their one day of rest. There was no required meal, no assembly, just pure peace. And since there was really nowhere to go in town, there was no reason to get up. So at eleven, when there was a knock on the door, they were still under their covers.

Luke incorporated the first knock into his dream, in which he was playing soccer in the World Cup and the knock was his coach banging on a bench and telling him to get a goal. But when the knock became louder and more persistent, he sat up.

"Come in," he shouted, rubbing his bleary eyes.

Oscar took his extra pillow and put it over his head. "Make them go away," he mumbled.

The door opened and there on the threshold stood Mr. Weymouth, Oscar's father. He was clad in a blue blazer and a tie, and everything about him from his hair to his polished shoes was meticulous. Basically, he was the exact opposite of Oscar.

"Mr. Weymouth," said Luke.

Oscar shot up in bed, his hair sticking out in every direction. Mornings were the only time Oscar didn't look completely photo-ready.

"Dad, what are you doing here?"

"Hello, Luke," Mr. Weymouth said, nodding at Luke. "Oscar, get dressed. We need you downstairs as soon as possible."

"What's going on?" Oscar slept shirtless in his boxers, and seeing him barely clothed almost seemed too much for Mr. Weymouth. He looked as if he wanted to reprimand his son, but then he glanced at Luke and remained silent.

"I can go . . ." began Luke, getting up.

"No need, Oscar will find his clothes and be down shortly."

"Just tell me what's going on?" demanded Oscar.

"Your mother and I are here with Stan Grossman. You might know him because we play squash together at the club. He's a lawyer. Headmaster Thompson and the police would like to talk to you this afternoon, and Stan—Mr. Grossman—thought it best that we have a chat prior to this," said Mr. Weymouth clearing his throat.

"They think I killed Mrs. Heckler," said Oscar in disbelief.

"I'd rather have this conversation with you in the presence of our lawyer," said Mr. Weymouth.

"This is so unbelievable."

"Mr. Weymouth for what it's worth, I can totally vouch for Oscar," said Luke anxiously. "It was my scarf, not Oscar's."

"That's nice of you to say, Luke. Right now we'll figure things out then get back to you on that. You're a good friend."

Oscar rolled his eyes at his dad, and stood up. Luke watched Mr. Weymouth glance around the room, and immediately felt self-conscious at what a pigsty it was. There was a large pizza box with two slices left on his desk—last night's post-sleuthing delivered dinner—as well as several empty Coke cans, a half-eaten bag of Doritos and a bunch of Milky Way wrappers. Both Luke and Oscar's laundry was overflowing out of their accidentally matching laundry bags, and textbooks were sloppily stacked on every surface. Since they were due for a room inspection this week they'd have to clean it up tonight for sure.

"I'll wait for you downstairs," Mr. Weymouth said.

"Fine."

When he had left, Oscar grabbed his khakis from a pile on the floor and pulled them on.

"This is surreal," said Luke.

"Dude, imagine how I feel?"

"Just stay the course. You're innocent. But don't tell them . . ."

Oscar turned and glared at Luke. "Of course not."

They stared at each other without saying anything for a beat. Both of their minds were racing. How did they fall into this mess? They should have never been out there.

"Good luck," said Luke.

"Yup," answered Oscar, before heading out the door.

Luke quickly showered and dressed. Then he paced around his room, attempted to clean up but only got as far as collecting the food wrappers and containers, all as he checked the window thirty times to see if Oscar was back. He chucked the trash in the bin down the hall and then, after making his bed and folding some shirts, he finally put on his coat and left the room. He was of no use to Oscar in the dorm. The only thing he could do was try to find the real killer. When he had read about Joanna Heckler, it mentioned that she had been married before, and it even had a quote from her ex-husband's ex-wife. Apparently Mrs. Heckler had broken up *their* marriage and she was mighty bitter. She lived only two towns over, and when Luke had found her address online, he decided to pay a visit. He called for a taxi (less trackable than an Uber, and cheaper) and was told he'd have to wait forty-five minutes for it to meet him on campus. Ah, the joys of living in the suburbs. It was a lot easier grabbing a cab or an Uber back home in Georgetown.

Since he had time to kill, he decided to get a bacon, egg, and cheese on a bagel at the Jig. When he entered, Andy Slater was sitting with Gupta and Oliver Brooks, another classmate, poring over the newspaper and chowing down on a grease fest of French fries, jalapeño poppers and bacon.

"Over here," Andy called.

Luke walked over to their table. "Hey."

"What's up with Oscar? Cal said he saw his parents going in to meet with the headmaster?" asked Andy.

"Yeah, um . . . they just want to talk to him. I don't know."

"Was he busted again?" asked Brooks.

"Nah, nothing like that," lied Luke.

"He's already got one strike. Leave it to him to do something stupid," said Andy.

Luke just shrugged. The less he said, the better.

"Did you check this out?" asked Gupta, sliding a copy of *The Southborough Courant* toward Luke.

The headline said: *Strangler Linked to Prep School Murder.* Luke scanned the article. It said that all leads pointed to the Southborough Strangler. There was the position of the body, which was apparently the same as the other two victims, as well as the time of night. It even knew that she had been strangled with a scarf, although it said it hadn't been able to confirm for sure if it was a St. Benedict's scarf, but off-the-record reports said it was. This was great news! This could totally exonerate Oscar. Luke wondered if the headmaster had gotten a chance to look at today's paper. Maybe he had already called Oscar's parents before it came out, and it was all a big misunderstanding. He hoped that was the case.

"Wow, major drama," said Luke, playing it cool.

"If it's the strangler, there's going to be mayhem around here," said Andy, picking up a gooey cheese fry.

"I think my parents might pull me out," Brooks said. "But

how can I write my college essay on surviving a murder if they yank me out now?"

"I know, my mom is all panicky too, like, *sweetie, honey, you take care of yourself,*" Gupta said. "*Sleep with a weapon under your bed, I know you're not allowed cutlery but maybe a flashlight, which can also be used to bang someone over the head . . .*"

"*Your* parents must be crazed," Andy said to Luke. "Once bitten, twice shy."

"They know I can take care of myself," said Luke quickly before changing the subject. "How old do you think this strangler is? If he killed someone ten years ago, he has to be at least what, twenty-eight at the youngest? Or do you think he's older?"

"Says here in the article they suspect him to be a white male between the ages of forty and fifty-five," said Andy, pointing to a part of the article that Luke had skipped.

Forty to fifty-five. Dean Heckler fit that profile. Could he have been the strangler long ago? thought Luke.

"Well, I gotta go," Luke told his friends.

"You just got here!" said Brooks.

"I know, but I've got stuff to do."

"Dude, you really are a mystery man these days," said Andy.

"Must be a girl," Brooks said knowingly.

"I'll leave you all guessing," said Luke, slipping away to the counter to order his breakfast before dashing to meet his cab.

16

"I'm going to 22 Piedmont Street, in Woodville," said Luke to the cabdriver. He had to repeat it a few times; the driver was blasting a radio station that was transmitting in some unidentifiable foreign language. He either had a hard time hearing or he didn't understand English very well, but after a few tries and a few mentions of nearby landmarks, the driver nodded his head.

Suddenly, the other door swung open. Instinctively, Luke slid to put his back against his own door, ready to face the threat. Luckily, he stopped himself from doing anything before realizing it was Pippa.

"Budge up," Pippa said to him, sliding in and telling the driver, "we can go now."

"What are you doing?" asked Luke.

"I needed to talk to you in private, without your dumber half around," she said.

Pippa looked intense. She was wearing a dark black wool

coat and her matching beret with a long white scarf. Luke didn't want to give Oscar creds, but with her pale skin and long, nearly white hair, the black and white outfit did make her look pretty edgy.

Pippa stared at Luke, as if challenging him to refuse. They hadn't left campus yet, so he could still tell the driver to stop.

"Okay, fine," Luke said.

"Tell me where we're going."

"To church," said Luke.

Pippa frowned. "For real."

"First, you tell me what you want to talk about. You're the one crashing my cab."

"All right," said Pippa. She turned her head up to the ceiling of the cab, focused intently on the spot where the sun was shining, and took a deep breath.

"Tamara and I were best friends. Really, truly. On the day of her . . . death . . . well, we had quarreled. I told her to sod off, and then she begged me to forgive her and we made up. But I told her I needed time. I couldn't be her instant best friend again after what she had done . . ."

Her voice trailed off. Luke watched her with curiosity, waiting for her to continue. "What had she done?" he prompted.

Pippa remained silent for what seemed like ages. "I don't want to go into that now," she said finally.

"Come on, you can't give me half the story."

"Honestly, it's better that you don't know. Things are still . . . unsettled."

Luke watched her fumble for words. She appeared genuinely upset but he didn't want to let her off the hook yet. "Okay, well, just continue. Then what?"

"Then . . . I really did leave her there. I know everyone said, oh, it was dark, what a terrible thing to do, but I needed to think things through, and she had to meet someone."

"Someone?"

"It's complicated. But I believe the person she met killed her."

"Who?"

"I can't tell you."

"Why not? I obviously won't know whoever it is."

Pippa just shook her head.

"Okay, but why didn't you at least tell the police you think that person did it?"

"I did!"

"Then why can't they arrest him, or her?"

Pippa stared at Luke and her lower lip trembled. "Because that person has an alibi. But the alibi is unreliable."

"Can't the police prove that?"

"They will. It's just a matter of wearing him down. Trust me, my parents have a team of lawyers working on that."

Luke sighed and glanced out the window. "I don't know, you're not really telling me anything. I'm way confused."

"Luke, please," implored Pippa. "I'm really not supposed to be talking about it, but please believe me. I didn't kill Tamara. She was my best friend."

"How can I believe you when you keep telling me that you can't tell me anything?" Luke stormed.

"Don't get mad," she said, alarmed.

"I just don't get it. If you didn't kill your friend, then who do you think did, and why can't you talk about it?"

Pippa stared at him and he saw tears spring into her eyes. For a second he almost backed down. He never thought he'd see Pippa cry.

"I just can't." Tears slid down her cheeks.

"Why?"

"Because, because . . ."

"Because what?" Luke's heart quickened. Why couldn't she tell?

"Because I feel ashamed. Because I had trusted him! I should have known better. I was always an outcast; I should have seen the signs. But I totally bought it. He was important to me, and then I find out that he and Tamara . . ." Pippa's voice caught and she couldn't finish. She put her hands over her face and her body shook from sobs. Luke felt instantly guilty. He had made a girl cry. Granted, he wanted to make sure she wasn't a killer, but still. He felt lousy. And no doubt she was talking about a boyfriend or something, which made him feel worse. He didn't like thinking of her with another guy.

"It's okay," said Luke, patting Pippa on the back.

Pippa kept her face in her hands for another minute.

"I'm sorry I made you cry."

Pippa was silent while she collected herself. When she finally looked at him she had wiped away her tears. "I miss my friend. I miss my life. I feel so sad all the time, that's why I seem like a bitch. I'm trying to do everything not to lose it."

"I'm sorry, I didn't realize . . . First Mrs. Heckler, then the article on you. I jumped to conclusions." He took her hand and she let him hold it carefully.

"Do you really think that the authorities in England would have let me leave the country if they thought I did it? Do you think St. Benedict's would have accepted me?"

Luke thought about it. He supposed not. "No."

"It's been dreadful. This whole thing, with the press and everything. That's why I had to leave the country. Everyone thinks I'm evil."

"I know you're not evil," he said, looking her straight in the eye.

Pippa returned his gaze. "Thank you," she said, squeezing his hand.

"And I know how messed up the press is. It's all projection. One minute they want to build you up—and they're only too game to call you a hero, and the next second they want to bring you down. That's what I figured out after I escaped; they had me on all these shows and stuff, wanted me to be a star—like better than a regular person." Luke shook his head. "It was unsustainable. My shrink told my parents that doing the publicity would be good for me. Like, I'd own the story; it would be *my* message, or something like that. But I didn't want to be the golden boy and then wait for them to come after me to tear me down. I came to St. Benedict's to disappear."

It was the most Luke had said to anyone about his abduction. Pippa smiled at him.

"Then you and I are alike," she said. "I sort of thought so. You have the haunted look of someone who has seen too much."

"That's just because my eyes are so light blue. It makes me look intense, that's all."

Pippa smiled and pressed her lips together, as if trying not to laugh. "It's true, you have pretty eyes, but you didn't need to fish for a compliment. That's not exactly what I meant about seeing too much."

Luke had been so absorbed in their conversation that he'd forgotten they weren't technically alone, but luckily the driver was preoccupied with his music. He looked down at their hands, now clasped together warmly.

He still had one last question.

"What about Kelsey? Why did you leave her out there?"

"I didn't think I left her out there," said Pippa with exasperation. "It's so American for girls to pee with each other, but I find it quite gross. I went off to the other side of the tree. When I finished, I saw a glimpse of her green coat in the moonlight over on the other side, kind of lying down, so quite honestly I thought she might, you know, need more privacy."

"You mean her Patagonia?"

"What?" Pippa looked confused.

"Kelsey was wearing a fleece. A dark blue Patagonia fleece jacket. She wears it all the time," Luke said. "But you just said you saw her out there in a green coat."

Pippa squinted. "I saw her out there in a coat . . ."

The minute she said it, they both knew that Pippa had not seen Kelsey when she was going to the bathroom. She had seen Mrs. Heckler. Who was, no doubt, already dead by then, lying in the bushes.

"Oh my God," said Pippa. "I thought she was murdered after we left!"

"I did too. But I think this means it happened when we were there."

It took a few moments to sink in. Luke again felt that eerie sensation that there was a missing piece to this puzzle that was right in front of them, but he couldn't see it.

"So maybe Kelsey was right. Maybe, when she came back all crazy angry saying someone was out there, maybe it was the killer," said Pippa.

Luke thought of Mr. Tadeckis. He was definitely out there, he had told Luke. But why would he kill Mrs. Heckler? Had he been the mystery man? He couldn't imagine that he was Mrs. Heckler's lover. Was the dean out there? Had anyone seen Kelsey? Luke didn't want to tell Pippa all that he knew. It was all conjecture. Plus she definitely didn't have Oscar's best interest at heart.

"Yeah, that would be weird if the killer saw us."

"Maybe he's just biding his time and he's going to come after us one by one," said Pippa.

"No way. That sounds like the plot of a horror movie."

"Seriously, it could happen. We could all be targeted."

"I don't even want to go there."

"Okay, then go here, and tell me where we're going now and why."

Luke told her everything about the impending visit. Pippa thought he was insane to attempt to meet with the woman, but luckily she was game to participate.

"Excuse me, Mrs. Johnson?" asked Luke.

"It's Ms. Johnson," said the capable looking woman who was raking the leaves on the front lawn of a small, white traditional house. "*Mr.* left years ago," she said, flashing a toothy grin.

It was the opening they needed. As Ms. Johnson waited expectantly, Luke gathered his thoughts on how to best approach the sensitive topic.

"Well, regarding *Mr.* is exactly why we're here," interjected Pippa. "We're students at St. Benedict's, and we work on the school newspaper. We know it's terribly bad form to just show up unannounced and try to ask you all sorts of questions, but we have a very aggressive editor who is determined to get into Harvard, and she has sent us novices out here to try and solicit some information from you."

Ms. Johnson glanced at them as if she was deciding what to do.

"Do you think we could take a minute of your time and ask you some questions?" asked Luke in his politest voice.

"All right," said Ms. Johnson, throwing down her rake. "I've talked to everyone, a few more shouldn't matter. Come on inside. What did you say your names were?"

They followed her inside, making brief chitchat along the way. The house was warm and well decorated. Luke had for some reason expected a dirty house, a weepy and bitter ex-wife, and a scene out of a low-budget movie. But instead, the house was clean with nice framed black-and-white photographs of landscapes hanging on the wall, comfy sofas and armchairs upholstered in cranberry with several throw pillows, and a large Chinese-style coffee table with lots of books on it. In fact, the décor kind of resembled those Pottery Barn catalogs his mother received in the mail.

"Would you like something to drink?" asked Ms. Johnson. "Coke? Tea?"

"Um, anything," said Luke.

"Tea would be lovely," said Pippa decisively.

Ms. Johnson went to the other room, the kitchen presumably. Luke glanced around the room, hoping to find a voodoo doll in the shape of Mrs. Heckler, or maybe a dartboard with her image plastered in the center, but there was, of course, nothing of the sort. He turned and looked at Pippa who arched her eyebrow at him. She'd recovered from her tears, and now seemed quite composed.

"So, how can I help you?" said Ms. Johnson, returning and plopping on the armchair across from them. Almost immediately, a fluffy white cat appeared out of nowhere and hopped on her lap.

"Adorable. What's his name?" asked Pippa, reaching over to pet the cat under his chin. The cat purred quietly, his tongue darting in and out of his mouth.

"Mr. Whiskers," said Ms. Johnson proudly. "The only male I let near me these days." Then she turned to Luke and added, "No offense."

"None taken."

"He's precious," said Pippa.

Wow, she's good, thought Luke. Thank God she'd jumped on board. Small talk was never his thing, as he'd learned at all of those insufferable parties that his parents hosted through the years.

"Well, we don't want to take up too much of your time. We just wanted to ask you, and we know it's sensitive, about Mrs. Heckler," said Luke.

"Oh, the late great Joanna Volk Johnson Heckler. She finally pissed off the wrong person." Ms. Johnson laughed with unrestrained malice.

"Do you mind if we get a little history from you?" asked Pippa. "I mean, forgive us if we're being too audacious."

"No, everyone knows the story," she said. "I'm a physician's assistant, and when I met Joanna we were both working for a small medical practice. She was in pharmaceuticals, you know, one of those people who drags a little roller suitcase around with samples. We became friends, very good friends. She confided in me about how she was having an affair with the older doctor that we worked for—married, I might add—and in turn, I talked to her about my life. She spent more and more time at my house with me and my ex—I refuse to call him by name. I mean, every weekend, dinners, movies, everything. I was so naïve. Next thing

I know, they sit me down and tell me they are in love and *sayonara,* sweetie."

"Wow," was all Luke could say. He was surprised by her candor. Most of the adults around him—his teachers, his parents, their friends—were much more formal. He couldn't imagine them confiding in him as if he were the host of a talk show.

"You must have been furious," said Pippa.

"That's the understatement of the decade," Ms. Johnson said, as she got up to go attend to the screaming kettle. She disappeared into the kitchen and again Pippa raised her eyebrow at Luke.

"What's that supposed to mean?" he whispered.

"Shhh . . ."

Ms. Johnson returned with two steaming mugs.

"Listen, I know what you're thinking. That I murdered her. Believe me, I would have loved to! She is—was—the most cunning, manipulative, selfish and awful person I have met in my life. She insinuated herself into my world, then destroyed it. I wanted her dead. And don't worry, I told the police this," she said, placing the mugs in front of them and giving them a look to make sure they both heard her.

"We didn't think you murdered her," said Luke quickly.

"I would have if I could have gotten away with it!" she laughed. Then she got serious. "But listen, again I want to reiterate that I went through all this with the police. They didn't think I had anything to do with it, but because of our history, they had to pay me a visit. I work at Memorial

Hospital now, and I was on duty all night last Tuesday. And now that she ditched my ex and made his life miserable, I've moved on. Everyone gets his or her comeuppance. I have faith in karma."

"Me too," said Pippa nodding.

"Why did she leave your ex?" asked Luke.

"I think he ran out of money!" said Ms. Johnson with a laugh. "He doesn't have the big bucks. He owns a sporting goods store in town. Joanna liked to live large, and even though her family had money, she liked to be spoiled by men." Ms. Johnson made a gagging gesture and Pippa smiled. "My ex was handsome as hell, I have to give him that as much as I hate to, and he also talked big. He probably duped her into thinking he was a hot shot."

"Then why would she go for the dean?" asked Luke.

"Well, Joanna walks—walked—that fine line of wanting stability and wanting danger. Needing danger. I heard she got some money from her father for marrying Carl Heckler. He wanted her settled down; he withheld money from her because he thought she was unstable."

"Her own father paid her off to get married?" asked Pippa.

"I wonder if Dean Heckler knows that?" Luke murmured.

Ms. Johnson looked at both Luke and Pippa. "Are you sure this is appropriate for a school newspaper?"

"Well, we just want background," said Luke quickly.

"I guess. But please don't humiliate Carl. He was pretty shocked when I told him all of this."

"You told him?" asked Luke, aghast. "When?"

"He came by a few weeks ago. Asked me all sorts of questions about Joanna. The poor guy had no idea what a predator she was. Joanna was that talented." Ms. Johnson stared into the distance, her eyes glazing over as if she was remembering.

"Was he here before or after she died?" asked Luke.

"Before."

Luke and Pippa exchanged glances.

"Do you think he knew she was cheating on him?" asked Pippa.

Ms. Johnson scrunched up her nose and thought. "He said that he recently learned she wasn't the person he thought she was. I think he was upset about that."

"Upset enough to murder her?" asked Luke.

Ms. Johnson stopped and her face became angry. "Joanna could make anyone upset enough to murder her. Especially those closest to her."

Luke and Pippa paused, unsure of what to say next. Sensing their discomfort, she softened. "Sorry, but you can see how crazy she made me. Luckily, I'm not a psychopath."

"Yeah," said Luke with nervous laughter.

Pippa looked pensive. "Did Dean Heckler say anything else?"

Ms. Johnson glanced at the ceiling, trying to recollect. "Not really."

"Anything about how he found out that she was unfaithful?"

"Hmmm. No, just something about her being nervous and stressed. Funny, sounds like she may have grown a conscience. Finally realized that what she was doing was wrong."

"But it was too late," said Pippa with genuine sadness.

17

It took an embarrassingly long time for the taxi to come and pick them up from Ms. Johnson's house, so when they had finally exhausted all of their questions and small talk, Luke and Pippa left to wait at the curb. Ms. Johnson protested a little out of politeness, but confessed she had things to do so let them linger outside. Luke offered to rake her lawn since she had given them so much of her time and managed to fill two garbage bags full of leaves before the cab finally collected them.

On the way back to school, Pippa peppered Luke with questions. She wanted to know who else he had been talking to, and why he had decided to embark upon his own private investigation. Luke deflected as much as possible, but finally confessed the reason behind his trip to Mary Heckler's house and his suspicion that the dean and possibly his ex had something to do with the murder. He kept his information about Mr. Tadeckis and Oscar to himself.

When they pulled into the loop in front of Wilcox, Oscar and his parents were loading Oscar's suitcase into his car. After handing the driver some cash, Luke dashed out of the taxi.

"Hey, what happened?" asked Luke.

Oscar's eyes got wide when he saw Pippa get out of the car.

Luke turned back to her. "Catch you later, Pippa?" He gave her an imploring look, praying she would not take his brusque dismissal as a blow-off.

She stood frozen for a minute, looking like she might protest, but then nodded, adjusted her beret and turned briskly on her heel, heading off in the direction of her dorm. Oscar took Luke's arm and led him over to the front fence, out of earshot of his parents.

"They're making me leave," said Oscar.

"No way!"

"Not necessarily forever, but the administration thinks I had something to do with it. They can't prove anything, but they want me to leave campus while they complete their investigation."

Oscar seemed pale and jittery, but worst of all, he refused to make eye contact with Luke.

"I need to go talk to them. We can tell them everything about sneaking out . . ." said Luke.

"They found that bottle that I threw."

"What bottle?"

"At the Dip. Don't you remember the bottle that Kelsey

tripped over? Well, it had my fingerprints on it. That, with the scarf . . ."

Luke was stunned. *The police were doing fingerprint checks? Why hadn't he thought of that? What next?* Luke's mind raced.

"We can explain that."

Oscar shook his head vehemently. "No. It'll just open up a can of worms and get all of you in trouble."

Luke sighed, conflicted. This couldn't be happening. He wanted to help, but now to bring Pippa and Kelsey into it . . . it didn't seem fair. But then again, nothing was fair. "But why would *you* do it? What is their reasoning?"

"I don't know. They wouldn't tell me in so many words, but my lawyer believes that Mrs. Heckler was definitely having an affair . . ."

"Duh."

"And someone told the police that she was having an affair with a student. And therefore when they put two and two together I guess that student is me."

Oscar stopped and for the first time since Luke had known him, he looked beaten.

"Dude, you don't have that much game," said Luke, attempting a joke. It rang hollow. Oscar was way too devastated. "Listen, I want to tell them I was out there with you. We don't have to mention the girls, just me. I'll come forward."

"No," said Oscar quickly, as if he had considered this. "You'll only get yourself booted out."

187

"But I can't let you go down for this."

"No, you can and you will. I need your help; I need you here. They think it's me, so they're not looking at anyone else. I need you to stay. You have to find the real killer."

"Okay."

"I'm serious," Oscar said. "Put your super-hero righteousness to good use. You saved yourself once, and it was a goddamn miracle. I need you to do it again. For me. My *life* depends on it."

18

Luke felt rage growing inside him as he watched Oscar's car pull out of the driveway. It was so unfair. Oscar a murderer? Maybe they were just looking for an excuse to boot him. He would have been long gone without all the money his parents poured into the school, that's for sure. But were they seriously going to accuse Oscar of murder?

Luke heard someone clear his throat behind him and turned around. It was Mr. Hamaguchi. He was wearing Yale sweatpants and an old St. Benedict's sweatshirt and had clearly been out for a run judging by the sweat pouring down his face and the steam behind his glasses.

"Was that really Oscar leaving?" he asked.

Luke nodded.

Mr. Hamaguchi shook his head. "Wow, tough break. You okay?"

NO! Luke wanted to scream, but instead he shrugged. "I'll be fine."

Mr. Hamaguchi stared at him closely. "It's not a good time for us here at St. Benedict's."

"That's for sure."

"It just goes to show."

Luke nodded, and stared at the ground. Suddenly, he looked up. "It just goes to show what?"

"That if they want to get you, they'll find a way."

And with that parting advice, he resumed his run, jogging into the distance.

Luke watched him go and became angry all over again. It was true. The administration wanted Oscar to go, and now they had found a way. This couldn't happen. Luke couldn't let it happen. He would clear Oscar's name. He owed it to him and he knew Oscar would do the same for him. The first thing he was going to do was march into the headmaster's office and try to put this investigation back on track.

"Luke, what can I do for you?" asked Headmaster Thompson when Luke was ushered into his office.

The headmaster had on his reading glasses and was writing something down in his notebook. An avowed Luddite, the headmaster refused to use a computer, so his octogenarian secretary typed up all of his speeches and letters to parents after he had written them out in his rickety handwriting on a yellow legal pad.

"I wanted to talk to you about Oscar," said Luke nervously.

The headmaster peered up at him from above his glasses and motioned for Luke to sit down.

"Sir, with all due respect, I can honestly say that Oscar had nothing to do with Mrs. Heckler's murder."

The headmaster took off his glasses and stared at Luke for what seemed like an eternity. "And why are you so sure?"

"Well, he just . . ." There was no way Luke could say how he knew for sure. The only key would be to prove someone else did it. "Look, I think the police are focusing on the wrong person." He paused, then burst out, "What about Dean Heckler?"

The headmaster remained silent.

"He had motive. She was, from what I hear, cheating on him . . . and then, her dad had all that money. Doesn't he stand to inherit it as her next of kin?"

The headmaster bristled. "Luke, you're out of line."

"I'm sorry sir, I know he's a colleague, but my friend's life is on the line here. Shouldn't every angle be explored?"

"I think we both have to have faith in the police. They know what they're doing."

"But what about how the dean and his ex-wife are so friendly? That's just weird. Since when do exes get along?"

The headmaster sighed deeply. "I understand you are worried about your friend. Since we have been talking to you off the record, I will address some of your concerns, but this has to be strictly off the record as well."

The headmaster gave Luke a warning look.

"Sure," said Luke.

"Upon Mrs. Heckler's death, Dean Heckler told the police and her family that he would waive all rights to her estate, life insurance, everything. He wanted to make it crystal clear that he was not involved."

"He did?" Luke paused. "Okay, fine. But maybe money was never his motive. Maybe he just wanted her dead."

"The dean was at a dinner with the admissions officers from Boston University that night. In Boston. Three people can vouch for his whereabouts."

"Well, Boston's not that far. He could have left after dinner, come back here and murdered her."

The headmaster didn't answer. Luke stared at a small square of light reflected on top of his dark, shiny head.

"I am sure the police checked every angle."

Luke's mind was racing. He was feeling desperate. "What about Mrs. Heckler? The first one? I saw her walking her dog that night. Um, out my window. Why would she do that? Doesn't she live off campus?"

"Not that it's your business, but Mrs. Heckler—Mary—had been working late in the library trying to update the card catalogs."

"Yeah, but that late? Until two in the morning?"

The headmaster stopped and stared at him. "How do you know what time she was out there?"

Uh oh. Luke had to be more careful. "Um, that's when I saw her coming back. Like I said, I couldn't sleep."

The headmaster stared at him before continuing. "The library system is antiquated and the board of trustees has decided that all revisions have to be done as quickly as possible. As Mrs. Heckler has children now, she prefers to put them to bed and work late into the night while her sister looks after them. She is an insomniac, and this schedule works better for her. We are only too happy to accommodate."

"Well, why did she bring her dog?"

"She brings the dog to keep her company. I think it makes her feel more protected."

"Protected from what? So there is a sense that there might be a strangler out there?" asked Luke, his voice rising.

The headmaster frowned. "No, Luke. Just in general, when she drives home, parks her car, that sort of thing."

"I don't know, it just seems like a coincidence," said Luke, still not entirely convinced.

The headmaster looked angry. "Do you really believe a fifty-eight-year-old woman with rheumatoid arthritis could strangle a fit young woman like Joanna Heckler?"

Arthritis? This was the first Luke was hearing about that. Was it true? If so, maybe it was time to cross Mary Heckler off the list. "I guess you're right."

The headmaster placed both of his hands on the table and looked at Luke carefully. "Luke, I know you want to help your friend, but this is not an episode of a television show that can be solved by a high school student. You have to trust our criminal justice system. Don't worry; the police are looking at everything. This is, by no means, a closed case."

"I know firsthand that leaving investigations up to the police, or the FBI, for that matter, is useless," said Luke harshly. He knew he shouldn't speak to the headmaster in that tone but he couldn't help himself.

The headmaster softened. "Luke, what happened to you was terrible. And I know you want to be a good friend to Oscar, which you are. But this is different. This is murder. And the police will solve this. You have to have faith in them."

Luke stood up. "With all due respect, sir, I've learned that the only person I can have faith in is myself."

And with that, he walked out of the room.

19

Vegas! As soon as Luke exited Archer and started back toward his dorm, he realized that he'd forgotten to mention Las Vegas. If he told the headmaster that he knew Mrs. Heckler had vacationed there with someone, that she was whispering sweet nothings to her lover on the phone and that the dean had never been there, then for sure they would know that she had some boyfriend and try to track him down. Elated, Luke was about to turn around and go back to the headmaster's office but then he stopped.

No, there was no way he could tell the headmaster. The person who told him that Mrs. Heckler had been talking lovey-dovey with someone about Vegas was Oscar. And Oscar was their main suspect, so they wouldn't believe him anyway. It was only a dead end. Dejected, Luke turned back around toward Wilcox. He'd have to find out who went to Vegas with Mrs. Heckler on his own.

Luke walked into his room to see a police officer on his

knees searching under Oscar's bed, and another standing on a stepladder searching through the top shelf of his closet. Mr. Crawford was sitting at Oscar's desk, but when he turned around Luke realized that it wasn't Mr. Crawford at all. It was Mr. P. Luke had never noticed how much they looked alike until now. They both were slight but sinewy, with dark hair and those strong features that girls loved. But where Mr. Crawford looked like he could star on a soap opera, there was something a slightly askew in Mr. P.'s looks that made him less handsome. Luke wasn't sure what it was, but there was a flatness to him. Maybe that's what all this responsibility did to someone, Luke thought. Mr. P. was the same age as Crawford, but he had a bigger job and wife and kids to look out for; he seemed more preoccupied and serious. He possessed none of the insouciance or spontaneity that Crawford had.

"Oh, Luke, hello," said Mr. P. immediately putting down the printed copy of Oscar's student handbook. He saw that it was open to one of the faculty pages, where Oscar had been very liberal with offensive and disparaging remarks about his least favorite teachers in the margins.

"What's going on?"

"Luke, I'm sorry but these officers need to look through your room."

Luke glanced around the room nervously. They'd finished the vodka at the Dip, and he knew there wasn't any other contraband in the room, but still, it was unsettling to have people poking through his stuff.

"Don't the police need some sort of warrant for this?"

"Not when a search falls under safety purposes, which is the unfortunate situation we find ourselves in today."

"Oh." Luke knew faculty always had the right to search his room. He just hadn't realized police could too.

"Isn't it a little late to be here? Why wouldn't they have come the other day?"

"Let's just say that some new information made it necessary." Mr. P. held up Oscar's student handbook. "Oscar has a lot to say about several people at St. Benedict's."

"Yeah, but it's just a joke," said Luke quickly.

Mr. P. nodded then turned to the faculty page with Joanna Heckler's picture on it. "So, Oscar thought Mrs. Heckler was 'smokin' hot.' "

Luke felt the blood rush to his face. "He did? I mean, I guess in comparison to a lot of the faculty. I mean, no offense, he was just messing around."

Mr. P. nodded again. "Luke, let's take a walk while the police finish."

The last thing Luke wanted to do was take a walk. He was so exhausted and emotionally wrought that he just wanted to dive into his bed and sleep, sleep, and sleep. He thought back to this morning when he was deep in sleep, naïvely dreaming about the World Cup. It already seemed like a lifetime ago.

"I have so much homework," Luke said when they stepped outside.

"Don't worry. I'll talk to your teachers. Have you eaten dinner yet?" asked Mr. P.

"No."

"Do you want to go to the dining hall?"

"Nah, I was just going to hit the vending machines later."

Mr. P. put his hands in his pockets and smiled kindly. "They assure me that this will be finished shortly."

As they walked along the paths, Luke could tell that passing students were eyeing him with curiosity. It was a little weird to be hanging with Mr. P. on a Sunday night. But then they probably all knew about Oscar by now. It was impossible to keep secrets at St. Benedict's. Everyone knew everything about everyone because they all spent every waking minute of their lives on campus. It could get claustrophobic if you let it.

"Luke, I'm sure this is hard for you, but don't worry, it will all work out."

"Yeah, maybe for me, but what about for Oscar?"

Mr. P. swallowed and didn't say anything. Then finally he said, "I think everything will be okay."

"So you don't think he did it?"

"I . . ." he paused as if he was about to say something but stopped himself. "Look, you know I can't discuss this with you. I'm sorry."

"It's so crazy. All this suspicion . . ."

Mr. P. stopped and looked at him. "What do you know about this, Luke? Have you been truthful?"

The question caught Luke off guard. "Yes. Of course."

"What is the connection between Oscar and Mrs. Heckler?"

"No connection. It's all bull . . . it's not true. He's being framed."

The dean put his hand under his chin and rubbed his beard growth. "Do you have proof? What do you know? What has Oscar told you?"

Luke stared into Mr. P.'s eyes, which were filled with urgency. He was tempted to break down to him, tell him everything, but then something held him back.

"He told me nothing, but that's because there was nothing to tell."

"Why did Mrs. Heckler request him?"

Luke was confused. "What do you mean?"

Mr. P. appeared momentarily disconcerted. "Nothing, I misspoke."

"She wanted Oscar to work off his demerits in her office?" asked Luke, unwilling to let him off the hook.

"Luke, forget what I said. Let's move on."

Luke didn't want to, but he knew that Mr. P. had shut down. He had obviously slipped up and told Luke something that he wasn't supposed to. So there *was* some sort of connection between Oscar and Mrs. Heckler, "Joanna." Luke remembered that Oscar always referred to her by her first name. That was weird. In fact, everything was getting weirder.

That night Luke had horrible dreams. He kept seeing Mrs. Heckler in the woods and he kept trying to warn her. But she wouldn't listen; instead she laughed at him and told him he was being stupid. And he kept hearing the voice, the lover's voice. The falsetto voice that said *he's going to hurt you.* At the time, Luke had thought it meant emotionally, but was the man warning her? And was he talking about the dean?

Several times throughout the night Luke awoke in a sweat. At one point he could swear someone was in the room with him. It was as if something changed in the air and alerted him. He lifted his head, but his body was so tired, every limb heavy, that he couldn't sit up to see who it was. He fell back into a deep slumber and dreamt that Mr. Tadeckis was sitting on his windowsill, watching him.

When he woke up he realized that he had slept through first period, American Lit with Mr. Turner. With just twelve students in every class, there was no chance of an absence not being noticed. Oh, well. The other eleven kids (including Pippa) would have to manage the roundtable discussion of *The Scarlet Letter* without him. He'd talk to Mr. P. about it. Surely there'd be some leniency considering they'd just booted out his roommate and accused him of murder? Wasn't it true that if your college roommate offed themselves you automatically got all A's for the year? Maybe this would be the same as having an accused murderer live with you; which was, if anything, more taxing. Since Luke had both second and third period free on Mondays, he decided to shower, grab a Pop-Tart, and set out to find someone. The time had come to have another conversation with Mr. Tadeckis.

Mr. Tadeckis's "office" was located in the basement of

Pearson, the Humanities building, one of the older buildings on campus. As Luke made his way down the narrow hall, ducking under low-hanging pipes and avoiding a small puddle that was forming underneath one of them, he could see why Mr. Tadeckis was so frustrated. By putting him down in this hellhole the administration was certainly making it clear that he did not occupy a place of importance.

"Come in," said the voice on the other side of the door. Luke hadn't even knocked. How did he know he was there?

When Luke opened the door, he half-expected to find some sort of torture chamber, or at the very least a room full of taxidermied animals, but he was pleasantly surprised to find neither. The room was extremely tidy. On one wall, bookshelves were methodically organized with neatly labeled binders and photo boxes. On the other wall there were several file boxes stacked on top of each other, again with a strong semblance of order. There were a few framed photographs of Mr. Tadeckis with some of his wilderness students, no doubt taken on expeditions.

Luke surveyed the room and finally focused on Mr. Tadeckis, who sat with his arms folded behind a wooden desk. The desktop was empty except for an accessories caddy in the right-hand corner containing some small color-coded pushpins, paper clips, pens and staples. Everything was organized immaculately.

"Hello, Luke," said Mr. Tadeckis with a knowing smile. "What can I do for you?"

"I wanted to talk."

"Excellent. Have a seat," said Mr. Tadeckis, motioning to the chair in front of the desk. It was only when Luke sat down that he realized the chair was really low. Like really low. He now had to sit up straight as a rail to see Mr. Tadeckis over the desk.

Luke squirmed awkwardly. He could see Mr. Tadeckis trying not to laugh, which made him determined not to express his discomfort.

"I wanted to talk to you about the murder."

"I'm listening," said Mr. Tadeckis quickly, as if he had been anticipating this conversation.

"Okay," said Luke, rubbing his hand through his hair. "Sorry, I just . . . I had the weirdest dreams last night. I thought you were in my room. In the middle of the night . . ." Luke let his voice trail off.

Mr. Tadeckis looked at him evenly and waited for him to continue.

"Anyway," said Luke, changing the topic. "Did you hear about Oscar?"

"Yes."

"Well, can you believe it?"

"I told you the police were morons, Luke. Now can *you* believe it?"

Luke rubbed his hands against his pants. "Yeah, preaching to the choir. But look, we both know Oscar didn't do this."

Mr. Tadeckis stared carefully at Luke and remained silent.

"I mean, you know who did it, right?"

"I won't play that way, Luke."

"Okay . . ."

"Who do you think did it?" said Mr. Tadeckis. Luke thought he sounded like a child who refused to cooperate.

"Me? I think . . . well, I think it was the dean."

"Which Dean?"

The question caught Luke by surprise. "Dean Heckler. Maybe he and his ex-wife cooked up something when he found out the new wife was cheating."

Mr. Tadeckis remained expressionless.

"I talked to Pippa," continued Luke. "I don't think she had anything to do with this. She's in enough trouble at home, and besides, she didn't have a motive."

"She told you that?"

"No, but I mean, I talked to her about this. I think she's telling the truth."

"Other thoughts?" asked Mr. Tadeckis.

"Well, of course I want to know who the boyfriend was. Who Mrs. Heckler was arguing with. I'm not sure he did it, I think he took off, but maybe . . ."

"Jealous rage?"

"Yes."

"Did it look like a jealous rage to you?" asked Mr. Tadeckis, arching an eyebrow.

"You don't think so?"

"I'm asking you."

Luke thought back to the pictures. "Maybe. How would I know? You're the one who witnessed the murder."

"Never said that. But you saw the pictures."

"How'd you know that?"

"Please, let's not waste our time on how I procure my information."

"Mr. Tadeckis, if you know who did it, why don't you just tell the police?" asked Luke with exasperation.

"I don't want to get mixed up in all this."

"But, if you know something . . ."

"*You* know something and *you're* not coming forward," said Mr. Tadeckis calmly.

Luke sighed deeply and shook his head. "Yeah, but you're a teacher. An adult."

"That's an insufficient excuse. Look, these are all incredibly flawed people we're dealing with, Luke. Everyone had broken a rule. The victim herself, one Joanna Heckler, was a loose woman. Immoral. Broke up marriages, cheated, manipulated. Then there is Dean Heckler. I have no love lost for Dean Heckler. He's a pompous, arrogant bore who thinks he is better than everyone. He still has his ex-wife, the demure little librarian Mary, do his bidding, perhaps spying for him. The boyfriend—Joanna's lover's name withheld—he was knowingly committing a mortal sin. Finally, there are the four of you; Oscar, Kelsey, Pippa and Mr. Goody Two-shoes himself, the hero of St. Benedict's, Luke Chase. You had broken a major school rule as stated in the St. Benedict's handbook on page seventy-six 'no one is to leave the dormitory after hours.'"

"But you said that you thought it was good that we were sneaking out!" interjected Luke.

"I think it is industrious. But let's face it: if we are going to break it down: you were violating the rules of the school. My opinion of those rules is irrelevant. In fact, all of the above mentioned were either lying, cheating, or snooping around where they didn't need to."

"But no one deserved to die!"

"There are consequences," said Mr. Tadeckis definitively.

"Why don't the consequences apply to you? You were breaking the rules also! Isn't your spying the same as Mrs. Heckler's spying?" said Luke, leaning forward in his chair. Now more than ever it bugged him that his chair barely reached the desk. Half of Mr. Tadeckis's face was obscured.

"Excellent point. You have me there," said Mr. Tadeckis calmly.

"So are you going to be penalized?"

"You never know. Are you?"

"I hope no one is. Only the killer . . ."

Mr. Tadeckis laughed. "Luke, you are either naïve or a genuinely nice person. What you don't realize is that they are all lying to you. All of them. *Lying.* Your own roommate included."

Luke felt stung. "I don't believe you."

"Don't. I don't care. But clearly you came to me because you needed help and guidance. I offer the truth and you reject me, imply I am just heartless."

Luke sunk back in his chair. "Okay, then give me guidance."

"Don't deviate from the victim."

"What's that supposed to mean?"

"Live her life and you will know who killed her."

"That sounds like a crock. Aren't the cops doing that?"

"They are, but you know things they don't know. You have access that they can't ever have."

"Me? I'm just a student."

"Exactly."

"So, what can I do?"

Mr. Tadeckis shook his head vehemently. "Luke, you don't understand. The reason I am assisting you is because you are more capable than you think. You're smarter than these security guards wandering around, more competent than the police."

"Come on," said Luke.

"I don't believe I have to remind you of your great escape in the Virginia woods when you were a mere thirteen. You outwitted professional criminals."

Luke shrugged. "It was a fluke."

Mr. Tadeckis bristled. "I don't understand why you want to undermine your strength and fortitude."

"I just don't want to be classified as something I'm not!"

"Why? Too much responsibility?"

"Maybe," snapped Luke. "Maybe I was just lucky. Maybe they didn't tie the ropes firmly enough. Maybe they were tired and I just picked the right moment. I don't want to have this burden of living up to the expectations that I am somehow special just because of one thing I did!"

Mr. Tadeckis cocked his head to the side and studied him

carefully. Finally, he spoke. "Luke, it took me an immense amount of time to perfect that obstacle course that you completed during freshman orientation. I laid very distinct traps, concealed clues, and placed the zip wire at the highest and most treacherous point. And yet you were able to complete it."

Luke's mind raced back to that day. It was true; the course had been a challenge. Most of the kids who got as far as the zip wire bagged when they saw there were no safeties. But it was just the sort of challenge that he enjoyed.

"That was different."

"I don't see how. It's all in your mindset, Luke. You have to trust yourself. And only yourself."

Luke's head was spinning. He felt tired, very tired. He stood up to go. As he turned the door handle, he glanced back at Mr. Tadeckis, who was sitting with a smug look on his face.

"Were you in my room last night?"

Mr. Tadeckis smiled. "No."

Luke pulled the door open. "Had to ask."

As Luke made his way out, Mr. Tadeckis called after him. "I was there the night before."

Jesus. Luke closed the door behind him firmly and leaned against it. Things were definitely getting weirder.

20

The next few days were all catch-up for Luke. He was so behind in all of his schoolwork that he buried himself under textbooks. For the first time, he was glad that they had mandatory study hall. Sometimes, without parents to crack the whip and tell you to get your stuff done, it was easy to fall behind. But in general Luke enjoyed being away from home. Nothing against his parents, he just appreciated the independence. And he generally liked boarding school life. Sure, Saturday classes were a drag. But it was fun living in a dorm, and the sports teams were more competitive than at his school back home, so that appealed to Luke, too. It was also more intimate living with your teachers day in and day out. You knew their kids, their spouses; in fact, most of the spouses were teachers, too. It was almost like an extended family.

But with all of this going on, school became strange. It was odd for Luke to be living in the midst of all this, and unable to leave. It was oppressive. Not to mention lonely with no Oscar around to hash it out with. His texts and Facebook messages to Oscar had gone unanswered. He called Oscar a few times on both his cell and his home phone but every time Mr. or Mrs. Weymouth said he was unavailable. He'd even tried emailing him, but those weren't replied to, either. It seemed they were really locking him down. How about a little benefit of the doubt?

The rumor mill was in overdrive. Everyone had theories about who killed Mrs. Heckler, why she was killed, and who was going to be arrested. Luke listened to everything with skepticism. Although she hadn't been at St. Benedict's that long, it seemed that everyone had a story about Joanna Heckler, and as often happens with the dead, she had been elevated to sainthood. Stories of her letting students off for minor infractions dribbled in, as well as small acts of kindness and words of wisdom that she bestowed upon people. Luke found them all hard to believe.

There was one story that piqued his interest. Liz told him that she had gone to the Palmers' house to babysit their kids and overheard Mr. P. and his wife arguing about Joanna Heckler.

"They didn't hear me come in," explained Liz. "Their daughter Becky let me in and they were upstairs. I heard voices and then they got louder and it was clear they were talking about Mrs. Heckler."

"What did they say?" asked Luke.

He and Liz were sitting in their usual spots at the table

in the Spanish classroom waiting for Señor Diaz. A light fall rain drizzled outside. Liz had been giving him the cold shoulder ever since the episode at the pond, so Luke had decided to apologize for offending her. He was glad he did; he had missed hanging out with her, not to mention she was turning out to be a pretty decent source of information.

"She said something about refusing to go over to Dean Heckler's with him—I guess there was some sort of reception to greet people or something. She was like, that whole marriage was a disaster and Dean Heckler was a bad guy for ditching the first wife and leaving her out in the cold."

"She said that?"

Liz nodded before continuing. "She also said Joanna was immoral and after everyone's husband and there was no way, no matter how Christian it was, that she would be a hypocrite and go over there and pretend to be sorry that she was dead."

The words stuck with Luke for the next few days. He wondered just how many people were pretending to be sorry that Joanna was dead but were secretly pleased. It's not something many people would admit. He was deep in thought as he stood in the hallway waiting for the previous history class to be let out so that he could enter the room when Pippa tapped him on the shoulder.

"You've been avoiding me."

Luke was psyched to see Pippa. His stomach gave a funny kind of flip. "I haven't been avoiding you. I just have been busy with homework and stuff."

Pippa looked at him in disbelief.

"I swear."

"Does that mean you haven't done any investigating since we were last together?"

Luke took Pippa's arm and gently escorted her away from the door, where student traffic was streaming in and out. It struck him that she smelled good. She was wearing that rose perfume again; not the overbearing stuff that you'd smell in a magazine or the kind they spray in the department stores his sisters sometimes dragged him to, but a light, summer's day kind. It was nice.

"I have been totally slammed with work so I haven't done jack. Not to mention, they booted my roommate, so I've been dealing with that fallout."

Everyone over the past few days had been bombarding Luke with questions regarding Oscar. There was a lot of speculation. The school said it was just an "academic suspension" and nothing to do with the murder, but rumors were still flying. Luke shot down every one of them, and refused to engage with anyone who was accusing Oscar of killing Mrs. Heckler. He avoided all of their texts and stayed off all his apps. No Snapchat, no Facebook, no Instagram, nothing. It was strange not to be checking those things every few minutes, but at the same time it was sort of liberating. He didn't mind being out of touch as much as he thought he would.

"How *is* Oscar?" asked Pippa.

Luke raised an eyebrow.

"Look, we both know there's no love lost between me and

that idiot, but I know he didn't kill Mrs. Heckler," said Pippa with genuine sincerity.

"He's fine. I mean, I guess he's fine. They won't let me speak to him."

"So odd. Do they really think he was capable of that? I don't see any motive."

"Me neither. I have to admit, the only good thing about him being away is that I don't have to worry about him blowing Kelsey off in person and making her so mad she does something to retaliate."

"Would he do that? They were all over each other at the Dip."

Luke gave her a sheepish look and shrugged.

Pippa rolled her eyes. "Wow. Nice guy. I really don't understand your friendship."

Luke thought for a second. "Oscar's always had my back. I mean, look at the situation now. Anyone else would have ratted us out, told the deans that he wasn't out there alone. We're his *alibis* and he's not exposing us! That's the kind of stand-up guy Oscar is."

"I think 'stand-up guy' is a way too generous description of Oscar," said Pippa. "And you have to wonder what Oscar's motive is. Why isn't he telling them that we were all out there? Maybe he doesn't want them to question us."

Luke hadn't thought of it that way. She had a point. "I don't know. Honestly, it's hard for me to reconcile the two supposed sides of Oscar. I've only seen one side in the three years that I've lived with him. That's the person I know and the person I'm inclined to help as much as I can."

Pippa smiled. "You're a good friend, Luke."

The bell rang and Luke motioned toward the door. "I've got to bolt."

"All right, but if you want me to help you out, let me know. I'll poke around and see if I can learn anything else."

"Thanks."

"I assume you've already talked to your buddy who worked in Mrs. Heckler's office?"

Tariq! He headed up the student-alumni committee and worked closely with Mrs. Heckler. Luke had forgotten to talk to him. "I'm on it."

"All right then," said Pippa, turning to go.

"Hey, Pippa," Luke said. "Thanks."

She smiled and Luke watched her walk down the hall. He enjoyed the view.

"You coming, Mr. Chase?" asked Mrs. DeStefano, poking her head out of the classroom.

"Yes, ma'am."

"**D**ude, I've told everything important to the police. Mr. P. also gave me the third degree. There is nothing else I can think of."

"Tariq, there has to be something," insisted Luke.

It was study hall, and Luke had spent the last twenty minutes in Tariq's room trying to get him to remember something about Mrs. Heckler. Tariq was not being very helpful. He was one of those self-righteous annoying types, who was always complaining about getting left out of group chats and that sort of thing. He would be cool if he would just drop the chip on his shoulder.

"Nothing. I could always tell when she had a personal call because she'd start whispering, but frankly I wasn't that interested in her social life so I didn't pay much attention," Tariq said, leaning back against the wall and blowing a lock of his dark hair out of his eyes.

"Okay, well tonight after study hall we're going to the alumni office," said Luke.

"Dude, not cool. The police were all over that place. They won't want me snooping around."

"You can tell them you forgot something."

"But the security guards . . ."

"Come on, everyone knows the security guards are a joke! First of all, they've totally reduced the number, there're only like five left, and they are totally clueless."

"I don't know. What if they ask why I'm bringing you there?"

"They won't. But if anyone does, we can pretend that we were just hanging out and you remembered you needed to come back for something so I came with you."

"I'm not sure . . ."

"Tariq, I'm not taking no for an answer."

Main Hall was thronged with students during Animal Hour. It seemed like it had gotten more popular than ever since the murder. There was an urgency to everyone's socializing that hadn't been there before.

Luke followed Tariq around the corner to the hallway perpendicular to Main Hall. Mrs. Heckler's office was located at the very end on the right, past a giant bulletin board advertising upcoming alumni events. Luke could tell that Tariq was nervous even though he was trying to play it cool. He kept glancing furtively over his shoulder as if someone would nab him. Tonight, Mr. Hamaguchi was on duty, but he had his head down as he sat at the front desk reading a book. A few security guards passed through, but everything seemed secure under the fluorescent lighting so they kept on moving into the shadows of the building.

Tariq took the key out of his pocket, snuck a surreptitious look from side to side to make sure the guards had passed, then opened the door.

"I'm surprised the police didn't change the locks," said Tariq.

"They probably took what they thought they needed."

The office was dark so Luke flicked on the light and closed the door.

"I think we should turn off the light," said Tariq nervously.

"That's way more suspicious," said Luke, scanning the room. It was a pretty straightforward office. There was a main desk with a chair and a computer, clearly Mrs. Heckler's. Luke walked around to the back of the desk and examined it. He was sure he wouldn't find anything majorly incriminating but he needed to see it. There were no framed pictures, which for some reason relieved Luke immensely, and the only personal item was a St. Benedict's coffee mug. Luke felt sad, the way he had when he'd seen the crime scene photos. Did Mrs. Heckler feel anything differently when she took her last sip of coffee? Probably not.

"Okay, can we go now?" asked Tariq in a high voice.

"Relax."

"Dude, I'm the one who will get busted, not you."

"I'll take responsibility, don't worry."

Luke suddenly noticed a startling lack of paperwork on Mrs. Heckler's desk. He opened her drawers, and aside from some old yearbooks, they were empty.

"Did they take all of her stuff?"

Tariq walked over to the desk. "Well, she had alumni files in the file cabinet."

Luke opened the file cabinet. "Empty."

"They probably have to go through everything. Hey, maybe some mad alum killed her."

"Did she have a date book?" asked Luke.

"She had a calendar on her desk."

"Gone," said Luke, once again checking the drawers.

"Hey," said Tariq snapping his fingers. "She also used Outlook on the computer."

Luke started to turn on Mrs. Heckler's computer.

"No, not this computer. She used my computer—well, the student computer."

Luke stared at Tariq.

"Why would she use the student computer?"

216

It started to dawn on Tariq. "I don't know. The first time she said she was having problems with her computer, and then it just became a habit. But maybe she was emailing with someone or making appointments and didn't want anyone to see."

"Did you tell the police this?"

"No!" said Tariq with growing excitement. "Should we call them now?"

Luke got into Tariq's face as closely as possible. "Are you insane? No. We can't tell them."

"Why?"

"Listen, don't worry. Just show me where the student computer is."

Tariq took a deep breath. It was moment-of-truth time. Would he be a total loser and not go along with it? Luke stood up straighter.

"It's not here," said Tariq.

"Don't be a—"

"I mean, it's in my room. I have it. I'm not technically supposed to remove it from this office, but I had so much work to do so I brought it home with me last week. I figured with Mrs. Heckler dead, no one would notice."

"You, my friend, are a genius."

21

Meet SDI Three o'clock.
SDI Five.
SDI Seven.
Change SDI.

Who was SDI? Luke had spent the last two hours poring over Mrs. Heckler's schedule in her Outlook calendar, and the only red flag was SDI She entered it several times over the past few weeks so it was clearly important. What did it stand for? Tariq had been no help. He didn't think it had anything to do with alumni stuff, and was pretty much useless at offering suggestions. Luke dismissed him as quickly as possible and they were both relieved to lose the other's company. Tariq could be so spineless. All he cared about was doing whatever he could to get into Yale or Princeton. Luke, on the other hand, was determined to vindicate his friend. He wished he could put *that* on a college application.

What could it stand for? Was it the creepy-voice guy's initials? Luke looked through the entire handbook and found no one whose initials were SDI. He even reversed it and there was one person whose initials were IDS, but it was Isabel Sanderson, a freshman, and Luke doubted that was whom Mrs. Heckler was meeting up with. But it was clear that she didn't want anyone to see her schedule, that's why she used the student computer. By one o'clock, Luke was having trouble focusing on the screen so he switched off the computer. He texted Oscar, asking to talk, but heard nothing. It was so frustrating to have this radio silence. He wanted to update Oscar on everything, see how he was doing. It was the first time he'd actually been at St. Benedict's without Oscar and it felt weird, abnormal. Finally, exhausted, Luke fell asleep. Again he dreamt about Mrs. Heckler. She kept motioning for him to follow her, and he kept trying to catch up with her. He'd get close, so close he could almost touch her, but then she'd run away. Still, when he woke up, he didn't feel frustrated, he felt somehow hopeful.

"Hey Luke," said Kelsey. They were both on line at the dining hall, waiting for the orange juice machine.

"Hey, how are you?"

"I'm okay." Kelsey glanced around to make sure no one was listening. Luke figured she was going to ask about Oscar, and predictably, she did. "So . . . how's Oscar?"

"Your guess is as good as mine. Haven't talked to him."

Kelsey flipped her hair behind her shoulder and took her turn getting juice.

"Well, to be honest, I'm actually glad he's not here now. Matt's coming down this weekend to visit, and it would just be awkward."

"Yeah," Luke agreed. He filled his glass and they made their way back toward the junior area tables.

"I'd hate for Matt to find out and there be, like, a confrontation," added Kelsey with another hair flip.

Luke shook his head with disbelief as Kelsey moved to the next table to join her friends. She was either delusional, or a great actress. She had to have known Oscar had been pulling away. There's no way he would have gotten into a fight with anyone over her.

When Luke sat down to eat, Pippa slid into the chair opposite him with her tray. He grinned, glad to see her. When this was all settled, he'd like to spend some time with her alone. Maybe take her out to dinner in town at Antonucci's, just the two of them.

"Okay, give me the latest," she said.

Luke filled her in on everything about the Outlook and the initials SDI.

"Interesting," said Pippa, spearing a piece of French toast with her fork.

"I know."

Suddenly there was a loud bang. Everyone was startled and glanced around the room. A freshman was standing there looking guilty; his tray and his entire breakfast were splat all over the floor. At first, there was dead silence—everyone's nerves were a bit shot since the murder. But when people realized what it was, they applauded. Kelsey and her friends immediately broke out in giggles while the red-faced freshman bent down to clean up the mess.

"That's so cruel," said Pippa. "I can't believe Kelsey would laugh at someone like that and cause him further embarrassment."

"What I don't get is that she's so upset about Mrs. Heckler flirting with her dad, and yet, she's cheating on her boyfriend with Oscar," Luke said, quietly so Kelsey wouldn't hear him.

"True. Rather hypocritical, I would say," Pippa agreed.

Suddenly, a thought occurred to Luke. He leaned out into the aisle toward Kelsey's table. "Hey, Kelsey. What's your dad's name?" he called.

"Steven, why?"

"Nothing, just wondering," said Luke.

Kelsey gave him a quizzical look, but Luke shrugged and she returned to her friends.

Luke leaned in toward Pippa. "That's got to be it!"

"What?"

"Kelsey's last name is Ingraham. Steven Ingraham is her father. Those must be his initials SDI that were in Mrs. Heckler's Outlook! She must have been meeting him. Maybe Kelsey's hunch was right?"

Pippa thought before she spoke. "Do you know whether her dad's middle name begins with D?"

"I think it's obvious."

221

"Huh," said Pippa.

Luke started to feel annoyed, like his great sleuthing work had been undermined. "What? You don't?" he asked, pushing his tray to the middle of the table and folding his arms.

Pippa looked up at the ceiling as if she was thinking. "My guess is that *SDI* stands for Southborough Days Inn. She was probably meeting her lover there."

Luke stared at Pippa, who stared back. Suddenly a huge smile crept across his face. The Southborough Days Inn: a small, one-story run-down motel on a tiny street off County Road 674 in the hamlet of Woodville. It was perfect. "You're right."

"I thought so," said Pippa, putting a large bite in her mouth.

They had one hour between the end of Luke's soccer practice and chapel to make it over to the Southborough Days Inn. Because Pippa didn't play sports, she was able to call a taxi in advance and have it waiting outside the athletic center for Luke to hop right in.

"You smell," said Pippa holding her nose.

"Sorry, I didn't get a chance to shower."

"Next time we'll have to arrange our schedule to include mandatory bathing."

"Shut up!" said Luke, punching her playfully. "Hey, did you sign us out?"

"Yes. I signed out with Ms. Chang in my dorm, and then

I didn't see Mr. Crawford but Mr. Hamaguchi was coming out of Wilcox so I asked him if it was okay if you and I went on a brief excursion."

"And he was cool?"

"Yeah, he was sort of wondering why, but I told him your parents were coming up to stay because they were worried about the whole Mrs. Heckler thing, and we needed to find them decent accommodation because all the regular places were taken by the reporters who had come to town. He said okay."

As the taxi pulled out of the athletic entrance on the school grounds, they could see the cluster of media trucks by the front gates.

"I wonder when they'll get bored and move on," said Luke.

"Are you mad? They love this stuff. Rich kids, beautiful corpse. They will never leave. Trust me."

Luke felt bad. "Sorry. I guess you'd know."

The taxi swept down the road and they sat in silence for a minute, both of them glancing out the window. Rolling hills, now becoming shrouded in dusk, dappled the landscape. There were scattered houses, mostly split-level ranches with a few white clapboards thrown in, and a mixture of farms and old run-down barns. They passed an old water mill that had long since been abandoned. "Southborough is such a depressing town."

"Aw, come on, don't you find it scenic?" Luke asked sarcastically.

"Not in the least. It's very grim. There is nothing quaint or charming. It's not even country, just impoverished suburb masquerading as country in order to make up for the lack of commerce."

"You just hate everything in this town."

Pippa turned and looked at him. "Not everything."

Luke felt himself blush. He was intrigued by Pippa, whoever she was. It was odd. Here he was searching for a killer alongside her while she had been accused of homicide back home. But he didn't see how she could have done it. She was reserved, for sure, and not very emotive, but he felt it was more of a suit of armor with her. He believed she was actually very vulnerable. Once you cracked the tough exterior, there was a really nice person underneath. Not to mention smart, funny, and sexy.

"So, did you bring the student handbook?" asked Luke after he realized he was staring at Pippa.

"Right here," said Pippa tapping her bag. "What's our strategy?"

"I was going to wing it."

Pippa laughed. "You'll have to do better than that."

22

The man shook his head.

"You're sure?" asked Pippa again.

"I'm sure."

"And there's no one else who would have been working here at those times?" asked Luke with urgency.

"Just me. My brother has the night shift."

Luke and Pippa both sighed in unison. The middle-aged man behind the front desk, who was both balding and short, had not proven very informative. Luke and Pippa were immensely disappointed.

"Can you tell us who checked in at those times?" asked Luke. He wasn't going to let this go. To come all the way here and not get anything . . . there had to be something this man could tell them.

The man held his datebook protectively. "I can't tell you who our clients are, that's our policy. I can only tell you that I haven't seen this woman before."

"Does that mean she wasn't here?" asked Pippa. "Or that maybe she had the man collect the key and she slipped in the room when you weren't looking?"

"It's possible," shrugged the man.

"Well, was there a guy at those times? Who maybe rented the room for a few hours?"

"There may have been," said the man behind the desk.

Suddenly, Pippa put her hand on Luke's wrist and pressed firmly. "Excuse me one second, sir."

The man shrugged again and went back into his little office. Luke watched him pick up a pastrami sandwich and take a large bite. A small dribble of mustard hung on his bottom lip while he chewed.

"Come here," whispered Pippa.

Luke followed her to the side of the lobby. It was a fairly run-down operation that had clearly seen better days. Paths were worn into the rug by extensive foot traffic, and the walls looked like they could use a fresh coat of paint. Even the fake flowers in the vase on the front desk looked forlorn. Luke knew that it used to get a lot of bookings from St. Benedict's parents who came up for games or parents weekends, but ever since they built the Courtyard Marriott in Kensville this hotel had been left in the dust. Luke couldn't imagine who would choose to stay here. Desperate lovers? It had the word "tryst" written all over it.

"He wants money," said Pippa.

"What?" asked Luke in shock, glancing back at the guy. "I don't think so."

Pippa nodded firmly. "I swear to you that bloke wants to see some cash."

"That's not real. People don't want handouts. That's just in the movies."

"Well, why don't we try it and see if it's just in the movies. How much money do you have?"

Luke fumbled for his wallet in his pocket. He pulled it out. "Forty bucks."

"All right then, I have a hundred. I will give it to you—men prefer men to do this—and then you'll pay for the cab."

"You brought a hundred dollars with you?"

"I was prepared," said Pippa.

Pippa was way more sophisticated than Luke was, that was for sure. It was nice being with someone who was one step ahead. Luke walked back over to the desk. The man put down his sandwich and came back over.

"Listen, sir, if there's any way we can get more information," said Luke, sliding the hundred-dollar bill across the counter toward the man.

The man hesitated and then put it in his pocket. He looked up at Luke and smiled.

"There was a guy who used to come in at those times. I suspect he's the guy you are interested in."

Pippa immediately joined Luke at the counter. "Who was he?" asked Pippa and Luke in unison.

The man was startled by their sudden enthusiasm and put his hands up. "Hey, wait a minute, this doesn't have anything to do with that murder on campus."

"No, no," said Luke and Pippa shaking their heads.

"'Cause I don't want to get mixed up in that. Maybe I should just call the police."

"No, it's not that, sir," said Luke.

"It's about my daddy," said Pippa, kicking Luke under the counter. Luke was amazed to watch her eyes fill with tears. She was quite the little actress. "I think he's cheating on my mum, with this man."

The man looked at Pippa with surprise. "This guy isn't English."

"Oh," said Pippa quickly. "They sent me to boarding school in the UK when I was young. That's where I picked up the accent."

The man shook his head. "No, this guy looked too young to be your father. No offense."

"How young?" asked Luke.

"Early thirties, tops."

Luke turned to Pippa. That ruled out Kelsey's dad as the lover. Luke pushed the student handbook back at the man. "Could you please look through this and see if it's any of the faculty."

The man sighed. "Look, I don't want to get dragged into this. I have a feeling that you guys aren't being straight with me."

"We are, we promise," said Pippa.

The man stared at them then finally picked up the handbook. "I really shouldn't be getting involved. I just had a woman here two months ago freaking out on me, saying her husband had been cheating on her here. Not my problem!"

"What did the woman look like?" asked Pippa. She turned and raised her eyebrow at Luke.

"A mousy brunette. Definitely not a homicidal type if that's what you're thinking."

The man started flicking through the pages, not in any particular order.

"It's always the mousy ones," said Pippa. "I think . . ."

The man interrupted her. "Could have been this guy," he said pointing.

"Mr. P.!" said Luke. He turned and looked at Pippa. Could Mr. P. really have been the one having an affair with Mrs. Heckler? He certainly didn't seem the type.

"Do you think?" asked Pippa, incredulous.

"I can't imagine . . ."

"Wait, wait, could have been this guy also," said the man.

"Mr. Hamaguchi?" asked Luke. "Wait a second, those guys couldn't look more different. One is white and the other is Asian."

"Well, I told you, he wore a baseball hat and sunglasses. It was hard to tell," said the man with exasperation. "I try not to look too carefully at them, makes them nervous. I don't want to scare them off, I need the business."

"All right," said Luke. "Who else?"

The phone rang and the man picked it up swiftly.

"Southborough Days Inn?" he asked hopefully.

"Yeah, let me look. Where did you leave it?" He paused waiting for the person on the other end to respond. "What room were they in, do you remember?" Again a pause. He began writing something down. Then he started opening drawers.

"I have to look in the safe, just a sec."

The man disappeared into the back room.

Pippa gave Luke a look. "We have to get back to campus before dinner," she whispered. "I promised Ms. Chang."

Luke nodded.

The man reentered "Naw, I'll go check out the room."

Luke made a motion toward the man.

"Hang on a sec," said the man into the phone. "Yeah?"

"Do you mind checking now? We really have to go."

The man shook his head. "Sorry, dude, I can't. It's my boss. I have to locate something or he'll have my ass."

"We really need to get back," said Pippa, glancing at her watch.

Luke was frustrated. "Okay, we have to go, but maybe you can keep the handbook and look through it a little more. Something might pop out at you. Call me please if anything," said Luke, scribbling his cell phone number and name on a Post-it note.

The man held up the Post-it. "Luke Chase. The Kidnapped Kid. I thought you looked familiar."

Luke normally cringed at the media's pet name for him, but this time he smiled. "That's right."

"You're like a real like Houdini."

"You know it," said Luke, playing along. He felt Pippa's eyes burning into his face, but he refused to turn and look at her.

"Wow, all right. I finally meet a celebrity," said the man. "For you, I'll take another look at that book."

"Thanks," said Luke.

The man returned to his phone call while Luke and Pippa walked toward the front door of the motel.

"What do you think?" asked Luke.

"About you being a Houdini?" asked Pippa.

Luke glanced at her quickly, then looked away. "No, about everything else."

Pippa shrugged. "I find it terribly hard to imagine Mr. Palmer as Mrs. Heckler's lover."

"I know. I lived in Nichols and he seemed like a totally devoted family man."

"Also, wouldn't it be a little hard for him to be out there in the middle of the night? How would he explain it to his wife?"

"Right. But you know what? His wife was no fan of Joanna Heckler's. She made that clear, according to Liz. Maybe there was a reason."

"Worth pursuing," said Pippa.

Luke held the door open for Pippa. A large gust of wind scuttled leaves across the parking lot.

"Wow, it's really picking up," said Pippa, zipping up her jacket. Her hair was blowing in the wind, and she turned and gave Luke a smile as they exited the motel office. He smiled back. She looked gorgeous.

The sky was now completely dark. It took a second for their eyes to adjust to the gloom, aided by two lampposts that marked the entrance of the parking lot. The scattered leaves were sucked up by a mini-tornado of wind and frantically whipped around in small circles as if in a blender. There was a chill in the air, the lick of winter.

"Where's our taxi?" asked Luke, surveying the lot. In the two slots against the Inn were two parked cars—a green Chevy and a red Toyota—but no cab.

"You told him to wait, right?" asked Pippa.

"Yeah, I handed him twenty bucks and told him we'd be right back, just sit tight. This blows!"

"That's for sure," agreed Pippa. "Maybe he's around the corner?"

They walked a few steps to glance hopefully around the side of the building, but there was no taxi.

"What the hell?" said Luke with annoyance.

"Hmmm . . . he's not there," said Pippa. "This stinks. I need to avoid drama, and Ms. Chang is extra strict about off-campus since the murder."

"I guess we could walk, but I don't want to walk back to school in this windstorm. It's friggin' cold!" Luke's formerly sweaty shirt now felt damp and clammy next to his body. He was aching for a nice, hot shower. "Let's call the taxi."

"Okay, but can we do it inside? I'm freezing!"

They returned to the entrance of the motel. Luke opened the door, allowing Pippa and about a hundred leaves back inside. The man was now off the phone and came out from the back office.

"Our cab took off."

"Hey, glad you're back. If it helps, this guy was here asking a few questions too."

Luke and Pippa walked over to where the man was standing, his greasy finger pointing to a picture. Dean Heckler. Luke lifted up his face to look at the man. "Are you sure?"

"Yeah, this guy was for sure. He had that military look. I definitely recognize him."

Pippa and Luke exchanged wide-eyed glances. "What did he want to know?" asked Pippa.

"Just, you know, if I saw the broad, who the guy was. Same as you."

"Why didn't you mention it before?" asked Luke.

The man shrugged. "Why bother?"

"Do you remember exactly when this man was here? Was it recently?" asked Pippa.

The man looked up at the ceiling as if there was a calendar there. "It was about two weeks ago."

Pippa and Luke stared at each other. Two weeks ago. Before the murder. So Dean Heckler had been on to his wife!

"Brilliant," Pippa said. As she continued to interrogate the man behind the desk, Luke called the taxi company. It took a few minutes but they paged the driver and connected him to Luke.

"Sir, why'd you leave?"

"That man came out and told me you changed your mind. Gave me twenty bucks to take off."

Luke felt a chill go up his spine. "What man?" He turned and looked out the window. Despite the dim streetlights, it was impossible to see if anyone was out there. All he saw was the green Chevy. The Toyota was gone.

"I don't know. Some guy."

"What did he look like?" asked Luke, he voice rising with fear. Even Pippa noticed something was off and stopped her inquisition to turn to Luke. "What?" she mouthed, but Luke put up his finger to silence her.

"I dunno, baseball cap. Sunglasses. He just handed me the dough. I was on the phone so I didn't really look at him too hard."

"Okay. Well, can you come back and pick us up?"

"I'm all the way in Rodon now. On the way home. Don't want to turn around. Sorry."

Luke hung up the phone and turned to the man. "Sir, is that your Chevy out there?"

"Yeah."

"Whose Toyota was out there?" asked Luke.

"Dunno. Maybe a guest."

"What is it?" asked Pippa.

"We need to get back to school," said Luke.

"Can't we call a teacher?"

Luke glanced at his phone. "It's six. We'll get in trouble for being out this late."

"Great. What should we do?"

Luke wracked his brain. Dinner was in fifteen minutes and they were required to be there. Sure, you were allowed to miss two dinners, but as it was only October, it was awfully early in the year to use one of those misses. He texted his friend Henry Price, who was a day student. Maybe he could pick them up.

"Hopefully he'll text me back."

"And in the meantime?"

"In the meantime? We walk."

They braced themselves and set off outside. It was a definite windstorm. Tree branches heaved and flailed in the wind above them.

"This is fishy. Who would tell our cab to take a hike? And why?" wondered Luke.

"Who do *you* think it was?" asked Pippa, looking around. The parking lot was empty. There was the wall of trees encompassing it, and a chain-link fence on the far side, but it was so dark and shadowy that it was hard to see beyond.

"More importantly, what's he going to do next?" asked Luke, grabbing Pippa's hand and crossing the street, suddenly protective. They were now walking against the traffic flow on County Road 674, not that there were any cars on the road now. On this side of the blacktop, there were clusters of trees and bushes dappled about randomly. Nothing was visible in the darkness, although there were some faint lights far in the distance that probably belonged to farmhouses. It was only about a mile and a half to campus, but they'd have to pass through long stretches of desolate areas to get there. They walked quickly, thrusting out their chests against the crisp air, determined to make this journey as hastily as possible. For a few minutes they didn't speak.

"Do you think we're being followed?" asked Pippa, glancing over her shoulder.

Luke looked back. He squinted and scanned the road and sidewalk. All completely abandoned.

"I don't see anyone."

They continued walking with Luke every so often glancing at his phone, hoping like hell Henry would get back to him. The darkness had now completely enveloped them, and the crescent moon had come out in full force. Suddenly, they both froze in their tracks. Distantly behind them they could hear the soft but growing hum of a car's motor. It was getting closer. Luke pulled Pippa closer toward him and quickened their pace.

"Do you think it's the man who dismissed our taxi?" whispered Pippa in a hoarse voice as she trotted alongside him.

"I don't know, but I don't want to find out."

"Should we hide in the trees?" Pippa pointed to three large oaks ten feet ahead.

Luke hesitated. He didn't want to come off as a wimp, but there definitely was someone out there who didn't want them to get back to school on time.

"Okay," he said.

Luke and Pippa walked briskly over to the trees and bent down. The car was getting closer now; they could make out the headlights. Luke's knees started to hurt from bending down so close to the ground. Pippa turned and grabbed his hand, squeezing it.

The car came closer and closer as the wind blew. They pushed themselves back into the wooded area and huddled together, as low to the ground as possible. Pippa was clinging on to Luke, so close he could feel her heart beating. Slowly the blazing headlights swept past where they were hiding. False alarm. Pippa glanced up at Luke, her eyes pleading. They paused for a moment, adrenaline and fear still pumping in their veins.

"Phew!" said Pippa finally. "He's gone."

"I think we're psyching ourselves out," said Luke.

"Yeah."

They stared at each other for a beat longer, before they both awkwardly glanced away. Neither wanted to admit how scared they really felt. Pippa moved slightly back and shivered.

"Sorry I practically jumped in your lap."

Luke grimaced. "No worries." *Silver lining*, he thought, but he didn't say.

She stared at him again. "Um, I guess we should go?"

Luke stood up and held out a hand to help Pippa up. He didn't let go after she rose, and he clasped it firmly as they walked together. It didn't feel awkward—he'd already held her hand a couple of times. He felt protective. They walked along in silence.

They passed a mailbox, its hinge squeaking in the wind. The wind had picked up a plastic bag, which was scraping along the road, dancing with the fallen leaves. Every noise was amplified.

Luke pulled Pippa toward him to avoid a ditch. It was then that Luke sensed something. He glanced over his shoulder, and saw the flash of someone jump behind a tree. Luke's muscles tensed. They were being followed.

"Don't turn around, but someone *is* behind us," warned Luke. "On foot."

He saw Pippa's neck stiffen. "Who is it?" she whispered.

"Not sure, but let's speed up."

They started walking as fast as possible without running. Luke felt as if there was a bullseye on his back. Was the person who was following them crazy enough to do something to harm them? What if he had a gun?

They were about a block away from the nearest streetlight. Luke feared that if they walked under it, they would be completely exposed to whoever was following them. It seemed safer to remain in the shadows. He abruptly pulled Pippa diagonally across the street. They picked up their pace and stayed on course.

"We'll be able to see who it is when they pass the streetlight," said Luke.

"Do you think he crossed, too?"

Luke pricked his ears. He could hear a distant tap, tap. Footsteps. "No, he's on the other side."

They walked past the streetlight and up about thirty feet before stopping short and turning around. For a split second, they saw a figure bathed in the light, but then it darted to the side. It looked like a man, in a baseball hat. But he was too fast for them. Luke grabbed Pippa's hand tightly.

"We need to run."

They both took off down the street, adrenaline driving them every step of the way. Luke could have gone even faster, but kept pace with Pippa so as not to abandon her. Their legs moved swiftly, pounding hard against the pavement.

Luke wasn't sure how far they had run before they hit a fork in the road.

"It's faster if we cut over on Wilmington," said Luke, motioning toward the street that intersected them. "But it's sketchy."

"Okay," said Pippa, breathing heavily. She wasn't much of an athlete. "Let's just get there."

They veered off right and continued running. This street had one lone streetlight in the distance, and other than that, utter darkness. Luke craned his neck to see if they were still being pursued, but he was moving too quickly to gauge. He didn't want to take any chances, so he kept moving. He glanced at Pippa, who was definitely struggling.

"We're almost there," encouraged Luke.

They continued running down the side street before they reached another street. They veered right and finally reached a residential block full of split-level houses.

"Can we slow down?" asked Pippa, out of breath.

"I think so," said Luke.

They slowed to a fast walk. Luke looked behind them but didn't see anyone.

"At least if something happens, we can scream and people will hear us," said Pippa. She was so winded she could barely get the words out.

"Yeah," said Luke.

Their pace got slower as they walked by parked cars and more houses. The cul-de-sac eventually dead-ended into a large metal fence covered with overgrown bushes.

"St. B.'s is on the other side of this," said Luke. "We just have to jump it."

Pippa glanced up at the large fence, her eyes wide. "Easier said than done."

"Come on."

"I don't think I can make it. Can't we just go back the other way?"

Luke turned and glanced back at the end of the road. He could swear he saw someone duck behind a mailbox. At this point, it may just have been someone who lived on the street, but he didn't like the odds.

"Don't worry, I'll help you over the fence."

"I have vertigo."

"You won't have to look down. Close your eyes if you want."

Pippa looked tentative. But glancing back at the street behind him, debating which was the lesser of evils, she turned back to Luke and agreed. "Okay."

Luke adroitly pulled himself up on the fence. He went a few feet before leaning back and putting out his hand to Pippa.

"Don't worry," he advised. "Trust me. I've got you. I won't let you go."

Pippa took his hand, and with the other, clasped her fingers around the metal fence.

"Ow, this hurts," she said, snapping her hand back toward her as if she had been burned.

"Hold on to me with both hands."

"Are you sure?"

"I can carry you."

Pippa took a deep breath and did as she was told. At first, it was difficult for Luke to steady himself with one hand while pulling Pippa up with the other, but he soon balanced himself. He dug his sneakers into the gaping holes and with one hand deftly climbed up; he used the other to pull Pippa. He'd carried backpacks heavier than Pippa on his climbing expeditions; this should be a piece of cake.

"Are you okay?" asked Pippa.

"I'm fine," said Luke.

He swiftly reached the top of the fence.

"Hold on for one second while I go to the other side."

"Okay," said Pippa, she glanced down and then recoiled in fear. "We're so high up."

"Don't look down."

Luke maneuvered himself to the other side and shimmied down several feet. Pippa was still teetering on the top.

"Jump down," he advised Pippa.

"I can't," she said, her voice tight with fear.

"Trust me, I'll catch you."

Pippa opened her eyes. She looked conflicted. But she had nowhere else to go. So she closed her eyes and jumped. Luke caught her with one arm, all the while holding on to the fence with his other.

"Whoa! That was the scariest part!" she said.

"I wouldn't have dropped you," said Luke. He held on to her for a second longer, before gently sliding down the fence and placing her carefully on the ground.

"Thanks," said Pippa. It felt like she might be doing the same, keeping her hand on his back longer than she needed to.

"Anytime," said Luke.

Glancing around, they found themselves near the rear entrance of the St. Benedict's gym.

"We made it," Pippa said.

They smiled at each other. Luke felt warm inside, with heat that had nothing to do with the recent physical exertion. He tried to remember if he'd ever felt like this around anyone else, but he didn't think so. All this fear was definitely heightening his feelings for Pippa. *This must be why guys take girls on dates to horror movies,* he thought.

"We did. We made it."

They continued along the path down the hill toward their dorms. The campus was quiet; most of the students and faculty were already at dinner. There was an eerie stillness. Both Pippa and Luke were breathing heavily. Luke's hands were burning; they'd been ripped up entirely by the fence and were most likely bleeding. He didn't want to check so as not to alarm Pippa. He was proud of himself for protecting her like he had.

"You going to chapel?" asked Luke.

"It's probably too late now. I'll just slip into dinner."

"Yeah. I guess we'll have to suck it up and get demerits."

"Lovely," said Pippa.

"What are you going to do?"

"I don't know. Try to bring down my blood pressure! I've never been so scared," she confessed. "That was worse than the other night."

"All right. Yeah, I'm gonna shower, try to calm myself down. This was . . . interesting."

"Any thoughts on who dismissed our cab, and who was following us?" asked Pippa.

"No. I want to say the murderer, but I honestly don't know . . ."

"No one knew we were there, right?"

"Right. But someone might be on to us."

"Dean Heckler?"

"Could be."

Pippa shivered.

"Now we know for sure we have to watch our backs."

"I don't get it. We don't really know anything. Why would the murderer want to come after us?" asked Pippa.

Luke shook his head. "I'm not sure. That is unless . . ."

"Unless what?"

"Unless we do know something. Maybe something is right in front of us, and we're unable to see it."

Pippa distractedly tucked a piece of her hair behind her hair. "Bollocks. That's freaky."

"I know."

They had reached Hadden, and were lingering on the steps. Luke had an intense urge to kiss her if he got the chance.

"Yeah, but don't worry. You're safe now," Luke motioned to two passing security guards, who were immersed in conversation and completely oblivious to Pippa and Luke.

"Oh, yes, brilliant security," said Pippa sarcastically.

"Well," said Luke. He stared at Pippa, who in turn, stared back.

"I just want you to know that I'm not going to press you on the Kidnapped Kid stories. I mean, of course I heard all about your notoriety when I arrived here, but that's not why I agreed to go to the Dip with you."

"Okay," said Luke.

"Unlike most, I don't have a morbid curiosity about horrific things that happen to people. And it didn't impress me that you managed to free yourself and evade detection and run fifty miles and all that."

"Forty-six," corrected Luke.

"Oh, was it only forty-six? That does change things," she said teasingly. "But seriously, I just want to make it clear that I am not trying to hang out with Luke Chase just because you're 'Luke Chase.' "

"Then why *are* you trying to hang out with me?" asked Luke with a crooked smile. "Why did you agree to come to the Dip that night?"

Pippa smiled and tipped her head back, as if looking for the answer in the night sky.

"Because I thought there was something about you, Luke Chase, something different. And you know what? I wasn't wrong."

She leaned in quickly and kissed him. It was a soft kiss, but Luke quickly brought both hands up to cup her face then gave her a deep kiss. Their nerves were fraught, their limbs were tired but right now a surge of energy moved through both of them. Finally, they broke away and stared at each other.

"Now go, or you'll get in even more trouble." And with that, Pippa turned and entered the building.

Luke stared after her for a minute before walking down the path toward his dorm, trying hard to wipe the smile off his face. If any of the guys ran into him and saw him smiling by himself, they'd know he was thinking of a girl and never let him hear the end of it.

He slipped into the hall as quietly as possible. By now everyone would be at dinner, but he didn't want to draw attention to himself and have to answer questions. He started to make his way up the stairs when someone called his name.

"Luke?"

He turned around. It was Mr. Crawford, standing on the base of the stairs in his bathrobe.

"Oh, hi," he said.

"Why aren't you at dinner?" asked Mr. Crawford.

"I um . . . lost track of time. I was out and didn't look at my watch."

Mr. Crawford gave him a look. "You're putting me in a bad position. I need to give you a demerit."

"I know . . ." said Luke, before adding hopefully. "But maybe give me an out because of all the stuff happening this week?"

Mr. Crawford looked like he was debating. Luke knew he hated to be the bad guy. "I suppose I can. The whole thing is surreal. I'm heading to the shower now because I just returned from filling in on an alumni event that Mrs. Heckler was supposed to host."

"That's a bummer," said Luke.

Mr. Crawford straightened his posture. "Listen, Luke, even if it seems stupid, if there is something that worries you, let me know. This killer is still out there, and although the faculty is supposed to make everyone feel safe and go along with it, I'm not so sure about that approach. They've never caught the Strangler, and now this. Why should we feel safe?"

"Geez, Mr. Crawford, way to make me feel better!" said Luke.

"Sorry, sorry. I'm just thinking out loud. I wish I could remember more about all the Strangler from when I was a student here. Maybe I could think of some details that would be helpful now."

"I don't think the police think it's the Strangler."

"Yeah, I know they don't think that. But come on, you and I both know Oscar had nothing to do with this. It's ridiculous. No, it's up to us to figure it out. And I just want you to know I'm on it, man. So don't worry."

"Thanks."

Suddenly, the door swung open. Luke whipped his head in its direction. It was a security guard. Tall, black hair, mid-twenties. Luke had seen him around campus. The guards were starting to become part of campus; all of this was starting to feel normal.

"Just doing rounds and checking in here, everything okay?" asked the guard.

"Yeah," said Luke.

"We're just dandy," said Mr. Crawford, winking at Luke.

"Okay, then," said the guard, before leaving.

"I guess I'll go shower," said Luke.

On the way up the stairs to his room, Luke glanced out the window. He saw Mr. Hamaguchi hurrying along the courtyard toward the dining hall. It gave Luke pause.

23

Monday's soccer practice was brutal. Endless drills, fifteen laps all topped off with fifty push-ups before quitting time. When the coach finally blew the whistle, Luke started to follow his teammates to the locker room.

"Hey, Chase!" It was Coach Saunders.

Luke walked over to the bench. "Yes, Coach?"

"What was going on out there? You seemed a little sluggish."

"I'm just tired today, not sure why."

"Look, I know things are going on with your roommate, but you have to keep your head in the game."

"I know, I'm sorry."

Coach Saunders stared at Luke, weighing a decision. "Want to give me another few laps around the field?"

Luke smiled wearily. "Can I say no?"

The coach shook his head, "Got to keep on you."

"All right."

Luke ran one lap before deciding to go back to his locker

and get his music. They weren't supposed to listen to anything during practice, but technically practice was over.

The locker room was empty. Everyone had most likely rushed down to the dorms to get in a little free time before dinner.

Luke walked over to his locker and started to turn the dial but the door flew open. He must have been so distracted when he was changing that he forgot to lock it. He realized the coach was right: his head wasn't in the game. It was everywhere else. There was just so much going on, with Oscar, the murder, Pippa, the guy who followed them. Not to mention schoolwork. He was totally overwhelmed.

Luke bent down to retrieve his phone, which had fallen to the bottom of his locker. As his hand grasped it, he felt something else that was cold, like metal. There, in the back corner of his locker was a delicate gold bracelet. Luke picked it up. It was a thin band of gold, with a diamond nestled into the side opposite the clasp. It looked expensive, and very definitely out of place in the boys' locker room. Whose was it?

Suddenly the door of the locker room banged open. Luke thrust the bracelet in the pocket of his running shorts without thinking.

"It's over here."

It was the coach's voice. Luke heard footsteps approaching. Just as he was pulling his undershirt over his head, they rounded the corner. It was Coach Saunders, Chief Corcoran, and Mr. P.

"Luke, we didn't realize you would be here," said Mr. P. with genuine surprise.

Chief Corcoran narrowed his eyes and looked at Luke with curiosity.

"Just came back to get some tunes," Luke said, with feigned cheerfulness, holding up his phone and headphones.

"Well, Luke, this is a bit awkward, but the police would like to search your locker," said Mr. P.

"*My* locker?" Luke croaked. Had Coach Saunders known they were coming and sent him out to do more laps?

"Is that *okay* with you?" said the chief in an accusatory tone. No doubt it wouldn't have mattered if Luke said yes.

"Sure," said Luke. He backed away from his locker toward the second row of lockers and leaned against them. Discreetly, he put his hand in his pocket and clasped the bracelet between his fingers. Was this what they were after?

The chief gave him a careful look. "You don't seem surprised that we want to check your locker."

"Well, I figure with everything that's going on with Oscar, I'm sure you have your reasons," said Luke. Could they tell that his voice was wavering?

"I'm sure there's nothing there, Chief," said the coach in a show of support. He gave Luke a slight nod.

"We'll see," said the chief. He started on the top shelf, taking out Luke's deodorant and extra towel. Then he rubbed his hand along the shelf to make sure there was nothing else there. There wasn't. Following that, he removed Luke's shirt, sweater and coat that were hanging on the peg. He felt around on the wall. Finally he bent down. He picked up Luke's shoes and put them on the bench. He reached into his belt and took out a flashlight, which he shined around the locker.

Luke started perspiring. This was intense. He felt his fingers clutching the bracelet and knew he had to get rid of it as soon as possible. He glanced around the room. What would be the best hiding place? His eyes focused on the lockers. In between each one was a very slight gap. Perhaps the bracelet could fit in there?

Luke started moving back toward the row of lockers behind him. He moved as slowly as possible, so as not to attract attention. Fortunately, the coach and Mr. P. were leaning in and carefully watching the chief's every move. Luke discreetly took the bracelet out of his pocket and quickly flattened it against his palm. Then he casually pressed his hand against the wall of lockers behind him, as if he was just leaning on it casually. He deftly wedged the bracelet into the tiny gap between two lockers. Quietly, but with as much small force as he could muster, he pressed it in. Most of it slid through, but there was still a slight edge sticking out. He was manipulating it when the chief spoke, causing Luke to start.

"It's clean," said the chief standing up.

"Are you sure?" asked Mr. P. skeptically.

What was that supposed to mean? Did Mr. P. really think he had anything incriminating in his locker?

"Do I have the right to ask what you were looking for?" asked Luke.

The chief turned and stared him in the eye. "Just had a report that there might be something of the victim's in your locker. You haven't seen anything that wasn't yours in there, have you?"

Luke returned his gaze evenly. "No, sir."

The chief's eyes continued to linger on Luke's face. "Do you mind if I search you?"

Luke gulped. "Of course not."

"Is that really necessary?" asked the coach.

"If he doesn't mind," said the chief.

"Go ahead," said Luke.

"Turn around."

Luke turned around. The chief moved his arms out, and patted down his body. Luke's eyes locked on the bracelet. If they really looked around, they might see it. His stomach started to turn as fear crept up his spine. He hoped, more than anything, they wouldn't notice.

"He's clean," said the chief. "Waste of time."

"Sorry about this, Luke," said the coach.

Mr. P. patted Luke on his shoulder as he walked away.

"You're a good sport," he said with a smile.

Luke gave him the fakest grin he could muster. He was furious that he had been questioned. Who told him Luke would have "something of the victim's"?

"You understand, though. Right, Luke?" asked Mr. P. "You're Oscar's best friend, his roommate, and we know how thick you are. We just had to make sure you wouldn't cover anything up for him."

"Oscar's innocent, Mr. P. So I wouldn't have to cover anything up for him."

Mr. P. gave him a long look, which Luke returned defiantly. He was starting to think a bit differently about him. Maybe Mr. P. wasn't such a nice guy; maybe he was fake. And maybe it was possible he *was* the one who had been having the affair with Mrs. Heckler.

"Be careful, Luke," said Mr. P. finally, before joining the chief as he left the building. Luke listened as their footsteps got farther and farther away. Before he made any move, he waited until he heard the locker room door slam. He breathed a sigh of relief, and collapsed onto the bench. He had escaped that one. But now what? What should he do with the bracelet? Where could he put it for safekeeping? But more importantly, who had put it in his locker? Could it have been Mr. P. trying to frame him? He didn't feel like doing those extra laps anymore. Instead, he dressed quickly, without even showering. Before he left, he slid the bracelet back out of the crack and pocketed it.

When Luke returned to the dorm, he decided to try Oscar again. Maybe he had some idea about the bracelet. Since Oscar had been avoiding him, he had little hope that he would answer this time, so he was stunned when he heard his friend's voice on the other side of the phone.

"Hello?"

"Oscar! Dude, why haven't I heard from you?"

"Luke," Oscar whispered. "Hold on one second."

Luke waited and heard rustling on Oscar's end of the phone. He glanced at his watch. He had about five minutes to get to dinner. He couldn't miss it this time. He'd get detention this time for sure.

"Luke, it's a bad time. I can call you back in about fifteen minutes," said Oscar, when he returned to the phone.

"I can't, I have dinner. What's the deal? They won't let you talk on the phone at all?"

"It's complicated," whispered Oscar. "I gotta go."

He hung up quickly and Luke replaced the phone. What was going on? Luke glanced around the room in a daze. For the first time since Oscar's departure, Luke noticed that he had not taken his prized lacrosse stick with him. In fact, most of his things were still there. Which would maybe mean that he thought he was coming back sooner rather than later.

Luke went downstairs, pushed open the front door and felt the cold on his face. The wind howled and it was then that he thought of Mr. Tadeckis's words: "What you don't realize is that they are all lying to you. All of them. *Lying*. Your own roommate included."

24

During study hall, Luke discovered that he didn't have his history textbook. He had vague memories of taking it out during lunch to finish his assignment, but couldn't remember if he had left it in the dining hall or somewhere else. His head really was in the clouds. Unfortunately, he had a quiz first period tomorrow, so he'd have to go to the library to borrow their copy.

"Sup, Chase. Wanna hit Main Hall?" asked Andy when Luke got outside.

"Nah, I gotta go to the library and get a book. I'm slammed."

"Dude, what's wrong with you? You've been under a rock lately," said Andy. "You sneaking around collecting community service hours I don't know about? I still need another eighteen to meet the grad requirement. Guess I'll have to work at the Autumn Fair or something."

"I only need about five more," Luke said. "I'll get them over the summer. I've just been busy."

"I hear you. All these American Lit essays have been killing me this term. So what's up with Oscar?"

"Don't know. His parents won't let him talk or anything. They're being really harsh," said Luke.

"That's weird. Brooks's brother just went to an Imagine Dragons concert with him in the city. They can't be that harsh."

Luke turned to Andy. He felt his stomach drop. "Really?"

"Yeah, I saw them on Snapchat. Oscar's living the life. I'm sure his dad will just make a call and he'll get into Harvard or Yale or wherever everyone in their family went for generations, so what does he care? Supposedly he's been hooking up with some older chick, too. A teacher from his old school."

Luke had a sinking feeling. An older woman? A *teacher*? Oscar had made it clear he wasn't into older women. In fact, hadn't he said directly to Luke's face, *Do I look like a cougar lover to you?*

"Seems like you know more than me," confessed Luke reluctantly.

"The roommate's always the last to know, Chase. Catch you later."

So it wasn't his imagination. Oscar had been dodging him. What the . . . ? Luke didn't even want to go there. Had Oscar been playing him all along? Couldn't be. Maybe Oscar's parents were being really lenient. Maybe they didn't think it was a big deal that he was accused of murder. But that certainly didn't sound like the Weymouths. They were always all over Oscar for everything.

At the very least, Oscar could have the courtesy to send him a message. Why was he totally avoiding him? Was it because of this teacher he was seeing? Luke's mind raced but he couldn't remember Oscar ever alluding to a teacher from home that he was interested in. It didn't make sense. If only Oscar would be honest with him. Luke continued to the library but couldn't help feeling seized by anger. Oscar had totally frozen him out.

Once again, it was nerd-city in the library. Luke noted that if he ever got serious with a girl, the library at ten o'clock would be the prime place for alone time. Old Mrs. Pemberly was at the desk, and she was so clueless that you could be doing keg stands in front of her and she'd have no idea.

"Hi, Mrs. Pemberly. Can you tell me where *Civilizations and Communities* is? It's on hold for Ms. DeStefano's class."

"I think that's on the second floor, near the back."

"Thanks."

If the first floor had seemed deserted, the second floor was even more so. Luke walked along the padded carpet to the very back wall where there was a low row of bookshelves. Each section was marked by a teacher's name and filled with books from the various classes. Luke spotted his book right away and picked it up.

"Just turning off the lights up here," said a voice.

Luke was behind several bookshelves so his view was obstructed. He leaned forward and saw Mrs. Heckler walking toward the other side of the room. She was wearing a long skirt and a turtleneck and moved slowly. He watched as she pressed the light switch, and within seconds the fluorescent lights flickered and then went black. The only light now came from the walkways outside.

Luke picked up the book and started to leave.

"Mary."

Luke froze when he heard the voice. He peeked his head out and saw through the shadows that it was Dean Heckler.

"Carl, what are you doing here?"

"I wanted to talk to you," he said in a low voice.

Luke's heart started racing. What had he stumbled upon? He stealthily crept as close as he could to his side of the shared bookshelf and pressed his ear against a row of encyclopedias, craning his neck to hear everything.

"They're looking for something of Joanna's," whispered Dean Heckler.

"What are they looking for?"

"A piece of jewelry, I think, but I don't exactly know," said the dean.

"Why are they looking for it?"

"They think . . . her killer took it."

"Do you have it?"

"Of course not."

"Come with me," said Mrs. Heckler. "I'm just turning off the lights."

"I'll help you."

The bracelet! The dean was talking about the very thing that was burning a hole in his pocket. He hadn't known what to do with it since he found it, so he'd kept it on him at

258

all times until he could figure it out. He had to get rid of it.

Luke could see through the slats in the bookshelf that the dean and his ex-wife had started walking toward the front row of bookshelves, where Luke would be instantly spotted. Should he walk up to them and expose his presence, or would they then know he had been eavesdropping? He snuck along the row of bookshelves parallel to them. He'd have to cross through the light to get downstairs and they might see him. He looked left. There was the tower. He could just go up there and pretend he was stargazing or something. Luke quickly walked up the spiral steps. He stopped when he knew he was in complete darkness. He leaned forward to listen.

"You did the right thing," said Mrs. Heckler.

"You think?"

"Of course," she said, her voice consoling.

"I mean, it was Joanna's money, and she left clear instructions as to what she wanted done with it when she . . ." the dean's voice trailed off.

"The circumstances of her death shouldn't change that," said Mrs. Heckler. "She wanted you to be in charge."

So the dean had taken the money after all! *There's motive right there*, thought Luke.

"Let me put this book away," said Mrs. Heckler.

It sounded like she was getting closer. Luke didn't want them to know he was there, but where to go? Frustrated, he glanced up at the tower. He hadn't been up there in years. Curious, he started quietly walking up the spiral steps.

When he reached the top, he glanced around. It was totally dark, so Luke had to wait for his eyes to adjust. Only light from the moon and the lights below illuminated the room. The space itself was very small; it could maybe fit two people. It was a purely decorative adjunct to the building, another feature that the architect was famous for. Luke felt around in the dark. He touched something, and realized it was a video camera, set up on the ledge. Luke leaned close to it and squinted. "Digital Yearbook" was written on a piece of masking tape that was attached to it. That was weird. Usually the Digital Yearbook was a video made at the end of the year compiled from hundreds of student videos taken on their phones. This must be something new. Luke glanced outside to see what direction the camera was pointing in. The woods.

Luke leaned down again and put his eye on the lens. It was a direct view of the woods. The very woods where Mrs. Heckler was killed. Perhaps the Digital Yearbook camera had a recording of someone heading there. Her killer. Luke clicked it open and slid out the memory card. He pocketed it. Excited, Luke started down the steps. Just as he got to the bottom: *boom!* He almost walked straight into Dean Heckler and Mrs. Heckler.

"What are you up to?" asked the dean with a frown.

"You nearly scared me to death!" said Mrs. Heckler.

"Sorry, um, I was up in the tower. Checking out the stars. It's a beautiful night," said Luke. He thrust his hands in his pockets, praying that they couldn't see the guilt on his face.

"It is beautiful," said Mrs. Heckler. "There's a wonderful view up there. I don't know why more people don't use the tower."

"I know. It's great."

The dean looked at him skeptically. "I find you in the most unusual places, son."

"Really?" asked Luke, blowing his bangs out if his eyes. "Well, um, now I'm heading back to my dorm. Found my book," said Luke, holding up the textbook.

"Good night," said Mrs. Heckler.

"Good night," said Luke, bounding down the stairs.

When Luke got back to his room, he borrowed a MacBook from a foreign exchange student down the hall instead of taking the risk of watching the contents of the memory card on his own computer. He was still paranoid that the school could somehow access his Mac. Better safe than sorry. He watched the footage on fast-forward. There was nothing incriminating at all. He watched a few couples strolling around, but no sign of Mrs. Heckler. Luke was disappointed until he noticed the date that was on the corner of the memory card: October 19. This footage was recent. It was useless. He had to get his hands on an earlier memory card and see if his suspicions were right, because he had a feeling that Mary Heckler had taken a break from sorting card catalogs that night and gone up to the tower. And from there she saw her ex-husband's wife walk into the woods, and then set out to find her.

25

In the middle of the night Luke woke up with a start. The bracelet! How could he have forgotten that it was in his pocket? He jumped out of bed and walked over to the chair where he had dumped his pants. It was still there. He pulled it out and held it up to the moonlight. What should he do with it? He needed it to be in a safe place. A place where no one would find it. He felt weirdly paranoid about tucking it away in some cubbyhole or under some rock. What if the person who was following him saw him hide it?

Luke sat down in the chair and twirled the bracelet between his fingers. He glanced out the window. There was an eerie stillness. Luke started to feel overwhelmed by everything that was going on. Maybe he was in over his head. Maybe he should just go to the headmaster and confess everything. Or call his parents. They were cool. They would help him get through this. Or maybe one of his sisters? They were totally reasonable. But then they would all probably ask him why didn't he tell them before. Why had he spun this web of lies and continued it? Why was he foolish enough to think he could catch the killer? His mind raced through all of his options. When he finally came up with a plan for the bracelet, he replaced it in his pants pocket and collapsed into a deep sleep.

After breakfast, Luke set out toward the science building. It had started to drizzle, so Luke pulled up his hood. It would be a gloomy practice in this weather. He was just passing the pond when he ran into Andy.

"Hey, Chase, the headmaster's looking for you."

"Me?" asked Luke.

"Duh, just said so. I just ran into him by the science building. He's there waiting for you."

"Great," said Luke.

"Are you the killer? Ha ha."

Andy laughed and kept going toward his class.

Why does the headmaster want to see me, wondered Luke He began walking to class but with a slower pace. Suddenly, fear seized Luke. He still had the bracelet in his pocket! What if they wanted to search him? What if they were searching his room again? Think, Luke, think!

He noticed two girls were walking toward him. At first it was difficult to discern who they were because they were in full rain gear, but as they moved closer Luke realized that one of them was Kelsey.

"Hey, Kelsey, can I talk to you for a second?" Luke gave her a plaintive look.

"Sure," she said. "I'll catch you later, Blair."

"Okay," Blair said, giving Kelsey a wide smile. She probably thought Luke was going to ask her out or something.

"What's up?" asked Kelsey.

"Listen, it's really important. I need you to do something for me. For all of us, actually."

"Okay," said Kelsey, suddenly nervous.

"Can you give this to Pippa for me?"

She swatted his arm. "If you want to give her jewelry, you should give it to her yourself! And no offense, but don't you think this is a little too early for jewelry anyway? You guys just got together."

"Oh, God, Kelsey. I'm not giving this to Pippa as a gift. I found it. Listen, its complicated, but can you just give it to her and ask her to hold onto it for me?"

Kelsey looked down at the bracelet. "Oh. It's hers, isn't it?"

Luke knew whom she meant.

"I don't know. It might be, but that's what Pippa and I are trying to figure out."

Kelsey touched the bracelet, almost tenderly. She nodded.

"Thanks," said Luke, before walking away.

"Luke, this all must seem confusing," said the headmaster.

"What's that, sir?"

"You know . . . Oscar leaving, room searches, the police searching your locker. Everything that's going on."

They were now in the headmaster's office. Not wanting Luke to miss his quiz, the headmaster had asked Luke to meet him after science class. Of course that made Luke entirely distracted and stressed during the quiz, which he most likely blew as a result.

"Why did you search my locker?"

The headmaster tapped his pencil on the desk. "We had some information."

"Can you tell me what kind?"

The headmaster attempted a smile. "I wish I could. But all these matters are out of my hands."

"Am I a suspect too?"

"No, I wouldn't worry. We would have contacted your parents if that were the case."

"I don't understand. Is there a reason that Oscar's not allowed to talk to me? Because it seems like he can talk to a lot of other people."

The headmaster gave Luke a blank smile. Luke could see in his expression that he knew the answer, but wouldn't tell.

"I don't know about Oscar. Perhaps his parents think it's best for him to avoid people from school right now."

"But he is coming back, right?"

"Luke, I can't discuss other students with you, I'm sorry."

A thought occurred to Luke. "You know, it was a rumor that Mrs. Heckler was having an affair with a student. Someone supposedly overheard a teacher mention it, but the teacher in question denies it." Luke thought it was best not to mention Mr. Crawford's name.

"Luke, the police are conducting a thorough investigation. I cannot comment on it."

Luke kept his eyes locked on the headmaster's. He refused to break the stare. The headmaster would have to look away first. Then Luke would know that he was not being honest. Finally, the headmaster looked down at his pencil.

"Do you have any more questions?"

"No," said Luke.

"Then I think you can return to class."

Luke started to get up.

"Oh, and one more thing. Dean Heckler is under the impression that you are conducting your own investigation into his wife's murder. Is that the case?"

So that's why he was really here. "No, not at all."

"Are you telling the truth?" asked the headmaster, cocking his head to the side and giving him a quizzical look.

"Absolutely," said Luke with a smile.

The headmaster hesitated. "Luke, just be careful."

"I will," said Luke. His throat was completely dry behind his fake smile.

26

"**I** think the person responsible for this should face serious consequences. I mean, *serious*. Because, obviously, the guilty party is morally bankrupt and has no soul, and we have to take a stand and say that we will not tolerate that sort of behavior. Like honestly? I think they should have to face a firing squad . . ."

"Let's tone it down, Willow," said Mr. Hamaguchi.

"I'm sorry, Mr. Hamaguchi, but the school is not dealing with this at all and it's up to us to do something. A crime is a crime. If you throw a can in the trash and not in the recycling bin, you are basically killing a baby seal. And who are we to kill baby seals? Just because we're bigger and stronger, we feel like we have the right to murder all of the rest of the creatures on this earth. If you ask me, we should one day let all the animals have a go at murdering us . . ."

"Willow," said Mr. Hamaguchi, in a warning tone.

It was the STEAM club meeting and they were gathered

in Mr. Hamaguchi's science lab, an antiseptic room that smelled of formaldehyde and the sawdust that lined the pet rats' cage. The walls were dotted with posters of the periodic table and various portraits of renowned scientists, but the room was pretty generic as far as science labs go. As usual, the activists in the group had a lot to say tonight. Luke always found himself somewhat amused by their passion—it was always the hippie girls and the guys with the dreads and prairie skirts (yes, the *guys* in prairie skirts) that got all worked up about everything. Luke admired their passion, but sometimes they took it a bit too far.

Willow, a petite blond dread-locked freshman, self-described vegan, and card carrying PETA member, ignored Mr. Hamaguchi. Suddenly even more emboldened, she raised her tone to plead her case.

"Seriously, people! We are killing our planet! We may as well be stabbing it in the back or burning it alive. We need to crank up our efforts. Mother Earth is like, crying now. We are all complicit in this mass murder! We are no worse than the killer who strangled Mrs. Heckler to death . . ."

"Willow! That's enough!" bellowed Mr. Hamaguchi, jumping to his feet.

"But Mr. Hamaguchi . . ."

"No, that is enough. I don't want to hear about this."

"I just want to make a point," whined Willow.

"Well stop making that point NOW."

"We need to stop the murder!"

Mr. Hamaguchi slammed his hand down on the cold

marble table. It made a smacking sound—and would have been far more dramatic if the table was wood or plaster—but he made his point. All eyes in the group were upon him. He had worked himself into a bit of a rage and was sweating and wild-eyed.

"Listen to me, young lady. You don't know what you are talking about and you are being very cavalier. Murder is when you snap someone's neck or plunge a knife in their heart and watch them bleed out, or fire a gun into their head and shatter their skull into a million tiny pieces. It is very different from throwing a can in the wrong garbage bin. So take a seat and be quiet."

You could hear a pin drop. Everyone was stunned and motionless. Willow stared at Mr. Hamaguchi, as if debating her next move, before shrugging her bony shoulders and reluctantly ceding the floor. Luke watched the interaction with intense curiosity. He had never seen Mr. Hamaguchi so riled up. It wasn't like him. Luke glanced over at his friend Cynthia Chin, a pretty senior in charge of the group, who widened her eyes and raised an eyebrow in return. What was happening?

Mr. Hamaguchi watched Willow sulk back to her seat before barking out, "Cynthia, take over the meeting."

Cynthia rose and stood in the center of the room. Luke twisted in his stool to watch Mr. Hamaguchi return to his armchair next to the wall and pick up his notebook. Without glancing up Hamaguchi began to write furious notes.

"Um, thanks, Willow. We're all grateful for your passion,"

Cynthia said, her voice a bit uncertain. "And Willow does have a point, that we need to up our recycling efforts. The dorm-recycling contest is still far from being over and we have to push people to really make an effort. I think we have to check with the headmaster and see if we can get the winners something really major, like a free day pass or a trip to the city. So far, Noonan is in the lead—I mean come on, older students; we can't let the freshmen beat us. Not far behind is Whitaker . . . ."

As Cynthia continued listing the dorms, Luke discreetly watched Mr. Hamaguchi out of the corner of his eye. His jaw was clenched angrily and his expression was still furious. This whole Mrs. Heckler murder had really touched a nerve with him and Luke wondered why. He was definitely broken up about it, but what did that mean? What was his relationship with Mrs. Heckler?

After the meeting Mr. Hamaguchi left abruptly. Luke had wanted to come up with some pretext to talk to him, but he didn't get a chance. By the time Luke exited the science building Mr. Hamaguchi was turning down the path near the infirmary. It was as if he couldn't get away fast enough.

"FEED!"

The stampede began. It sounded like four hundred people were pounding down the stairs rushing to the common room, when Luke knew in reality it was really only twenty. Faster than the speed of light, there was a mass of people grabbing for sodas and sandwiches as if they had never been fed before in their life.

Feeds happened sporadically and were organized by the dorm head along with the student prefect. During study hall, the prefect would place a huge order from somewhere like Pizza Hut or Dunkin' Donuts, the dorm head would pick it up, and students would be excused from study hall to binge together in the common room. The funny part was that it was only about an hour or two after dinner, but everyone gobbled up the food as if their last meal had been a week ago.

"Hey guys, settle down, there's enough for everyone," laughed Mr. Crawford. Tonight Luke had ordered grinders, aka "heroes" or "subs," and he and Mr. Crawford were giving the giant sandwiches out hand-over-fist to the starving students.

"Dinner wasn't *that* bad," laughed Luke, popping open a can of Coke and collapsing on a couch.

"What are you talking about?" sneered Andy, plunging his hand into an open bag of barbecue potato chips. "Tofu tacos? Disgusting. I actually had to add lettuce and tomato just so I'd be able to recognize what I was eating."

After everyone was well sated and had flopped around on various sofas and upholstered chairs, the talk inevitably returned to Mrs. Heckler and her murder.

"Should we be freaked out that they haven't arrested anyone yet?" Gupta asked.

"Yeah, we could all be axed in the middle of the night," said Andy, shoving more chips in his mouth.

"Relax, people, that's not going to happen," Mr. Crawford

reassured them. "There are so many security guards around and a huge police presence."

"Yeah, but why do they keep us at school? How can they be certain that we won't be killed?" asked John Fritz, a kid who lived down the hall from Luke.

"Because they think Oscar did it," shouted Jordan Price, one of the hockey players in the dorm.

"Yeah! Oscar's going down!"

People began to chant and whisper. Luke tried to brush off the talk, which annoyed him. Mr. Crawford gave him a sympathetic look. "Guys, don't rush to judgment. It's all going to work out, and we have to assume that the administration knows better than we do."

"But shouldn't we be looking over our shoulder?" asked Gupta.

"I'm pretty certain if the school thought that someone here was the murderer they would remove them," replied Mr. Crawford.

"Like Oscar," repeated Clive. Others started laughing.

Luke rose and chucked his can in the recycling bin. He didn't like to hear Oscar being dissed like that. He began to start collecting garbage and swooping it into a giant Hefty bag.

"Dude, lighten up," said Andy as he ambled over to him.

"I'm fine."

"You're not. Look, if Oscar made just the tiniest of effort with people, he wouldn't be under suspicion."

"I can't believe you think that's true."

Andy pitched the soda can into Luke's trash. "He's a jerk. Maybe he's a murderer also."

Luke removed the can from the bag and shoved it at Andy. "This is for recycling. If you throw it in the garbage, you're a murderer, too. Of a baby seal."

Luke walked away.

Within minutes, as if a bomb had exploded, almost everyone had returned to their rooms for the last gasp of study hall, leaving Luke and Mr. Crawford to haul out the garbage.

"Don't worry about Oscar," said Mr. Crawford. "He can take care of himself. He's always done his own thing."

Luke nodded. Suddenly, he thought of something. "Mr. Crawford, this may be inappropriate, but today Mr. Hamaguchi got really worked up about murder and Mrs. Heckler. I didn't know they were . . . friends."

"Did he?" asked Mr. Crawford. He raised his eyebrows and looked pensive. "You know, now that you mention it . . ."

Mr. Crawford stopped abruptly.

"You were about to say . . ."

He shook his head. "I probably should keep my mouth shut."

Luke waited, his interest piqued. "Come on . . ."

"Okay, not from me. But he once said something to me about Joanna . . . I thought I had misheard him, but now that you say that . . ."

"What?"

Mr. Crawford smiled. "Sorry, I should take the fifth. But your instincts are good, Luke. There might be something there."

Interesting, thought Luke. He'd have to find out exactly what was there.

27

"**H**ey, Higgins," said Luke, sliding into line at the Jig the next morning. He had waited until he heard George Higgins place his order of bacon, egg and cheese on a toasted bagel and hand over his debit card before he spoke.

The slight nerdy guy with big glasses turned around and noticed him. "Oh, hi, Luke."

Annie, the older counter lady with frizzy gray hair who always donned the wildest sweatshirts (today's was gray with puffy rainbow-colored lettering that said "Sassy!" on it) asked Luke what he wanted. She was always brusque and rude and never smiled, but was somehow beloved by everyone at St. Benedict's. Someone had even started a *Shit That Annie Says* tumblr, and it was a point of honor to be on the receiving end of an insult.

"I'll just have a chocolate milkshake, thanks, Annie," said Luke.

"Now I gotta start up the blender? Who orders milk-shakes for breakfast," she grumbled.

After he had paid, he rejoined Higgins at the other side of the counter where they would wait for their orders. Several tables at the Jig were full of students who had opted to forgo breakfast in the dining hall and were carbing up between classes. The giant panoramic windows that faced the pond showed off the gloomy weather, and the paths were empty. There was always a stillness that settled on campus when most people were in class. Luke had a free period, and decided to use it to continue his search for the killer.

"Listen, you're head of Digital Yearbook, right?"

"That's right."

"Can you tell me how long have you been filming from the library tower?"

"Hmmm . . ." George Higgins put his fist under his chin to prop it up. He always did this when he thought carefully about something, and it had earned him much ridicule from his classmates. Everything about the guy was so geeky, that he was almost a cliché. "About a month."

"Good!" said Luke, excited. "I need to borrow the memory card from a few days ago."

"Which one?"

Luke leaned in close to him and responded in a low voice, "The one from the day Mrs. Heckler was killed."

"Sorry, Luke, can't do it."

"Why? Dude, come on."

"A freshman filmed over it."

"You've got to be kidding!" exclaimed Luke.

"Yeah. These newbies are morons sometimes. He at least should have let me review it before he deleted it."

"That's a bummer. Why were you filming there anyway?"

"Truthfully?" asked George Higgins.

"Yeah."

Higgins glanced around furtively, as if someone was eavesdropping.

"Well, officially, I wanted to get a complete day-in-the-life of our school. We've put cameras in various parts of campus so we can capture what goes on there."

"What's the unofficial reason?" asked Luke with interest.

"Well," said Higgins, raising an eyebrow. "I mean, you can find out a lot of stuff. Like people having relationships that were not supposed to be having relationships."

"Students or teachers?"

"Students of course," said Higgins, straightening up. "Teachers? I never thought about that. I would have noticed something." Again, he put his fist under his chin and rested his head on it, pensive.

"Where are the other cameras?"

Higgins stood up straight. "Look, I can't tell you. It will ruin the experiment. It's going to be the grand finale. All this funny footage . . ."

Luke tried to appear as buddy-buddy as possible. "Come on, you can tell me."

"You're putting me in a bad position."

"Am I? I thought we were friends."

Higgins gave him a curious look, then sighed. "All right, but promise me you won't tell anyone . . ."

"Swear."

Twenty minutes later they were in the Digital Yearbook studio, going through old DVDs. The room was completely maxed out with state-of-the-art equipment, from televisions to a professional editing machine. It was as sophisticated as any real editing facility. There was a wall of shelves that was meticulously organized with all of the past yearbooks—when they were in video form—to recent footage that was so small that it was in tiny sleeves categorized by date and location.

"How about this one?" asked Luke, holding up one dated the day before Mrs. Heckler died.

"Right, that's from the mailboxes."

"The mailboxes? So, mostly just students."

"Right."

"Does anyone really ever hook up there? It's so exposed."

The small area with the student mailboxes was just off Main Hall near the front desk and was so open that it didn't even have a door.

"You'd be surprised," snorted Higgins. "But mostly, it'll be fun to capture seniors when they open their college acceptance and rejection letters. Then we'll see some drama!"

Luke gave him a look. "That's hardcore."

"Makes for good footage."

"Does the administration know you have all these hidden cameras?"

"They know about some. They sort of vaguely signed off on everything. Our adviser is Mr. Ogilvy, who's basically out to lunch."

"Mr. Ogilvy? The guy is like a hundred years old. Does he even know what a digital camera is?"

"Not really," said Higgins with a smile.

It was always the seemingly weak and nerdy guys who ended up being the forces to reckon with, Luke thought. He'd have to remember that. One day, Higgins would be some famous tabloid TV entrepreneur, like the guy who did *Girls Gone Wild*. And he'd be laughing his way to the bank.

"Where are the other cameras?"

"Let's see . . . you know about the library tower, the mailboxes. Um, we have one by the vending machines, one in the photo lab—lots of stuff goes on there—one in the gym, oh, and one in the Main Hall Xerox room."

Luke thought for a minute.

"Xerox room?"

"Yeah, that one's kind of a waste. Nothing much goes on."

"Can I see it? The one that was from the day before Mrs. Heckler got offed?"

"Sure, but let me assure you, it's not that exciting."

Higgins retrieved the memory card from that area and put it in the camera. He took the remote and clicked on the giant Sony HD TV that was mounted on the wall in front of them. The empty Xerox room appeared on the fifty-six-inch screen. Luke had a tremor of excitement as they waited. And waited.

"Can you keep it on fast forward?"

"I told you, nothing happens."

A figure came into the screen. Mrs. Holliway, one of the school secretaries. She started copying something.

"It's like this all day long," said Higgins, folding his arms. "It was kind of a mistake to put it there. I think one of the freshmen picked this spot."

"Let's just look at it for a while."

They watched on high speed over the next ten minutes. Basically, it had recorded several school administrators coming in and out of the room to make copies.

"That's it," said Higgins when it clicked off.

"Let me see the day before," said Luke.

"Really?" asked Higgins.

"Please," said Luke.

"Okay, but I have a class in twenty minutes."

"You'll make it."

Higgins removed the first memory card and replaced it in its sleeve. He took out the second one and popped it in. Again, they had to wait a few minutes to see any action, and the first person was again Mrs. Holliway.

"She makes a lot of copies," said Luke.

"She's single-handedly killing off forests with all of her memos."

They watched for a minute more before something attracted Luke's attention to the screen. "Stop here," he said, pointing to the screen.

It was Dean Heckler. He walked into the Xerox room and

discreetly looked around before taking something out of his inside coat pocket and putting it in the copier.

"What's that?" asked Higgins.

Luke squinted and looked carefully at the screen. "Rewind one second."

Higgins did as he was told. Luke pressed his eyes as close as possible to the screen. "It looks like a photograph."

"Hmmm . . . interesting."

Suddenly, another person walked into the Xerox room. Dean Heckler at first looked concerned, but then relieved.

"That's Mrs. Heckler," said Higgins. "The first one."

"Turn up the sound," commanded Luke at full attention.

They both watched rapt as Dean Heckler wordlessly lifted up the cover of the Xerox and showed his ex-wife what he was copying. Unfortunately, her body obstructed their view of what it was.

"What are you doing in here?"

"Ran out of paper in my office. Wanted to copy this."

Mrs. Heckler sighed. "That's bad."

Dean Heckler raised his eyebrows. "Evidence."

"What do you plan to do?"

"You know what I plan to do. And I need your help," said Dean Heckler.

Then he and Mrs. Heckler both walked out of the Xerox room.

Higgins and Luke looked at each other with amazement.

"You don't think . . ." said Higgins.

"I don't know," said Luke, shaking his head vigorously.

"Oh my God."

"Well, the good news is this will be a nice little finale to Digital Yearbook this June," said Luke, attempting to joke.

"So, now what? Do we tell the police?" asked Higgins.

Luke didn't answer him directly, instead he mused out loud "I wonder if he had some incriminating picture of his wife. Probably having an affair or something . . ."

Luke thought of the Southborough Days Inn. The man behind the desk specifically said that Dean Heckler was asking around about his new wife. He knew. But what about his alibi in Boston? And what about his ex-wife's arthritis? He couldn't imagine her having the strength to murder Joanna Heckler. She had seemed tired just from making dinner for her foster kids.

But maybe . . . who knows? Perhaps they put it out there that Mary Heckler had arthritis. It could have been a part of the plan. She may play the weak middle-aged lady, but for all he knew she was a black belt at karate. And maybe if they added it up, Dean Heckler could have quickly come down from Boston to meet his ex-wife in the woods to kill his current wife. It happened at two in the morning; did he really have an alibi until then? Did meetings with school administrators last until the wee hours? It was all possible.

While Luke was thinking, the digital video continued playing. Out of the corner of his eye, Luke caught a glimpse of the next person to enter the Xerox room. It was Mr. Tadeckis.

"Wait a sec," said Luke.

He turned his attention to the screen. Mr. Tadeckis pressed several buttons and then a copy came out of the side.

"He didn't put anything in there," said Luke.

"Yeah, but you can just hit reverse and have it recopy whatever was printed before you."

"Are you telling me that Mr. Tadeckis also got a copy of the picture that Dean Heckler just Xeroxed?"

Higgins nodded.

Luke felt like his head was swimming. Could Mr. Tadeckis have been toying with him all along to throw him off the track? Maybe he was the other man? Or maybe he had just killed Mrs. Heckler for sport? He was in the woods that night.

"I think we have to show this to the police," said Higgins, his voice now quivering. "This might be important."

"Hang on," said Luke. "Let me think."

Even though this was a major red flag and certainly something the police would want to see, Luke still couldn't believe that Mr. Tadeckis was the killer. He was weird, for sure, and creepy, but Luke didn't sense that he was dangerous, just a misfit. But could Luke trust his instincts? He had been so clueless about everything else. Maybe they should show this to the police. Between the footage of Dean and Mary Heckler conspiring about something and Tadeckis being on to them, there was definitely something going on. And maybe this could exonerate Oscar?

"I don't think we need to say anything," said Luke finally. "It's not a big deal."

"But you heard the dean say he had evidence."

"What does that mean, really?" asked Luke, cocking his head. He wanted to confuse Higgins so that he would not show the cops the footage.

"I thought you implied that—"

"I'm just messing around."

"I have to be cautious," said Higgins firmly. "I should tell the police."

Luke had to make sure he wasn't. "If you do that, you know they'll make you take down all your cameras everywhere, confiscate everything . . ."

"Not necessarily."

"Of course they would. It could even be the end of Digital Yearbook. Everyone is so litigious in this day and age and you don't have signed permissions from everyone to use this footage. You haven't even informed people that they're being filmed at all, and *that's* against the law. They might jump all over you."

"I don't think they would," protested Higgins.

"For sure they would. Then the faculty would totally be all over you and you'd lose control over this little fiefdom you've built. It would be a big hit to your college applications."

Luke watched as Higgins digested this information. He furrowed his brows and his eyes flitted from side to side. He was a nervous guy, but he also had a sneaky side—the one that had put all the cameras around so he could be a voyeur. It was that side that Luke was counting on to help him.

"Okay," Higgins finally relented. "I'll hold on to it for a few days and put it somewhere safe."

"And don't tell anyone."

"Okay."

"Thanks," said Luke, preparing to leave. He once again scanned the room and the high-tech equipment as well as the comfortable leather chairs and sofa. He hadn't noticed but there was even an elaborate cappuccino maker, and a fridge stocked with various sodas and sparkling waters.

"This place is pretty fancy. Who donated it anyway?"

"My dad," confessed Higgins.

"Nice."

"Yeah, he'd be pretty pissed if it got shut down. We only just got it set up."

When Luke exited the Digital Yearbook room and turned the corner, he saw Dean Heckler leaning against the wall. Waiting for him.

"What are you up to, son?" he asked menacingly.

Luke felt a growing sense of dread.

"Nothing much," Luke said, feigning nonchalance. He was getting good at sounding cheerful when that was the last emotion he was actually feeling.

Dean Heckler stared at him wordlessly. Luke shifted on his feet. If he could just hang in there and play it cool, all would be okay, he thought.

"Doesn't look that way," said Dean Heckler finally.

"Oh, well, I was just hanging with Higgins. Checking out his new Digital Yearbook."

Dean Heckler walked toward Luke and stared at him. He was so close Luke could almost feel the heat emanating from his body.

"I'm warning you. Stay out of this. Mind your own business if you know what's good for you."

"Yes, sir, of course."

"After what happened to you before, I'd have thought you would have wised up."

Luke didn't know what to say. He didn't want to lie but if he explained himself, it would seem suspicious. "I have, sir," Luke replied after a pause.

Dean Heckler's breath was hot on his neck. He was still obstructing Luke's way, so Luke had to take a step back and around him to pass. As he did so, the dean swiveled around and stared at him.

Luke could feel the dean's eyes boring into him as he walked away, but Dean Heckler didn't make a move to stop him. Luke's heart was pounding.

28

"**D**ude, get this, Brooks just got a text from a friend from home and found out that the teacher that Oscar's been hanging with is *married*," said Andy as they made their way into dinner.

"Fishy," said Luke. How the hell did everyone else get an update about what Oscar was up to except him? And obviously, there was a lot that Oscar was not sharing with him. "Probably means nothing's going on."

Andy laughed. "You are so naïve, Chase. You think Oscar would turn down a hookup?"

"Well, sure. But . . . older and married?" asked Luke with skepticism. "I doubt it. He told me he's not into cougars."

Andy shook his head again. "Ah, my friend, one day you'll wake up."

Luke was both distracted and tense when he sat down at his assigned table with Mr. Crawford and the rest of his friends. And to add to the misery, tonight was a sit-down dinner. Not only was it a total drag to don a coat and tie after a long day of sports and classes, but he just wasn't up for small talk. The thing was, over the past few weeks, Luke had been searching so desperately—even putting himself in danger—to find Mrs. Heckler's killer. And his main reason for doing that was to exonerate Oscar. But it seemed that lately there had been a slow trickle of revelations about Oscar that made him question his friend. Too many inconsistencies were starting to add up. Luke was confused and angry, even.

Chicken again, sighed Luke staring down at his plate. You couldn't avoid seeing chicken almost every other meal. Lemon chicken, chicken in white sauce, chicken in red sauce. Chicken for lunch, and chicken for dinner. And if not chicken, then tofu or some other fake chicken. Luke wished for the good old days, before everything had to be organic, when there was always a loaf of white bread and a tub of peanut butter next to the coffeemaker. At least tonight they were serving some sort of pesto flatbread. Any sort of bread was always a plus.

Luke was on his third piece of flatbread when Mr. Tadeckis approached.

"Hello, Luke," said Mr. Tadeckis in his brisk manner.

"Hello, Mr. Tadeckis."

Mr. Tadeckis glanced around the table, then turned his attention back to Luke. "I would be interested in a progress report," he said in a low voice.

Luke squirmed in his seat. "Yeah, um, not much to report."

Mr. Tadeckis waved his finger at Luke. "Tsk, tsk. Don't kid a kidder."

Mr. Crawford, who was seated a few seats down chimed in. "Hello, Dwight."

Mr. Tadeckis barely glanced in his direction. "Hello, *Skippy*," he said tersely, before returning to Luke.

"Luke, have you forgotten what I told you?"

Luke gave him an imploring look. "What?"

"Are you sure you don't remember?"

"I remember," said Luke, gazing up at him. Mr. Tadeckis had told him they were lying, to not trust anyone. Basically, Mr. Tadeckis wanted him to become the same kind of suspicious loner that *he* was.

"I guess I expected a little more follow-through from you."

"I'm doing the best I can."

"Is that good enough?"

"For me."

Mr. Tadeckis leaned closer to Luke. "Don't forget. They are not as they seem. Watch your back. Look at what is right in front of you."

Luke could tell the guys sitting around him were wondering what the heck was going on. Luke cleared his throat and said a little too loudly. "Sure, Mr. Tadeckis. Watch my back. Yup. I'll do that."

Some of the guys started laughing but stopped when they realized Mr. Tadeckis was not. Mr. Tadeckis stood up very straight and gave Luke a look of outrage. "Very well then. You'll get what's coming to you."

When he walked away, Luke suddenly felt awful. He shouldn't have spoken to Mr. Tadeckis like that. He was after all, a teacher of sort. A grown-up. But in Luke's mind, he was also a suspect.

"Is Tadeckis your buddy these days?" asked Andy, his mouth full.

"No, please," said Luke in disgust.

"What's up with the friendly little chat then?"

"It's nothing, he's weird."

"Come on, you aren't joining his club, are you?" asked Gupta. "Are your extracurriculars really that light?"

"Seriously, don't you have enough outdoor stuff to talk about on your apps without having to go on one of those *Deliverance* trips with his posse of nerds?" asked Andy.

Luke sighed. How could he explain? "I wouldn't do it just for colleges, but, yes. I'm thinking about it."

"No way, dude! You're going to go all Discovery Channel on us?" asked Gupta.

"I hear weird stuff goes down out there," said Andy. "And not weird in a good way."

"Hey, some of those camping trips can be fun. When I was a student here we had some pretty wild times," interjected Mr. Crawford.

"Really?" asked Luke with surprise.

"Yeah, 'cause in those days, plenty of girls went," said Mr. Crawford raising his eyebrows suggestively.

"You're the man, Mr. C.!" said Andy.

The other boys started to whoop suggestively. Luke rolled

his eyes, thinking of what Liz or his sisters would say if they were here.

"Keep it down over there," said Mr. P., who was seated at the next table.

"Sorry, Robert," said Mr. Crawford over his shoulder. He turned back to the boys and whispered conspiratorially: "Guys, don't forget, we're not allowed to have fun at these dinners."

All the guys laughed. Luke was surprised that Mr. Crawford would be so brazen in his dismissal of Mr. P. But he recalled that he had once heard that they didn't like each other. Something happened back in the days when they were both students. Apparently, Mr. P. was kind of a dork and Mr. Crawford was one of the "cool guys." Well, at least according to Mr. Crawford. It must be weird now that Palmer was a dean, and in effect, superior to Mr. Crawford. Luke didn't see teaching in his future but he tried to imagine himself in Mr. Crawford's shoes, if he were to fast-forward ten years from now. It would be a bit uncomfortable if he had been passed over to be a dean for someone like, say, Higgins. It would just be a strange dynamic. He didn't think he'd handle it well either. Then again, he doubted he'd act as immature as Mr. Crawford did if he were a teacher.

"Let's hit Main Hall," said Andy as soon as dinner was done.

"I don't know . . ." began Luke in protest.

"Chase, you're such a bore these days!"

"Shut up," said Luke. "I'll go as far as the vending machines. I want some chips or candy to wash away the taste of whatever that dinner was."

"I hear ya," said Andy.

They walked together toward the vending machines where Luke stopped and bought some M&Ms and Andy got a Kit Kat. Thank God the organic food police hadn't gotten rid of the vending machines yet, but Luke was willing to bet that when he returned for his first alumni weekend they'd be long gone. It was only a matter of time. The boys continued their stroll down Main Hall. Luke searched for Pippa, but there was no sign of her.

"These security guards are beyond worthless," Andy said, pointing to three guards clustered outside of Main Hall.

"What do you mean?"

"Apparently, they're a total joke. They're all wannabe cops who failed their test. Totally clueless. Fisher snuck out of his dorm the other night to go meet his girlfriend, and they just, like, nodded at him. I mean, they don't even realize that we have a curfew and aren't allowed out after lights out!"

"That's kind of scary when you think of it. Aren't they supposed to be protecting us?"

"Yeah, right. I heard they all hang out in the bike room downstairs, playing poker. I tell you, no one here is safe."

Luke frowned. Andy had no idea how right he was.

"Hey, I want to check my mailbox," said Luke, guiding Andy in that direction.

"What, you waiting for the new J. Crew catalog?"

"Victoria's Secret."

"Ha."

"No, really, I want to get my American Lit paper. Mr. Turner said he'd put them in our boxes tonight."

They went into the area where all the student mailboxes were. As Luke approached the back wall where his was located he saw Mrs. Palmer, shoving something into a box. It was too far away to discern whose it was. She glanced up and quickly slammed the box shut and before moving toward them.

"Hello boys, just returning some papers for Mr. P.," she said rapidly, before pushing her glasses up on her nose. "Have to get back to the twins now."

"Have a good night," murmured Luke and Andy.

When she was out of earshot Andy leaned toward Luke and whispered, "She is one mousy lady."

"Yeah, but nice."

"I bet Mr. P. wished he could have had a hottie like Joanna Heckler."

Luke sighed. "Dude, it's not all about what chicks look like, you know."

"What do you mean?" asked Andy, truly perplexed.

He's beyond help, thought Luke.

Luke walked to his mailbox and bent down to open it. He put his hand in the box and pulled out his paper. He got a 93. Not bad. Now he had a chance of getting an A in this class. He put his hand back in his box and felt a small rectangular slip of paper. He'd probably received a package; that was usually the form they used. He pulled it out and saw that it wasn't a package form. It was an index card. There, scrawled in black ink was a message:

You are playing a dangerous game. You think you know better than anyone else. This will end badly for you. Watch Your Back.

"Whadja get?" asked Andy.

Luke quickly put the index card on top of his English assignment and folded it in half. "Oh, nothing, I just have a package . . ."

"No, I mean on the paper."

"Oh, 93."

"Nice. Never got that kind of a grade from Turner, myself."

"Thanks," said Luke. "Listen, I'm going to head back to the dorm. Prep for study hall. Interested?"

"No, man, I'm playing this out until the very end. I just saw Lily and Kira arrive and I want to let them fight it out over me."

"Right, that's gonna happen. Catch you later."

"You don't want to be my wingman?" said Andy.

"I'm out of here," said Luke, over his shoulder.

He took a deep breath as he walked down Main Hall back to his dorm. *Watch your back.* That's what Mr. Tadeckis had warned him at dinner. He had clearly been offended by Luke's tone and had taken it a step further. There was no proof at all, of course. The handwriting was indecipherable and probably disguised very well. It was all coming together. Luke felt stupid. All of Mr. Tadeckis's clues had been to throw him off. Perhaps Mr. Tadeckis had thought Luke had seen him that night, so he had tried to mess with Luke's mind.

Something flashed in Luke's head. He remembered when he and Oscar were climbing back into the dorm and he had looked up at the hill and saw a figure. It had to have been Mr. Tadeckis. He had the same large build. Luke shivered at the memory. Mr. Tadeckis was a trained outdoorsman, a hunter. He knew how to wait for his prey and then attack. There could be no doubt.

Luke headed for Nichols, the freshman dorm where Mr. Tadeckis lived.

"May I help you?" asked Mr. Tadeckis sharply, when he saw Luke at his door.

"Mr. Tadeckis, I was hoping to talk to you."

"I'm on dorm duty. I have to check in these newbies and make sure they're glued to their desks, not using their cell phones and are in compliance with all of the rules and regulations."

"This will only take a minute."

"A lot can occur in that minute. I could be distracted by you, and one of the freshmen could use that opportunity to open their door, retrieve their cell phone, and text someone."

Freshmen were supposed to leave their cell phones outside their doors in the hallway during study hall. It usually took them until winter break to realize they could leave an old, nonworking phone in the hallway as a dummy phone.

"But if you're on dorm duty, aren't you technically supposed to be available for any academic help? In which case, the same thing could happen. I could be asking you a question about science and one of the freshmen could open their doors and sneak their phones. Same thing. Or that could also occur when you are doing impromptu room checks. You could have your head in one room and someone could slip past you . . ."

Mr. Tadeckis thought a minute. "Touché," he said. "You may enter." He moved ever so slightly to the side to allow Luke entrance.

Luke had been surprised by Mr. Tadeckis's office and was once again surprised by his apartment. It was actually very well-decorated. The walls were hunter green and there were large framed poster-sized photographs of all sorts of animals—tigers and bears and lions. He had two leather club chairs and a beige couch with zebra-stripe throw pillows. It felt more like a home than some of the other dorm teacher's apartments, which felt more like, well, dorm rooms.

"Wow, did you take these pictures?"

"That is correct," confirmed Mr. Tadeckis.

"They're awesome. Were you on safari?" asked Luke, almost forgetting why he was there.

"Yes, one of my many trips to Africa."

Luke turned back to Mr. Tadeckis. Suddenly, he felt nervous. "I know it was wrong for me to be sort of rude to you tonight, but there's no need for threats," said Luke, summoning up all of his courage.

"Threats?"

"Yeah, you know, 'watch your back,'" Luke said.

"That was advice, a warning."

"Yeah, but I mean, to write me the note—"

"What note?"

"You know, the one in my mailbox."

"I did not write you a note. Please let me see the evidence."

Luke handed the index card to Mr. Tadeckis. He adjusted his glasses and read it silently.

"Very interesting."

"You wrote it, right?"

Mr. Tadeckis stared at Luke. "I did not write this."

Luke started to feel nervous. "Then who do you think did?"

"The murderer, no doubt," said Mr. Tadeckis matter-of-factly. Luke couldn't believe he was being so cavalier. It was as if he were discussing the weather.

"Really? You think?" said Luke, his voice rising to a squeak.

"Most likely."

Luke sat down with a thud in the chair. He felt weak. The murderer was now threatening him? "But why would he say 'watch your back'? That's what you said. It's what you said tonight."

"Maybe he overheard me."

Luke sat in a daze. Then something occurred to him. "How do I know you're not the murderer? I know that you followed the dean and his first wife into the Xerox room and saw the picture they copied of Mrs. Heckler."

"True. And does that make me a murderer?"

"Well, why were you following them? Why were you in the woods?"

296

"Curiosity."

"Maybe you had some sick obsession with Mrs. Heckler also! Maybe you were her boyfriend!"

Mr. Tadeckis went and sat down across from Luke. It seemed as if his body relaxed, and he leaned back in his chair. "I was not her boyfriend."

"How do I know?"

"Because I am a socially awkward oaf that could only dream of being with a woman like Joanna Heckler."

"Huh?"

"That's what she told me, anyway," said Mr. Tadeckis, his eyes shining under his glasses.

"She said that? When?"

"I will be straightforward with you in order to put your mind at ease that I would never commit homicide or engage in threatening index card correspondence," said Mr. Tadeckis clearing his throat. "Joanna Heckler was a very wily woman. Cunning. I am usually very good at reading people, but she had me fooled."

"How?"

"She came down to my office last month, just before school started. As you know, it's rare that I receive visits, particularly from adults. She turned on all of her feminine charm and told me she admired my work, my trips, that she'd been watching me from afar. She was very good. I'm really impressed, in retrospect, by her acting ability. She asked for my help in teaching her some rock climbing skills. I took her out a few times, taught her the fundamentals."

"Rock climbing?"

"Yes. Several times she made allusions that rock climbing was the best way to get a man you had your eye on. I took that to mean me. Later, when I tried to address her infatuation, she laughed and inquired as to whether I really thought, and I quote, that 'a socially awkward oaf like myself would enamor a woman like her?' She told me she was out of my league."

Luke didn't know what to say. "Oh. So, um, then what?"

"She had used me to get the skills she needed to impress someone. Then she moved on. I imagine it wasn't the first time."

"Was it to get the guy in the woods?"

A small smile flickered across Mr. Tadeckis's face. "No. She was using him as well. That became clear. And he didn't like that very much. Sometimes you pick the wrong person to mess with."

"Why won't you tell me who it was? Why won't you tell me who murdered her?"

"You already know."

"Is it Mr. Hamaguchi?"

"Why do you say that?"

"Well, he seems pretty broken up about her death."

"Flimsy," interrupted Mr. Tadeckis.

"And he got really mad when people talked about the murder. And then he said they don't know what it's like to kill someone. He sounded like he knew what it was like."

"What it's like to murder? Or witness a murder?"

"I don't know. Murder, I think."

Mr. Tadeckis wiped an imaginary dust line off the side of his table with his index finger and blew it away. "I think Mr. Hamaguchi has great fantasies about murder. I think he is consumed by it. Actually, I don't just think, I know."

"Then you think he's the one who killed Mrs. Heckler?" asked Luke hopefully.

"No."

"But that doesn't make sense . . ."

Mr. Tadeckis stood up. "I will have to terminate our conversation now. It's been exactly seventeen minutes since I checked on the freshmen, and my routine is to check on them every fifteen. You need to return to your dorm for study hall."

"Please, Mr. Tadeckis. Give me a hint."

"Nothing was ever handed to me, Luke. I had to learn survival skills. The boys here are soft. None of them could take a killer down. But you could, Luke. We both know that. That's why I gave you the knife. Don't forget about it."

Luke's mind raced to the knife. He had hidden it in the radiator in the stairwell in his dorm. It was probably time to remove it now that he was getting threats. Luke followed Mr. Tadeckis out the door with frustration. Sometimes he just didn't know what Mr. Tadeckis was talking about.

"But what if he tries to kill me?"

Mr. Tadeckis turned toward him. "It wouldn't be the first time that's happened. Defend yourself. It worked before."

29

So Mrs. Heckler was a serial seductress, thought Luke as he lay on his bed, arms folded underneath his head and eyes glued to the ceiling. There was no way he was doing homework tonight. No way. Not after receiving a threat, telling him to "watch his back." And not after cracking Mr. Tadeckis's robotic sheen and realizing that there was a living, breathing human underneath it. He was way too wound up.

It was clear that Mrs. Heckler could really make men crazy. Crazy enough to kill her. He couldn't imagine a girl having power over him to that degree. Sure, he liked girls, but could they really make him homicidal? He remembered Kelsey, bringing Matt up in an attempt to make Oscar jealous. Some girls did mess with your head a lot, true. But who would hurt a girl? You'd have to be a sicko. Even if a girl was really being mean to him, Luke knew he would walk away rather than fight, although he had never been in love. Maybe love was the problem. That's why Dean Heckler couldn't be ruled out. He was obviously in love with his wife, he'd obviously known she was cheating on him, and he was obviously bitter.

Was Oscar the type to get crazy about a girl? Luke had never seen that side of him, but maybe he kept it hidden. Maybe Mrs. Heckler somehow got to him. How insane did you have to be to kill someone, wondered Luke? What did Mrs. Heckler do to the guy in the woods? She hurt Mr. Tadeckis's pride, made him feel embarrassed, scorned him. But he seemed okay. The other guy was clearly not. Had she *done* something really bad to him, or was there something wrong with him from the start?

Luke's mind sifted through all of the evidence, trying to focus on anything that would have revealed what Mrs. Heckler might have done to her lover. Did she call him a mean name? Was it just that she broke up with him? She was married; he must have known they had no future. Had she promised him a future? Maybe in Las Vegas, when they were at the pool kicking back some margaritas, she told him she'd leave her husband. Then changed her mind. Luke was getting increasingly frustrated trying to figure it out.

And what did Mr. Tadeckis mean about Mr. Hamaguchi being "consumed with murder"? How does that *not* make him the murderer? How could Luke find out?

"Sometimes you pick the wrong person to mess with," Mr. Tadeckis had said. The words kept floating back to Luke, and he couldn't figure out why. He thought of all those TV detectives and how they'd always advise each other to "Put yourself in the killer's shoes." His mind continued racing.

301

He remembered that Ms. Johnson, the woman whose husband Joanna Heckler had stolen, had told them that Dean Heckler said Mrs. Heckler was stressed before her death, and that she was "surprised she grew a conscience."

Luke shot up in his bed. It was simple. He shouldn't have been focusing on Mrs. Heckler, but instead, her killer. Maybe it wasn't something that Mrs. Heckler *did* to the killer per se; maybe it was something about *him*. And maybe Mrs. Heckler knew that, and that's why she ditched him. He had a hunch.

Luke walked over to his closet and pushed aside all of his winter sweaters that were folded on his shelf. Behind them he had hidden the computer from the Alumni Office, which he still hadn't returned to Tariq. He took it down and switched it on, waiting impatiently for it to boot up. When it finally did, he clicked on the WiFi, sighing in relief as it came through strong. Maybe if he sifted through Mrs. Heckler's search history, he'd find out something about the killer. Something that had made her "stressed and nervous."

He went alphabetically, typing one letter at a time to see if anything showed up on the search bar. The first few letters brought no luck. Turns out Mrs. Heckler was a fan of celebrity blogs such as Crazyfamous.com and Dlisted.com, all of which seemed to focus on people on reality shows. Of course, it could have been Tariq running those searches but Luke doubted it. When he got to the letter "H," it started to get interesting. There had been a search for the Hard Rock Hotel. Luke clicked on the link, which brought him to the home website. That must be where she stayed in Vegas. He clicked through the pictures of the pool and it all looked pretty glitzy. But unfortunately, there was no information about her reservation.

Luke was about to move forward when he distractedly clicked on "dining." Pictures of the various Hard Rock restaurants fluttered onto the screen. Luke's eyes widened. The Pink Taco. Holy moly. The restaurant from the Post-it note. Oscar had said it was a restaurant in Los Angeles, but here it was in Las Vegas. Had he lied? Had Oscar been the one accompanying her to Las Vegas? Luke tried to rack his brain. When could Oscar have gone to Vegas? Over the summer? It was possible, but he certainly didn't mention it. Maybe they had hooked up there, and then when they were back in school, Mrs. Heckler—or "Joanna" as Oscar called her—slipped him a little Post-it reminding him of the good times they had at The Pink Taco. Luke had the crushing feeling that he had been lied to. And now he was being avoided.

Desperate to find more clues, Luke continued his search. When he got to the letter "P" he was about to keep going but he noticed something that made him stop. Mrs. Heckler had done a search on "psychopaths." Luke immediately clicked on the link. When the page came up there were over 2,790,000 results. But there was one result that was in a light shade of violet, which meant that it was the link that Mrs. Heckler had clicked on. And the title was "Are You Involved with a Psychopath?" Suddenly, Luke remembered that Andy had referred to the murderer as a psychopath. And Ms. Johnson had said she would have killed Joanna but she "wasn't a psychopath."

The word was often used in a cavalier manner, but the true meaning was harrowing. It was a person with no conscience.

Luke opened the article. The traits of a psychopath include "superficial charm," "self-centered," "prone to deception." It stated these traits can often go undetected, but clearly Mrs. Heckler had noticed them. Someone had probably charmed her, and then become desperate when she learned he was dangerous. Luke knew he might be grasping, but for the first time he put himself in Mrs. Heckler's shoes. He finally realized what kind of person he was up against, and it made him shudder.

Was Oscar the psychopath that Mrs. Heckler feared? He appeared totally normal to Luke, yet if he was a true psychopath, he could have a twisted evil side. Had Luke ever been in danger from Oscar? What would have happened if he had ever really pissed Oscar off? But maybe Oscar's hidden rage, if he had any, was directed only at women. That's why he moved from one to the next so quickly, why he loved them and left them. At the same time that he was with Kelsey, he was smugly derisive of her and the fact that she was cheating on her boyfriend. Not to mention he was still flirting with every girl in sight. Oscar must hate women, right? Was that what happened?

But even if that was true, there had to be someone else, someone now on campus who had something to hide. The person who was leaving Luke notes and following him. Dean Heckler? Luke wasn't sure.

Luke slipped out of his room and went to the radiator in the stairwell. The knife was still there. Maybe it would be a good idea to carry it with him. Just as a precaution.

30

After practice the following day, Luke made his way at a steady run down the hill from the playing fields to his dorm. Night was setting in earlier and earlier, winter gloom was hovering. The air was crisp, the trees had shed most of their leaves, and the grass was stripped and raw. It was almost the time of year when students buckled down and spent most of their time indoors. Luke turned up the volume when Green Day came on and pushed himself to sprint the last bit. He wanted to be transported somewhere else, in a bubble of sound, where he didn't feel alone. Anywhere else but here.

He was so focused on *American Idiot* that it was a shock when he felt a hand touch his back. He shoved it off, then whipped around, prepared to fight until he saw who it was. Pippa. Luke pulled off his earphones.

"Jesus! I could have really hurt you!"

"I was shouting your name forever. On what level are you listening to that music? You'll ruin your ears!"

Luke bent down and held onto his knees.

"Sorry," said Pippa. "I didn't mean to catch you off guard, but I have to admit it was a bit of a thrill to see you in action."

Luke stood up. Pippa had her hair pulled back in a ponytail, which made her green eyes seem large and bright, her face less pale. Why had Oscar dissed her looks? She had to be the best-looking girl at school. Especially when she was looking at him like that, with admiration. Luke wasn't sure why she would have thought anything he'd just done was admirable—he'd probably looked ridiculous, lost in the music, letting her sneak up on him like that, hopping around like a scared rabbit.

"Anything to report?"

"Everyday there's something," said Luke.

"Brilliant! Fill me in. I assume you'll start with the bracelet?" She held up her arm, where it sparkled on her wrist. "I didn't want to leave it in my room, now that I know the police are searching for it. If I'm wearing it, no one would think twice."

"You're probably right." Luke told her about everything, from how he found the bracelet to the video yearbook. He told her about Mr. Tadeckis's revelations about being spurned by Mrs. Heckler. Pippa listened with rapt attention. Luke liked the way Pippa took in information. She was thoughtful and didn't interrupt just to push her two cents in. When he had finished, she waited before she spoke.

"Why don't you want to turn in the memory card to the police? Let them take over."

"I don't know. I feel like, if I do it, they'll keep too close an eye on me and I won't be able to finish finding the killer."

Luke thought of Oscar. He hadn't told Pippa about Mrs. Heckler's search for "psychopaths" on the computer. Despite all of his doubts, some sort of loyalty was preventing him from betraying Oscar.

Pippa was pensive. "But it's getting dangerous, Luke. We're being followed, and you're getting threatening letters. Even Mr. Tadeckis advised you to carry a knife."

Luke nodded. "I know, it sounds crazy. But I have faith that I can find the killer. We're just one step away."

"You're not scared?"

"I'm tense as hell, but not scared. I think I could take him down."

"I would say you were mad, but the truth is, we both know that you can't leave it up to the police."

"Yeah, if I had three years ago, I'd still be locked up in a cabin or dead," said Luke. He surprised himself by bringing up his abduction. He *never* brought it up. But it felt natural to discuss it with Pippa.

"You're probably as bored with banging on about your sordid past as I am about mine," said Pippa quickly. "But if you want to have a session where we hash everything out that's happened to us, I'm all ears."

Luke smiled. "Thanks. It's weird that we're both freaks in that way."

"Yeah, but in my case I'm an outcast, and in your case, you're a legend."

"I'm not a legend!"

"You are!" protested Pippa. "It was the first thing the girls informed me when I got to St. Benedict's. *Look, there's Luke Chase, the hero. The bravest boy in America.* No offense, I hadn't heard a whit about you before then. Your fame didn't exactly make it across the pond."

"Thank God!" He shook his head and continued walking down the path. Pippa followed. "I really hate this reputation. I keep waiting for it to fade away, to never come up again, but it's always there."

"So, solve Mrs. Heckler's murder. Give everyone something else to talk about," said Pippa.

They walked along in silence, Luke reviewing his conversation over and over. He liked Pippa. Her honesty was refreshing, sometimes to the point of unnerving, but it was also mature. He felt like they really communicated without all the stupid high school games.

They were passing a bench when Luke abruptly took Pippa's hand and pulled her over to it. He sat next to her and stared into her surprised face.

"Do you really want to know what happened?"

Pippa nodded. "I do."

Luke hesitated. Could he tell her? He had never spoken to anyone at St. Benedict's about it. Even Oscar only knew what he had read in the paper.

"Three years ago, this month actually, I was walking home from school in Georgetown. Suddenly, a black SUV with tinted windows pulled up. I didn't think much of it, I mean, it's D.C. and all. Every official person there has a car like that."

He looked at Pippa and waited. She nodded, coaxing him to continue.

"But the next thing I know, these masked men grab me and pull me inside. I didn't even have a second to register before I was tied up and gagged. I should have been scared, but I was more thinking that it was a prank or something.

"All of a sudden we're driving. And it's scary then because no one says anything. Then after about forty-five minutes, the car stops and I think we're there but then they put me in another car and drive on and on for what must have been hours."

"Had they said anything to you at this point?"

Luke shook his head. "It wasn't until we get out, to a cabin in the woods I later learned, that they start talking. Actually, it was only one guy, this British guy—"

"British? Are you sure? He could have been South African or Australian."

"British. Don't get defensive," said Luke with a slight smile. "But he didn't have one of those posh James Bond accents, like yours. It was more, you know, rough. Anyway, he tells me not to speak, not to yell. He says if I do as I am told, I will be safe. He's sent a list of demands to my parents and when they pay them, I'm free. Then he unties me and tells me not to open my eyes until I hear the door close."

"Then what?" asked Pippa. She was leaning toward Luke, hanging on his every word.

"I do what he says and when I open them I see I'm in a wooden room with a metal cot. The window is bolted shut. There's a rustic table and two chairs. He had left me a pizza . . ."

"Plain?"

"Pepperoni," said Luke. He was distracted now, picturing the pizza. He wished he were able to tell the story with detachment, as if it was something that happened long ago and didn't really matter. But it still conjured up dread for him.

"Sorry, I get obsessed with the details," said Pippa.

"That's okay," said Luke. He was staring into the distance, his mind focused on the events of three years ago.

"Then what happened?" asked Pippa softly.

"I don't know, really. Two days went by with no one there at all; that was the worst part. Then, the next thing I know, two masked men come in and drag me out of bed and put me in a cage outside."

"Was one of them the British guy?"

Luke shook his head. "No. They were meaner. Scarier. I never saw the British again . . ." Luke's voice trailed off. He had heard fighting outside the cabin when the two bad guys (*worse* guys) arrived; he had actually felt relief when he'd heard the British guy's voice. Luke had been waiting for him to come back—had thought he'd die there alone, in fact, if the guy didn't come back. But the other guys had won, and the Brit did not return again.

"You trusted him?" asked Pippa.

Luke rubbed the scar on his jaw. He couldn't go there with her. It had taken him a year of therapy for him to realize that he had experienced Stockholm Syndrome—where a victim identifies with his or her abductors. The therapist had said it was because his captors were playing good cop and bad cop, but he felt it was something else. The British guy had needed something from Luke. He hadn't intended harm. It was almost like the British captor had regarded him as an ally.

"Whatever. The bottom line was the British guy disappeared. The second two guys treated me badly, and then I escaped."

Luke knew he wrapped up the story quickly, but it was painful for him to analyze it. Plus, Pippa would have questions that he didn't like to think about.

"How did you manage it?"

"That's a story for another time," sighed Luke.

"I did hear that you had to hike through the woods for days. That you managed to kill the attack dog they had sent after you, and that you," she paused, "seriously injured one of your abductors. She reached out and softly touched the spot under his ear where the scar began. "Is that how you got this?"

Luke winced, and his reaction must have startled Pippa because she got a panicked look on her face.

"I'm sorry, Luke. I know I'm very blunt."

Luke shook his head. "It's okay."

"Seriously, I shouldn't push you on this."

Luke glanced at the darkening sky that was now the purple and black color of a heavy bruise. "I'm supposed to talk about it, actually. My parents made me see a therapist after and he said it would help."

"Does it?"

Luke pondered this. "Well, perhaps it can help me clear up the myths. I mean, it wasn't such a miracle that I hiked through the woods. I spent every summer and every vacation I could at my grandparents' farm in Virginia. My grandfather knew everything about the outdoors. He would take me camping and hiking on the Appalachian Trail. He taught me about tracking and marking, noticing distinct wildlife. He helped me with maps and taught me how to mark time by the sun. He could identify medicinal herbs, edible plants, and everything one would need to stay alive."

"It's weird, but . . ." interjected Pippa.

Luke turned and stared at her quizzically. "What?"

"It's almost like he was preparing you for this."

Luke's heart raced. He'd never shared that idea with anyone, not even his parents.

"I've thought the same thing," he admitted. "You know, my grandfather was a POW, so maybe he didn't want history to repeat itself, or maybe he worried that it would. I wish he were still around so I could ask him."

"It's almost . . . destiny. Like he knew your fate."

That's exactly how Luke had thought of it. It felt good to have someone agree with him for once. His parents were always trying to tell him it was random, a fluke, a one in a million shot of terrible luck.

Luke rubbed his face again and realized he never answered Pippa's original question.

"Yes, that's the long answer for how I got this scar. I've got a few on my arms, too, and a mean one on my ankle."

He held out his arms for her to inspect. There was a short, raised scar on his right forearm, and the top of his left arm had a few light lines where his skin hadn't quite healed before the sun had changed the pigment color.

"Terrible," she said sympathetically. They drifted into silence. Finally, Pippa spoke again. "So, did your parents pay the ransom?"

"They sent it the second day. They tried to pay immediately but the FBI wouldn't let them because they wanted to catch the guys and make sure I was okay. When the feds caught the two guys, they eventually made them confess and return the money."

"What about the British guy?"

"They never found him," said Luke quietly.

"And the other two guys didn't give him up?"

"Nope. They denied there was anyone else. Said it was just them."

"Why do you think they took you? I mean, are you supremely rich or something?"

"Hardly! No, there were a ton of richer kids than me in my class. And also kids with super important parents—diplomats and government officials."

"All the more reason to wonder, why you?" asked Pippa, her eyes searching his face.

"I . . ." Luke hesitated.

"What?"

He shook his head. He couldn't tell her. Not yet. It was something he never spoke about, and only once with his parents. A few months after the kidnapping, he'd intercepted an email with a UK domain name. Something about it made him sure it was from the British kidnapper. It was addressed to his mother and hinted at what the kidnapper had really been after. He hadn't wanted the money; that was a pretext. He'd needed something that had been with Luke's grandfather, and there were references to family secrets and old grudges that Luke hadn't understood. When Luke had tried to talk to his mother about it, she had shut him down, claiming the police had confirmed the email had been a hoax. Luke didn't think it was, but he didn't want to press. He was better off putting his energy on moving forward, and even now he still didn't want to open that door and face any of those implications.

"Aren't you scared he'll come back to kidnap you again?"

Luke shook his head. He had always gotten the feeling if the British man came after his family again, kidnapping wouldn't be the method. "I don't think he will. I never did. The other night, though—I admit while we were in the woods I was worried a bit. But once I realized Mrs. Heckler was the target? No. I think I'm safe."

"Are you sure?" pressed Pippa.

"Well, we have wonderful security here at St. B.'s. Nothing

ever happens here!" joked Luke, attempting to lighten the mood.

Pippa didn't fall for it. "This murder must have terrified you."

"Apples and oranges," said Luke quickly.

"What do your parents think?"

"My parents?" asked Luke, stretching casually. It had felt great to share some of his past with someone in a real way, but he was ready to move on. "They ask me more questions about my love life than the murder."

Luke saw Pippa blush. She glanced down at her knees, removing an invisible piece of lint from her skirt.

"Typical parents, then."

"So, um, are you going to the Autumn Fair this weekend?" Luke asked casually.

"Does this mean you don't want to talk about your past anymore?"

"I guess. It also means . . ." Luke cleared his throat. "I want to know if you'll go to the Autumn Fair with me."

"I'd love to, but what is it?"

"After Saturday classes end at noon, everyone is invited across the street to Gordon Farm. If students need service hours, they can work there running booths where people can play stupid games like knock down all the bottles or squirt water guns at clowns' heads. There's pumpkin carving. Shaved ice. You know, fair stuff."

"Right."

"But they also have hay rides and the cool thing is the farmer makes a maze out of his cornfields. And we're talking a totally elaborate maze. Last year Gupta was stuck in it for something like two hours. It's serious."

"Sounds like a worthy way to spend an afternoon."

"Great, then. Why don't we meet there at, say, twelve thirty?"

"Okay."

Luke couldn't keep the smile off his face for the rest of the night.

After dinner, Luke was sprawled out on his bed attempting to translate a short essay into Spanish. Languages just weren't his thing, but at least the subject reminded him of Pippa now. Then he realized they never did watch that telenovela together. Maybe this weekend.

There was a knock on Luke's door.

"Come in."

It was Mr. Crawford. He came in gingerly and glanced around the room. "Well, it's not that much neater without Oscar here."

"I know," said Luke. "But I can say one thing in my defense. I may be messy, but I'm not dirty."

"Unfortunately, I'm here for room inspection, and with that garbage can filled to the brim and that pile of laundry, you've earned a failing grade."

"Mr. C., please," Luke said with a grin.

Mr. Crawford shook his head. "Luke, I gave you a get-out-of-jail-free card for missing dinner the other night. I can't do it every week."

"I promise," said Luke.

"If next week is better, I might erase this one," said Mr. Crawford.

Suddenly, Luke's cell phone began to ring. He glanced down quickly enough to see that it was a local number and declined the call.

Mr. Crawford shook his head. "Cell phones off during study hall."

"I'm sorry. I forgot. Everyone who calls me knows it, not sure who that was."

"What was the area code?"

"203."

"Be careful, Luke. A lot of the press is trying to reach students for comments. I hope you're not talking to them. There have been some students leaking information . . ."

Luke shook his head vehemently. "No, no. It wasn't me. Was probably the Southborough Inn."

He glanced down at his phone and saw that a voice mail had been left.

"Why would they be calling you?"

Luke's mind raced. "I have some relatives coming to visit. I wanted to book several rooms for them."

"You must hate them if you're booking there," said Mr. Crawford with a chuckle. "That place is a dump. Don't even change their towels."

"Have you stayed there?" asked Luke with suspicion.

Mr. Crawford smiled. "Once. We had our tenth reunion there. We didn't do much sleeping. It was a total party. Even Dean Palmer tied one on."

"Mr. P.? I can't imagine him letting loose."

"You'd be surprised. Usually only when his wife isn't around. She keeps him on a tight leash."

"Yeah, she seems kind of . . . nervous."

"To say the least." Mr. Crawford did one last glance around. "Okay, then, I'll catch you later. And please, Luke, clean up your room."

"I will."

When he left, Luke jumped up and began pacing. Twenty minutes left of study hall before he was allowed to make a phone call. Why had the guy called him? He probably recognized who had brought Mrs. Heckler to the motel. Either that, or someone else came asking and he wanted to tell Luke. That hundred-dollar bill had been a good idea. Kudos to Pippa.

When study hall was over, Luke listened to the voice mail.

"Hi, it's Charlie from Southborough. I think I recognize someone from your picture. I'm heading out for the night, I'll try you back."

Luke quickly dialed the number. The phone rang and rang before a woman answered.

"Hi, is Charlie around?"

"He left."

"Do you know when he'll be back?" asked Luke with urgency.

"He's off until Saturday morning. Had to take his wife to her crafts fair over in Fairfield."

"Saturday?" repeated Luke with frustration. Today was Thursday. That would be two days! "Does he have a cell?"

"I can't give it out."

Luke's mind raced. "Okay, can you please give him the message? It's pretty urgent."

Luke gave the lady his name and number and just to be extra sure he also gave her Pippa's name and dorm number, which he looked up in the school directory. He didn't know her class schedule but maybe he'd catch one of them and tell them what he knew. This could be the break they needed!

31

"**H**ey, Chase, I found something you might be interested in."

Luke glanced next to him on the lunch line and saw George Higgins holding his tray.

"Oh, yeah?"

"I'll wait for you to grab your lunch," said George, walking off to the side.

After Luke had filled his tray—grilled chicken fajitas—he made his way over to Higgins. "What's up?"

"After we saw what we saw in the Xerox room, I became very interested. I've just spent every waking moment of free time reviewing old footage. I want to show you one part before I take it to the police."

Fifteen minutes later they were in the Digital Yearbook room. Luke had gobbled down his lunch and then waited anxiously while George Higgins took his sweet time attempting to doctor up his grilled chicken with things from the salad bar. Finally, they were ensconced in the chairs in front of the monitor.

"It's huge," said Higgins.

"I'm ready."

Higgins pressed play and Luke watched as the Xerox room flickered onto the screen. At first there was nothing, but then a second later there was a blur as people came in. One of them was Mrs. Heckler—the dead one. Luke squinted. It was hard to see whom she was talking to; all that was visible was the sleeve of a blue-checked button down. But her face said it all. It was clear she was very angry with the person in question.

"Listen, I want you to get the hell away from me. It's over. Stop harassing me!" she said, before waving her finger in the person's face and marching out of the room.

The person didn't move.

"Can you tell who it is?" asked Luke eagerly.

"Just wait."

Luke watched as Mrs. Holliway entered.

"*Oh, hello, there,*" she said to the person Mrs. Heckler had just yelled at.

He or she must have nodded hello, or at least not rudely or suspiciously, because Mrs. Holliway stepped forward to the copier machine and commenced her daily routine of tree slaughtering.

The blue-checked sleeve disappeared. Whoever it was left without showing their face.

"Mrs. Holliway was blocking him!" said Luke. "Can you rewind?"

"I can, but I can tell you I sat here and watched this thing about twenty times last night. I even broke it down to slo-mo. Fat Mrs. Holliway is blocking the guy completely. All you see is a flash of blue and dark hair."

"Well, at least that's something! We know he has dark hair!" said Luke.

"Do you know how many faculty members have dark hair?"

"No."

"Seventeen. And I'm talking full head."

"You counted?"

"Totally. And that's also not to mention that there are students with dark hair. If the rumor is true that she was with a student. I mean, Oscar has dark hair."

Luke's pulse quickened. It was true. Oscar has dark hair. And a blue shirt like the one the guy was wearing.

Luke's mind raced. "Let me talk to Mrs. Holliway before you give this to the police."

"I don't know," said Higgins.

"Come on. I'll go right now."

"Fine, but I'm giving it to them by the end of the day."

"Whatever," said Luke, leaping out of his chair, as he did so, the knife dropped out of his pocket.

"What's that?" asked Higgins with astonishment.

Luke quickly picked up the knife. "Oh, nothing, just a knife."

"I think it's illegal to carry a knife here."

"Is it? Well, it's Swiss Army. It's also a corkscrew."

"It's illegal to drink also."

"Thanks, Einstein. I just need to carry this around for . . . um, my survival course."

"Your survival course?"

"Yeah, I'm taking one with Mr. Tadeckis. Planning on going camping, in training now, so I need it."

"Oh," said Higgins.

"Yeah. Thanks for showing me this," said Luke, quickly exiting. He put the knife into his back pocket. From now on he'd have to be more careful about where he kept it.

"**M**rs. Holliway?" asked Luke in his most polite voice.

"Yes, dear, what can I do for you?"

Mrs. Holliway was a stout woman with a strong Boston accent. Luke noticed the stacks and stacks of neatly organized papers on her desk. She must have an addiction to copying, he thought. This might be something to bring up at the next STEAM meeting.

"I was wondering if you remember who you said hi to a few weeks ago, I think it was October 2nd, in the Xerox room?"

"Excuse me?" she asked with confusion.

"I thought you might remember, I know it's a long shot."

"I don't know if I could possibly remember who I said hi to in the Xerox room. Lots of people. What is this about?"

"Yes, Luke, what is this about?" said a voice behind Luke.

Uh oh. Luke turned around and was face to face with Mr. P. His heart sunk.

"I just was wondering . . ."

Luke tried to think of an excuse fast, but nothing would come to his head.

"Luke, I think you need to come with me," said Mr. P., putting his arm on Luke's shoulder and walking him out of Mrs. Holliway's office. "If my suspicions are correct, you're proceeding with your own investigation. The headmaster told me about this."

"No sir . . ."

"Luke, we have an honor code. I don't want you to lie."

Luke remained silent. Mr. P. shook his head.

"Is there something you want to tell me? Have you discovered any information?" pressed Mr. P.

"No."

"Nothing at all? I need to know everything. What do you know?"

"I don't know anything."

Mr. P. examined Luke's face carefully. "You are putting yourself in danger if you are not truthful. Why did you want to know who was using the Xerox room?"

"I . . ." but Luke didn't know what to say. He was just curious? Yeah, the dean would never buy that. "I don't know."

"No good will come of this. You can't be poking your nose around in other people's business."

"I'm not. I won't."

Mr. P. changed tack. "Look, why don't you come to my

office on Monday and we'll have a chat. Who's your adviser?"

"Mr. Crawford."

"Great. I'll let him know that I would like to see both of you. I'll see you at three o'clock."

"Yes, sir," said Luke, dismayed. Great. This was just what he needed. It was overwhelming, and he felt like he was starting to crack. Maybe he did need to disclose what he knew to someone.

On his way back to his dorm, Luke decided to stop by Mr. Hamaguchi's office for a consult. He was having trouble writing up the dissection lab.

"If you're looking for Hamaguchi, he's not there," said Liz on her way down the path from the science building.

"He's not?"

"No, and it's super-annoying. I don't get any of the stuff that's going to be on the quiz and he said he would be there today to go over the study guide."

Liz dropped her knapsack on a bench by the entrance and shoved her thick chemistry textbook inside.

"Did he leave a note?"

"Said he was in Archer and he'd be right back," she said, blowing a strand of her dark hair out of her eyes. "But I waited at his office for, like, ten minutes and he was AWOL. I'm going to email him and see if I can meet him after field hockey, but I'm supposed to be skyping with my SAT tutor tonight already."

"I'll roam around Archer and see if I can find him."

"You may want to check downstairs. Please tell him I was here. If I can't meet with him, maybe he'll still give me credit for trying."

"Will do."

Luke crossed over to Archer and descended the stairs. C Level—which was basically the basement—housed the woodshop, three photography darkrooms and the pottery studio, as well as a number of utility closets. Luke walked across the carpeted floor and glanced into the woodshop. Mr. Kessler was conducting a class and holding a giant saw. Luke saw various freshmen he recognized but no Mr. Hamaguchi. He continued onwards and peered into the window of the pottery studio and the first darkroom. Again, no sign of Hamaguchi.

It wasn't until he reached the last darkroom that he found him. The darkrooms had a lightbulb outside that was illuminated orange if someone was working and didn't want you to come in. That meant they were at a sensitive stage of the development process and exposure to light would compromise their film. It was all super-retro in this age of digital photography but lots of the really artsy kids loved it.

The bulb outside the third room was orange so Luke waited. He hoped whoever was developing would be finished soon. Sure enough in about three minutes the orange light went off. Luke opened the heavy metal door and walked into the room. The entrance was shrouded in a thick black curtain and darkness. This was to ensure time to announce yourself in case the person in the darkroom was still doing something with the film.

"Hello?" Luke called out.

There was no response.

He slowly opened the curtain and peered in. The room was dark and it took his eyes a few seconds to adjust. But he saw Mr. Hamaguchi standing over a tray of glossy prints, swirling them in the developing liquid.

"Mr. Hamaguchi?"

Luke took a few steps toward him, careful to close the curtain. He squinted his way through the murkiness until he could see Mr. Hamaguchi closer. He was wearing huge noise-canceling earphones, and Luke could hear the faint murmur of music.

Luke moved toward him and was about to reach out his hand to touch Mr. Hamaguchi's shoulder when he stopped. The pictures stared out at him from their trays. They were almost all of Joanna Heckler, yet there were some of another blond who vaguely resembled her, but younger. *Jeez*, thought Luke. *Why was Mr. Hamaguchi printing these pictures? This was all so creepy.*

Luke slowly retraced his steps and walked backwards as quietly as possible, feeling his heart thumping. He got out before Mr. Hamaguchi saw him.

Luke was now late for sports and furiously throwing on his clothes with his shaky hands when his phone rang.

"Hello?"

"Dude, it's me."

Oscar. Luke was caught off guard.

"Oh, hi."

"Look, sorry we haven't talked, I've been under surveillance forever. I haven't been allowed to talk to anyone."

"Anyone?" asked Luke, dripping with sarcasm. "Because that's not what I heard."

"What do you mean?" asked Oscar.

"I hear you're living the life. I'm busting my butt trying to exonerate you and you're at concerts . . ."

"Whoa, whoa, slow down. I went to *one* concert. My parents made the exception because their friend's daughter was in from out of town and needed someone to go with her."

"Right," said Luke harshly. "So was she the teacher everyone says you're banging . . ."

"What?" exclaimed Oscar. "I'm not banging a teacher."

"That's not what I heard."

"What do you mean?"

"I keep hearing reports that you're all over town with some older, *married* teacher. Wow, Oscar. You act all wide-eyed and innocent, insist you'd never go there, and you're totally lying to my face."

"I'm not hooking up with anyone, but if I was, it definitely wouldn't be Sheila, who is probably the person you're talking about."

"Oh, her name is Sheila?"

"Yes. And she's my *tutor.* That's why I've been quote unquote everywhere with her. I'm trying to keep up my grades so I can come back to school."

Since when had Oscar cared about keeping his grades up? "Well, what about the Post-it that I found? From Mrs. Heckler or, as you like to call her, Joanna."

"What Post-it?" asked Oscar. "Wait, are you talking about the Pink Taco again?"

"Yes."

"I explained that . . ."

"Yeah, but you told me it was a restaurant in Los Angeles. It's in Vegas," said Luke.

"It's in Los Angeles *and* Las Vegas," said Oscar. "She'd been to the one in Vegas and was going on and on about it. She asked me if I'd been and when she found out I was going to L.A. she got all excited and told me I had to go to the Pink Taco because it was so awesome."

"Oh," said Luke. "So you guys talked a lot?"

"Luke," said Oscar with exasperation. "I told you I was in there working off demerits. That's it. That's all I was doing. I could tell right away that the woman was trouble. Short skirts, all flirty, and totally bored at her job. All she wanted to do was talk. I don't think she was so much into me, she just can't relate to guys without coming on to them. I've said it before and I'll say it again: that woman knew how to push people's buttons."

Luke didn't know what to say. Oscar had answered all of his questions. A flood of relief, sorrow, and confusion crept over him. He felt sorry he had doubted Oscar, but also defensive. He paused, letting the tension between them linger.

"You still there?" asked Oscar finally.

"Yup."

"Look, I'm sorry I couldn't call. I didn't realize you were hearing all this stuff and it was getting so twisted. But I'm the one stuck at home with a couple of angry parents until the school lets me come back."

Luke's shoulders dropped. He felt tired. "Okay."

"There are still things I can't explain yet, but I will soon."

"Like what?" asked Luke.

"Well, for one thing, I've got some good news. I heard the police are moving in on someone and it's not me. My lawyer just called and said an arrest is imminent."

"What? Who?"

"I don't know. But it is all happening."

"Did your lawyer say if it was someone from campus?"

"No, all he said is that there would be an arrest. No details. Nothing else."

An arrest. Interesting. Who? Dean Heckler? "Let me know if you find out more."

"Sure," said Oscar. "We still friends?"

"Always, dude," said Luke. And he truly meant it.

32

"**S**orry to bother you, Mr. C., but I need to talk to you."

Luke had stopped by Mr. Crawford's apartment before study hall, when he generally held office hours.

"Sure," said Mr. Crawford from his armchair. "Come on in."

Unlike Mr. Tadeckis's apartment, Mr. Crawford's apartment was sparsely decorated and had that transitional feeling as if he might have to pack up all of his belongings in one afternoon and move somewhere else. There were two mismatched chairs, an old steamer chest of the sort you might take to camp that had now transitioned into a coffee table; a few cinder-block and plank bookshelves filled with books and electronic equipment; and a small table for eating. On the walls there were some tapestries, a bulletin board jammed with papers and newspaper clippings, as well as several picture frames, mostly snapshots of Mr. C. with his friends on various camping or fishing trips. He'd thrown down a striped Indian rug over the standard gray wall-to-wall carpet, and had a few Target-style floor lamps, but other than that, it didn't have very much personality.

Physically, it consisted of a tiny kitchen, a living room, bathroom, and bedroom. Small quarters for sure, but completely rent-free. There was a lot of turnover with faculty because most came right after college and taught for a few years then moved on, living up to the mantra "those who don't know what to do, teach." But Mr. Crawford had already been at St. Benedict's for several years, and lived in this dorm the whole time. Most teachers who had been there as long preferred to move into one of the several faculty houses off campus, but those were usually the ones who were married and had families.

"Thanks, sorry, I'm not bugging you or anything?" asked Luke.

"No, have a seat. What's up?"

Luke sat down on the armchair opposite Mr. Crawford. He'd spent many an evening there with other guys from his floor, having pizza and watching the Giants or the Rangers.

"I need to go see Mr. P. on Monday and he wants me to bring you because you're my adviser."

"Oh no. What did you do?" asked Mr. Crawford with a grimace.

"Well, before I tell you, I should start at the beginning."

"Okay."

"I need to talk to you in confidence. How much of what I say do you have to tell the administration?"

"Well, that's a tough question. If you are suicidal or homicidal, I am required by the laws of the school to immediately report you to health services."

"I'm not either," said Luke with a grin.

"Okay. If you confess to me that you have broken any of the major school rules like cheating or plagiarism or theft, I have to report you to the school administration."

"It's nothing like that."

"Okay," said Mr. Crawford smiling. He was preparing to recite more of his caveats before Luke stopped him.

"Look, what if, say, I did break a school rule. But that's not the part I need to discuss. The point is that I may have some information about Mrs. Heckler's murder."

"Oh, listen, I love this part." He turned up the volume on his speakers. It was a song by the Grateful Dead, one of those with the really long guitar solos. Luke was not a big fan. He watched as Mr. Crawford closed his eyes for a minute and swayed to the music.

"This is a great song."

"Yeah," said Luke halfheartedly.

"Okay, Mrs. Heckler. You did something and you know who killed her?"

"I didn't say that. I just mean I think I have some idea."

"Who do you think killed her?" asked Mr. Crawford.

Luke hesitated. Could he really trust Mr. Crawford? What if he was forced to turn him in for sneaking out?

"Okay, Luke, let's just say for a moment that this is a safe place. I won't tell anyone. Now tell me who you think killed her."

"Well, the thing is that I was out in the woods that night."

"*You* were?" asked Mr. Crawford.

"Yes."

"You mean Oscar was," said Mr. Crawford.

Luke hesitated. "I was with him."

"You were *both* out in the woods that night?"

So they did know, thought Luke. *That's why Oscar was out of here. He did tell them he was in the woods that night.*

"Yes."

"Was anyone else with you?"

Luke stared at Mr. Crawford. "No."

"You're certain?"

"Yes. But I mean, Mrs. Heckler, the first wife, was out there walking her dog."

"Did she see you?"

"No."

"Are you sure?"

"Yes."

"What did you see out there?"

"Well, I didn't *see* anything. I heard something."

"What?" the tone in Mr. Crawford's voice was rising.

"I heard the second Mrs. Heckler talking to some guy. Seemed like they were having a fight."

"Okay, hold up. This is going to take some time to sort out. Would you like a soda or something?" asked Mr. Crawford standing up and walking to the kitchen.

"Um, sure, great," said Luke. He could hear Mr. Crawford open the cupboard and then the refrigerator. He glanced around the room. In the corner was an assortment of baseball bats and mitts. Mr. Crawford was the baseball coach. There were also some science textbooks stacked against the wall.

"Here you go," said Mr. Crawford returning to the living room and handing Luke a glass of Coke.

"Thanks," said Luke.

Mr. Crawford sat down next to him.

"Continue. You were in the woods and heard Mrs. Heckler arguing with someone. A guy. Did you see him?"

"No."

"Do you know who it was?"

"No."

"Any ideas?"

Luke hesitated. "Well . . ."

"Tell me," said Mr. Crawford with urgency.

"Well, initially I was thinking Mr. Tadeckis . . ."

Mr. Crawford gave him a quizzical look and then started to laugh. Heartily. "Come on."

"Really."

"You think Joanna Heckler would go for a guy like that? No way."

That was weird. Joanna Heckler had reacted the same way toward Mr. Tadeckis.

"But who'd have thought she'd go for Dean Heckler? She clearly had bad taste in guys."

"I'll give you that much. I mean, Dean Heckler is a pretentious windbag. Don't quote me on that, if you know what

I mean. He's kind of my boss. But Dwight Tadeckis? The guy's a freak."

"Pretentious windbag?" repeated Luke. He had heard that phrase somewhere before.

"Sorry to interrupt, Mr. C. I'm here for the biology book?"

It was Pippa.

"Oh, Pippa, hello," said Mr. Crawford, standing up. "I knew you were coming for it."

"Thanks. I'm on my way to the new Bereavement Club," said Pippa.

"The Bereavement Club?" asked Luke. "What's that?"

"Mr. Hamaguchi started it. It's a support group for people who suffered a loss."

"Did you suffer a loss?" asked Mr. Crawford. "I'm sorry to hear that."

"Thank you," Pippa said somewhat awkwardly. She glanced over at Luke. "I feel like it could be helpful to um, open up and come to terms with things."

"Hopefully it will help Mr. Hamaguchi. The guy cannot get over his girlfriend who was murdered in college," interjected Mr. Crawford. "Sad story."

"That's awful."

That explained Mr. Tadeckis's comments about Mr. Hamaguchi being consumed by murder. The photographs he'd been developing must have been of his girlfriend! Mrs. Heckler's murder must have brought it all back. Luke felt terrible for suspecting him. He certainly knew what it was like to be tortured by old memories.

"They never caught the killer, and he's obsessed, poor guy," Mr. Crawford said. "I'll get the book, Pippa."

Mr. Crawford went toward his desk to retrieve the biology textbook. Pippa smiled at him and made a gesture toward Mr. Crawford. The bracelet slid down her arm.

"Here you go," said Mr. Crawford handing her the book.

"Thanks," said Pippa, stretching out her hand for it. The diamond in the bracelet caught the light and glinted.

Mr. Crawford didn't move.

"Mr. C.?" asked Pippa, waiting.

Luke turned and looked at Mr. Crawford's face, which appeared frozen. Like he was in shock or something.

"Sorry, here you go, Pippa," he said, recovering.

"And can you show me again which sections I need?"

"Sure," he said before turning to Luke and adding, "this will just take a second."

"No problem."

Luke took a large sip of his Coke. It was flat. Gross. Then he stood up and walked over to the other side of the room while Mr. Crawford helped Pippa. His eyes fluttered over the photographs in the frames. Mr. Crawford was surrounded by a pack of guys in most of them, and they all looked like they were having a blast. There were even some pictures of them sitting at tables with hundreds of beer bottles in front of them. Luke wondered what the administration would think of that.

"I'll get going. Mr. C., are you going to the fair tomorrow? I can't wait to try this famous maze I've heard so much about," said Pippa.

"Yes, the maze. Easy to get lost there," Mr. Crawford said.

"I can't wait," Pippa said. "Thanks, Mr. C., and um, catch you later, Luke?"

He nodded. "See you at Animal Hour."

"I'm going to grab something from the other room," said Mr. Crawford. "Be right back."

Luke nodded. He heard the door slam. He took another sip of soda and walked to the other side of the room, where Mr. Crawford's bulletin board hung. He glanced at the bulletin board. There was a small red felt flag that said "St. Benedict's" on it, as well as a track team schedule, a menu for Pizza Hut and several other food delivery services. There was a cocktail napkin from The Hard Rock in Las Vegas with a heart scrawled on it in blue pen. There was the school holiday schedule and an invitation to someone named John's fortieth birthday party in New York.

A chill ran down Luke's spine. He felt weak under the realization. The pieces of the puzzle that he had been trying to solve had all come together at once, with complete clarity. The Hard Rock Hotel Las Vegas: where Mrs. Heckler had gone to meet her lover. "Pretentious windbag": that was how the man Mrs. Heckler had argued with in the woods had referred to her husband, exactly as Mr. Crawford just did. Mr. C. was on duty that night; *they'd even seen him outside.* And Mr. Crawford was the one to introduce the rumor that Mrs. Heckler was sleeping with a student. She'd been sleeping with *him*! Now that Luke thought about it, Mr. C. had been everywhere. He had access to his room, he would have been the one to steal Oscar's scarf.

Mr. Crawford was Mrs. Heckler's lover. And her killer.

"Sorry about that," said Mr. Crawford, returning to the room. "I just needed to get something. Are you okay? You look a little pale."

"Um, Mr. Crawford, I should go," said Luke. It was strange, but he started to feel a little sluggish, as if he was talking but the words weren't coming out. His legs felt like jelly.

"Not yet, Luke. We need to finish our conversation."

"You know, really, it's just stupid."

"No, it's not," said Mr. Crawford strongly.

Luke put an arm out to steady himself against the wall.

Mr. Crawford came closer. "You okay, buddy? Here, why don't you sit down? You don't look okay."

Mr. Crawford led him to a chair, and despite his wishes, Luke collapsed into it. He tried to get up to leave but his feet seemed glued to the floor. What was going on? It was like he knew what was happening but was unable to react. He heard the study hall bell ring. Animal Hour. That meant students would be flooding out of their dorm rooms and heading to the main building to decompress before bed.

"Now let's get back to our discussion," said Mr. Crawford. There was something strange about his voice. It was distorted, high-pitched.

Luke felt his stomach pitch. It was the voice he had heard in the woods that night. Mr. Crawford stared at Luke carefully. Luke stared back. Where once he had considered Mr. Crawford an attractive guy, he now looked grotesque. His face seemed out of proportion. His eyes had become very small, and his jaw tense. It was as if he was morphing into a monster. Luke was almost afraid, except that he could feel the knife in his back pocket.

"Luke," said Mr. Crawford taking a step toward him.

He felt so strange. Weak. Light-headed.

"Are you okay?"

His head was spinning. Everything was blurry.

"Is there something between you and Pippa?" asked Mr. C. "Was she out there in the woods with you?"

Luke tried to shake his head no. The bracelet popped into his brain! *Mr. Crawford had frozen when he noticed it on Pippa's wrist.* At the same moment that Luke was staring at him, Mr. Crawford slowly turned his head and stared at Luke. Their eyes locked. Luke gulped. He knows. *He knows!*

"I sensed something between the two of you. I think you're lying."

The vein on Mr. Crawford's temple was pulsing. He had changed dramatically over the past few minutes. His voice was affected. He spoke in short clipped tones. He stared at Luke. Luke stared back, wishing he could rise, but his strength had abandoned him. What was going on? Finally, Mr. Crawford spoke.

"You do look pale, Luke," said Mr. Crawford, walking over to his door and locking it. Luke watched him, barely able to register what was happening. Normal things were happening, things like conversations, but not-normal things were happening, too. Doors getting locked. Luke's brain fuzzing up. Mr. Crawford behaving differently.

"I've given you a roofie. You'll be fully aware of what's going on, but unable to do anything. Then you will black out."

Luke knew he should be scared, but he couldn't feel anything. His body was heavy. He wanted to get out of there, or at the very least to shout out, but he couldn't speak. How had he let this happen to him again? Shouldn't he have been able to figure out who was dangerous by now? God knew he had a lot of experience.

"See, here's the thing. I've had enough of you and your little investigation," said Mr. Crawford. "If I had seen you out there that night, I would have pinned it on you as well, but I only saw Oscar."

He pushed Luke, and Luke fell over in the chair, helpless to keep himself upright. Mr. Crawford produced a rope and began to tie Luke's hands. Luke wanted to protest but he couldn't. He was frozen.

"I'm sure you're used to being tied up by now," said Mr. Crawford.

Luke opened his mouth but no sound came out.

"You smug little brat. Snooping around, trying to play detective. Luke Chase, the Kidnapped Kid, trying to maintain his image as a hero. And how pathetic, clinging to your friend Oscar. It would have been fine if you hadn't interfered. Everyone wanted to believe it was Oscar. No one was sorry to see him go. But you had to come along . . ."

His voice was contorted, again in that crazy girlish tone.

That scared Luke more than anything. Mr. Crawford was the psychopath. He had no conscience.

"And now Pippa also! That makes her an accomplice. We'll have to see about that."

Luke's eyes widened.

"The thing is, I did love Joanna. And I would have been better for her than anyone else," said Mr. Crawford with defiance. "But she was a snob. She wanted better and better. She met some retired gazillionaire. A heli-skiier. A pretentious jerk who was into extreme sports. She was going to leave the dean and me for him. Didn't matter that he looked like a horse and was about sixty. All she cared about was money and power."

Mr. Crawford made a tight knot with the rope and Luke felt his wrists burn. It was a déjà vu. The sense of irony was both hilarious and outrageous. But what was Crawford planning on doing to him? Would there be another cabin in the woods? Another murder? Luke wanted to shout and scream but who would hear him? And he couldn't even speak.

"You went too far, Luke. And here's how it ends."

Luke closed his eyes in fear. Everything went black.

33

His head was throbbing. It felt like he was in a tunnel. When Luke opened his eyes, he was completely disoriented. Where was he? Why was it dark? What had happened? Was he back in the Virginia cabin? Had the past three years been a dream?

Time was playing tricks on him. He was drowsy, coming in and out of consciousness. All he knew was that he had to remember. There was some urgency. Something bad had transpired. He needed to wake up. But what was it?

Then it all came flooding back to him. Mr. Crawford was the killer! Mr. Crawford, the "cool teacher," the one everyone worshipped had murdered Mrs. Heckler. And now it looked like he planned on murdering Luke.

Luke tried to move around but he discovered that his hands were tied behind his back and his feet were tied together. Not only that, but he felt dizzy. Where was he? He turned his head and looked around. It was pitch black; he couldn't see anything. He bent forward searching for light. He found the faintest trace of it under what must have been the door.

Luke wanted to scream, but there was tape on his mouth. It twisted and yanked at his skin when he tried to open his mouth. He pulled himself forward, but his arms were pinned behind him and tied to a pole. Where was he? In a cave?

When he twisted his body again something brushed against him and he recoiled. *Keep cool*, Luke reprimanded himself. *Remember that you've been through this before, and you got out.* He moved his body so he could once again graze against whatever was in there with him and was momentarily flooded with relief when he realized it must be clothes. He was in a walk-in closet. But now he had to escape.

His heart started beating rapidly. He felt that wave of nausea that comes with claustrophobia. He had to remain calm. He pulled again at his arms, but the knot was secure. His fingers traced the rope and indeed it was taut. There was no way he could untie it by yanking. He rubbed his arms against the pole. What was it? It felt like metal. Maybe it was a table?

He had to calm down. He didn't want his fate to be the same as Mrs. Heckler's. Last time he had been tied up, he had used extreme patience to whittle away at the ropes with a small safety pin. It took days, but he finally cut through. He needed to summon that quiet determination to keep his head sane and find a way out of this mess. Luke leaned forward again and tried to reach his feet. No luck. He shimmied down the table, trying to lift it up, but it was securely bolted to the floor.

Maybe someone would realize he was gone? If only he had a roommate! Was it already Saturday? Maybe his teachers would wonder why he missed class? But he only had two classes and the person they'd be notifying was his adviser, Mr. Crawford, so that wouldn't do any good. Maybe Pippa would look for him? He had promised to meet her at Animal Hour. Or would she think he had blown her off? Was he really trapped?

Luke jiggled his body and felt something against his butt. The knife! It was still in his back pocket. Hope rushed through his veins. He was suddenly so elated his blood pressure quickened. All he had to do was retrieve it and try to cut off the ropes. Luke bent his knee, hoping the movement would propel the knife out of his pocket. No luck. What if he slid back and forth and back and forth? Luke tried it. It didn't seem to help; the knife remained firmly in his pants. He arched his body forward and tried to place his butt and his back pocket against the pole that he was tied to. His abs and glutes were burning. It took several minutes, but finally Luke was able to shimmy the knife to the top of his pocket. Just once more push. Yes! The knife fell with a clink to the floor.

Luke felt around for the knife with his upper arm, frustrated that he didn't have the use of his hands. When he located it, he bent his elbow, and dragged it along to his fingers, which he splayed out in order to catch it. He had to stop for a second. It was hot, and sweat was pouring down his face. His throat was sore and parched, and he found himself craving water. Just a drop would feel so nice! He had to remain strong; it was the only way. He took some deep, controlled breaths through his nose to calm himself.

He resumed his efforts, and tried to snap open the knife. It took several attempts with shaky hands, but he finally opened it. Now was the tedious part: sawing through the rope. At first, Luke used slow strokes to cut it. He had to stop several times to relax; his body was tensing up from the small motions, and his fingers were cramping. Finally, the first layer of rope started to crack. Excited, Luke beefed up his effort. Back and forth, back and forth. Luke was feeling more and more comfortable with the knife. He'd used hunting knives tons of times with his grandfather, gathering firewood, setting up camps, and dressing game. This shouldn't be a problem.

Dammit! He'd cut himself. He cockiness had made him careless and now he could feel the blood trickling down his left hand. It burned like hell. He prayed he hadn't nicked a vein. Luke's body started to perspire more. He took some deep breaths then restarted his cutting. Every time he flicked his wrist, he felt a sting. He ignored the pain, and slowly kept to the task at hand.

The fact that Mr. Crawford had this rope made Luke's blood curdle. What had he planned on using it for? How could everyone be so taken in by this psychopath? He had dismissed Mr. Crawford completely. He was a good ol' boy.

Out of the same mold as Luke and Oscar. Suddenly something in his mind stirred. Mr. Crawford was here in the nineties as a student? What if *he* was the Southborough Strangler? What if he got his start back then? Who knew what kind of monster he could be?

He had to track him down. Before . . . Oh God! Before Mr. Crawford went to the fair and found Pippa. In the maze. It would be the perfect place to kill someone. And for sure he thought Pippa was involved since he had seen her wearing the bracelet. The bracelet that he had no doubt planted in Luke's locker.

Luke worked furiously on the rope, as if his life depended on it, which it did. The blood was pooling into a sticky mess in the palm of his left hand. It was impossible for the blood to coagulate since he kept moving, but he didn't have time to spare. What time was it? And was Pippa safe? *Must work harder*, Luke chanted in his head. *Must work harder!*

Broken! Yes, he had freed one hand! He immediately ripped off the tape that covered his mouth.

"Hello!" yelled Luke. "Hello?"

Silence. Wherever he was, there was no one else there.

Quickly, Luke glanced at his watch. Luckily the numbers glowed in the dark. Almost twelve o'clock. Pippa would be at the maze already, wondering where he was, and not knowing what danger she was in.

Rather than scream, which he somehow knew would be futile, he decided to continue his efforts to free himself. That way if Mr. Crawford were somewhere close by, he'd be ready to take him on. Luke did small circular motions with his shoulder in order to loosen it up. He'd definitely be sore if he made it through this ordeal.

Luke took his right hand and grabbed some of his shirt to press on his cut. He held it there for a few seconds, hoping the pressure would make the bleeding stop. He could feel the blood seeping into his shirt. He was hurt badly, but he had to keep going.

It was much faster to free his feet. He worked at top speed, ripping through the threads with his knife. Then, Luke glanced around the darkness, trying to establish where he was. He was terrified to touch the walls or any other part of the room, for fear he might touch another body, but he had no choice. He felt around on the floor but didn't come across any corpses, thank God.

When he hoisted himself up, his head banged into the pole that held rows of shirts on hangers. Luke felt around on the walls, trying to locate the exit. They were padded, in some sort of felt material. When he found the doorknob it was of course locked. He pulled it back and forth but it wouldn't open. There had to be a light switch, thought Luke, running his hand along the wall. Bingo!

It took a second for his eyes to adjust to the light. Luke's eyes flitted around. If someone were to open the door, it would appear that it was a normal walk-in closet. Mr. Crawford's clothes hung neatly, and on the side there were a few pairs of shoes. But in the back, what Luke had been tied to, was a metal table. And hanging over it, was a rack, which held various masks. They were mostly ski masks, but there was one leather hood. Luke shuddered. What went on here? Had Mr. Crawford been up to something sick, right in the dorm, just feet from where students slept?

There was not a moment to linger; it was time to escape. Luke stuck his knife in the lock and tried to open it but it wouldn't budge. He bent down, and slid the knife between the door and its hinge. He moved it up and down, jingling it at a side angle, jimmying the lock. Finally he heard a pop. The door was unlocked! He had been lucky twice in his life, at the most important moments.

Still clutching the knife in one hand, he pushed the door open with his other hand, stumbled out, and found himself in Mr. Crawford's bedroom. He was alone. He glanced at the digital clock next to the bed. It read 12:15 p.m. Everyone was at the fair. Including Pippa, waiting for him in the maze. Mr. Crawford probably planned on grabbing Pippa, before murdering both of them. Luke had to help her.

He ran out of the dorm, praying he wouldn't be too late. The campus was empty. A thick layer of fog had nestled over the school, swallowing the tops of buildings. In the distance, a security guard was emerging out of the heavy mist. Luke was tempted to run to him, tell him to call for help, but he didn't have time to waste; he had to get to the fair. He had to save Pippa.

Luke dashed down the path to the stoplight that would allow him to cross Route 443 to the farm. He jogged in place waiting for a passing car to go by. He was tired, but he knew he had no choice. Suddenly his attention was drawn to the row of white clapboard faculty houses to his left. Luke squinted to see what the commotion was. A large crowd had gathered in front of Dean Heckler's house, and more people were pouring out of buildings making their way toward it. Police cars with flashing lights surrounded the house, and policemen were erecting barriers to keep people at bay. Luke ran toward them.

He scanned the crowd. "What's going on?" he asked a baby-faced freshman.

"They're arresting Dean Heckler for his wife's murder!" the freshman said with excitement.

"What?" asked Luke, stunned.

"They found some major evidence and nailed him. They're in there right now cuffing him!"

"They're wrong!" said Luke. He pushed past a throng of students and made his way to a police officer.

"What's happening?" asked Luke, frantically.

"Step back, please, young man."

"If they're arresting Dean Heckler, they've got the wrong guy. It's not him: it's Mr. Crawford. Skip Crawford is the killer!"

The policeman gave Luke a dismissive look. "Young man, you have to step back."

"Seriously, where's the chief? I need to talk to him!" implored Luke.

"He's not available, and this is the last time I'm going to ask you, *get back*," said the policeman, firmly pushing Luke behind the police barrier.

Luke was swept along with the aggressive crowd. He felt as if he were in the ocean, caught up in rough waves and pulled by a strong undertow. Every time he saw someone he knew, someone he wanted to confide in, he was hurled in a different direction before he could get to them. The crowd was aggressive, thirsty for blood and justice.

"What's going on, man?"

It was Andy. Luke turned to him and felt a surge of relief. "Andy! We've got to tell them, they're arresting the wrong guy. Mr. Crawford killed Mrs. Heckler. He tied me up in his room, he threatened me."

"Dude, what happened to your arm?" asked Andy, recoiling.

Luke glanced down at his wrist, which was still gushing blood. "I cut myself trying to escape."

Andy gave him a strange look. "Escape?"

"Yes! Mr. Crawford tied me up! He's the murderer."

Andy gave Luke a quizzical look. "But they say it's Heckler. They found his wife's bracelet in his glove compartment. The one some witness said she was wearing the night she died, when he was supposedly in Boston."

The bracelet! That meant Crawford had gotten it from Pippa! Luke's stomach churned. He had to get to the maze.

"Andy, tell the police to come to the maze and get Crawford! He tied me up, tried to kill me!"

"Dude, are you sure you're not having some sort of PTSD?" asked Andy.

"He's going to kill Pippa!"

Andy stared at him again and then his eyes widened. "What's with the knife?"

Luke glanced down. He had forgotten that he was still clutching it. He slid it into his pocket.

"It's nothing."

"Luke, I think you should go see the nurse," Andy said slowly, as if he were talking to an idiot.

Luke sighed with extreme frustration and took off. He didn't have time to convince people that he wasn't insane. Why couldn't they just believe him? Was he really considered so delicate that he would have a breakdown and freak out?

Luke shoved his way through the crowd that was now several layers deep. It looked like everyone on campus—from town even—had come to witness this arrest. But they didn't know the police had the wrong man! A cold-blooded killer was still lurking in their midst.

Luke extricated himself with effort from the bystanders and ran opposite the flow back to the streetlight and waited again for it to turn. He saw two passing security men and shouted out to them.

"Tell the police to come to the maze! There's going to be a murder at the maze!"

But his warning fell on deaf ears. They both just gave him an odd look and continued on their way to Heckler's house. People continued to flood past him, some even jogging briskly. It was like an accident, people couldn't look away. They all wanted to see the dean taken down.

As soon as the stoplight turned green, Luke ran across

the street and through the entrance where there was a giant banner proclaiming "Autumn Harvest Fair." The fair was deserted. Everyone had clearly heard the news of the imminent arrest and abandoned their post to go see it firsthand. Luke made his way past rows and rows of booths where anonymous farmers and organic food sellers had only moments ago been purveying their goods. Everything from produce and breads to fresh jams had been forgotten. The place was a ghost town.

Luke kept up his speed and raced toward the maze. He passed a table that was set up for face painting and pumpkin carving. It was empty. On another table, children's art projects had been hastily forsaken by parents eager to witness a murderer being taken into custody. *But it's the wrong man! The murderer's still on the loose!* Luke wanted to shout. *Probably here inside this very fair!*

By the time Luke got to the back of the fairgrounds he was out of breath and heaving so hard it felt as if his lungs would collapse. The maze was situated at the very edge of the cleared field. The entrance was a small gash that had been hacked through the enormous overgrown stalks of corn. Luke stared at the imperious fortress and felt a sense of foreboding. The farmer had let the corn grow as high as possible, and their tangled leaves wove together into a thick, impenetrable wall. Was Pippa already here? Would he even be able to find her if she were?

Clutching his stomach, which had a sharp pain from his running, Luke hobbled into the maze. Immediately, his surroundings darkened. He glanced up at the sky, and saw that the pregnant clouds were gathering and ready to burst. The day was rapidly growing grayer, gearing up for the dreaded rain that the weathermen had promised. The air hung heavy over the cornfield.

Luke stared at the paths in front of him. He could go left or right. Taking a gamble, he gathered his energy and started down the dirt path to the left. He moved as quickly as possible, rendering the stalks of corn a whirling sea of beige in his peripheral vision. He followed the path to another left and then bang! He stopped in his tracks. It was a dead end.

"Dammit!" cursed Luke.

In order to contribute to the Halloween effect, the caretakers of the maze had added skeletons and lifelike ghouls in every corner. At this corner was a plastic skeleton hanging in a makeshift noose with a sign tacked on it that said, "Try again, Sucker!" Luke ripped off the sign in frustration and turned back to retrace his steps. When he got back to the entrance, he made a right turn. He jogged a bit before he was confronted with another choice to go left or right. This time, Luke went right.

The path was narrower this time and Luke had to push through drooping corn stalks that were obstructing his way. The wind picked up and starting lifting leaves off the ground. Luke quickened his pace.

"Help!"

Luke heard a voice in the distance. He froze. "*Pippa*! Is that you?"

He waited, but there was silence. Luke started running in the direction of the voice, smashing the stalks from side to side. They fell aside, then hurled back and whipped him in the face. He felt blind, like a rat in a cage. He got to an opening and glanced left.

"Help!"

Luke jerked his head to the right, just in time to see Mr. Crawford dragging Pippa down a path before whipping around a corner. Luke followed in pursuit.

"Pippa! I'm coming!" he yelled.

Luke could feel his heart thudding in his chest. He felt pain all over his body, but adrenaline was pushing him forward.

Pippa screamed again. Luke flung himself around the corner and *wham*!

Extreme pain.

It took a second for Luke to realize that he had fallen on his face. His eyes flickered open and he saw only darkness. Suddenly, a large throbbing ache gathered in his forehead and burst. Luke rolled himself over, writhing in agony.

When his vision returned, he hoisted his body up enough to see Mr. Crawford running forward, dragging Pippa with him. He had obviously laid in wait to knock Luke out.

Luke sat up and clasped his head in his hands. Then he stared at his wrist, where dirt and pine needles now clung to the crusted blood in his open wound. There was no doubt it would get infected.

Taking a deep breath, Luke pulled himself up. His legs

were resistant, and almost gave way. But he had no choice. He summoned his energy and followed the direction that Mr. Crawford had taken. All he could think of was the look in Pippa's eyes. Extreme fear. Had Mrs. Heckler had that same look when she was strangled?

The town had prided itself that the maze was the biggest in Connecticut, boasting that it was almost two miles long. What had once seemed cool to Luke was now his worst nightmare. People got lost in here for hours; there was no way to tell who came in or out. Would he be able to get to Pippa in time? And if Mr. Crawford was able to get out of the maze before him, he would have no problem dragging Pippa away to a waiting car, everyone was over at Dean Heckler's house—it was the perfect diversion. Luke shuddered.

Hobbling along like a wounded bird himself, Luke got to another fork. A witch's head was hooked on a branch, her googly eyes rolling in circles. Still no sign of Pippa or Mr. Crawford. There were so many twists and turns; it was outrageous. Luke glanced at the ground, trying to see if there were any tracks. On the right, it looked like there were large shoes, and next to it, marks that looked like something had been dragged. Pippa. He followed, them. A large clap of thunder sounded and Luke glanced at the sky. It looked angry, dark, and mysterious. In a minute there would be a downpour. Then everyone would disperse and head home and there would be no chance of getting help.

Luke pushed himself harder. He was dizzy and light-headed. He hadn't eaten or had anything to drink for hours, and that—along with the drug he was given, his cut, the hit to his skull, and subsequent fall—was severely draining. His adrenaline kept him moving but he felt as if he were fading. He had to hang on. He had to save her.

Finally, after racing around, gasping for breath, Luke rounded a corner and saw them.

"Luke!" screamed Pippa, but her voice was muffled by Mr. Crawford's hand around her mouth.

With every ounce of courage and strength he had left, Luke ran after them. When he spun around the corner, he saw that Mr. Crawford was still hanging on to Pippa. He had his arm tightly secured around her neck, so that she was almost choking. Mr. Crawford was moving quickly, but he was at a crossroads, and would have to move fast.

Luke was closing in on Mr. Crawford, and they both knew it. Mr. Crawford was leading them down a path, but the plastic ghost at the end of the alley alerted them to the fact that it was a dead end. Finally, Luke had Mr. Crawford trapped.

Suddenly, Mr. Crawford stopped abruptly and turned around. He firmed his grip around Pippa's neck. Her arms flailed wildly, and she began thrashing around trying to free herself. She was starting to suffocate.

"Let her go!" yelled Luke.

Mr. Crawford smirked. "Back off, Chase. I want you to stay here and count to a thousand while we take off."

"Why would I do that?"

"Because if you don't, I'll kill Pippa."

Mr. Crawford bent his elbow even tighter around Pippa's neck.

"Let her go! If you kill her, it's just one more body. Everyone knows it's you who did this!"

Mr. Crawford threw his head back and laughed.

"That's where you're wrong! When Pippa dies, they're going to think it's *you* who killed her."

Luke's eyes remained on Pippa. Her hands were wildly trying to unclench Mr. Crawford's grip from her neck. She didn't have much time. Mr. Crawford was slowly asphyxiating her.

"How's that?" asked Luke, slowly taking a small step toward Mr. Crawford.

"When the police search your room, they'll find a shrine to Pippa. Love letters, photos, stuff like that. They'll think she rejected you, you went crazy, and attacked her."

"They'll never believe it."

"That's where you're wrong. Everyone expects you to snap one day. After what happened to you, it's impossible to be normal. You're a ticking time bomb!"

Luke's eyes flitted to Pippa. She was struggling to breathe.

Luke lunged, and Mr. Crawford had no choice but to release Pippa. Luke heard her gasp for air just as Mr. Crawford dug his nails into Luke's gashed wrist and kneed him in the chest. Luke recoiled in pain. Mr. Crawford started to scramble away, but Luke grabbed his leg and slid him back under him, pressing his body down to hold him. Next, Mr. Crawford freed his arm and punched Luke in the face.

Luke howled in pain. He used all of his strength to push Mr. Crawford's arms down to his sides. Luke could see his own arms shaking, and his cut from the knife had reopened and started to gush again. The knife! Luke tried to pull it out of his back pocket but before he could, Mr. Crawford spat at Luke, causing him to twitch and momentarily lessen his grip, and Mr. Crawford used that moment to his advantage. Rolling to his side, he swiveled out from under Luke and stood up, putting his fists in the air and doing a dance around Luke.

Luke, in turn, stood up and grabbed the knife from his pocket.

Suddenly, there was another clap of thunder and then the rain began to fall. It came on strong, pouring down in angry and aggressive pellets.

Luke held up the knife. "You know I'm not afraid to use this. And look around. Pippa's gone, probably to get the police. It's over."

Mr. Crawford laughed. It was an eerie, empty laugh. He seemed deflated, but not yet defeated.

Luke felt the rain washing all the dirt off of him, and he finally started to relax. Pippa was alive. He had a knife. The police would arrive soon. He bent down to steady himself and just as he did out of the corner of his eye he saw Mr. Crawford's foot. It knocked Luke to the ground, but more importantly, knocked the knife out of Luke's hand.

"You think I'd be that easy?" asked Mr. Crawford. He grabbed the knife and flashed it over Luke. How could Luke have been so stupid? Anyone knows you never let down your guard. Could it really end this way?

Suddenly, something caught Luke's eye. Mr. Tadeckis, his long face illuminated in the flashing lightning, was standing against the corn behind Mr. Crawford. Luke's eyes widened and Mr. Crawford followed Luke's gaze.

"Skippy, you really shouldn't," said Mr. Tadeckis, picking up Mr. Crawford and slamming him against the ground. Luke scrambled and grabbed the knife back from Mr. Crawford and placed it against Mr. Crawford's throat.

"One move and you're toast, and I mean it this time," said Luke.

Mr. Crawford's eyes flitted from Mr. Tadeckis to Luke.

"Don't even try it," said Luke.

Mr. Crawford's body went limp. This time, Luke knew he wasn't going to fight.

"Was it really worth it?" asked Luke.

Mr. Crawford turned his head away.

Luke held him down. A flash of lightning flickered across the sky, and the rain continued its heavy descent.

"Thanks, Mr. Tadeckis," Luke said, looking around.

But Mr. Tadeckis was gone.

Just then, Headmaster Thompson rounded the corner with the police. They immediately rushed over and took Mr. Crawford from Luke.

"Are you okay?" asked Chief Corcoran, putting a protective hand on Luke's shoulder.

"I will be," said Luke, rising and wiping hay from his shirt.

"What happened?" the chief asked.

"Mr. Crawford's the real murderer."

The chief yanked Mr. Crawford up while his deputy cuffed him. Luke watched zombie-like as they read Mr. Crawford his rights and whisked him away. Mr. Crawford had a small eerie grin on his face the entire time. Something about his calm, satisfied demeanor gave Luke a chill.

Luke looked down at his wrist. Blood was still pouring out of it; this would leave a worse scar than the one he already had.

"Pippa," he said urgently to the headmaster. "Where's Pippa?"

"She's safe," Headmaster Thompson said. "The medics are attending to her now. She's near the maze entrance; she told us where you were."

Luke followed the direction of the flashing red lights and found her on a stretcher outside an ambulance.

They hugged each other tightly, not caring about the police or the medics who were surrounding them.

"You're a hero," Pippa gasped, her voice barely audible. "There's no getting around it this time. You're an actual hero."

34

Late that night, Luke and Pippa were sitting in the headmaster's office listening to him and Chief Corcoran explain everything that had happened. Luke's wrist had been slashed significantly and he'd had to go to the hospital to receive seventy stitches, meeting up with Pippa who was bruised and battered, but well enough to check herself out of the hospital.

Luke felt exhausted and ached to his core.

Mr. Crawford had been taken into custody. Luke's parents had been called and were on their way from Georgetown to see him. He could go home, but he wasn't sure he wanted to.

Luke was tired. Very tired. But he wanted to hear an explanation of everything; he needed to know what had really happened. Thankfully, Pippa was on her toes enough to lead the inquisition, putting her natural haughtiness to good use.

"If you could please start from the beginning that would be brilliant," Pippa told them.

"Yes, and make sure to tell us exactly why you were about to arrest the wrong man for the murder," Luke added.

"We knew it was someone from the school," said Chief Corcoran defensively.

"But the wrong guy," said Luke.

The chief ignored him.

"If you knew it was someone from the school, you were putting all of the students in danger," said Pippa. "Including, and most especially, Luke and me."

"Not exactly," said Chief Corcoran. "We had undercover people all over this place keeping an eye on everyone."

"Not me," said Luke.

The chief turned and stared at Luke. "You don't even know how much we were watching you. We were all over you. I only took my men off you last night when we were closing in on the dean."

"And I was almost closed in on by a killer," muttered Luke. He felt he had a right to be petulant, especially toward the chief.

"How did you know it was someone from campus?" asked Pippa. "And not, say, the Southborough Strangler."

"The Southborough Strangler is a myth," said the chief. "Something the kids scare up on Halloween."

"Are you sure Mr. Crawford isn't the Southborough Strangler? He was a student here back then," said Luke quickly.

"Mrs. Holliway just looked up Mr. Crawford's records,"

interjected the headmaster. He pushed his glasses up his nose and stared down at a file on his desk. "He was on semester abroad when the first murder occurred."

"But I'm sure he knew about it, and probably used the premise of it to his advantage," said the chief.

"Then it could have been someone else off campus who knew about it," said Pippa.

The chief shook his head. "No. We knew it was someone from St. Benedict's, because it was clear from the beginning that they were trying to pin it on Oscar. We had an anonymous call telling us he was involved."

"And it was Oscar's scarf," said Luke.

"Yes, and what you didn't know is that the caller told us there was a piece of her jewelry in your room."

"The bracelet?" asked Luke.

"No, an earring. The bracelet came later."

"Did you find the earring?" asked Pippa.

"We did, but we knew it had been planted. It was stuck in the pocket of a freshly laundered shirt on top of Oscar's hamper. But underneath was all dirty laundry. We knew Oscar wouldn't just launder one shirt and not do the rest. It was too suspicious. That's when we talked to him."

"And what did he say?" asked Luke.

"He confessed he'd been out there. But I can assure you; he didn't give you up easily. And we had no idea you were out there, Pippa. But he told us about Luke when he realized it was for your own safety," said the chief.

"Great," said Luke.

"And that's when it was clear to us that we had to remove him. That it could be very dangerous for him," said the chief.

"We agreed with his parents that we would have to make people believe he had been suspended. It was for his own protection," said the headmaster.

"So that's why he couldn't talk to me! He wasn't allowed to tell me anything," said Luke. *And that's why Mr. Tadeckis said he was lying.* Suddenly Luke felt awash in gratitude for his friend. His best friend. He was now more certain than ever that Oscar appreciated him as much as Luke appreciated Oscar. He couldn't wait to have him back as his roommate.

"The more we kept him out of it, the faster we could close in on the killer," said the chief.

"You didn't seem to get very close at all," said Luke.

"It's true we focused our investigation on Dean Heckler. The same red flags that alerted you, also alerted us," said the chief.

"Yeah, he was really in my face," said Luke.

"When we questioned him, he said he thought you were in grave danger. I think he knew the police were looking at him, and he knew you were wide open, conducting your own investigation," said the headmaster. "He did everything he could think of to keep you out of it."

So the dean was trying to protect him? Huh. Who'd have thunk it?

"I thought it was strange how close he was with his ex," said Luke.

"Not that it's any of your business, but Mary was the one who ended the marriage. She loves children and didn't want to miss her chance to make a difference in a child's life, but Dean Heckler wasn't prepared to make that commitment. I figure after the maturity you've shown, you can handle some adult truths," said the headmaster.

Luke felt guilty, thinking of how much Mrs. Heckler had remembered of him from last year, and yet she had barely even registered on his radar. She had called him one of her students, and he hadn't ever given her a second thought. He was glad she'd made the decision to become a foster mother. It seemed like she would be a good care-taker.

"Dean Heckler and Mary remained close. Mary made sure of that, because she told us she had invested too much of herself into the school and her students to lose it all over a bad end to their relationship. In turn, Dean Heckler confided in her and asked her to keep an eye on Joanna. He knew Joanna was being unfaithful. That night, when Mary was working at the library, she happened to see Joanna go into the woods and followed, but became frightened so she immediately left," the headmaster said.

"What I want to know is how you found out it was Crawford," the chief asked.

Luke and Pippa looked at each other. "I wasn't sure until it was almost too late," admitted Luke.

"We would have found him, but you found him first. In fact, just this morning we got a call from Las Vegas PD with confirmation that Skip Crawford was the boyfriend who accompanied Joanna to Nevada. The staff at the Hard Rock identified him."

"Yeah, still it might have been too late for me," said Luke.

"You really took your time," Pippa said.

"We would have found you," said the chief with confidence.

"I guess no one gets away with murder," said Luke.

"No," said the chief.

"Oscar will be back at school tomorrow. I'm sure you'll both be happy to be reunited," said the headmaster.

It was the best news Luke had heard all day. "Can't wait," he agreed.

"You've beaten the odds twice in your life, Mr. Chase. I hope that's it for you," said the chief.

"Me too."

"Luke, you look exhausted. Why don't you go get some rest and we'll fill you in on everything else later," said the headmaster.

"Okay." Luke did want to ask some more questions but he was tired from his head to his toes. He wanted to go relax, get rid of the stress that had been eating at him for weeks.

As he and Pippa walked to the door, Luke turned back. "And what about Mr. Tadeckis?"

"Mr. Tadeckis?" asked the headmaster.

The chief looked equally blank.

So, they didn't know everything. Maybe he was a better detective than they were after all.

"My mistake," said Luke. "I'll see you later."

"Thanks, Luke," said the chief. "You did good."

When Pippa and Luke left the building, Luke took a deep breath. He relished his newfound sense of peace. Even though they were making him spend the night in the Infirmary, he had his freedom again.

"I owe you everything," said Pippa, as he walked her back to Hadden. "You know, I've never met anyone like you, Luke. You go above and beyond."

"Don't embarrass me." But Luke was pleased that Pippa had said it. When he heard it from her, it meant something to him. He felt like she really understood him, and didn't just want to assign him the role of superhero. It felt nice to be recognized.

"Let's go to the Jig tomorrow," Pippa suggested. "Chocolate milkshakes, my treat."

Chocolate milkshakes at the Jig. Perfect. Something uncomplicated and normal, that's exactly what Luke wanted to do.

"Well done, Luke," said a voice behind them on the path. They both whipped around.

"Mr. Tadeckis," said Luke.

"May I have a word?"

Luke looked at Pippa who shrugged. Luke followed Mr. Tadeckis over to a clearing so they would be out of Pippa's earshot.

"Good work," said Mr. Tadeckis.

"Thanks for your help. You saved my life," said Luke with gratitude.

"You saved your own life," said Mr. Tadeckis with confidence.

Luke smiled. "If you knew, why didn't you tell me?"

"You didn't need my help. You needed my knife, but not my help," said Mr. Tadeckis in his usual brisk manner.

"I could have died."

"Please. Don't be dramatic."

"Was this all some sort of a game for you?" asked Luke. "I don't get it at all."

Mr. Tadeckis straightened upright like a soldier. "Luke, I am a survival instructor."

"I didn't think I needed to prove myself again."

"Of course you did. You were brainwashed into believing your first escape was just luck. You refused to acknowledge your heroics. Now you can't deny them. You can now know that you are truly special."

"So what next?"

"You're ready for the big time."

"What's the big time?" asked Luke. He didn't think he could take anything else.

Mr. Tadeckis smiled. "Stay tuned."

He started to walk away.

"What does that mean?"

Mr. Tadeckis turned around. "It means, you're going to help me clean up this campus and this town. Just wait." He continued walking.

"I'm not sure about that!"

"Just wait! You'll see."

Luke returned to Pippa. It was strange, feeling the same familiarity with her that he had with Oscar. He'd never thought that sort of a connection could happen with a potential girlfriend.

"That dude is crazy," said Luke, but he meant it affectionately.

"Homicidal crazy?"

"No. Vigilante woodsman crazy."

Pippa shrugged. "That could come in handy."

"I'm so glad this is over," Luke said. "And I'm psyched for Oscar to come back. Ready for life to return to normal."

"I'm sure he'll be just as glad to see you," Pippa said.

"Oscar will grow on you, I promise."

"Look, if you think he's so brilliant, I'm sure there's something decent to him."

"There is, trust me," Luke said with a smile, taking her hand. He liked the way she tucked in her thumb so that her whole hand was inside his.

"So you've got this courageous exploit thing down pat. Maybe you'll be FBI or something," she teased him, lightly swinging their arms.

"Never. I'm retired."

"That's a pity."

"Why?"

"Because I was going to ask you to come to England with me over Christmas and help me find Tamara's murderer. Clear my name."

Pippa's tone was still light, but she was looking at him intently.

A thrill swept through Luke's body. Maybe one more murder case wouldn't be so bad. They did make a great team.

He smiled at Pippa. "Brilliant."

THE END

About the author

Chuck Vance grew up outside Washington, D.C. where both of his parents worked in government agencies. An avid outdoorsman who would rather be rock climbing and snowboarding than sitting at a desk, Chuck spent his high school years at an east coast boarding school that became the inspiration for St. Benedict's in *Sneaking Out*. This is his first published novel.

Visit Chuck's author site at **chuckvanceauthor.com** or learn more about Chuck (and Luke, Pippa, and Oscar) on **www.dunemerebooks.com**.

Please visit
www.dunemerebooks.com
to order your next great read or just to hang out
with Luke and hear what he has to say about
boarding school, crime, and the outdoors.

DUNEMERE
Books